A *REAL* MAN

Panic whispered in her ear. Where was she? Who was he? *What* was he?

"If ye think to keep me here by spiriting awa' my plaid, ye've made a mistake." Climbing from the sleeping pad, he towered above her in all his naked glory.

A jagged scar ran from the top of his thigh to within several inches of humanity's salvation. Staring up at him, she admitted the unthinkable, the truth her instincts had immediately recognized. No fake could have so many imperfections and yet feel so . . . perfect.

He was *real*.

For the moment, it didn't matter who he was or where he'd come from. His untainted sperm could bring males back to a dying human race. She blinked away sudden tears.

Me first. Me first. She shoved aside the selfish thought. "Who are you?" Her whispered question carried all the hushed awe due the most important human on earth.

AN ORIGINAL SIN

NINA BANGS

LOVE SPELL BOOKS NEW YORK CITY

To Gerry Bartlett, Donna Maloy, and Kimberly Raye Rangel. Thanks for keeping the dream alive.

LOVE SPELL®

July 1999

Published by

Dorchester Publishing Co., Inc.
276 Fifth Avenue
New York, NY 10001

ISBN 0-505-52324-8

The name "Love Spell" and its logo are trademarks of Dorchester Publishing Co., Inc.

Printed in the United States of America.

AN ORIGINAL SIN

Prologue

War. Been there.

  Famine. Done that.

  Pestilence. Ho hum.

  Drought. Boring, boring.

  Life's the pits when you're the best damn cosmic troublemaker in the universe. You scratch and claw your way up the ladder, think you're top dog, and then what? You have to maintain quality, never relax because someone's always lookin' to bring you down.

  The best, that's me. But after a couple of thousand years it starts gettin' old. Know what I mean? One more flood and I'll puke.

  I can't quit, though. Lifetime contract. I quit, zap, I'm gone. Let's be honest, I've sorta gotten used to existing.

  But I've gotta think of something. Ten thousand

more years of the same old, same old and I'll slit my throat. Figuratively speaking, of course.

Problem is, I'm too good. We're talking talent here. The universe's numero uno pain in the butt. Can't get better than that.

So what's the big deal, you say? The big deal is . . . there's nothing left. *Would you believe? Not one new sin.*

OK, so I've done them all. But I'm not ready for the big Crockpot Down Under yet. There's gotta be one more. One more sin.

Look, I'm a creative kinda guy. There was that time in . . . Guess you don't wanna hear about that. But take my word, if anyone can think of a dirty deed, it's me.

So why not go small, you say? Why always mass chaos, devastating destruction? Good question. This is tough to admit, but . . . I've got a weak stomach.

Big is easy. I go in, whip up a hurricane, then get out and watch from far away. No blood. No gore. No Maalox.

Small is harder. I can't see things from far away. Hey, I'm a professional. I gotta stick around to make sure every detail's perfect. Close up is, well . . . not a pretty sight. Major Maalox moment.

So what in heaven's name—Did I say that? Sorry. What the hell can I do that hasn't been done?

Got it! Am I inspired or what? I'll whip up a disaster of the heart. All emotional catastrophe, no upset tummy. Something small, intimate, with room for growth. First, I'll choose two of the least compatible people on earth, guaranteed to hate each other's guts. Now it really gets good. I'll cleverly encourage them to fall in love; then when they're pant-

ing for each other, I'll rip them apart forever. Brilliant.

Since I'm a sporting kinda guy, I'll give myself a time limit. Three's a cosmic sorta number. Let's say three weeks. That'll give me until midnight on October 31 to wreck their lives. Halloween. I like it. Great symbolism.

One's gotta be a real babe, though. What can I say, I love women. Hey, a guy's gonna be a guy.

Final detail. I need a form. Something they'll trust. Something that'll get me close so I can watch, manipulate.

Then I can relax, do my thing, and see what shakes out.

Ah, young love. Just call me the great cosmic Cupid.

Chapter One

Man-maker conventions were hell.

First, Four-Two-N woke to find that her sleeping pad had drifted to the floor during the night. Scientists could build a floating city on Mars, but they couldn't make a sleeping pad that would stay suspended three feet in the air. Of course, scientists had screwed things up for centuries, so she shouldn't be surprised.

Next, there was the far wall she'd stared at for the last five minutes. *Strange.* Had she gone to sleep in a museum? An antiquated picture of the galaxy hung above a bureau. A *wooden* bureau. With the scarcity of trees, no one had used wood for at least a hundred years. A fake? Maybe. People had become masters of imitation. She could attest to that.

Finally, there was the small matter of something

sharing her sleeping pad. Something large. She could feel it move against her back, hear it breathe. Which was why she'd stayed frozen for five minutes, staring at the stupid wall.

Added to everything else, she couldn't feel her cross at her neck. Peering over the edge of the sleeping pad as far as she could without moving, she spotted the silver chain, with her Celtic cross still safely attached, lying on the floor.

Four-Two-N heaved a sigh of relief. Grandma Two-Z had given her the antique piece, and she treasured it.

Now what? She could turn over, face what lay at her back, and order it off her sleeping pad. *Problem*. She had a vivid imagination. She needed imagination in her line of work, but not for facing unidentified sleeping partners.

Maybe she'd wandered into the wrong rest-over room last night after the party. Maybe a large carnitak had followed her in and curled up beside her. Maybe she was a galaxy-size wimp and should just turn over.

Unfortunately, her imagination reminded her the rest-over was close to NASA, and NASA frequently entertained unusual visitors. With her luck, a Saralian poison pig had escaped and chosen her out of all humankind to cozy up to.

Her thoughts scuttled in every direction. What to do? She didn't know where she was, or what horror happily slept at her back. If she screamed, she'd wake it. *Scrap that idea*.

That left . . . Holding her breath, she slowly turned over.

She would've preferred the pig. At least then she'd know she wasn't hallucinating.

A human male. A man. Just like her Dark and Dangerous Dick model, only better. She let her breath out on a puff of disbelief. A fake? She'd never seen one this perfect. Even *she* couldn't create something so lifelike.

Of course, he had to be a fake. Men had gone the way of the Dexovil rock burrower, extinct for fifty years or more. Another scientific screwup.

Studying the man, she couldn't squelch a small stab of professional jealousy. A master creation.

What kind of a party had she gone to last night, if she didn't remember *him*? One of her friends, probably Three-Six-H, must've put the man next to her as a joke.

What a joke! Long, dark hair lay in a tangled mass across incredibly broad shoulders that had a perfectly tanned skin tone. Hmm, the hair looked like the real thing. Reaching out, she stroked it. Raw silk. She allowed herself a sensual shiver.

His face was molded perfection—knife-edge cheekbones, straight nose, full lips, long lashes. His eyes? She longed to know their color.

She had to speak with his creator. Never had she been able to make a face look so real, as though warm blood pulsed beneath the skin—soft, touchable. *Wonderful!* She almost hated the woman responsible for him.

But was he anatomically correct? A lot of cheap models weren't very detailed. She'd check.

Scooting down, she ducked under the cover. Warmth and essence of male surrounded her. She frowned. How did his maker get that scent of desire and dark erotic nights? It left her heart pounding, her mouth dry. She'd never experimented much with aromas. Maybe she should.

Running her fingertips across his chest, she marveled at the textures—smooth flesh over muscle, hair-roughened areas, and nipples that actually pebbled beneath her touch. Amazing.

A shudder ran through the body. Must be a short somewhere.

When her fingers touched his stomach, his muscles contracted and rippled. Unbelievable technology.

She finally reached her destination. This was what separated true artistry from assembly-line cheapies.

Utter brilliance. She couldn't suppress a small coo of admiration. Large, round, firm. Long, thick, hard . . . *Hard*? She didn't remember anything hard down here when she'd first ducked under the cover. *Hmm*. Must be a clever use of sensors.

Unable to resist, she ran her fingers lightly along his length, then clasped him. Liquid heat flooded her, then settled heavily into a bubbling pool of want in an area that had never experienced any kind of bubbling.

She choked back a surprised gasp and closed her eyes in shocked horror. *Impossible!* She'd created customized men for years and never once had a sexual reaction to any of them. They were fakes—a mass of Toglor fibers and electrical impulses. She prided herself on never forgetting that.

She teased her friends when they panted after her great-looking Hot and Horny Hal or Stud Muffin Stuart models. Now who'd have the last laugh?

Three-Six-H would never let her forget this if she ever found out. Nervously, Four-Two-N searched her memory. Had she seen any sign of a scan-glow? *No*. She relaxed slightly. Even if her friend had set this up, she wouldn't defy privacy rules by watching. No one would ever know.

She'd know. She had to admit it. Her sex drive was on automatic pilot and begging for permission to land.

So close, so warm, so convenient. She closed her fingers more tightly around him. Sex. She'd seen the disks, knew the basics of the ancient ritual. All she'd have to do was . . .

Appropriate muscles spasmed at the thought of him filling her, touching every dark, wet, yearning space. Reflexively, she kneaded him like a cat with eyes half-closed in feline bliss, while she imagined a joining she'd never know. Warm flesh sheathed in satin-smooth skin that slid slickly into—

With a discipline forged from her society's expectations, she ruthlessly clamped down on her useless fantasy. She might as well accept it. Men were gone, so she'd never experience that particular pleasure. And she'd never get so desperate that she'd lose herself in a fake. A make-believe man.

She opened her eyes. *Liar*. She could with *this* fake.

Suddenly the body jerked. *Oops*. Had she broken him?

"God's teeth, woman, I dinna know how much more I can stand. Cease cooing like a mating dove and show yerself."

She froze. *Dinna? Cease?* What a strange dialect. And his voice—harsh, arrogant. This didn't sound like any programmed response tone she'd ever heard.

Possibility sprouted and grew with the speed of a Pelmar choke-weed. It curled inside her stomach, making her feel the way she did each time she started a new creation. Putting out feelers, it touched her heart. Not satisfied with the mad pounding it left behind, the possibility wound around her lungs and squeezed. She gasped for breath. Her brain tried to fend off the invader, but to no avail.

Real? Could this be a real man?

No way. Nah . . . Maybe? She shot from beneath the cover, flinging it aside as she emerged.

"Easy, lass. Dinna look so daft. Have ye ne'er seen a man before?" His deep chuckle made light of the suggestion.

"No." *Green*. He had eyes the color of jade, spectacular with their frame of thick, sooty lashes. "Not a real one."

His slashing white smile disappeared, but she'd already noticed one slightly crooked tooth. Customers never asked for flawed men. OK, they *did* want men with oversize—

"Nay, I'll not believe ye were raised in a nunnery." He smiled again. "Not when I wake to find ye rooting beneath the cover like a wee pig."

"Wee pig!" She never programmed anything but polite chitchat and a few orgasmic groans into her creations. But fine, she could fling a few insults of her own. "I don't know who you are, but I've made men better than you." A lie, of course.

"Made men better?" He narrowed his gaze, and she noticed a small scar above one dark brow.

"Aye, I can well believe yer touch would cure a man of what ails him. Ye've talented hands, ones I'd lief feel again." His gaze turned hot, aggressive.

Fakes were never aggressive. She felt a trickle of sweat slide between her breasts, a reminder that she wore no clothes. Pulling the cover and her anger around her, she tried to ignore her body's embarrassing demands. Amazing he didn't notice them.

"I was *not* under the cover rooting around like a 'wee pig.' I was . . . checking out the competition. I'll tell you something, too. I've made a lot *bigger* men." OK, she'd admit they were a tad too big— big enough to double as rocket nose cones. But that was what her customers paid for.

"Ye *make* men?" The corner of his expressive mouth turned up. "With yer hands? Like a man would fashion a sword?"

A sword? She frowned, trying to ignore the sexual implication in his words. *Forget it. Everything* about him shouted sex. "Customized models. Very expensive."

"Aye." One dark brow rose to match his mouth. "And I'm King William."

As he nodded, a strand of hair fell forward, and he raised his hand to push it aside. Fascinated, she followed the motion. Male bodies were her business, but this one interested her more than usual. He had broad hands with long, lean fingers. Strong hands used to hard work, yet hands that would be gentle on a woman's body. Where had that thought come from? Only one thing should interest her— real or ultimate imitation?

Mentally, she shook herself. He couldn't be real.

Men were extinct, victims of a gene-directed virus gone amok.

He glanced away from her, then suddenly stiffened and drew in a harsh breath. Sitting up, he stared at the room.

"What manner of demon's lair is this?"

"Demon's lair? Sure, the room's a little old-fashioned. I bet the rest-over keeps it as a novelty for travelers who want to get the true feel of living in the past. Cute idea. But 'demon's lair' is over-dramatizing a bit."

" 'Tis like naught I've seen before. How came I here?" He fumbled beneath his pillow. " 'Tis gone! I canna find my dirk. Who . . . ?"

Uh-oh. He sounded upset. She never programmed her models for extreme emotional responses. Well, maybe once. Six-Nine-R wanted her man to sing the commercial for Healthy Hot and Spicy Sausages—no fat or caloric content—while she climaxed.

His gaze returned to her—accusing, threatening. "Ye shouldna have done this deed. D'ye think to keep me here, witch?"

"*Witch*? Like in bad hair and a broomstick? You have to be kidding, right?"

"It doesna matter if ye've ne'er seen a real man before. Ye have no right to conjure one for yerself. Ye and a score of virgin witches canna force me to yer will."

"Virgin witch?" She slid her gaze across his muscled arms and shoulders. So wonderful. So flawed. Maybe if she bashed him over the head with her broomstick it would correct his obviously faulty circuits.

17

"Yer familiar awaits, but 'twill do ye no good."
He pointed toward the bureau.

Shifting her gaze, she met the fixed amber stare
of a large black cat, a cat that hadn't been there a
few minutes ago. Her thoughts fragmented. She
pressed her suddenly clammy palms flat against
the base of her throat, feeling the warmth, the
steady throb of her pulse, the *realness*. No, she
hadn't been tossed into some sort of virtual world
gone mad.

"Dinna try yer devil's spells on me, witch." He
made some strange signs as he slid to the edge of
the pad. His eyes blazed with fierce anger and behind the anger . . . fear.

He wasn't kidding. This could get scary fast. "It's
your lucky day. I'm all out of devil's spells." She'd
kill Three-Six-H if her friend had put this maniac
beside her. *Kill?* She never had violent thoughts.
Breathe deeply. Stay calm.

He nodded. "Since ye canna use me, tell me
where ye hid my weapons, then free me."

Fascinated, she watched him swallow hard, lingered on the strong column of his neck. She
blinked. *Weapons? Plural?*

Crossing his arms, he leaned back, obviously
waiting for her to fulfill his demand.

He'd have a long wait.

Returning her attention to the cat, she fought to
hold on to reality. *A dream? Could be.* Like a
dream, unrelated oddities seemed to float by with
no particular pattern.

She had to ground herself in things she recognized or else listen to the whispers of her faceless
fears. Four-Two-N gazed up at the galaxy painting.

The planets were comforting old friends. *Hmm*. She peered more closely. The cat was seated right beneath one of Jupiter's moons. "Ganymede. That cat is—"

" 'Tis a strange name for a cat." The man's brows drew together in a puzzled frown. "And what be yer name, witch?"

Her heart missed a beat. A fake would never be puzzled. The men she created existed for only one purpose: sexual release. They didn't need extraneous emotions. "Four-Two-N."

His brows almost met. "Fortune?"

She sighed. "No, Four-Two-N."

" 'Tis settled. I'll call ye Fortune."

Stubborn. Why would anyone want a stubborn fake? Every word he uttered drove her toward a conclusion she feared, didn't believe—wanted to believe.

Pushing himself erect again, he gazed around the room, then stared at her with an intensity that made her pull the cover higher. Yanking it up to her chin, she did a quick survey of the room. No clothes.

Panic whispered in her ear. Where was she? Who was he? *What* was he?

"If ye think to keep me here by spiriting awa' my plaid, ye've made a mistake." Climbing from the sleeping pad, he towered above her in all his naked glory.

A jagged scar ran from the top of his thigh to within several inches of humanity's salvation. Staring up at him, she admitted the unthinkable, the truth her instincts had immediately recognized.

19

No fake could have so many imperfections and yet feel so . . . perfect.

He was *real*.

For the moment, it didn't matter who he was or where he'd come from. His untainted sperm could bring males back to a dying human race. She blinked away sudden tears.

Me first. Me first. She shoved aside the selfish thought. "Who are you?" Her whispered question carried all the hushed awe due the most important human on earth.

His dark scowl dismissed her question. "Leith Campbell, as ye must well know." He turned and strode toward the door.

"Wait! Your clothes. Don't go off half-cocked. . . ." Poor phrasing.

His pointed gaze swept the room, then returned to her. "Do ye see my plaid? I grow tired of this playacting, witch."

Cautiously opening the door, he peered left and right, then slipped quietly from the room.

Where did he think he was going? He couldn't just . . . "Come back! Millions of women need—"

"Shush, witch." He appeared in the doorway again. "Yer blather will lead our enemies to us." With that cryptic whisper, he silently closed the door on any further arguments she might muster.

Frantic, she leaped from the sleeping pad, then rushed to the bureau. She couldn't let him get away. The future of the human race depended on her.

Pulling open the drawers, she searched for something, anything she could wear. Empty.

Glancing up, she met the cat's stare. He winked.

No, she hadn't seen that. It must've been a trick of the lighting.

She slammed the drawer shut, then closed her eyes, breathing deeply. *Don't panic*. Her eyes opened wide, and she stopped breathing altogether as the telltale squeak of the door announced Leith's return.

She didn't need to turn to verify his identity because she could *feel* him; his gaze was as potent as a trail of fingertips down her spine. Sudden heat and the urge to clench her thighs tightly made her swallow hard. How could his mere entrance into the room do this to her, make her feel as though her body belonged to someone else, someone filled with fierce, primitive hunger?

"Why . . . why did you come back?"

In the sudden stillness, she could hear his breathing—harsh, rapid with an unnamed emotion.

"Where would I go? 'Tis all like this room."

She could almost feel his frustrated gesture.

"Ye've entranced me, witch, and only ye can release me."

She breathed deeply, and wondered who had entranced whom.

"I brought ye clothes. Ye must cover yer body so ye dinna tempt . . . a weaker man." His voice was sandpaper rough, deeply thick with something that spun her around to face him. For a moment, his stare burned with the green flame of a Norian cantu pit, then was banked as he looked down at the clothes he held.

" 'Twas all I could find. The woman cleaning the

21

room across the hall foolishly left the door open
while she went elsewhere."

"A thief. Wonderful. I'm stuck heaven-knows-
where with a thief." *Where* was the operative word.

"I do what I must to survive, witch." His words
held a warning.

Some footwear he'd wrapped in a towel and
slung across one shoulder fell from his grasp. He
turned, closed the door, then bent to retrieve them.

Even as she rushed to the sleeping pad, yanked
off the cover, then wrapped it around herself,
snatches of thought fought for attention. Before
he'd shut the door, she'd glimpsed the inside of the
room across the hall, exactly like theirs—archaic
yet new-looking. That meant something, if she
could only focus. And the cat, where had it come
from? Where had Leith come from?

Automatically, she scooped her chain from the
floor and secured it around her neck. Beloved and
familiar, it felt like a talisman, protecting her from
the craziness surrounding her.

Her logical, reasonable self screamed for her to
think. Something strange and potentially dangerous lurked, waiting to pounce. But the part of her
that pulsed with need, that cried tears of depriva-
tion, wouldn't let her concentrate. Not with an
unobstructed view of Leith Campbell's strong buttocks—smooth, hard, silently begging for her to
run her hands over them. Following the path of
least resistance, she slid her gaze down the backs
of his muscled thighs, lingered hopefully as he
spread his legs a little more to reach the fallen objects.

"Yer gaze could draw blood, witch." He straightened and turned to face her.

"What?" Regretfully, she steered her attention away from his lower body.

His heavy-lidded glance raked her, leaving a trail of unexpected goose bumps. "Ye could drain a man dry wi' only yer stare. Verra strong, verra tempting." He scowled. "But 'tis dangerous to lie wi' a witch. If I dinna please ye, I might leave yer bed wi' my manhood a wee shriveled berry. Release me from this enchantment so I may go."

She huffed and puffed, ready to blow him away with her denial, even though it would be a false one. What did he know about desire? Wherever he'd been, she'd bet he hadn't been without sex for twenty-eight years. "A wee shriveled berry's too good for you. How about an organ transplant? We could take your berry and put it . . . Oh, never mind."

He smiled coldly and she lost her train of thought.

"Cat and mistress have much in common. Ganymede enjoys a wee peek now and then, too." He nodded toward her feet.

Glancing down, she gasped. A black tail stuck out from beneath her trailing cover. Mesmerized, she watched it twitch back and forth, back and forth.

With a horrified squeak, she yanked the cover up to expose the black cat. He peered at her, then yawned.

Pulling the cover more tightly around her, she stepped away from the animal. When she looked up, she saw that Leith had dumped everything on the sleeping pad. He stared at the pile for a moment, then picked up one piece of clothing. "Men wear these?"

How would she know? "Men wear nothing. They're—"

His coldness vanished as his eyes lit with laughter, and he grinned. "And do women wear nothing, also?"

Wow! Talk about a meteor-shower smile. *OK, forget the smile. Focus*. "Extinct. Men no longer exist. They haven't existed for more than fifty years. Scientists thought they were so successful with their cloning until . . ."

She blinked. Of course they weren't extinct. She was talking to one. "So where *did* you come from? I—"

He heaved an exasperated sigh. "Cease yer babbling, witch. My head aches with yer false tales." Before she realized his intent, he strode to the window and drew back the covering to peer outside.

"Ohmigod! Get back. You're naked. Everyone will see you." She prayed the window was high enough to cover the obvious.

Instead of returning to her, he stood staring out the window. Dozens of emotions whirled in her head as she watched his sun-bathed silhouette. He reminded her of a warrior from some distant past. *Some distant past*. Taking a deep breath, she glanced around the room, thought of the room across the hall. Antiquated.

For an eternity of time, he continued staring at the outside world while she waited behind him— afraid to ask, afraid to know. Terror settled at the back of her neck and squeezed. This felt like her

24

first visit to Hanus when she was seven years old. She'd hidden her face the entire trip, then screamed like a warren cat when she'd seen the planet's natives.

"Come here." His command vibrated with an emotion she couldn't identify, feared to identify. He didn't turn from the window.

No! She didn't want to face the reality that waited for her beyond the window. If she ignored it, it might dissolve into the bright light of morning; then she could have a laugh with her friends over her dream.

"Fear is a shadow lie. Drag it into the light, and it isna so fearsome," he murmured, then turned to face her.

She swallowed hard. *Easy for him to say.*

His expression didn't encourage her. In the dim light of the room, his face appeared harsh, dangerous. She could imagine him a warrior, viewing the carnage of battle, with the same expression— a mixture of horror, fear, and fierce determination.

Slowly, she forced herself toward the window, step by torturous step. She sensed, in the dark, hidden places of her mind where frightening truths huddled, that each step took her toward . . . What? The unknown. *Please, please let me look out the window and see something familiar!*

She reached the window and stared at the view below. She spoke no words; none were needed. The street was alien, a scene from centuries ago, one she'd seen only on history disks. But one detail riveted her attention. Men. Dozens of men walking on both sides of the street. Men driving four-

25

wheeled vehicles that had disappeared from earth hundreds of years before.

And in the distance, a lake. She knew the lake—its shape, its color. Clear Lake. But God help her, that was all she knew.

The heart of fear was a cold place—no one around to soothe her with promises that this was all a misunderstanding, that everything would be fine in a little while. She grasped the windowsill in an attempt to still her shaking hands.

The sudden warmth of Leith Campbell's body against her back was such a relief she wanted to cry. *Not alone*. She wasn't alone in her empty terror.

She allowed him to turn her into his embrace, and it seemed natural for her to lay her head against his chest. The solid pounding of his heart calmed her.

"Release me, witch," he murmured, then gently raised her head to meet his kiss. She never considered rejecting him.

She closed her eyes. Amazing how weird thoughts hit you at the strangest times. She was the first woman in fifty years to kiss a real man.

Then all thoughts fled, and she allowed her senses to drift free on a current of discovery. His lips, soft yet firm against hers, moved in a way that demanded a response. He traced her lips with his tongue until she softly moaned and opened her mouth to him. He explored her, and she tentatively returned the touch.

A world of sensation blossomed, the rhythmic caress of his hand on her back, the male scent she'd never known—had always known—and the exciting hardness pressed against her thigh.

She stood tottering on the edge of a new and startling universe when he released her and stepped away. She fought against a feeling of abandonment.

"I dinna need to do this." He stared at the ceiling and raked his fingers through his hair. "Ye are no witch, so I dinna need to pleasure ye to gain my freedom."

She breathed deeply, trying to control her anger, her need, her . . . disappointment. She'd kissed him only to take her mind off what she'd seen outside the window. He'd more than succeeded as a diversion.

"Just to satisfy my curiosity about how the savage mind works, would you tell me why you decided I wasn't a witch?" *Uh-oh*. She stepped back. She'd better watch her insults. A true savage could crack her head like a Coro egg.

With something suspiciously like a smile touching his lips, he nodded and his hair settled like a cloud across his gleaming shoulders. "I saw this when I kissed ye." He reached between her breasts and lifted the Celtic cross from where it lay partially hidden by the cover. "A witch wouldna wear this."

"Oh, so you thought you could kiss me, and I'd melt away like the Wicked Witch of the West?" Even furious with him, she couldn't control the hopeful pebbling of her nipples. It seemed she didn't control any part of her world right now.

"Wicked Witch of the West?" Frowning, he clasped the cross in his palm and rubbed his thumb across the intricate silver design, then gen-

27

tly laid it back between her breasts. She absorbed the heat from his palm, a brand seared into her memory.

"Forget it." He'd treated her like a booster rocket—use it; then lose it.

Amusement flickered in his glance. " 'Twas only a wee kiss."

"A wee kiss? It felt like all systems were go to me."

He studied her with narrow-eyed intensity. "Is it that I kissed ye or stopped kissing ye that has ye bleating like a sheep?"

He held her with his gaze, too intimate, too disturbing. "I wanted to believe ye a witch rather than . . ." He gestured toward the window. And for an unguarded moment she glimpsed fear in his green eyes, a fear that touched the woman in her more than a hundred fierce denials ever could. She forced down the urge to lay a comforting hand against his cheek, pushed away the picture of him turning his head until his lips touched her palm and—

She didn't want to soften toward him. Tearing her gaze from his, she walked to the door and opened it. A woman pushing some strange machine hurried past in the hall. Four-Two-N cleared her throat of the rock that seemed lodged there and called to the woman. "Excuse me, can you tell me the date?"

The woman stared at her blankly. "What the heck you doin' in there, sugar? Room three thirty-three's supposed to be empty." Then as the woman's gaze swept over the cover she wore and continued on to where Leith stood behind Fortune, her expression cleared. "Never mind; I get the picture. He must be one hell of a man if you'd take a chance on being caught makin' love when you oughta be working. Better be out in fifteen minutes, though. Big convention comin' in at noon, and this room's gonna be occupied."

"The date?" Fortune reminded her weakly.

The woman laughed. "He must be damn good if he made you forget the date." She winked at Leith over Fortune's shoulder. "Gorgeous, you ever get tired of your lady, look me up. When I'm finished with you, you won't even remember your name."

She glanced back at Fortune. "Today's October tenth, and I've got this whole floor to do, so I better get movin'. Remember, out in fifteen minutes." She started to turn away.

"The year?" Fortune prodded.

The woman looked at her strangely before answering. "Two thousand."

Fortune slammed the door shut and leaned against it. *Stay calm. Don't hyperventilate.* "It can't be 2000! When I went to sleep last night it was 2300. There's no such thing as time travel. Oh, scientists have played with the idea, but . . ." She must be the victim of some gigantic hoax. But what about Leith Campbell? What about the world outside their window?

She glanced at Leith to see his reaction.

His curse was low, graphic, and—she suspected—physically impossible. He closed his eyes for a long moment, and she watched his expression change. When he finally opened his eyes and stared at her, she wanted to turn and run from him, from his battle face. She had no doubt this *was* his battle face—all shadowed planes and hard, gleaming eyes.

"Dinna waste yer time denying what's plain to see." He walked back to the sleeping pad, then glanced at the black cat, who returned his stare with unblinking amber eyes. "Where is this place?"

"I saw Clear Lake in the distance. So if this were really the year 2000, which it isn't, then we'd be near the city of Houston in the state of Texas."

"Houston? Texas?"

He looked at her. Confusion clouded his gaze, and that frightened her as much as what she'd seen from the window.

"Texas was part of the United States of America," she clarified in an uncertain whisper. *Please let him recognize the name.* She didn't want to be trapped in this room with a madman, and she'd have to believe him a madman or else accept a truth that logically could be no truth at all.

He didn't answer, but merely shook his head, then picked up a garment from the sleeping pad. "Men *do* wear these in the year 2000?"

"Jeans. I remember now. One of my history disks. They were called *jeans.* Men and women wore them in . . ." *No!* She struggled against her rising panic. "I don't believe it. The whole world has gone crazy. It's not—"

" 'Tis! Use reason, woman. I dinna want to believe it either, but I canna deny what I've seen wi' my own eyes."

He moved close to her and she stepped back, away from his heat, his power.

Feeling as though her throat had permanently closed, she could only nod.

While she watched him struggle into the jeans, her pounding heart slowed, and she grew calmer. This was ridiculous. There had to be a reasonable explanation. She lived in an advanced civilization. She should laugh at the idea of being whisked back in time. More likely she'd eaten some bad tagan dip last night that had caused this strange dream.

Leith continued to struggle with the jeans. Aside from the fact that they were too tight, he didn't seem to understand how to fasten them.

Now calm and convinced that this whole thing was a nightmare, she could afford to be charitable. "Need some help?" Her offer was out before she thought of the consequences.

"I need no woman's help." He continued to fumble.

Patience. He's only a barlo seed in some bad tagan dip. Gritting her teeth, she reached for him. "This is a zipper, an old-fashioned fastener." She expected him to push her hand away, but surprisingly, he stood still.

The moment her hand touched his flesh, she knew she'd made a mistake. Her fingers shook as she pulled the metal teeth together. Each time her knuckles grazed his stomach, her lower regions clenched in gleeful anticipation. He didn't make it any easier when he sucked in his breath without warning.

"Enough, lass. Between yer shaking hands and these cursed metal teeth, I'm in danger of losing my future bairns." He put his fingers over hers.

Yanking the zipper up, he then chose a piece of clothing from the bed and handed it to her. "Put this on."

31

"No." This was a dream, a dream, a—

"After ye dress yerself, we can leave this room."

"No." What if it wasn't a dream? "I want to stay here."

She could almost see bits and pieces of his patience breaking away from him like the heat plates during a primitive rocket's reentry into earth's atmosphere.

"I willna hide in this room. Hiding solves nothing, and it leaves the foul taste of the coward in my mouth. 'Twas a lesson hard learned, but I learned it well."

"Fine. Leave. I'll stay here." What was she saying? She couldn't let him walk away. He was womankind's salvation, a living sperm bank. She *wouldn't* lose him.

His last bit of patience shot into hyperspace. "Ye *will* come wi' me!"

She flinched away from his thunderous pronouncement. "Why?" She hoped he didn't hear the quaver in her voice.

Roiling emotion darkened his gaze, pushed her backward with its power. "Ye dinna need to know why. Ye need only know that I willna abandon a helpless woman. I *willna* leave ye."

She opened her mouth to tell him what he could do with his "helpless woman" label, then closed it. What did it matter what he said? "I'm sure this is a dream."

He turned beseeching eyes to the ceiling. "Deliver me from a stubborn woman." Lowering his gaze, he reached out and cupped her chin with his large hand. "What were ye doing last night?"

She blinked at his unexpected question. "I . . . I

was discussing marketing trends with Three-Six-H. Muscular men are out. Potbellies are in. The comfort factor," she explained in response to his blank expression.

"God's teeth, woman. Ye would confuse Saint Peter himself."

She steeled herself to resist the rasp of his callused thumb rubbing back and forth against the side of her jaw.

"Before waking here, I fell asleep wi' Mary McDougal warm beside me and . . ." He shook his head. " 'Tis no matter. 'Twas a long time ago."

"No! I don't believe you. This is a dream, nothing but a dream. I swear, tagan dip will never touch my lips again." She jerked her head from his hand, then stumbled back—from the truth in his eyes, from the reality of his touch. A touch that seared her as no dream touch should.

She didn't want to know, had purposely not asked him, because knowing might make it true. Look at the ostrich, she thought. It stuck its head in the sand to avoid unpleasantness, and it had survived just fine when all those perky birds who poked their inquisitive beaks into everyone's business were extinct. No, nothing could force her to ask.

She asked. "How long ago?" The quaver in her voice embarrassed her.

"Three hundred years." He raked his fingers through his hair. His hand shook.

The black cat watched with slit-eyed interest, then began to purr.

Chapter Two

Leith was dead. He'd died last night. If he'd known ahead of time, he would've put more effort into his last good brawl, savored his last drop of ale, killed a few more cursed MacDonalds. If he had to go to hell, he'd like to have taken some of those thieving rogues with him.

The clergy had lied about hell, or maybe each person's hell differed. The devil was a canny one. Leith could bear fire and brimstone. He'd endured enough physical pain in his life to know. But fear?

He hadn't felt such terrible fear since he'd watched his parents slaughtered during that long-ago midnight raid. *Helplessness*. He'd hated the feeling then; he hated it now. Only a bairn, he'd cried a bairn's tears—for the loss of his mother's love, his father's gruff kindness, for his own alone-

34

ness. He'd learned several important lessons that night.

Tears couldn't bring back those you loved, couldn't make anything better. He'd never cried since. Tears were a weakness, and strong men didn't cry, didn't show weakness. Strong men didn't waste time on useless emotions. They took action.

Why was he here? *Glencoe*? No matter how deeply he tried to bury the memory of Glencoe, of the massacre, it waited, ever ready to condemn him. He need only close his eyes to relive the pain.

The cold February morn. His brother waking him to whisper that King William had issued Letters of Fire and Sword against the MacDonalds of Glencoe because the small clan had been late in pledging its allegiance to the king. The Campbell soldiers quartered at Glencoe were to rise and put to the sword all under the age of seventy, then burn their cottages.

God's blood, the MacDonalds had shared their hospitality with him, and now Leith's brother expected him to slaughter them as they slept. He couldn't do it. Even though he'd fought many a MacDonald in fair fight and bore them no love, he would *not* murder unarmed men, women, and children.

But he hadn't been able to stop the killing, and that would forever be his shame.

Leith forced away the remembered horror. This wasn't about Glencoe. He owed much more than this for Glencoe.

Mayhap one of his lesser sins had earned him

this punishment—doomed to lug behind him a stubborn innocent who claimed to make men. He'd rather shoulder a ten-stone rock. The rock wouldn't argue.

No matter. He'd do what he'd always done—*survive*.

"We canna stay here, Fortune. Put on what I brought ye."

He glanced around. A weapon. He wouldn't leave without some means of protecting them from whatever dangers lay beyond this room. Striding to the small table beside the bed, he studied the object that rested there—it had a solid, squarish base with numbers on it, with a smaller piece cradled on top. The top was connected to the base by a curled cord. It would have to do.

Lifting the cradled piece, he almost dropped it when it buzzed at him. With a jerk, he yanked the cord loose from the base. Satisfied, he wrapped the end of the cord around his hand.

"What do you think you're doing?"

He turned to face Fortune's outraged tone.

"We must have a weapon. 'Tis the best I can find." He swung his newly made weapon to demonstrate its possibilities.

She ducked even though he came nowhere near her. "I don't believe you. There's never an excuse for violence. Any disagreement can be solved with reasonable discussion."

Amazed, he stared at her. "Ye're a fool, woman."

"And you're a savage."

She looked a little uncertain about her insult, and well she should. He'd beaten men senseless for less. But how could he deny the truth? In her eyes he must seem both primitive and savage. "Aye. Now dress yerself." He headed for the door.

He'd opened it, then stepped into the hall before he realized she hadn't moved. He turned to find her still planted in the center of the room, feet spread and arms crossed defiantly.

"This woman's not moving, primitive person."

He silently groaned. Would his punishment never end? What had he done during his life to deserve this woman? It had to be more than just his wish to send a few MacDonalds to hell. His last raid? Maybe. He'd relieved several clergymen of their worldly goods—helping them live up to their vows of poverty. *No*. More likely it was the willing women he'd taken. He savored the memories. There'd been a lot of women in his life, all willing.

"Come wi' me, lass, so I can protect ye from danger. Ye need a strong man to fight for ye. Trust me." He smiled the smile that had convinced Mary McDougal a heated night spent in his arms was worth the loss of her questionable virginity.

Fortune looked him up. She looked him down. She sniffed her disdain. "Not only primitive, but violent. The only danger I see is standing in front of me. Any problem I meet, I'll solve in a civilized way—calmly, logically."

He should leave her. The temptation called to him, but he'd sworn on his mother's grave never to desert a helpless woman, and Fortune *was* helpless, with her fantasies of a world with no wickedness or violence. He might know nothing about this time, but he knew human nature. Men had laughed and raised drinks to each other before the blood flowed at Glencoe. The possibility of violence lurked in even the most peaceful setting.

"A peeping chick in a forest of hungry wolves," he muttered. Resigned, he returned to her side. "Why would ye stay here?"

She stared at him as though he were mad. "I don't know how this horrible thing happened, but it happened in this room and this is where I'll stay until someone sends me home."

A troublesome woman. A vexing combination of defiance and stubbornness with the body of an angel. He narrowed his gaze. The body of an angel with tousled hair the color of the vixen whose den he'd found last week, and eyes like a cloudless sky. The devil could at least have provided him with a shriveled crone, one who wouldn't torment him with her attractions.

He'd try reason, although it was a strategy that often proved useless with women. "Ye canna stay in this room. Ye heard the woman say others would soon arrive. Besides, what if ye ne'er return home?"

"Never go home?" Her horrified expression mirrored his own feelings.

Home. He pushed aside thoughts of Hugh, of Glencoe. He couldn't allow them to sour his memories. Home was the mountains, the glens, the heather. The women. He closed his eyes, remembering—heather like a purple sea flowing across the mountain, and Dora MacKay lying in its midst smiling up at him. After that day, heather had always owned a warm spot in his heart . . . and other places.

He opened his eyes. Perhaps if he did suitable penance to appease whatever powers had put him here, he might one day see the Highlands again. *Suitable penance*. What penance would satisfy a god or devil with such a strange sense of humor? If it was his love of women that had annoyed a jealous power . . .

Love of women He glanced at Fortune. Powers had cast him into this time with this woman for a reason. *Virgin*. She was a virgin. Could the powers want him to . . . ? Why choose him? He thought of all the women he'd pleasured. Who better? But Fortune? Teaching this woman the joys of love would be like drinking too much ale. It made a man feel wondrous that night, but exacted a painful vengeance the next morning. He exhaled sharply. Of course, if it were easy it would not be adequate atonement for all the times he'd sinned. Still, something about his penance seemed passing strange.

His thoughts splintered at Fortune's snort of disbelief. "Of course I'll go home. I refuse to spend the rest of my life here. Leave if you want." The slight tremble of her lower lip belied her brave pronouncement.

That tremble touched him. She was, after all, a woman, and he would never walk away from a lass, even if she rejected his aid. "If ye dinna dress yerself, I'll do it for ye."

She narrowed her eyes to slits the color of a storm-darkened loch. "Why're you forcing me to go with you?"

"Because I can." He smiled. " 'Tis one of the good things about being a primitive person. I do what I want—"

"Barbarian!"

"And ye canna stop me." He held up his hand against another barrage of insults. "Ye canna hide from life, Fortune. Hiding doesna save the bird from the hunter." *Hiding didna save me from my demons.* "Come awa' with me, whilst we try to make sense of what's happened."

"Extinction has its merits," she huffed, but reluctantly pulled the clothes on.

When finally dressed, she gazed at herself in horror. "I can't leave like this."

He thought her beautiful, but suspected she wouldn't accept a compliment from him. " 'Tis a wondrous gown."

"It's a wedding gown, and it's too long." She stared at the trailing folds of white material as though she still stood naked.

"Aye, 'tis a wee bit long, and I'd prefer ye in red."

She glared up at him. "Gowns like this are totally impractical, and red is an awful color on me. Besides being primitive, you have abominable taste."

Good. She was mad. A woman with red hair should have a temper. "Red is a passionate color, lass." He stared pointedly at her hair. "I admire passion in a woman."

"I bet you do." She tottered shakily back to the bed on the strange high-heeled shoes, then plunked herself in its middle. "That does it. I'm not leaving."

He sighed. He hadn't wanted to do this, but . . .

Reaching the bed in two strides, he scooped her up and flung her across his shoulder.

She rewarded him with a startled gasp as her body stiffened in protest. A woman in his own time would be kicking, screaming, and calling him foul names. But Fortune would not resort to such demonstrations. Kicking would be violence, and screaming would not be a calm, reasonable thing to do. Lucky for him, but sad for Fortune. Every lass should spend some time kicking and screaming. It was the womanly thing to do.

"Animal!" Her hiss reminded him of a tiny outraged snake—seemingly harmless, but with venom enough to fell a grown man.

"Yer curses lack bite, lass. Ye must learn to curse a man with strong words. Mayhap we should start with something simple—bastard."

"Bas . . ." She couldn't get it out. "Put me down before someone sees us and asks questions we don't want to answer."

Logical. He could learn to hate that trait in her. Carefully, he set her on her feet.

She glowered up at him. "I've decided to go with you. While you were playing caveman, I realized you were right this once. We can't stay here, and you're obviously not fit to cope with even this degree of modern life. You need someone to keep you from lopping off the heads of innocent strangers. Besides, we need to find a place to discuss why we were sent here together and how we can get back to our own times." She shrugged. "It's the only reasonable thing to do."

"I must have sinned greviously to deserve such penance."

"What?"

"When my penance is done ye'll be free of me."

Never. She didn't understand his mutterings about penance, but one thing she knew for sure— he was the one. *Him.* The man chosen to repopu-

41

late the earth with males. She'd forgotten that little fact during her battle of words with him. Luckily, she'd remembered while she hung over his shoulder. Must've been all that blood rushing to her head that had cleared her senses.

Why Leith? She didn't know, but humans had learned there were no random acts in the universe. He was the one. This stay in the year 2000 must be like a halfway house. She'd ease him into what to expect when he got to her time. No, Leith wasn't getting away from her. "We can come back here when—"

He made an irritated noise. "Powers strong enough to drag us from our time dinna need us in a certain room, lass."

His statement made sense, though she hated to admit anything he said made sense. "I suppose you're right, but there's an order in the universe, and I think we'll have to come back to—"

He smiled at her. Lord, that smile would mow women down by the millions. Of course it didn't affect her in the least. She touched her nose. Was it in that ancient tale of Pinocchio that someone's nose grew when they told a lie?

"Dinna fash yerself, lass. I'll take care of ye."

"Hmmph." Even as she rejected his easy assurance of male dominance, a second reason for staying with him poked at her—one she resisted: fear. The only fear she'd experienced in her life had revolved around the worry that her newest model wouldn't be sensual enough, marketable enough. She'd never felt the gut-wrenching fear she felt now. And Leith Campbell was the only familiar person, however aggravating, in a world gone crazy. She'd cling to a Rilior smoke devil right now, if he offered a familiar face. She glanced up at Leith. *Close enough*.

"Come, Fortune."

Come, Fido. Fear, confusion, and anger jigged in time to her pounding heart. Anger leaped the highest. "Four-Two-N. My name is . . ." Reason joined the dance. No, she'd be safer answering to Fortune. No need to call attention to herself.

She studied the man next to her. She'd never blend into the local populace as long as she hung around with him, and she intended to hang around him like Saturn's rings. She refused to admit any relief at the thought. No way did she need him.

And he had a lot of nerve assuming *he* should lead. She was much more qualified to think of a rational plan of action. She'd always been the one in control. Even as a child, she'd made her own decisions while her mother space-hopped across the galaxy.

OK, she couldn't match him physically, but she could punch holes in him intellectually. After all, she had a six-hundred-year advantage. *Punch*? She'd have to make sure none of him rubbed off on her. "For your information, Your Hugeness, intelligence is power, not size and strength." She felt like a child sticking out her tongue, but she couldn't help herself.

Leith grinned at her. "Mayhap in yer time, but we're not in yer time. And I'll always be bigger than ye."

Bully. "Fine. Lead on, oh primeval one. Should I stay two steps behind you?"

"Aye, although five would show more respect, ye ken."

He'd already turned, so she couldn't see if he'd smiled when he said that. She certainly hoped so.

"I realize you think you know best, but I'd like to make a few reasonable suggestions." She tried not to let the mesmerizing motion of his buttocks in those too-tight jeans distract her. "I've watched history disks of earlier societies, so I might have a better grasp of survival strategies."

She raced to keep up with him as he pounded down an endless flight of stairs. He'd gone right past an archaic, but perfectly good elevator. Of course, he wouldn't know what an elevator was.

"I dinna need yer help. It shouldna be hard to find a wee cave that's dry and free of vermin. Ye can start the fire whilst I kill some fearsome beast wi' my club. When I drag it home, ye can skin it, then cook the meat. 'Tis simple."

She didn't appreciate his sarcasm. At least she hoped it was sarcasm. She was too out of breath to make a cutting reply. The flow of blood must've been different in earlier humans. It obviously bypassed the brain and went right to the legs.

At the bottom of the stairs he opened a door, then stopped dead. The force of gravity from her warp-speed descent carried her into his back with enough strength to wring a grunt from her.

For one dazzling moment, she forgot everything in the cling wrap sensation of his back and buttocks melded to her breasts and stomach. The empty spasming of her lower regions reminded her they yearned for some melding too. If only he were a little shorter.

He was so darn tall. She wasn't used to looking up to people, literally speaking, of course. It made her feel . . .

No! It made her feel nothing. Evolving humans had to be physically large and strong to cope with their hostile environments. In an advanced civilization, mental capacity was more important than physical size.

A heavy weight landing on the trailing end of her gown interrupted her satisfying thoughts of anthropological superiority. Glancing over her shoulder, she met the black cat's enigmatic stare. "What's with you, cat?"

"He's taken wi' ye, lass. Are ye certain ye have no witches in yer family?"

She glared at Leith's strong back as he stepped into the rest-over's lobby. Dragging her feline hitchhiker behind her, she moved to stand beside him.

He turned in a circle, not bothering to hide his amazement. " 'Tis passing wondrous."

She gazed up at a huge skylight that let in the sun's harsh glare. Last night the rest-over's ceiling had glowed with soft, mood-enhancing light. She squinted at the walls. Wood paneling? Last night the walls had been a kaleidoscope of muted colors that shifted and flowed, responding to the energy levels of the many guests. Glancing down, she blanched at the red floor covering. Didn't these people know anything about the soothing influence of neutral color schemes? And everything was so . . . cluttered. Plants, paintings, statues. "Garish."

"Ye dinna like it?"

"I prefer lighter shades—unobtrusive, restful. In my society, we use our minds to work, and mental stress is tiring. Neutral colors leave me calm and rested." She started at his wide breadth of chest. What would he know of stress? She'd bet he solved his problems by hitting them over the head with his club. She'd make it simpler for him. "What I mean is—"

" 'Tis a fine carpet."

"What? Oh, yes, you have this thing about red."

"Ye'd look fine in red, lass, wi' a gown that dipped to here." He ran his finger from the base of her throat, where her pulse beat madly, to between her breasts—a line of sizzling, molten·. . . red.

Enough. He had this touchy-feely thing, and his touch bothered her. She wasn't used to someone touching her. Even her mother hadn't bothered with hugs, viewing them as unnecessary physical contact.

Besides, she was trapped in a strange time with an even stranger man, and all she could do was discuss color preferences.

Turning away, she dumped the cat off her gown, then started toward the main desk. The cat immediately returned to his seat on her train. She tried to ignore Leith's chuckle.

The few men who looked at her seemed more amused than admiring. She must be quite a sight with her uncombed hair and too-long gown, hauling a black cat along on her train.

The women were a different matter. They riveted their attention on Leith like a rocket's homing device. She supposed there was a certain residual fascination with the primitive male animal. Even she felt it . . . a little . . . very little . . . so little it wasn't worth mentioning.

She stopped at the desk, then coughed to get the white-shirted attendant's attention. He stared at her with wide-eyed interest, obviously too polite to ask questions. A big improvement over Neanderthal Man behind her. "Do you have a . . ."—she searched her memory for the right word—"newspaper?" Thank heavens she'd studied all those history disks.

The man pointed toward a metal dispenser. "Fifty cents."

"Never mind," she murmured, and started to turn away. Another problem. Humans still used money in the year 2000.

Leaning over the counter, the man peered at her train, and his polite expression changed to a grin. "How'd you get the cat to stay there?"

"We glued him." Still dragging the cat behind her, she walked back to where Leith continued to gawk at his surroundings, while every woman gawked at him.

"Umm. Sir?" Leith turned at the attendant's call. "You can't leave with hotel property. You'll have to return it."

"Hotel property?" Leith stared blankly at him.

"The phone receiver. You have the hotel's phone receiver." The man's face was turning an interesting shade of red.

Phone. Fortune searched her memory. Of course. Phones were primitive communication devices used before . . . she smiled up at Leith. "He wants your weapon."

As Leith's expression darkened, she moved to

47

head off an explosion. "Give it to him. We can't afford to make a scene and call attention to ourselves. You can find another weapon."

Leith's intense gaze made her want to squirm. Finally he nodded. "Aye. Ye're right."

They walked back to the attendant, and Fortune didn't know what surprised her more, that Leith gave up his weapon without a fight or that he'd actually agreed with something she'd said.

Once the attendant had the phone receiver, he dismissed Leith with a supercilious smile and turned his attention to Fortune. "Exactly what did you intend doing with this?"

Fortune glared at him. *Salian slug*. She didn't know why his patronizing attitude toward Leith made her mad, but it did. She could see Leith's thunderous expression. *Uh-oh*.

She grabbed Leith's arm and turned toward the door. Luckily, Leith allowed her to guide him. Glancing over her shoulder, she smiled sweetly at the attendant. "We were expecting an important call."

They'd leave the rest-over now. And as unreal as this place seemed, it felt safe compared with what they'd find outside. Fortune controlled the urge to race back to their room, then curl up in a fetal position on the sleeping pad. She was scared. She'd never known danger. There was nothing to fear in the year 2300, except perhaps the calm predictability of each day. Sometimes she'd wished for excitement. Perhaps she'd wished too hard. Perhaps this really *was* a dream. "Pinch me. I have to make sure this isn't a dream."

Leith's eyes lit up like those of a child presented

with a season pass to Planet Play. "Yer bottom is nicely fleshed. I'll pinch ye there and ye'll ne'er feel it."

"Pinch my bottom and you're space trash. Here." She pointed to her arm. "I'd do it myself, but it'll be more convincing if someone else does it."

He shook his head. " 'Tis useless. I think ye know this isna a dream." The light in his eyes faded, and she glimpsed turmoil in their jade depths before he turned from her.

They'd reached the automatic doors, and as the glass panels silently swung open, she walked outside. Glancing back, she watched Leith step gingerly past the doors. He'd paled, and a sheen of sweat covered his torso. Looking quickly away, she hoped he hadn't seen her staring; she sensed he wouldn't want a witness to his fear.

Sympathy touched her. She'd expected the doors to open, understood the four-wheeled machines that roared up and down the street. But to Leith, they must seem like terrifying monsters. He needed her. No matter what he said, he really *needed* her. She wondered at the warm glow the thought brought.

Still basking in the glow, she looked around her. When she turned back to the rest-over, Leith was gone.

Gone! Oh, no. Fear caught at her, cutting off all rational thought. She couldn't lose him. No matter that dozens of men walked around her. *He* was the one.

Intent on locating Leith, she stepped off the curb without noticing the traffic. Turning in every direction, she finally saw him. He was standing beside a little old woman with . . . blue hair? What was the old woman handing him?

The screech of tires jerked her attention away from Leith. Too late she remembered she wasn't in her own time, and vehicles didn't have sensors to guide them around things in their path. Frozen, she stared at the vehicle hurtling toward her and could muster only one thought: *Leith will be alone*.

If a person's life was supposed to flash in front of them, she was denied that treat as someone flung her from harm's way, then fell on her. The air escaped her lungs in a startled whoosh, and as she fought for breath she felt the mad pounding of her heart and heard the cat's surprised yowl.

Leith. She'd found him, and she was still in one piece. Life was good. Even with dignity and breath gone, her body refused to ignore the solid length of him pressed against her. Her nipples swelled in joyful reaction at the contact with real male flesh, and she didn't even want to think about the lower half of her body's response to a male leg lodged between her thighs. If she didn't move fast, she'd have a revolution on her hands.

"Get off me before I . . ." What had she read about ancient defenses against unwanted male advances? "Before I kick you in the groin." Of course, the manuals hadn't indicated what to do when said groin was pressed against her thigh.

"Ye're an ungrateful wench. Here I've just saved ye from one of yon devil's toys and not a word of thanks do I get."

"Devil's toys?" Fortune turned her head so she could peer beneath his muscled arm. She squinted at the four-wheeled vehicle marked TAXI that had pulled up to the curb beside them. There was a boxy vehicle—she thought it was called a truck—with ICE CREAM emblazoned on its side parked behind it. The singer on the truck's loudspeaker bemoaned his stay at someplace called the Heartbreak Hotel. A sad song about love. No one sang love songs anymore. Without men, what was the use?

Exhaust fumes engulfed her and she coughed. When she got home she'd appreciate her pollution-free hovercraft a lot more.

When she got home. The sudden reminder of her predicament made her response harsher than she'd planned. "If you hadn't run off with that blue-haired woman, I wouldn't have stepped into the street. Let me up."

He pushed himself off her and stood. The sudden flow of cooler air across her body made her shiver. She looked up and met his equally cool gaze.

"Dinna think because ye come from another age ye know everything. Blundering into the path of that cursed machine was foolish." A smile touched his lips. "I helped the old woman carry her things. She gave me some pieces of paper and told me to come to her room so I could light her fire. I dinna think 'tis cold enough for a fire." He held the pieces of paper out for her to see.

"Light her fire?" Money. The pieces of paper were money. "I think she wanted you to . . . Forget it. Her heart couldn't take it. You'd kill her."

"Aye." His smile widened. " 'Tis what I thought. I'd turned to leave when I saw ye needed saving."

He'd shielded her with his body. Unexpectedly, the thought thrilled her. That he'd sacrifice his body for hers was wonderful. Not logical. In her time people accepted the consequences of their own actions. But . . . wonderful.

She looked away. "I'm sorry." He'd saved her life. "I don't know what's happening to me. Sensitivity's part of my culture, but you make me want to scream and . . . Must be something in the air. Uncivilized oxygen molecules." She wished the answer were that simple.

He exhaled sharply and glanced around. "Mayhap we should—"

"That bum of an ice-cream pusher cut me off. Didja see him? Now he's runnin' away before I can plant my foot in his butt. Musta got his license outa a cereal box." A pair of skinny legs encased in jeans cut off Fortune's view of the street. "Yo, you guys want a taxi or not? Better let me take you someplace private, 'cause I think it's illegal to do it on the sidewalk. Know what I mean?"

Startled, Fortune shifted her gaze to the wiry little man who'd climbed from the taxi. His grating laughter galvanized her. Pushing down the gown that had ridden up to her thighs, she accepted Leith's extended hand.

After pulling her to her feet, Leith turned to the taxi driver. He'd seen these machines from the window, so he knew people rode in them, like carriages without horses. When he returned to Scotland, he'd never declare anything impossible again. "We must find clothing and shelter. Can ye help us?"

The small man's gaze darted to Fortune, then to

Ganymede, and finally returned to Leith. He lifted a cap with the words HARLEY DAVIDSON on it from his head, then slicked back his thinning hair. "I can take you to hell if you got the dough to pay for it."

"Gee, and here I thought we were there already," Fortune muttered.

Fascinated, Leith stared at the man. "Dough? Ye take dough in payment? 'Tis strange. Yer wife must do an uncommon amount of baking."

Fortune leaned toward him, and for a moment Leith forgot everything. Her eyes sparkled as she tried not to laugh. If he were home, he'd woo her with soft compliments, then lie with her in the heather. Though he suspected soft compliments would have little effect on Fortune. He also suspected her laughter was aimed at him. It wasn't a comfortable feeling.

"Dough is the common word for money, payment. Like the old woman gave you." She turned her attention back to the driver. "We don't have much money. We'd just gotten into town when creditors took everything we had except what we wore." She smiled weakly.

Leith groaned inwardly. Who would believe such a tale?

The driver slapped his cap back on his head and nodded sagely. "Yeah, those loan sharks don't cut anyone no slack. Lucky they didn't break your legs. Next time stick to finance companies. Lots of interest, but no broken legs." He peered at Fortune's chest, and Leith felt an urge to break some legs himself. "Nice cross and chain you got there. Worth some money. Why don't I take you guys to a pawnshop, see what we can do?"

Leith nodded. He didn't know what a pawnshop was, but if it would get them some of this badly needed "dough," he favored it.

Fortune shook her head. "Whoa. This cross has been in my family for generations." She clasped it protectively.

The driver rubbed his hand across his forehead, then heaved a sigh. "Look, guys. I'm tryin' to help you. No money, no ride, no nothin'. Understand? Besides, your cross isn't gone forever. Get some cash; then you can get it out of hock."

Leith watched Fortune consider the proposition while she held the cross in her clenched fist. He was glad she wouldn't part with it easily. It comforted him to know that in her perfect world, possessiveness still flourished. He'd begun to think no human traits had survived the passage of time.

Her decision made, she nodded. "OK. But as soon as we get some money, I'm coming back for it."

The driver adjusted his cap, then peered more closely at Leith. "Funny. You look just like a guy I used to drive to the library. Hugh Campbell. Real smart. Always looking up stuff about Scotland. Wanted to write a book about his ancestors. Old guy, but you sure look like him. You related?"

Leith felt the cold fingertips of fate dancing along his spine. Coincidence? He didn't think so. " 'Tis possible. Ye must tell me where this Campbell lives."

The driver shrugged. "He doesn't. Killed in a car crash a year ago. Too bad. Nice guy. I can tell you where his wife lives, though. She's real interested in Scotland, too."

Fortune still clasped her cross as she stared at a group of men walking past. She turned an uncertain gaze toward Leith. "Maybe we're moving too fast. Maybe we should go back into the rest-over. Maybe—"

Leith remembered the raid, his parents' dying cries. He'd cowered in his hiding place, frozen with fear and horror. Later, he'd lain awake agonizing, wondering if he could've helped, done something to save his mother, his father.

He'd saved his own life, but at the price of his conscience. He'd never hide again. "Ye canna let fate push ye around. Ye must take it by the throat and throttle it." He'd probably horrified her anew with his violent image, but it was how he felt.

The driver opened the vehicle's door, and Leith bent down to peer inside. Stale smoke and strangeness assailed him. His palms began to sweat, and he wiped them against his legs. The roughness of the fabric reminded him that his one piece of clothing belonged to someone else. He owned nothing. He was Adam in a strange Garden of Eden. His Eve? He glanced at Fortune. Unlikely. She'd probably explain to the serpent that she already knew everything and had no need of his apple.

"Are you getting in?" Fortune sounded impatient.

He didn't want to. He'd rather face a hundred MacDonalds than climb into this strange machine. But he was a warrior, and warriors faced death in battle without showing fear. Could this be worse? *Yes.*

Straightening, he stepped aside while Fortune

climbed in and slid to the far window. He took a deep, steadying breath, then eased in beside her. The cat leaped in after him and settled comfortably onto Fortune's lap. The driver closed their door, then climbed into the front seat.

When the machine roared, he wanted to fling open the door and leap to safety. Sweat trickled down his chest, and his breath came fast and shallow. Pressing his back against the seat, he clenched his fists. The machine slowly began to move, and he feared he might vomit.

Suddenly he felt Fortune's hand covering his clenched fist. Gently she pried open his fingers, then held his hand in hers.

He didn't want to look at her. Didn't want her to see the hated fear in his eyes. But he needed something to cling to, so he clasped her hand tightly, thankfully.

"This whole thing is crazy, but it's crazier for you than it is for me." Her voice was low, calm. She squeezed his hand.

He had to be strong. It was not right that she should comfort him. He felt less than a man. And because he could not accept this sudden weakness, he denied it. " 'Tis nothing."

"I know." Leith glanced at her, expecting mockery, but she gazed back at him with belief. He turned away to stare out the window and drew in a deep, calming breath, unable to speak any words of gratitude. She'd given him a gift beyond value—his pride.

He thought about this while Fortune and the driver were in the pawnshop getting money in exchange for the cross. When they returned to the taxi, Leith studied her forlorn expression as she dragged the ends of her gown inside, then closed the door. He controlled his urge to touch the spot where the cross had rested, and swore he'd find a way to rescue it.

"So you guys need clothes? You're newlyweds. What the heck do you need clothes for?"

Leith wanted to strangle the driver for his bold comment, but he couldn't anger anyone who'd offered to help them.

"You don't wanna go to a store dressed like that." The driver paused in his conversation long enough to glare at another driver and to give him some sort of finger signal. Leith understood that language perfectly. "Tell you what I'll do. I'll take you to a place you can stay cheap, then loan you something you can wear to go shopping. How's that sound?" He grinned into the mirror at them. One front tooth was missing.

Fortune's smile was relieved. "That's wonderful. We're so lucky we met you—"

"Blade. Just call me Blade." His glance shifted to Fortune's chest.

Leith's anger surprised him. "Mayhap ye should watch where ye're going." He cast Fortune a glance, but she seemed unaware of the sexual currents surrounding her. And she hadn't questioned Blade's willingness to help them. She might be at ease with machines, but she didn't know much about men.

"Why are ye doing this?" Leith shot a hard stare at the mirror.

Blade's joviality died. "Sorta owe Hugh Campbell. Lent me a few bucks when I needed it. Can't

57

pay him back, and his wife sure don't need it, so I'll use the money to help you guys and call everything even."

Leith nodded. "Aye. Honor. Now I understand ye."

No one spoke for the rest of the trip. Leith tried to relax as he stared at the wondrous sights they passed. He couldn't quite decide how he felt. His overwhelming fear now warred with awe and . . . excitement. Glancing at Fortune, he also admitted a sense of anticipation.

His penance. Assailed by so many emotions, he hadn't had time to think about it. He thought of it now. Narrowing his gaze, he watched the gentle rise and fall of Fortune's chest. He pictured himself peeling the cloth away from her breasts, exposing the creamy flesh, touching one pink nipple with his tongue, then watching it pucker, become a hard nub.

Something else was growing hard at a wondrous rate. Yes, he would look forward to paying for his sins. With penance such as this, he would be sorely tempted to raid a score of clergymen.

They finally pulled to a stop in front of a small white house surrounded by trees. It looked like heaven to Leith.

He climbed out, but before he could offer Fortune his hand, she'd clambered out the opposite door and walked around to stand beside him. The cat returned to his seat on her trailing gown.

Arching her back, Fortune stretched. Leith followed the motion and hungrily thought of the delights that swelled beneath the layers of white material.

An Original Sin

"How can people stand riding in things like that? I felt every bump in the road." She glanced at Leith and grimaced.

He couldn't help smiling. When she frowned, she had a way of thrusting out her bottom lip that was . . . enticing.

" 'Tis better than wrapping yer legs around a horse and plodding through a driving rain wi' no protection."

His smile widened, and she glanced away. Primitive men were easy to read. He wasn't thinking about wrapping his legs around a horse. It disturbed her that she wasn't either. Unbidden, she saw an image of him as he'd looked standing beside her sleeping pad, all smooth flesh and tight muscle. At a time like this she'd have thought she'd have better things to think about.

Like how was she supposed to get Leith to her time? And why had cosmic forces shackled her with a man from 1700? Why couldn't she just grab a man from this time? She glanced at Blade. *Maybe not.*

She wished cosmic forces had chosen someone else to do the dirty work. Of course, she was probably the most qualified. She knew women's fantasies, listened to them on a daily basis as she took their orders for customized men. She certainly knew men's bodies. No one could do a quality check like she could.

She let her gaze inventory Leith from his shining mane to his spectacular buns and muscular legs. *What a total package.* She sighed. *Fine.* She understood. Leith probably had superior genes, but—

"Let's get you folks inside so we can find you

something to go shopping in. Me and my old lady own this place. Just moved out yesterday. Got ourselves a double-wide on a few acres down in San Leon. She's inside practicing her— Hey, here she is now."

Fortune looked up . . . and up . . . and up. No human stood on the rickety old porch, but a Valkyrie, come to escort a fallen hero to Valhalla. Tall and broad, with bright yellow hair whipping in the breeze, she looked as though she could heft an army of fallen heroes across her wide shoulders. Obviously she'd come for Leith, so Fortune would quietly sneak away before—

"Welcome home, dumpling." With that greeting, the Valkyrie grasped one of the many knives secured to her person and let fly.

Once again Fortune ended up flat on her back staring into riveting green eyes. This position threatened to become habit-forming.

" 'Tis a dangerous time we've come to, but dinna fear; I'll protect ye." He glanced up to where the knife still quivered in the tree trunk above them.

His eyes glittered with excitement. He *enjoyed* this. She supposed she ought to expect that in a primitive mentality. But she didn't have a primitive mentality, and she was scared.

"You guys lie around on the ground a lot, don't you? Must really have the hots for each other."

She stared up at Blade. He grinned and winked at her.

"Get up and meet my wife, Lily. World-class knife thrower. Rated number eight in the whole country."

Leith climbed to his feet, then helped Fortune

up. Ganymede clung to her gown like a Shundi sucker. None too gently, she scraped him off and plopped him on the ground. He registered his displeasure with a low growl.

Doing a little low growling herself, she followed the males up the path to where the Valkyrie lovingly fondled another of her lethal weapons.

"Welcome to the year 2000," Fortune offered to no one in particular.

Chapter Three

I gotta tell you, plagues are easier. I could whip up one of those suckers in five seconds flat. Black Death. Sorta has a nice ring to it. Too bad it went outa style.

Physical *things are a snap. You want a hot-as-hell forest fire? Kid's play. How about a great tidal wave? No strain.*

But I sweat the emotional stuff. See, I can't mess with people's minds. Some stupid rule.

So far things are goin' OK. Not great, but OK. I didn't want that cross comin' along for the ride, but I can't touch religious symbols. Another stupid rule. I hate rules.

And where'd this Hugh Campbell come from? Co-incidences make me nervous. Somethin' about that damned ice-cream man bothers me, too. Big guy, fuzzy hair and beard. Reminds me of someone.

No one better be messin' with my show. Hey, I'm an artist, and I don't like anyone tryin' to paint my picture for me. Get the idea? Last jerk who tried that trick is lookin' outa someone's fish tank right now.

I'm not gonna think about it anymore. It'll just upset me, and when I get upset my tummy starts hurtin'; then I have to drink a gallon of that pink stuff. I'll think of somethin' else.

Is Fortune Cookie hot or what? Great babe. I can sure pick 'em. Hope she doesn't let me down and fall for some bozo she meets on the street. Shouldn't be a problem, though. Hey, Leith's a great-lookin' guy. Just like me. That's why I chose him. But he's a little old-fashioned. Know what I mean? Now me, I believe in women's lib. I love free and easy women. OK, so I love any kind of woman. What can I say; it's a weakness.

Right now, I'm starved. Hope they don't buy cheap cat food, the stuff that tastes like cardboard. But great artists gotta be willin' to suffer.

That's me. The Michelangelo of cosmic catastrophes. I'm just workin' on a different ceiling.

"Ye're beautiful, and I willna let anyone take ye from me. Ye make me a man again."

Fortune felt like covering her ears. She'd gotten what she deserved for listening at the door. She'd spent a few minutes exploring the small sleeping-room—wondering at lights you had to switch on, a sleeping pad with legs—then gone looking for Leith. When she'd heard his voice, she couldn't resist eavesdropping.

How had it happened so fast? She'd been gone for less than ten minutes, and he was declaring his love for the overabundant Lily. She should've known. When he'd first seen Lily out in the yard, his eyes had glazed and turned predatory.

Fine. She'd put a positive spin on this. If cosmic forces had decided to repopulate the earth with males, then they'd obviously need a man with a tomcat mentality. They'd probably scoured the time continuum for the most overactive libido they could find.

She blinked back unexpected tears. What did she care? She didn't even like him.

Of course the tears were for Blade. How would he take the news? After all, he couldn't possibly compete with Leith. Leith was . . . a rotten piece of space sewage! How dare he seduce their host's wife and put them in jeopardy!

Armed with righteous anger, Fortune flung the door open and charged into the room. She skidded to a stop when she found only Leith. He held one of Lily's knives in his hand.

"OK, where is she? Lily, if you're hiding, come out. I know everything." Fortune swung her gaze to take in the faded floral couch, the ripped leather recliner, and the coffee table cluttered with what seemed like hundreds of knives. *Hmm.* Maybe she'd been a bit precipitous. Lily with a fresh supply of knives would be a formidable opponent.

"Are ye daft? Lily and Blade are outside."

She narrowed her gaze. "Then who were you talking to?"

Humor flared in his eyes. "Ye listened at the door."

She glanced at the floor, noting a burned spot in the carpet. "I didn't." She inspected the ceiling, wondering about the hole right above the couch. "I absolutely wouldn't." She stared at the wall, pondering the slash mark right in the middle of the photo of a younger Blade. Either a bad practice session for Lily, or a momentary problem in paradise. "I was walking down the hall, and I staggered into the door. Weak from hunger, I think. Anyway, I couldn't help hearing."

"Ye dinna lie well, lass."

He smiled, and she fought to maintain her affronted, *who, me?* expression. "If you weren't talking to Lily, then you must've been talking to"—she peered at his hand—"the knife?"

He glanced away, but couldn't hide his embarrassed flush.

"Ye dinna understand the relationship between a man and his weapon." He lovingly caressed the smooth wooden handle.

She imagined his fingers sliding across the swell of her breasts. She shivered at the vivid image.

"A sharp blade protects a man from enemies." He touched the gleaming point with his fingertip.

She imagined his fingertip touching her nipples, her nipples puckering to exclamation points of yearning.

"A wise man keeps his knife close."

He glanced down at his jeans, and she understood his sudden look of frustration. Not even a blade would fit between skin and fabric. *Good thing.* She was jealous, and jealousy of an inanimate object did not indicate great mental health.

"Yes, but you *talked* to the thing."

"Have ye ne'er talked to something that couldna talk back?"

"Never. I mean, I said a few words to the cat, but it couldn't be termed a conversation."

"Never?"

He stared at her, and she resisted the urge to squirm.

"OK. When I was a kid, Mom wasn't around much, so I used to talk to Skirky." God, she'd forgotten all about Skirky.

"Skirky?" That slow, *I'm sexy as hell* smile spread across his face.

"I got him on a trip to Polius. He was a fuzzy yellow tube-toy with big purple eyes. He looked kind of like a giant caterpillar. Researchers had found that tubular-shaped stuffed toys comforted children more than any of our advanced play designs. The discovery sparked a craze for retro-toys. Every child wanted an old-fashioned stuffed toy exactly like her ancestors played with." Fortune laughed and shook her head. "I had educational toys that could probably build a space port in a pinch, but I only loved Skirky. I slept with him until I was seven."

"What happened to him?"

Her smile faded, and she stared beyond Leith into the past. "Mom came home unexpectedly and found me talking to him. She threw him away. Said I was too old to be talking to a mangy-looking toy." Fortune shrugged.

"She shouldna have done that." His voice turned soft, understanding. " 'Twas a friend, someone to ease yer loneliness."

Lonely? Yes, she could admit it now. An only child, she'd wished with a child's intensity for her mother—someone to talk to, to touch. *Forget it.*

66

Think about now. Mom had probably been right. Life was real, and she shouldn't waste it on nonsense. "Skirky doesn't matter. He's been gone a long time. Let's get back to you and your conversation with that knife."

He held it up. " 'Tis a beauty. When I showed Lily how I could throw a knife, she said I shouldna be wi'out one. I canna believe she gave this to me."

His smile would melt ice on Pluto, and she understood exactly why Lily had given him the knife. Lily had better watch it. Her sudden stab of fierce possessiveness surprised Fortune.

Before she could investigate that disturbing emotion, Blade entered the room. "Go take a look in the hall closet. Friends left a few clothes behind. You might find some stuff to wear."

Leith was confused. They both wore the garments called jeans with shirts and "sneakers." What a strange society where men and women dressed alike. But he had to admit the jeans showed Fortune's form even better than the gown. He allowed his gaze to follow her slender legs up to her nicely rounded bottom, then gave himself permission to continue his journey to the swell of her breasts. Their spectacular peaks reminded him of home. Thank heavens women's forms hadn't changed in six hundred years.

He could not allow lustful thoughts to distract him, though. There would be time enough later to consider his penance.

Survival. He turned to Blade. "Before we leave to find food and clothing, ye must tell me how much this dwelling will cost."

Blade ran his hand along the side of his face. "Well, it ain't fancy, but it's got a good location. Since this is paying my debt to Hugh Campbell, I'll let it go for two hundred a month."

Leith glanced at Fortune, and she nodded. He watched as she pulled the pieces of paper she'd gotten in exchange for her cross from her pocket and offered them to Blade. "Take what you need."

Leith closed his eyes. He couldn't watch. Her complete trust in everyone's honesty would be the death of them. But the pieces of paper were hers to lose, so he'd not say anything.

"Not smart carrying around a bundle like that. You might want to put some of it in a checking account." Blade waved away the offered money. "Pay me when you get on your feet. I can wait."

Leith opened his eyes. *Count Checkin*? He reached out, snatched the paper from Fortune's hand, then glared at Blade. Fortune stood with a dazed expression, staring at her empty hand. "I dinna know this Count Checkin, and I dinna trust my dough to anyone but myself. I willna answer for the fate of anyone who tries to take it from me."

Blade shook his head. "Hey, don't look at me. I wouldn't touch your money. I heard the Scottish were careful with dough, and now I'm a believer." He turned away. "I'll wait outside."

Leith felt his head would explode from all the new words. *Dough* and *bundle* meant money. He'd have to learn quickly.

"I want my money back."

Leith stared at Fortune's open palm poised at the end of his nose. " 'Tis better that I keep it, lass, so I can protect it."

"And who's going to protect it from you? It's mine. Give it back. Now." *Uh-oh. Open mouth and insert foot.*

"Ye'd trust Blade wi' yer money, but ye wouldna trust me." He slapped the money into her open palm. "Take it, but ye'd better guard it well so I dinna steal it when ye're not looking."

She studied his angry expression, glanced at his rigid stance. *Yep, big mistake. Time for honesty.* This wasn't about the money; it was about control. When he took the money, he also took command. She resented it.

He turned stiffly and strode out the door. She'd hurt his pride by depriving him of the one thing he had to offer, his protection. Again she remembered the feeling when her mother had thrown Skirky away—*powerless.* Leith must feel the same way now.

Sighing, she followed him. If she said she'd changed her mind about the money, he wouldn't believe her. She somehow knew he wouldn't accept her pity. History disks had shown her what men looked like and told her how they'd acted, but not one disk had said a thing about the emotional storms men created.

Leith climbed into the taxi, and she settled beside him. Leaping onto her lap, Ganymede curled into a comfortable ball. Blade started the taxi, then turned on some booming music with men chanting words in time to the rhythm. She winced.

Leith showed no sign of speaking, and Fortune realized she'd have to begin the conversation. "So you're from Scotland?"

"Ye didna know?" His expression gave nothing away.

"There was something familiar about your accent." She cocked her head to the side and studied him. "I'd read about Scotland on history disks, but it was so long ago that—"

" 'Tis gone?" He looked like he'd lost an old friend.

She'd said the wrong thing again. "Sort of. We don't have separate countries, only member states in a world nation, and everyone speaks the same language. No dialects."

He turned his face to the window. "Aye, I understand. A peaceful world where all are the same. Ye must be verra bored." He glanced back at her. "I'm not a quarrelsome man, lass, but I'd be lying to ye if I said I didna enjoy a good fight. The pitting of my strength against an opponent makes me feel alive."

Puzzled, she shrugged. "I guess you'd be unhappy then. We don't have wars. Everyone settles disputes in a civilized way."

He furrowed his brow. "If ye dinna fight, then ye have only sex for excitement."

She felt a need to defend her life, which was calm and satisfying in every way. Wasn't it? "Exactly the comment I'd expect from a primitive mentality." She leaned over until she was almost nose-to-nose with him. "We haven't had men for fifty years, and we've done just fine without sex with real males, thank you very much."

She started to move away, but he gently grasped her chin, holding her in place. So close, she could see forever in the depths of his jade eyes, and it bothered her that she even noticed.

"Ye canna turn awa' without explaining yerself. No fighting? No men to fulfill yer womanly needs? Are ye certain ye dinna live in hell?"

She nodded toward Blade, who'd turned the volume down on his music. Leaning close, Leith pushed her hair aside and whispered in her ear. "Ye'll explain yerself when we get home."

Fortune swallowed hard. His scent excited her even after the day they'd been through. A tantalizing mixture of cool air and warm male. She almost forgot to breathe when he softly kissed the side of her neck.

Fortune shuddered all the way to her toes. Primitive men must've had some potent pheromones. Surely that was the only explanation for the way Leith made her feel. After all, she didn't *want* to feel this tingly excitement every time he touched her. Maybe as with one of those ancient diseases, she could build up an immunity with constant exposure. She could hope.

"What do you guys want to do first?" Blade glanced in his mirror and winked. "Besides touch each other."

She felt heat rise to her face as Leith leaned back in his seat. She rushed into speech. "I think we'd—"

"Food. 'Tis long past time we ate."

There he went again, making decisions for both of them. "I'm not going anywhere to eat until I have some clothes of my own." His lordship would huff, puff, and bluster. She'd counter with cool reasonableness. He'd slink away, defeated by her superior logic. Then and only then would she relent, allowing them to eat first. Her stomach growled in anticipation.

"Aye. Fortune is right. I dinna need to eat. 'Tis many a day I've gone without food." He looked at Fortune and grinned.

He'd done that on purpose. Her stomach gurgled and grumbled its disappointment. No wonder. She hadn't eaten since last night, and she never missed a meal.

"What is that, Fortune?" Leith pointed, then turned from the window long enough for her to see the sparkle in his eyes, feel the tight-sprung energy that radiated from him.

His excitement reminded her of her own excitement after completing her first man, the thrill when she'd stood back and realized she'd created him with her own hands. The creative experience had remained the only thing in her life to give her that heart-pounding feeling of being able to fly. *Until Leith*. She pushed the thought away as she tried to control her urge to press her face to the window and share in his wonder.

Down, girl. She had to remain hard where Leith Campbell was concerned or he'd run over her like one of these old-fashioned vehicles, leaving nothing but tire tracks.

"Umm. I think that's a truck." Cumbersome. Amazing that things arrived anywhere in one piece.

"And that?" He stared, as close to openmouthed as he would probably ever get, at a tall building they zipped past.

"An office building." If she remembered her history, it would be another hundred years before the world discovered that building *down* was much more efficient and environmentally friendly than building *up*.

" 'Tis impossible!" He stared skyward.

She followed his gaze. "That's an airplane." Didn't people mind traveling so slowly?

"I didna know birds so large existed."

"It's not a bird. That's a machine that carries people from place to place through the air."

"No! People canna fly through the air."

His wide-eyed wonder was endearing. *Uh-oh*. She was getting mushy around the edges.

Blade coughed. "Where the hell have you been, big guy?"

Careless! "Tibet. He's been in Tibet."

Leith stared at her. "Are ye daft, woman?"

She sent him her *don't say another word* glare, then turned her attention to Blade. "Yes, monks raised him in Tibet. This is his first trip to the outside world. They had to send a Saint Bernard in after him. Exciting, isn't it?" What she found really exciting was how much historical trivia she remembered.

Blade had his mouth open to ask another question, but luckily they reached their destination.

Critically, Fortune studied the large store with its hordes of people streaming through the doors. She preferred shopping electronically. "We should be able to get most of our essentials here." She smiled at Leith. "Of course, this place is very—"

"Primitive. I know. But 'tis not primitive to me." He sounded annoyed.

Blade looked offended. "Hey, I could take you to

someplace swankier, but we'd have a longer drive."

"No, this'll be fine." She'd have to be more careful about what she said.

Blade nodded. "I'll wait here with the cat. Don't know why you brought him with you."

Fortune stared at Ganymede, and Ganymede stared back. "I didn't bring him. He brought himself. He's sort of attached himself to me." She shrugged. "I don't know why."

" 'Tis easy to see why he attached himself to ye," Leith murmured.

Blade frowned. "I don't have anything to do for the rest of the day, so I can take you where you need to go. But tomorrow you're on your own. Either one of you have a driver's license?"

Fortune opened her mouth to answer, but Leith placed his hand over hers, and she closed her mouth.

"We dinna plan to be here long, so 'twould be useless to get this . . . license." He opened the door and climbed out before Blade could think of another question. "We'll return after we've spent a bundle of dough."

She blinked. "Bundle of dough?"

"Aye. I must begin using the common language in order to blend with others of this time," he whispered.

Wasted effort. She skimmed all six-feet-plus of gleaming muscle. Every woman, in whatever time, would notice Leith.

Fortune climbed out, then closed the door firmly in Ganymede's surprised face. Glancing behind her, she saw the cat's mouth open wide and could hear his howl even through the closed window. Blade wore a pained expression.

As they entered the store, Leith put his arm across her shoulders and pulled her against him. She knew she should assert her independence by pulling away, but something about his protective gesture comforted her.

She felt him exhale deeply as he gazed around him. "There are too many things I dinna understand. 'Tis passing strange."

Amen. She doubted she could answer all his questions. The solid strength of him beside her seemed to be the only thing keeping her upright. Without him, she'd probably plop herself down in the middle of the aisle between "curling irons" and "hair dryers," then bawl out her confusion. And to think just a short time ago he was the strangest thing in her universe.

"Fortune, dinna look around, but someone is following us."

She looked around. "What? Where?"

"God's teeth, woman, when will ye learn to obey?"

"Never. Now who's following us?"

"I dinna know, but with a piece of yer dough hanging from yer pocket, 'tis like the stink of carrion to a buzzard."

"Oh." She stuck the money back in her pocket. "I'm sure no one's following us. You see criminals around every corner. It's called having a suspicious mind." She paused at a display. What did you do with an "ironing board"? Maybe you used it with your "curling iron." Why would anyone want to iron curls?

" 'Tis called having a warrior's instincts." He glanced over his shoulder, then relaxed. "The man is gone." He pulled her even closer against him. "Ye trust too easily. Ye need protection more than any woman I've ever known."

"Primitive reasoning." But her insult lacked bite because the heat from his body was doing its thing, and she was finding it hard to concentrate.

" 'Tis amazing! Light wi' no flame. Voices that come from the air. What is a blue-light special?" He grinned at her, making her heart bounce up and down with enthusiastic appreciation. "I favor a time where women show their legs almost up to their bottoms. Mayhap ye can—"

"No." Why should showing her legs bother her when he'd seen all she had to offer? Somehow, the more she knew him, the more she became aware of her body . . . his body. . . .

"This time has wondrous things." He reached into a bin and pulled out a wisp of silky red material. Before she could react, he held it against her lower body. "Aye, they'll look fine on ye, lass. Ye can purchase three for two dollars."

"Well, yes, I suppose so." They were only panties, nothing to get excited over. But the pressure of his hand against her lower stomach . . . She must be glowing like a Martian sunset. She quickly pulled out three white panties.

Gently he put his hand over hers. "Dinna buy white. Ye would look bonny in colors."

She freed her hand. "What does the color matter? You won't see them."

He smiled. "Aye, but I can imagine."

"Then you can imagine white." Cool white. Calm white.

Shrugging, he wandered over to another bin.

Making sure he wasn't looking, she put the white panties back. Colored ones *were* prettier. She wouldn't think about why *prettier* should matter now when it never had before. Just this once. She pulled out a blue pair, a black pair, and . . . a red pair, then balled them up in her fist so he wouldn't see. Somehow she didn't want to give him even this small triumph.

Trying for casual, she joined him beside another bin.

He glanced down at her with heavy-lidded intensity; then he smiled—a wicked grin her body understood instantly even as her mind fought the good fight. "I'll enjoy sliding the red ones over yer smooth thighs and down yer long legs."

"And what virtual world will you be visiting when this happens?" She tried to ignore the mental picture of his hands touching her, the sensation of his fingers. . . .

He frowned. "I dinna know what a virtual world is, but I must do penance before I can return to Scotland."

Now it was her turn to be puzzled. "Penance? What does penance have to with anything?"

His expression cleared, and he smiled. "Ye're right. 'Twill be no penance at all."

Somehow she'd lost control of this conversation.

Glancing down, she studied the contents of the bin beside them. Bras. Braving more comments from an intensely interested Leith, she defiantly grabbed three white ones.

"What are those?" The evil glitter in his eyes told her he knew exactly what *those* were.

"Bras." If he could play games, so could she. "Bras have a force field that's activated by the wearer's body heat. If someone touches me, poof, the toucher disappears." *Careful*. Violent images were not healthful images.

His playfulness vanished. "And who would ye fear touching ye, lass?"

You. "Who, indeed?" Time for a dignified retreat. "Wait here while I try on these bras." Relieved, she quickly escaped behind the curtain of a small dressing room.

Stripping off her jeans and shirt, she hung them on a hook, then slid on the red panties. For some reason they made her feel . . . protected. *Protected? Against what? Not what, whom. Leith*. No way did he have so much power over her, but she still couldn't bear to remove the panties. She'd tell the clerk she was wearing them and pay when she left.

Without warning, someone ripped open the curtain. Even as she instinctively crossed her hands over her breasts, a sense of inevitability overwhelmed her. "Jupiter's balls! Don't you dare look, Leith Campbell. Get out of here. Close the curtain."

From his dazed expression, she guessed he didn't know which command to obey first.

"Jupiter's balls?"

"I *never* use that kind of language, but you make me so . . . Get out!"

Carefully he pulled the curtain closed behind him. *No*. That wasn't the command she'd wanted him to obey first.

"I chose a bra for ye." He dangled a piece of cloth

from two fingers. He looked uncertain. She refused to melt even a little bit. He'd be lucky if she didn't remove his fingers along with the bra. "I meant only to hand it through the curtain, but then I spied the tail."

"Tail?" Fortune glanced down. Ganymede. Could a cat smile?

She glared at Ganymede. "Scat!"

Flattening his ears, whipping his tail from side to side, and growling his displeasure, he stalked from the room. Fortune wondered how well "scat" would work on Leith.

"How'd he get out of the taxi? You have to take him back." She glanced longingly at her shirt and jeans. Could she get them on without exposing her breasts to Leith's view? One look at his predatory gaze told her he hoped she'd try.

"But the bra . . ." He held it up. Only one finger this time. *Smart man*.

"There's nothing to it, just a little piece of lace. And can't you pick something that isn't red?"

His expression turned hurt, vulnerable, *practiced*. "Ye dinna like my choice?"

"Oh, it's very pretty, but I need a little more support, and . . ." Unbelievable. Even knowing his expression was fake, she was trying not to hurt his feelings. Where was her backbone? If it had disappeared, it was probably one of the only things Leith couldn't see right now. *Clothes*. She had to get dressed.

She watched, frozen like a small animal caught in the path of a hypnobeam, as he calmly hung the red bra on an empty hook.

Stepping forward, he wrapped his arms around

79

her and pulled her against him. "Ye dinna need support. Yer beauty should be free. The red bra will cup ye like a lover's hand. And the sign says the cloth breathes wi' ye." His soft murmur against the side of her neck wrapped around her like the silken threads of a cocoon. *Breathes. Yes.* That was good, because she wasn't doing such a great job of breathing on her own right now.

He moved back, his heated gaze promising, enticing, as he gently forced her hands away from her breasts. And she let him.

"Yer beauty would shine in any time, lass." He reached out to trace the line of her jaw with his fingertip.

She dragged a deep breath into her oxygen-starved lungs. If she could just breathe, she could move—could shatter whatever spell he'd woven.

His gaze followed the movement of her breasts as she breathed, and he groaned. The sound was an extension of his touch. Her nipples pebbled, yearning for his caress, the warmth of his mouth, and dark heat pooled within her.

Look away. She had to escape the searing need he'd loosed in her—powerful, compelling.

Swallowing hard, she glanced down. The fabric of his jeans stretched tightly across his arousal, an arousal that would do justice to her best creative efforts. But no man she'd ever made had tempted her to touch, to feel.

Her hand seemed detached from her will as she reached for him. Her mind's strident commands to stop had no effect.

She molded her palm to his length and felt it pulse, grow. Her lips tilted as an errant thought intruded. If he grew any larger his jeans would explode in a fiery display of cloth and metal teeth. She squeezed gently to see if it would happen.

With a sound that resembled a feral growl, he lowered his head and touched one nipple with his tongue.

His touch was exquisite pleasure, exquisite pain, flinging wide the locked door of long-denied desire.

She closed her eyes and threw back her head. She breathed in small pants through slightly parted lips. *Now. Let it happen now. She'd think later, much later.*

"Bloody hell."

His harsh mutter spoke of lost control. *Yes.* She felt the siren call of danger, the thrill of all those who'd hunted the long-extinct tiger.

His arms enfolded her, pulled her tightly to him. The scrape of her nipples against his shirt wrung a moan from her. She opened her eyes to the wonders of sensations she'd only imagined, never thought existed.

Lowering his head, he captured her lips. As he traced them with his tongue, she opened her mouth to the pleasure, allowing him to explore further, deeper.

She wanted him. She couldn't have him. In a last desperate effort to gain control, her mind shrieked that her duty was to bring him home, not sample what he had to offer. Forging a sexual bond with him would be dangerous, futile. *He's not meant for you.* Her emotions rose to do battle with her logic. It wouldn't be a pretty fight.

The decision was wrested from her as, suddenly,

someone jerked open the curtain and grabbed her shirt and jeans. With a small cry, she pushed Leith away and again covered her breasts with her hands. *Too late,* her mind suggested.

With a muttered curse, Leith whirled. "I canna believe it. A kiss like no other, and some bloody fool interrupts it."

Even his savage tone couldn't stop Fortune's glow. *A kiss like no other.*

"He's taken yer dough!" Leith ripped the red bra from its hook and raced after the thief.

Fortune came crashing down to earth. This is what you got when you lowered your guard, allowed your emotions to overrule your head, she thought. In a way, the thief had done her a favor, had kept her from making a massive mistake. It wouldn't happen again.

Attempting to remain calm in the face of impending financial ruin, she yanked the curtain down and wrapped it around herself. This was starting to become a habit.

As Fortune hurried from the dressing area, she met a bemused saleswoman. Obviously she'd sighted Leith. "A thief just stole my clothes, my money. Could you get the manager for me?"

Never losing her dazed expression, the woman nodded.

Fortune finally sighted Leith racing through what must be the menswear section in pursuit of a small man who looked like he was running for his life. *Rightly so.* Leith's murderous expression would lend wings to anyone's feet.

Fortune gained on Leith as he paused to reach down toward his leg. When he lifted the material at his ankle, a flash of metal warned her of what was coming. *The knife*.

No! "Don't do it, Leith!" Her words came in short gasps as she strained to run faster. "No violence!"

Whether he heard her words or feared the thief would escape before he could use his knife, Leith straightened, then flung the red bra he still clutched around the man's neck.

The man came to a gasping halt and clawed at the bra closing off his air, but he didn't drop Fortune's clothes.

"We can discuss this calmly, work out a solution." Fortune panted as she raced to reach Leith before he could . . . She didn't want to contemplate what he intended doing.

Salvation launched itself from the highest shelf of a display labeled JOCKEY SHORTS and landed atop the thief's head.

Ganymede! Fortune didn't question the why or wherefore. As the thief struggled with the howling mass of black fur intent on gnawing off his left ear, he dropped the clothes.

As Leith reached for the clothes, the thief disengaged himself from Ganymede long enough to take a swipe at the man who'd relieved him of his ill-gotten goods.

"Uh-oh," Fortune murmured.

Leith hit him with all the pent-up rage and frustration he'd built up over this fearful day. The man bounced off a wall and staggered toward the doors. He still wore the red bra around his neck. Leith watched with grim satisfaction.

* * *

Leith closed his eyes for a moment, allowing some of the anger to seep from him. When he opened them, it was to face a mob of curious shoppers who'd gathered, and an authoritative-looking man hurrying toward him.

Then Leith saw her. Wrapped in the curtain, Fortune stood wearing a confused expression.

He had no time to consider how Fortune felt, because the store authority had reached him.

"I can't tell you how sorry I am something like this happened in my store. I've been the manager here for six years and nothing . . . What can I possibly do to make up for it?" He wiped his hand across his sweaty brow and shook his head apologetically.

Leith glanced at Fortune, who'd worked her way to his side. "Ye can give us the clothes we choose free."

The manager nodded. "And I hope this won't discourage you from visiting our fine store again." His expression said *I don't want to be around if you come back.*

Without speaking, Fortune grabbed her clothes and headed back to one of the small, curtained rooms. Leith waited impatiently outside and wondered where Ganymede had gone. He hoped he wouldn't have to search for the cat, but he also knew he couldn't abandon the animal. Strangely, he felt a growing affection for the creature. Ganymede had shown a warrior's fierceness in attacking the thief.

Suddenly Fortune pulled open the curtain. His gaze collided with her wide-eyed stare. His glance slid down to her lips, still swollen from his kiss.

His body reacted to the memory of how she'd felt, tasted.

"You hit that man." Her tone suggested he'd boiled the man in oil, then torn him limb from limb.

He scowled at her. "Damnation, woman, the bastard meant to steal all our dough. What would ye have me do?"

She winced at his curses, and that made him even angrier.

"Maybe you could've discussed it, given him some options, before you hit him."

"*Discussed* it?" He snorted his opinion of that. "There are some things beyond discussion, and ye'd better learn that quickly if ye mean to survive here."

"I've never seen anyone hit before. We don't have—"

"Violence. Aye, I know." He was mad. He longed to slam his fist into someone's belly, blacken a few eyes. Where were the bloody MacDonalds when you needed them?

She hadn't shown a bit of gratitude for his rescue of their dough. "And I enjoyed it. 'Twould have been a bonny brawl if the coward hadna run away." He smiled evilly.

She seemed to shrink from him. "I have to show the manager the clothes we want. You'd better check on Ganymede."

Nodding, he walked from the store and headed for Blade's taxi. He couldn't contain a small, triumphant grin, however. She'd still held the colored panties clutched in her hand. Too bad about the red bra, though. Red suited her.

When he reached the taxi, he found Blade standing beside it with a harried expression on his face.

"Damn cat. Leave it home next time. I only cracked the window this much." He demonstrated how much with two fingers. "A roach couldn't squeeze through, but he got out somehow. Must be part greased pig." Blade glared into the backseat. "Anyway, as soon as I saw he was gone I went looking for him. Got all hot and bothered for nothing. Came back here thinking I'd lost your cat and there he was, asleep, looking as innocent as a newborn."

He spit on the ground for emphasis. "Give me a dog any day. Dogs are up-front. Cats are sneaky."

With that said, Blade opened the door and climbed in.

Leith could see Fortune swaying toward him. He loved the way her hips— He mentally shook himself. *Besotted*.

Forcing himself to look away, he opened the back door so she could get in.

Ganymede stretched, then gazed up at him.

Leith froze. For one searing instant, it seemed as though a mask had been torn from Ganymede's eyes.

Ganymede blinked, and the moment vanished.

Leith shook his head to clear it. He had to get something to eat soon. Hunger did strange things to his mind. Of course, he'd only imagined the ageless intelligence he'd seen in the cat's gaze. Ganymede was only a beast.

Ganymede purred his agreement.

Chapter Four

"I can't believe you *hit* him." She should feel disgust, indignation. Instead, for one frightening moment, she'd wanted to jump up and down and shout, "Take *that*, you dirty thief!"

"Ye're like a dog gnawing an old bone, lass."

"Violence is *always* wrong." OK, so Leith had saved their money. But her feelings of unholy glee at the mayhem made her uneasy, as though Leith had put his mark on her, making her forget everything she'd ever believed.

"If that is what ye truly think, ye're lucky to have a violent primitive along to protect ye and yer noble foolishness."

Ignoring his sarcasm, she stared out the window at dusk creeping up on her first day in this new world. Time to put philosophical arguments aside. "I'm hungry." She'd lived on a schedule all her adult life, and she'd already missed exactly—she glanced at the taxi's clock—two and a half meals.

"Aye. I feel as though I could eat an entire sheep." Leith leaned over to Blade. "Where might we find food?"

Fortune grimaced. An entire sheep? Leith was a walking ad for excess—too much emotion, too much aggression, too big an appetite. *Hmm.* She remembered his body's splendor. Probably too big an appetite for many things. "Nothing fancy," she added.

"If you want someplace fast, how about Mc-Donald's?" Blade pointed to a brightly lit golden arch in the distance.

Leith's expression turned thunderous.

Fortune moaned inwardly. Even though she'd known this man for only one day, she recognized the signs of an imminent explosion. Well, if she didn't get something to eat soon, her stomach would do some exploding of its own.

"McDonald's! Ye canna expect me to eat at a place named after my sworn enemies. 'Tis impossible." He glared at both Fortune and Blade in turn. "I thought the one good thing about this new world would be that there were no more cursed Mac-Donalds. Bloody burrs. Ye canna get rid of them."

Oh, boy. Just what she needed to end a perfect day, a berserk primitive challenging the chef to a fight in the name of clan honor.

She glanced into the taxi's mirror and met Blade's puzzled stare. She smiled weakly. "In Tibet, this MacDonald family lived next door to the monks. Real slobs—never mowed their lawn, let their dog run loose. You know the kind."

Blade shook his head and glanced away. Leith groaned his disgust. " 'Tis the worst excuse I've ever heard."

He was right. She wasn't doing such a great job thinking on her feet. That should put an end to her budding feelings of superiority. "Could you take us somewhere else, Blade?"

Blade nodded. He must think they'd escaped from some asylum. Maybe he was right. Maybe this whole awful experience was a figment of her warped imagination brought on by too much agonizing over her newest creation, Wicked Walter, the first bearded man she'd attempted. He wasn't turning out quite like—

"How do you feel about Burger King, big guy?" Blade sounded weary.

Leith nodded. " 'Tis . . . OK. I know King William rules England, but what land does the Burger King rule? Burger. 'Tis a land I've ne'er heard of."

Blade turned and grinned at him. "I like your sense of humor. Strange, but funny."

He stopped in front of a brightly lit building. "I'll drop you guys off here, then pick you up in half an hour."

Hesitantly, Fortune climbed from the taxi and stood staring at the building. The excitement she felt surprised her. She thought of her favorite restaurant, a soothing beige building with dim, stress-reducing lighting and thick, sound-absorbing gray carpeting, that catered to tranquil women dressed in calm, neutral shades. Serene. *Boring*.

Mournfully, Fortune watched Blade drive away with Ganymede's outraged face suction-cupped to the back window. Somehow the taxi had seemed a safe cocoon from the reality of this new time. She glanced at Leith, who stared at the Burger King as though it were a dragon he'd have to slay. Maybe for him it *would* be a dragon. "Let's get something to eat."

She automatically started walking ahead of him, but before she could react, he'd stepped in front of her.

"We must be cautious in this time."

When they reached the door, he held it for her, glancing around as though he expected a sneak attack. *Ridiculous*. The only danger they faced came from a direct hit by one of the noisy black birds perched on the branch above them.

Fortune controlled her irritation. He was taking this "protecting the helpless female" thing too far, but she was too hungry to argue about it now. She studied the menu.

Didn't they have *anything* that didn't involve dead animals? "I can't believe the stuff they serve here. My arteries are clogging just reading the menu. Where's the scientifically formulated imitation beef patty guaranteed to taste like the real thing even though it's made from inorganic material manufactured on Quellum?"

Getting no response from Leith, she turned to look at him.

He stood staring glassy-eyed at the menu, and he didn't look hungry anymore. "I dinna understand any of this." His admission seemed torn from the very heart of his pride.

Even though he'd cut out his tongue before saying the words, Fortune knew he needed her. Somehow the thought made her glad. No one had ever needed her before. Her friends shared their company with her, but they'd survive just fine without her. And her mother? She wouldn't think about her mother.

"Tell me what you'd like to eat, and I'll get the closest thing I can find." She reached out to touch him in a comforting gesture, but he jerked away from her. This man and his pride would drive her crazy. She sighed. "After you tell me what you want, find someplace for us to sit." *Oh, no*. Now he looked offended that she'd dared order him to do something.

"I want meat and potatoes with something cold to drink that willna poison me." With that declaration, he strode to a back table. A ripple of interested female glances followed his progress until he sat down. Fortune could almost feel the collective sigh of yearning.

She turned back to the perky-looking girl smilingly waiting for Fortune to give her order. *OK, meat and potatoes, cold drink, no poison*. From what she could see in this time, that last order would be hard.

A few minutes later, she tottered back to their table bearing a tray laden with death-by-cholesterol. She set it down in front of Leith, then plunked herself in the seat across from him. "Here's your dead animal, French fries cooked in goo, and cola, which can also take varnish off floors. I've read about the health habits of my ancestors."

Leith ignored her. He tentatively bit into the burger, then ate a French fry. His expression cleared as he took a cautious sip of his cola. " 'Tis delicious, even though it looks a wee bit strange. What are ye eating?"

She frowned down at her food. "A salad and orange juice." She cast a contemptuous glance at his half-eaten meal. "You won't live to old age eating that stuff."

He offered her a crooked smile, and once again she realized the power he wielded just by being male. All the rationalizations in the world couldn't stop her heart from thumping out a rapid rhythm of excitement.

If only she could capture the impact of his smile in one of her models. Maybe her Hunka Hunka Burning Love Leroy model.

"Aye, but I'll die happy." He broke off a piece of his burger and offered it to her. "Dinna ye even want to try it?"

Uncertain, she studied the food. She'd never had *real* meat in her whole life, only healthy imitations. Choice: eat meat or starve. She breathed a silent apology to helpless animals everywhere. Amazing how hunger could reduce her to the level of the savage grinning at her from across the table.

Leith watched as she took the piece of food in two fingers. She looked as if she expected the spirit of the cow to appear at any second and moo accusingly in her face. As she bit into it, her eyes widened in wonder. "Our imitations *never* tasted like this."

"Real is always better." He remembered she'd said she made men. Her eyes showed that she knew he spoke not only about food. He slid his fries over to her. "I'll purchase more."

When he returned laden with more food, his cola had disappeared and Fortune wore an expression of blissful satiation. He knew with a fierceness he couldn't deny that he would someday put that same expression on her face.

Before he could question his sudden need, a low growl sounded from under the table, and a black paw rose from the depths to swiftly swipe a fry off his tray. He froze.

In unison, they peered under the table. Ganymede stared at them while he calmly licked salt from his mouth. Leith sat up without comment. He met Fortune's gaze and she shrugged. Blade would be furious when he picked them up. He hoped their new friend didn't spend too much time searching for the wee devil.

Playing with her fries, Fortune didn't meet his gaze as she spoke. "Why all this anger about a place named McDonald's?"

He felt the customary fury flood him at the hated name, even in this distant time and place. "They are my enemies."

She finally looked at him, and he could see her puzzlement. "OK, I can understand that. But this is a long way from Scotland. Anyone named MacDonald here wouldn't be your enemy."

"The name carries bad memories, lass." How could he make someone who'd never known hate and betrayal understand?

She sighed, and he knew she found him unreasonable. The truth? He directed as much of his anger at himself as he did at the cursed MacDonalds. *If only* . . . He forced his thoughts away from the event that had made his only brother an enemy.

Wishes never changed anything. He'd learned that as a child watching the slaughter of his parents.

" 'Tis time to leave." His appetite gone, Leith handed his burger to the creature beneath their table. He pulled his fingers back quickly lest they be considered part of the offering.

Fortune nodded. She seemed strangely quiet. He didn't know whether to treat her silence as a blessed event or a warning of unpleasantness to come. It would do no good brooding upon it, though. Scooping Ganymede from under the table, he rose and strode from the Burger King while Fortune trailed behind.

Complications. Always complications. Fortune pulled herself from her reverie long enough to realize the taxi had reached home. *Home?* No, this little house wasn't home, would never be home. It was merely a temporary place to stay while she figured out how to get Leith and herself back to her *real* home.

She wouldn't think about that now. It was too soon. Much too soon. She remembered very well the old sayings about the bearer of bad news and shooting the messenger. From what she'd seen so far, Leith would *not* react calmly and logically to her revelation. *No, indeedy.* She'd just wait awhile.

Leith climbed out, then held the door while Fortune and Ganymede followed. He slammed the door, then turned to Blade, who rolled down his window and glared at an unconcerned Ganymede.

"Ye've taught me some curses I've ne'er heard before, Blade. For this I thank ye." Leith absently stroked the taxi's surface. "I could wage wondrous battles with this machine."

Blade ignored his last comment, intent on his own complaint. "You'll hear a lot more if you keep that mangy cat around. I tell you, I only rolled the window down this much."

Leith nodded. "I know. A roach couldna crawl through."

"Damn right." Blade scowled at the cat. Ganymede stood, yawned, then paced regally up the walk with his tail waving dismissively over his back. "Scruffy ball of hair and deceit."

Leith smiled. "Aye, I think I'll keep him."

Blade shook his head, then drove off with a squeal of tires.

Fortune waited for Leith to follow her in. She remembered to switch on the lights, then stood staring at the cracked floors, peeling paint, and worn rugs—all somehow softened in the dim light. She felt Leith behind her and suddenly the room shrank, dwarfed by the large man fate had cast her with.

He yawned. "This hasna been an easy day. We need a long night's rest so we may think clearly on the morrow. Where is our sleeping chamber?"

"*Our* sleeping chamber? We each have our own room, buster."

He smiled—not a nice smile. "There is but one."

OK, she could handle this. "You're used to primitive conditions, so you can sleep on the couch."

He wore his *you have to be kidding* expression. "If by couch ye mean that monstrous pink thing in the living room, I'd rather sleep on the floor."

She smiled brightly. "There you go. Problem solved."

Or not. She'd once seen the same expression on a mule.

"I'll sleep in the bed beside ye."

She briefly considered the couch and the floor for herself. Very briefly. She was used to some semblance of civilized comfort, and she refused to be ousted by a hulking savage. Her conscience chided her on the "hulking savage" label. He really wasn't. But he *was* an overbearing, dictatorial—

" 'Tis too late to stand here arguing. Come."

Come? Before she could react to the command, he'd grabbed her hand and pulled her down the hallway to the "sleeping chamber." He flung open the door and stepped inside, then remembered to flip on the light switch.

The sleeping pad—no, *bed* in this time—loomed huge in the tiny room. Until she glanced at Leith. Large, solid, and . . . disturbing, he leaned against the door frame. Swallowing hard, she looked at the bed again to find that its faded blue mass had miraculously shrunk to the size of a dwarum's head.

"Well, guess I'll clean up a little." Before he could respond, she grabbed her nightgown and rushed to the bathroom.

Minutes later, she tried to relax under the shower's warm spray. She didn't feel quite so panicky now. She'd approach this situation in a calm, rational— *No!* She absolutely, positively would *not* sleep in the same bed as Leith Campbell. And this wasn't about logic. It was about pure gut instinct. Sleeping with Leith would be a contradiction in terms. Her eyes would be glued open the whole night, remembering—his body with its smooth expanse of warm, golden skin stretched over supple muscle, his heat that would touch her, tempt her, even if she clung to the bed's edge. *Uh-uh*. She was no dummy. It was the couch for her.

"Dinna take too long, lass."

She screeched her shock, then caught herself before she could fling aside the curtain to confront the invader. "Get out!"

"Why?"

She could hear him turning the faucets on and off. He flushed the toilet, then opened and closed the cabinet door.

Why? "You're invading my privacy. You *do* understand privacy, don't you?"

"Umm." He pulled out a drawer, then slammed it shut. "Dinna be embarrassed, lass. Ye have a beautiful body, and ye should be proud of it. So why do ye want me to leave?"

Fine. Logical hadn't worked, so she'd try illogical. "Because I said so."

"Ye say a lot of things, lass. A man doesna know which to listen to." He opened the cabinet again, rattling things as he moved them around. "I think I'll just stay here and wait."

Wait until you take root. She wasn't coming out while he watched even if she turned into a wrinkled prune. Just the memory of his glance skimming over her body this morning raised goose bumps along the remembered path of his heated gaze. "OK, be stubborn, but at least turn your head while I get out."

She took his silence for assent and quickly flung the curtain open, then stepped out of the tub. She'd

97

Nina Bangs

almost reached her nightgown when she looked
up.

He stood watching her with an expression she'd
recognize if men had been extinct for a thousand
years. "You promised!"

"I didna," he murmured softly. "I wouldna make
such a stupid promise."

Lunging for her nightgown, she pulled it over
her head with a sense of relief that left her limp. "I
should've know I couldn't trust you. Primitives
have no sense of—"

"Beauty? Ye shouldna be ashamed of yer body,
Fortune."

"I'm not *ashamed*. I'm . . ." *Embarrassed*.

"Aye?"

She gulped loudly and considered making a
break for the door as he slowly peeled his shirt
from his impressive chest. *Why*? She *made* men.
But she'd certainly never felt this strange discomfort around any of her creations—an aching heav-
iness that left her craving something.

Sexual awareness? She'd read about it, and some
of her friends had talked about achieving it with
the men she sold them, but she'd never . . . Yes, she
had. She'd felt it this morning when she'd turned
over and found Leith beside her.

"Watch me, Fortune. Our bodies are wondrous,
able to give and receive great pleasure." His voice
had lowered to a harsh whisper that sandpapered
across sensitive nerve endings.

She had to get out of here!

"Dinna be a coward, lass." She heard laughter in
his voice. "A woman from yer superior society can
surely stand the sight of a man's body." He slipped

98

his sneakers off, then worked at the snap on his jeans.

She reluctantly abandoned her plan to flee the room. She wasn't a coward. Of course, she'd never had anything to fear before today. Fear? Yes, on a level she didn't understand, she knew this man was dangerous.

He started to slide his jeans down over his lean hips.

She swallowed hard. *Think of him as a duty, a man you have an obligation to bring home with you, a humanity-saving sperm machine.*

Sliding the jeans down his muscular legs, he kicked them off, then stood. Naked. Very naked.

Forget duty. Think of him as a prototype for Creature Comfort's newest, most spectacular line—a man who's fought to survive life's battles and has the scars to prove it. Primitive Paul? Nah. Warrior Wayne? Uh-uh. Doesn't flow. She'd think of a name later. When she could concentrate.

Concentrate. She'd just do a quick inventory of his finer points, the ones that made him so extraordinary, ones she could incorporate into her new model.

Head. What drew her attention? The heavy fall of dark hair framing his lean face was startling, and those mocking eyes danced with a life she'd have a tough time imitating. OK, his lips—full, sensuous. But inexorably, her gaze riveted on the faint scar above his right brow. She longed to reach out, trace the thin line, then draw her fingers down his hard, masculine jaw. The scar lent danger to the wicked beauty of his face, a danger that would intrigue women. It made him real.

Nina Bangs

"Ye're taking an uncommon long time to decide, lass."

He rubbed his hand across his chest, and her gaze followed the motion. "Umm, I'm thinking."

She admitted his chest's sculpted perfection rivaled her best effort, but that was not what held her attention. A thin white line ran beneath one pectoral. Too close to his heart. She shuddered at the pain he'd suffered. *Real.*

Mesmerized, she watched his chest rise and fall as he took a deep breath. Her models didn't breathe. She'd work on it.

"If ye think about everything this long, lass, 'tis a wonder ye get anything done."

He was laughing at her, but she didn't care. Her glance drifted down over his flat stomach, then stopped. She stared, unable to look away, as his erection swelled. No matter how analytical she tried to be, she couldn't control the heat building, pooling. . . . Frantically, she attempted to push aside her emotions and focus. Her men achieved arousal by touch. Maybe she could implant sound sensors that reacted to a specific voice command. Maybe . . . "Rise and shine." Maybe just heavy breathing would do it. She sighed. *But it wouldn't be real.*

"Ye have a powerful gaze, lass."

Startled, she glanced back to his face. His amusement had disappeared, replaced by something hot, elemental. Real.

It was hopeless. Even if she managed to duplicate how he looked, she'd never be able to achieve the raw masculinity that flowed from him, the intangible "lived-in" feel that made him *real.*

100

This wasn't working! She started to shake, but she couldn't have fled if her life depended on it.

With a fluidness that spoke of a man at ease with his own body, he turned and stepped into the shower, then stared at the gleaming knobs. "Bloody hell."

Ignoring his expletive, she stared. "A dimple. You have a dimple in your . . ."

He twisted his head to stare at the object of her intense interest. "Aye. When I was a wee laddie, I fell from my horse onto a sharp rock. The wound healed, but it left the dent behind." That explained, he turned his attention back to the knobs. "How do ye make these work?"

"Turn them to the left. The right one is cold; the left is hot." *The right one is dimpled, the left one is not.* A dimpled bun. She had to put one in her next model.

As in a trance, she watched him follow her directions. Water flowed over him, turning him into a gleaming statue. No, he was too warm and vital to be compared to a statue.

"Yer gaze is bold for a virgin, lass."

Had she shocked him? She glanced up. His heated stare was many things, but shocked wasn't one of them. "This isn't personal. Men's bodies are my business."

Her heart pounding, she couldn't tear her gaze from him as he soaped his body with smooth strokes. She yearned with an intensity that hurt to slide her hands across his body, to—

"Come here, Fortune." His harsh command belied his outward ease. He'd turned his back to her. "I need ye to soap my back."

For a moment her old spunkiness tried to assert itself. "Your back looks fine. Squeaky clean."

"I *want* ye to do this, lass." His voice lowered to an enticing rumble, promising unspoken delights.

Someone else moved robotlike toward his gleaming back. It couldn't be she, because no way would she be mesmerized by a hunk of primitive maleness. Someone else took the cloth and ran it tentatively down his warm, water-slicked back. She wouldn't consider giving in to sexual coercion, not when she knew perfectly well what game he played. Someone else moved the cloth lower. She'd *never* let herself be turned into a mindless robot by firm, well-shaped buns . . . with a dimple. *Don't forget the dimple.* She abandoned the cloth and slid her bare palm across his buttocks. Just to prove this was someone else, of course.

Without warning, he turned around. With her gaze still fixed at bun-level, she couldn't mistake the hard length that proved he was far from casually indifferent. Someone else reached out and stroked him.

She raised her gaze to his eyes. They burned with a million promises—all tempting, all terrifying.

Fortune jerked her hand away, freeing herself from "someone else," and turned tail. She slammed the door so hard that it bounced off the wall. "I've changed my mind. The couch will be great. I'll . . . I'll see you in the morning."

He watched her flee with a mixture of regret and wry amusement. He hadn't meant to frighten her. *That's exactly what you meant.* Honesty demanded he admit that her sometimes arrogant sureness in

102

dealing with everything today had made him feel like the primitive she declared he was.

He took a deep breath. His penance. Her heated gaze had reminded him that he must teach her the joys of love. The thought of his body joined with hers made him groan as he twisted the knobs, then stood stoically as cold water sluiced over him.

Not tonight. He'd frighten her to death. But soon.

The next morning, he sat on the edge of her couch and waited impatiently for her to awaken. He'd slept peacefully despite the previous day's events. Of course, he'd learned to sleep through the turmoil of battle, and this was not so very different. Now rested, he felt the need to earn his redemption quickly.

He smiled. Red hair tousled in sleep, she looked like an angel. The fact that she probably thought of him as a devil amused him. If he had his way, she'd soon be a fallen angel.

Ganymede had curled himself into a furry black ball and rested contentedly against her side. Without thinking, Leith pushed the cat off the couch and listened as the animal growled and grumbled his resentment. He watched the even rise and fall of her breasts as she slept. Soon his head would be pillowed between those soft mounds and . . .

He'd have to put her at ease first. He'd frightened her last night. He suspected she'd frightened herself. If she were to return to her time with the memory of glorious lovemaking, she would have to share equally in their joining. For this, he'd need patience. God's teeth, but he wanted her.

Nina Bangs

He'd first lull her fears by getting her to talk about her life. To be honest, he was curious about how females could live, or would even want to live, in a world without males. If the situation were reversed and there were no females . . . He grinned. There'd be a great increase in the popularity of sheep.

She'd said she made men. Now he understood. He pitied the women of her world who had need of such poor substitutes.

Her sleepy murmur put an end to such depressing thoughts. She opened her eyes and stared at him. "If you want me to wash any other part of your body, forget it."

Good. She sounded like the Fortune he knew once again. "Nay. I thought only that we should talk. We should learn more of each other."

"Hmm. I'm hungry."

The sudden spurt of joy her words brought died as their meaning sank in. Grumpily, he made his way to the kitchen and rooted through it. The box that kept things cold by some magical means surrendered several apples and a container of milk. He carried them out to Fortune, who still reclined on the couch. She wore an unusual expression of docility, but it didn't fool Leith. She was still lazy with sleep. Perhaps now would be the time to put his plan into operation, while she hadn't yet remembered she had for a companion a primitive savage. He grimaced.

"Tell me of yer life, Fortune. I'd lief know everything. 'Tis time for me to shed my barbaric past and learn all I can about the wonders of yer world." He glanced away so she wouldn't see the laughter

104

in his eyes. When he had himself under control, he looked back to meet her suspicious gaze.

"You're laughing at me. I know you're laughing at me." She bit into the apple, and he watched her lick the juice from her lower lip. His body reminded him this was no laughing matter.

He shook his head. "I am verra curious about yer life."

She impaled him with a searching look; then, apparently satisfied, she nodded. "It's simple, really. In the twenty-first century humans decided cloning wasn't such a bad thing."

"Cloning?"

She smiled. "That's creating exact copies of living things without . . ." Small lines of concentration formed between her eyes. She was probably trying to think of an explanation his feeble mind could grasp. ". . . without having sex. Men could be completely eliminated from the reproductive cycle."

" 'Tis witchcraft. And dinna look at me in that superior way. If what ye say is true about men no longer existing, then ye werena as smart as ye thought."

She closed her eyes for a moment. He was right. They'd been dumb, dumb, dumb. She opened her eyes. "There's an old saying: 'Don't mess with Mother Nature.' Long before I was born, even before we'd abandoned our old name system, one of our greatest scientists, Jan Kredski, developed what she believed to be a superior cloning technique. She was wrong. She forgot that for every action there's a reaction. Over the generations, Jan Kredski's mass cloning method reduced our bio-

Nina Bangs

diversity, and we became more susceptible to an-
nihilation by a single virus. When it finally
happened, it took only the males and any males
produced from their sperm. With men extinct,
we've been forced to continue the cloning process.
It's only a matter of time before another virus
strikes. That's why . . ."

She looked up at him with suddenly widened
eyes, and he had the feeling she'd almost said more
than she wanted to. But then she lowered her gaze,
hiding her expression from him.

He didn't pretend to understand everything
she'd said, but he'd understood enough to be horrified. "Ye have no father?"

She glanced at him from under lowered lids,
then shook her head. His question had been soft,
sympathetic. How could a man who'd lived as he'd
lived, probably killed to survive, zero in on her hurt
with such sure instinct? He was supposed to be
hard and insensitive, someone she wouldn't feel
guilty about dragging home to play stud to the
world's women.

"I'm not sure I had a mother either." Had that
admission really come from her? "I'm an exact duplicate of my mother, only younger. I think that
bothers her." She shrugged. "Everyone's expected
to have at least one child. I was Mom's token child.
Once she'd done her duty, that was that. I was on
my own."

She almost flinched from the sympathy in his
gaze. "It wasn't that bad. I could do what I wanted
to do. At least I was well fed and safe."

He looked at her as though he could see right
through her puny defense of her mother. "Ye

106

needed a mother to hug ye and tell ye she loved ye. And ye needed a father to tell ye stories and find a good man for ye to marry." He seemed slightly embarrassed by his outburst.

Fortune couldn't find it in her heart to argue with the part about finding her a good husband. He was trying to comfort her. It had been a long time since anyone had tried to comfort her. Not since Ten-X, the woman next door who'd found her alone and crying on her ninth birthday, had anyone really cared.

"Good. Ye must be feeling better if ye can smile."

She nodded, suddenly shy. "You seem to have strong opinions on parents. Now that I've bared my soul, tell me about your parents."

He might as well have put on a Mordian mask. The warm, caring man of a few minutes before was gone. "They died when I was only a wee lad. I dinna remember much about them."

"Oh, well, then how about brothers or sisters?"

He still had the mask firmly in place. "I have one brother. We dinna see each other verra much."

So much for the information highway. It obviously ran only one way. "So what do you want to do today?"

He seemed to relax once she got off the subject of his family. "After we dress, I'd like to find a place to eat. I canna exist on wee bits of fruit. Then we can find a place to purchase food to bring home wi' us."

He'd given her the opening she'd been looking for. Now was the time to tell him one of the things he needed to know. OK, so he didn't really *need* to know this, but she needed to tell him. "There's a McDonald's close by."

Once again, he glared at her with savage anger. "I willna eat there. They are my enemies."

"They are *my* ancestors," she said softly.

Chapter Five

I gotta tell you, Fortune Cookie made a big mistake. Don't get me wrong; I think she's a terrific babe, but sometimes women talk too much. Know what I mean?

Leith tells her he has this thing about the Mac-Donalds, so what's she do? Confesses she's a Mac-Donald. I love women, but damned if I understand them. Things were going great, too. That scene in the shower was hot.

Relax. I didn't watch. I have a few scruples. Very few. But I'd stopped to scratch a flea—I hate fleas— and couldn't help hearing.

Fortune's a virgin—I love virgins—so I expected a few nerves. I could deal with that.

But now Leith's gonna be a hard sell. My life would chug along a lot easier if I could do a little mind manipulating. I've gotta think of some way to get past this MacDonald thing, and I've gotta do it fast. If they split up, it'll be tough gettin' them back together again. I might lose. Nah. Never.

Another problem. That jerk of an ice-cream man parked his butt outside the house. I should go out, order a cone, then suggest a few creative uses for it. If he doesn't do a quick disappearing act, he'll find nuclear plants aren't the only things that can have massive meltdowns. How does chocolate fallout sound? I don't know what game he's playing, but he's playing with an expert.

First I patch it up between Fortune and Leith; then I figure some way to go shopping with them. I've got gourmet taste buds. Fries and burgers don't cut it with me. Besides, my weak tummy won't take too much fast food. So I've gotta point them in the right direction when it comes to cat food. It'll be a real challenge. They'll want to buy some of that pet-aisle garbage, and I want steak. Rare. And maybe salmon. Whole.

Hey, I'll manage it. They don't call me the Great Manipulator for nothin'.

"A MacDonald! A cursed MacDonald?" Out of all the women in the world, the powers-that-be expected him to teach the joys of sex to a *MacDonald*? He couldn't do it. Even if God struck him dead on the spot, he couldn't make love to a MacDonald. "I canna stay in the same house wi' a cursed Mac-Donald!"

"Is that one word, or two?" she shouted back at him. "I've never seen such a hardheaded, obstinate man in—"

"Ye've ne'er seen a man at all. Mayhap we're all

hardheaded and obstinate when there are cursed MacDonalds nearby." That hadn't come out exactly as he'd planned.

A glimmer of laughter shone in her eyes. "Well, at least you admit you're hardheaded and obstinate."

Anger heated his face. The last person who'd laughed at him had nursed a broken head. " 'Tis useless trying to reason wi' a MacDonald. Now I know why ye've aggravated me so. MacDonalds are aggravating by nature." He strode toward the door.

Just before reaching the door, he turned to hurl one last comment her way. She wore a startled look, and he felt an intense stab of gratification. She hadn't thought he'd leave.

"Leith, wait! You can't just walk out and—"

Suddenly Ganymede shot between his legs and he tripped, falling hard against the door he'd pulled open. Kneeling, he rubbed the bump rising on his forehead. The cursed cat should stay with its cursed MacDonald owner. They belonged together.

"Are you okay? Let me get some ice to put on that lump." Her voice had turned soft, worried.

"I dinna need ice. I dinna need yer help." He couldn't control the gruffness in his voice. He hated women fussing over him, except in bed, of course.

He used the door to pull himself to his feet, then stumbled down the path with Fortune following. A familiar voice made him look up. Ice-cream truck? He'd seen it somewhere before, heard the same voice singing, but now the singer begged that someone not be cruel. *Hmmph*. What did the voice know of cruelty? Cruelty was turning a bonny lass into a cursed MacDonald.

"Where does the voice come from?" he asked Fortune, who'd finally caught up with him.

"I think they call it a loudspeaker. It's a recorded voice made to sound louder." She attached herself to his arm. "We have to talk about your moving out. You can't move out. We . . . we were meant to stay together for some reason."

"To torture me, no doubt." He scowled down at her, but his heart wasn't in it. The fall had given him a moment to calm down. The red haze of fury had lifted, and he could think.

"No, I'm sure—"

"Why not settle your argument over one of my Heavenly Hash cones? There's nothing like something cold and sweet to cure what's hot and bitter in your soul." The deep voice was soothing.

Leith stared at the man. Dark hair that flew in every direction and a fuzzy beard framed a face with eyes . . . Leith blinked. The bump on his head must've addled his wits. He couldn't tell what color the man's eyes were, only that they were deep, penetrating, with a hint of mischief. Leith had the uncomfortable feeling they could see to his very soul. He looked away. His soul wasn't ready for visitors just yet.

"We'll take two cones." Fortune glanced at the nightclothes she still wore, then at Leith. "Do you have any money on you?"

He nodded, then winced. His head would ache from that bump. He reached into his pocket and pulled out some coins.

His enthusiasm for leaving dampened, he paid

for the ice cream, then followed Fortune back into the house. Maybe he'd been a little unreasonable. Fortune wasn't one of the lying, thieving Mac-Donalds he knew from Scotland. She was right; that had been a long time ago.

A long time ago. All those he'd known were dead, had been for hundreds of years. His brother, the MacDonalds. The pain of that realization hurt worse than the ache in his head.

He had to find a way back, even if it meant living with a MacDonald. He shuddered at the thought.

"You must have a killer headache. I'll get something for it; then you can lie down. Should I give Ganymede your cone?"

He nodded, then slumped down on the couch and closed his eyes. The lumpy cushions still held the warmth from her body, and he could smell the clean scent of the soap she'd used last night. His body reacted to the memory of last night, regardless of the name MacDonald attached to the memory. His body had no loyalty to clan.

She'd returned. Even with his eyes closed and no sound to announce her presence, he knew she'd returned.

"Here. Take this."

He slitted his eyes just enough to identify the glass of water she held. He took the glass from her and the small pill she handed him. Probably poison. But he cared not so long as it got rid of his headache.

As he drifted toward sleep, he sensed another presence—intelligent, assessing. The feeling was so strong that he opened his eyes. Only Ganymede sat beside the couch, watching him with large amber eyes.

He forgot about Ganymede as he fell asleep to dream of an endless line of MacDonald hordes waiting to be taught the joys of love, and each MacDonald bore Fortune's face.

Fortune gazed down at Leith as he slept. She had let him rest for several hours. Too bad she had to disturb him. He looked younger, somehow less threatening, especially with that bump on his head. She fought the urge to smooth his hair away from his face. Maternal feelings? *Hardly*.

As she watched, he murmured something, then slowly opened his eyes. Those jade eyes still made her catch her breath.

"Feeling any better?" she asked softly.

"Aye." His voice was husky with sleep. "Are ye still a cursed MacDonald, or was that a wicked dream?"

She sighed. Back to that again. "Sorry, I'm still your worst nightmare. Do you feel up to shopping for food?"

" 'Tis necessary." Sitting up, he winced, then glared at Ganymede, who stared blandly back at him. "Leave the cat here."

"You can try. Blade hasn't had much luck so far."

"Ye must be firm wi' the beastie." With that manly pronouncement, he strode to the door, flung it open, then waited for her to follow. "This place we can purchase food—"

"I think they call it a supermarket."

"This . . . supermarket is close. We passed it last night. 'Tis not a long walk." He slammed the door shut just as Ganymede tried to follow them. "That should hold the black demon."

Silence stretched between them during the short walk. Leith had his own thoughts, and Fortune didn't want to get involved in another discussion about the "cursed" MacDonalds.

How could a man have such intense emotion over a name? She'd never felt that emotional about anything in her whole life. Come to think of it, not much had happened in her life to trigger any kind of emotion—until she met Leith.

She breathed deeply. It was pleasantly warm. The trees, the brief glimpses of the lake, the man walking beside her, all made her feel lazy and . . . what? She should be frantic, but somehow, right now, she wasn't. She felt almost content.

"I dinna believe it!"

While Fortune had been lost in thought, they'd reached the store. *What now?* She looked around.

"Yer cat is a wee spawn of hell."

"*My* cat?" She looked down. Ganymede sat by the supermarket door, calmly washing his face. "How did you get out?" She picked up the surprisingly heavy cat. He lay contentedly against her chest and purred. His happy rumble shuddered through her as she glanced up at Leith. "He's not going to let us go inside without him, you know."

Leith scowled. "Mayhap we can heave the troublesome ball of hair into yon loch." The glimmer of admiration in his gaze belied his fierce pronouncement.

She grinned. "Let's see how far we get without him." Setting the cat down, she slipped through the automatic doors with Leith right behind her,

but to no avail. Ganymede was trotting happily behind them by the time they reached the first aisle.
When they paused at the cereals, the cat leaped
into the cart and sat, king of all he surveyed.

Fortune shook her head. "What are we going to
do with you, cat? I'm sure you're not allowed in
here. You'll get us all booted out." She looked helplessly at Leith.

"We could brain him, then hide his body behind
yon Cocoa Puffs." He grinned happily at his solution.

"Don't you think about anything but violence?"

His grin died. "Ye dinna know me verra well if
ye think I could do such a thing. Ganymede has
courage. I admire that in any creature." His smile
returned. " 'Tis easy to anger ye, lass. I dinna have
to work hard at it."

She hated that he found her so predictable. Not
wanting to explore why his opinion mattered, she
busied herself with choosing a cereal. With a satisfied exclamation, she whipped a box of Special K
off the shelf and studied the label. "We'll get this.
It has all the essential vitamins and minerals without a lot of sugar. At home we have morning foods
that are manufactured grains made from scientifically formulated—"

"I dinna know what that means, but I'd guess ye
mean the food isna real." He casually reached for
another box of cereal.

"You make it sound like if something isn't *real* it
isn't good. Our cereals are much healthier than—"

She finally realized what he'd plunked into the
cart. "You have to be kidding. Double Sugar Choco

Pops?" She snatched up the box and studied the label. Horrified, she firmly placed the box back on the shelf. "That junk is pure sugar. It would rot your teeth while you were still chewing on it. Yuck!"

With a forbidding glare, Leith returned the box to the cart. "I like sweet things." His scowl suggested he'd never choose her from a shelf of women. "I willna eat something just because 'tis good for me. Ye have no adventure in yer soul, woman."

She glared at the offending box. "Being with you is adventure enough for a lifetime." Some remote corner of her brain responsible for monitoring cosmic truths yelled *Bingo*.

Carefully, she arranged one box on each side of Ganymede. "There. At least he's hidden a little."

They stopped again at the dairy section. Glancing down the row of milk containers, Fortune carefully examined each label, then set a plastic container of skim milk in the basket.

Leith looked suspicious. "Which one is the complete opposite of the one ye've chosen?"

"What do you mean?" She busily scanned the yogurt labels.

"Ye've probably chosen the healthiest one, so I want the one that tastes the best."

She abandoned her search of the yogurt containers long enough to throw him an exasperated glance. "This skim milk is fortified with vitamin D and has all the milk fat removed—"

"It looks more water than milk. I'd not want to drink it. I like milk rich with cream that rises to the top. Milk that is whole." He picked up a carton of whole milk and placed it on the opposite side of the cart from the things Fortune had chosen. "Not filled with . . . vitamin D. What is vitamin D?"

"Vitamin D is something . . . that's good for you."

He grinned. "Like a warm woman after a cold day of killing and plundering?"

She smiled sweetly. "Exactly." She suspected that on life's shelf, he considered her pure skim milk. But what did she care? She'd be surprised if his heart lasted through the bakery section. She'd have to wean him away from all that fat.

Forget it. She wouldn't be with him long enough to impact his eating habits. Somehow that thought depressed her.

Ganymede joined the fray when they reached the pet section. His howl of outrage made Fortune quickly return the bag of dried cat food she'd tried to sneak into the cart. His cries were only slightly less strident when she piled six cans of guaranteed-to-please-your-kitty food in the cart. As they meandered toward the meat section, the cans mysteriously disappeared one by one.

Fortune got her first real taste of battle when she tried to sneak past the meat section. She knew from experience that Leith's threat to drag her kicking and screaming to the roasts wasn't empty blustering. And could a cat cry? She'd swear those were real tears sliding down Ganymede's furry face.

Fine. Let Leith fill up on enough fat for a lifetime, because when he reached her time he'd have only healthful choices. Something about that thought bothered her, so she busied herself rooting through the skinless chicken. Leith chose T-bone steak, and Ganymede chose fresh salmon—whole.

And so it went. Leith chose chocolate cream pie and Fortune chose fresh fruit. By the time they reached the checkout counter, the basket resembled an armed camp. Leith's fatty feast topped off with hot-and-spicy salsa—chosen because the words *hot and spicy* reminded him of a certain Moira McAllister—protected his end of the basket, while Fortune's healthy harvest converged at the other end. Fortune decided she held the advantage. With all the leafy green vegetables she'd chosen, she had a veritable forest to hide in.

"You know, you and that cat won't be able to walk home without bypass surgery if you keep eating that junk," she grumbled as she pulled out money to pay the clerk.

He shrugged and picked up the bags. "Ye take the cat."

Ignoring the clerk's horrified realization that a cat crouched between the spinach and the broccoli, Leith strode from the store, leaving Fortune to lug Ganymede. Luckily, the cat leaped from her arms almost immediately. She would've been puffing before they reached home, while Leith strode along under the weight of four bags of groceries as though he carried nothing.

She ran to catch up with him. "I can carry one of those."

He gazed at her with unexpected passion. " 'Tis all I have to offer, Fortune. Dinna take it away."

Pride. He had more than his share.

Fortune remained silent on the walk home. Her nagging guilt wouldn't go away—probably a prod-

119

uct of her society's attitude. Each person was part of the whole, and therefore had a responsibility toward those around her, etcetera, etcetera. Well, she wasn't responsible for the grouch beside her, other than making sure he went with her when she returned to her time.

Went with her. At last she'd identified the source of her feeling. The thought of what she had to do made her feel uneasy, guilty. He'd hate her if she didn't warn him. On the other hand, if she told him, he'd probably leave and never return. *What a mess*.

When they reached home, a two-wheeled vehicle—a motorcycle, if she remembered correctly—was parked in front. Blade bent over the vehicle while Lily heaved knives into a hapless tree.

"I'll take these inside for ye, and ye can put them away." Leith disappeared into the house.

Fortune stood with her hands on her hips. "What if I don't *want* to put them away?" she inquired of the closed door.

"Leave that man alone, honey." Lily had retrieved her arsenal and moved up beside Fortune. "Men like to feel in charge, so a smart woman doesn't sweat the small stuff."

"But that's not being honest." *What you're planning for Leith isn't honest either*.

Lily threw back her head and laughed. "Nothing's black or white. Sometimes gray's the kindest color."

Fortune frowned. She felt there was a profound truth in Lily's statement, if she could only find it.

Lily threw a companionable arm across Fortune's shoulder, blissfully ignoring Fortune's instinctive flinch.

Fortune drew a deep breath. She'd have to get used to touching. Obviously people in earlier times saw nothing wrong with it. They hadn't learned that invading another's space without invitation was unacceptable. *Then why don't you resent Leith's touch? Why do you find it so easy to touch him?*

"Let's you and I go inside. We can put those groceries away in a snap." Lily opened the door, then pushed a reluctant Fortune into the house just as Leith emerged.

A small black body trailed at Leith's heels. Ganymede had found a new hero. Leith and Ganymede had so much in common. Both were demanding males, and both had a death wish where food was concerned.

Resigned, she let herself be guided toward the kitchen.

Leith felt disappointed. He'd expected Fortune to react when he told her to put the food away. In some perverse way, he liked her fiery and disapproving.

He stopped beside Blade. "What manner of vehicle is this?"

Blade paused to wipe his hands on a cloth. "You really have been out of the loop, big guy. This is a Harley."

Leith touched the gleaming metal. He thought of sharing this experience with his brother. The sudden ache almost made him gasp. Hugh was gone, perhaps forever. The sadness he felt was old.

In truth, Hugh had been gone from him for many years. Time would not change that.

"You know, big guy, I have a question. If you were raised in Tibet with monks, how come you still sound Scottish?"

Curse Fortune's lie. "I lived with Scottish monks."

Blade scratched his head. "Scottish monks in Tibet?"

"How does this vehicle work?" Leith crouched to peer more closely at it.

"This bike's a Harley classic." Blade's narrow chest swelled with pride. "How about I take you for a ride, big guy?"

Leith nodded. Anything to get Blade's attention away from Tibet and monks. He watched Blade straddle the machine, and he did the same when Blade motioned behind him.

As the Harley roared away from the house, Leith's heart swelled with newly discovered love. *Wondrous.* He could ride it like a horse, with the wind whipping his hair, yet the amazing speed made his heart pound with excitement. He had to have a Harley of his own. *Ye willna be here long enough.*

The thought acted as cold water splashed in his face. He wanted to go home to the Highlands. He needed to go home so he could make his peace with Hugh. But even after two days, the thought of never seeing Fortune again weighed heavy on him. How could he feel sadness at the loss of a woman who despised him?

When Blade stopped the Harley in front of a building bearing a sign that read CAJUN CAFÉ, Leith got off and followed his new friend inside. Men wearing vests made of leather milled around the dark interior. Leith needed no one to tell him they were warriors. He immediately felt at home.

Blade sat down at a corner table and raised his hand. Immediately a woman came over with a tray of drinks. Blade set one in front of Leith. "Have a beer, big guy."

Leith took a tentative sip, then relaxed. It tasted different from what he was used to, but it was a man's drink.

Blade leaned back. "Feels good to relax." He took a gulp of his beer. "I ran into Hugh Campbell's widow today. Told her about you. She wants to meet you, so I said I'd bring you and the little lady over tomorrow. That okay with you?"

Leith nodded. Could this be connected to his reason for being here? He hoped not. Leith wanted no more surprises. He still reeled from the knowledge that Fortune was a MacDonald, and worse still, that it mattered not to his desire for her.

"This here's Tank. He's the president of our club."

Leith forced aside his thoughts to acknowledge the big man with the cold, assessing stare who'd sat down across from him. Leith recognized an equal. He nodded a noncommittal greeting.

"Leith just got into town. He ran into some bad luck, so I'm helping his old lady and him out a bit."

Tank continued to assess Leith. "Where're you from?" His voice was low, relaxed. A dangerous man.

Leith couldn't make his lips repeat Fortune's ridiculous story about Tibet. He shrugged. "Here and there."

Tank smiled grimly. "I respect privacy. You have a bike?"

Leith shook his head. *Be careful. Don't say too much.* "If I stay here, I'd like to have one." *If I stay here.* The words stirred a maelstrom of emotions in him. Thoughts of Fortune, thoughts of Scotland.

Finally making up his mind about Leith, Tank grinned. "When you decide it's time to get a bike, see me. I'll make sure you don't get ripped off. And if you need any help, give a shout. Any friend of Blade's is a friend of mine. Here's my card."

Leith looked blankly at the small piece of paper Tank handed him. "Attorney-at-law?"

"It comes in handy. If anyone hassles you, call me." He rose and walked away.

"What is an attorney?"

Blade chuckled. "A lawyer. He defends you if you get in trouble with the law. That's why we call him Tank—short for Think Tank. Get it?"

Leith didn't get it, but he understood the part about defending people who were in trouble with the law. He'd found from experience that the law could be as fickle as a beautiful woman. Which brought his thoughts back to Fortune.

He'd been away from her only a short time, but he found he missed her. How much more would he miss her when he returned to Scotland? He'd bedded so many women and rarely thought of them afterward, yet this woman haunted his every thought.

"Tank likes you. He doesn't tell everyone he's a lawyer. Surprises a lot of people." Blade chuckled at some memory. "Guess we better be gettin' back. Lily gets all nervous if I'm gone too long. Women."

Blade stood, then wound his way toward the door. Leith followed. This felt familiar, not much different from places he'd visited at home. Men didn't change, only women. Of course, that made women more of a challenge, and he loved a challenge.

"I absolutely, positively will *not* sleep on that couch again tonight." Fortune stood on tiptoe and tried on her most intimidating expression. Leith leaned indolently against the wall of the bedroom and stared across the disputed area.

"Ye dinna have to. This bed is verra large."

He widened his eyes, probably trying to look innocent. It didn't work. Even as a baby, she'd bet he lay in his cradle looking up at all the women who'd come to coo over him and mesmerized them with his touch-me eyes and wicked, sexy grin.

"OK, I'll sleep in the bed. Where are you going to sleep?" She did some eye-widening of her own.

"In the bed with ye."

She sighed. "Then I guess it's the floor for me. That couch killed my back last night." She hunched over, placed one hand on the affected area, and tried to look pathetic. She hoped her pathetic look was a little more sincere than his sympathetic look.

"The floor is verra hard, but 'twill do yer back good."

That's all? No chivalrous offer to abandon the bed for the sake of her aching back? She *always* programmed self-sacrifice into *her* men. "Right. See you in the morning." She stomped from the room with vengeful thoughts swirling in her head of the circuitry changes she'd make if he were one of her men.

Pulling a throw pillow from the couch for her head, she settled onto the floor. Nothing would make her budge. *Hmm*. There had to be a more comfortable position, though.

Rolling onto her side, she found herself eyeball-to-eyeball with . . . an insect! A huge insect with big, hairy legs and long, waving antennae. And behind it were assorted family members, all with evil intent.

Springing from the floor, she stood breathing hard. She'd been taught all life was precious, but she doubted that included big, ugly bugs with extended families. Clenching her teeth with determination, she headed down the hall.

When she finally stood beside the bed, she didn't have to wake Leith. He lay with his hands behind his head, and even in the room's dim light she could see his amused expression.

"Did you know there were bugs in this house?"

"Aye."

"Why didn't you tell me?" It was hard speaking through gritted teeth.

"Ye dinna like people telling ye things, so I thought ye'd rather discover it yerself." His wicked grin flashed in the darkness. "Climb into bed, lass. I dinna take up much space."

"Fine. But the space you take up had better not be on my side of the bed, buster." She couldn't believe she'd agreed to sleep in the same bed with him. It was like the ancient tale of the wolf and Little Red Riding Hood. Little Red Riding Hood had been dumb, but even she wouldn't have *slept* with the wolf.

Do it now. She made a flying leap into the bed that would've done a Havlan jumping-dorne proud. Quickly turning her back to his side of the bed, she waited tensely.

Did she hear a quiet chuckle? She felt the bed give beneath his weight as he shifted onto his side, then nothing.

It was too quiet. It was the silence of the jungle just before a predator leaped upon its helpless prey.

Oh, good grief. She'd always known she had a vivid imagination, but this was ridiculous. She couldn't help wondering, though . . . Was he naked? What was he thinking about? Was he naked? Would he try to move closer? Was he naked? *Get a grip*. She'd simply breathe deeply and think calm, rational thoughts. There, she was under control again.

OK, if she was so calm, why did she feel the need to fill the silence with nervous speech? "I guess everyone back in Scotland will wonder where you've gone."

"No one will wonder." His tone said *Drop it*.

She couldn't. She suddenly had an urgent need to know. After all, she was sharing a bed with this man, and she didn't know a thing about him. "OK, I remember you said your parents were dead, but didn't you mention something about a brother?"

"I dinna see Hugh often." His tone had turned glacial.

She couldn't let it alone. It was like poking a stick at a hibernating bear, all the while knowing the bear might very well wake and mistake you for a midnight snack. "Why don't you see him? He's your only relative, for heaven's sake."

Fortune could feel the tension. The air around her seemed to explode, twisting in tortuous coils of agonizing emotion.

Maybe she shouldn't have asked that last question. She felt the bed shift and knew he'd propped himself up on one elbow.

"Look at me, Fortune." His voice held a quality she'd never heard before, a pain so deep she couldn't even fathom it.

Without attempting to argue, she turned to face him.

A full moon shone in the window behind him, making him nothing more than a dark silhouette. The shifting shadows played across the dark walls, hinting at secrets. "You . . . you don't have to tell me about Hugh if you don't want to."

"Ah, but I do, lass. Ye canna call back yer question. Mayhap ye might wish ye had once ye hear my answer." He reached out and touched the side of her face with one finger. She resisted the urge to flinch away—from his touch, from the truth.

"Hugh hasna spoken to me for eight years, since the morning he slaughtered a host of unarmed men, without pity, without mercy. I was there, lass. I saw the blood. It stains my soul. Even three hundred years canna wash away the blood."

Shaking, Fortune closed her eyes. This would teach her to never again make light conversation in bed with a Scotsman from 1700. They didn't have the knack for idle chitchat. Everything had to be blazing anger, heart-wrenching emotion. Her calm, unchanging life hadn't prepared her for this.

But she'd asked, and now she knew. Sort of. She'd seen on history disks the kind of carnage he spoke of, but it had been distant, unreal. Now she lay beside a living, breathing man who'd experienced the horror. She could almost smell the blood.

Drawing a deep breath, Fortune tried to think logically. She'd spent only two days with Leith, but she'd seen him furious with Ganymede, with her. Not once had his fury taken the form of violence. She didn't doubt he could kill, but not unarmed men.

"You didn't kill the helpless." She spoke the quiet words with a certainty that amazed her.

"Do ye know me so well then, lass?" His harsh whisper sent tendrils of doubt skittering down her spine. What if she was wrong?

Logic had no part in her response. "I know you don't have that kind of savagery in your heart."

He lay down again, his body radiating brittle tautness that threatened to snap and shower her with unbearable emotions. He turned over, presenting his back to her, and her tension eased.

"Ye're too trusting, Fortune. Ye have no idea what evil walks the earth in the guise of man. Dinna ask more."

She wouldn't ask any more questions tonight, but they rattled around in her head, demanding answers. On another night they'd talk about Hugh again. When she'd recovered from tonight's overload of emotion. When she felt strong enough to accept the horrors that writhed in his past and had followed him to this new time and place.

If she and Leith were still together. Did she still want to stay with Leith? Could she bring a man with such a bloodstained history back to her peaceful world?

Fortune burrowed her face into her pillow. She didn't have to remain on guard against Leith tonight, because tonight Leith did battle with his personal demons.

She wished she'd been able to bring her Beautiful Dream Machine through time with her. She glanced at Leith's taut back. They both needed some beautiful dreams tonight.

Chapter Six

"Yer babe will be born verra soon, I think."

Leith watched Fortune's lashes flutter open, waiting for the moment her sleepy-eyed confusion would turn to awareness—of him, of the fact they lay in bed together.

"Babe?"

Her blue gaze darkened like cloud shadow over Loch Naver, and he knew she remembered what they'd spoken of last night, or rather the blather *he'd* spoken. The darkness and this woman must've stolen his wits. He could think of no other reason for baring his pain for her to see. He must distract her from thoughts of last night before she asked more questions. "Dinna ye feel him move? Methinks he'll grow into a braw laddie."

"Braw laddie?"

He watched in amused silence as realization

131

crept over her—of his nearness, and the fact that part of her had grown mightily during the night.

Her eyes widened as she stared down at the suspiciously rounded sheet. "My stomach is purring!"

"Aye." Leith could hear the contented rumble clearly.

"Ganymede!" The mound shifted; the rumble grew louder.

"Ye dinna look too pleased at the blessed event, lass."

"Blessed event, ha!" She reached for the sheet, ready to fling it aside.

Leith arranged his face in lines of mock horror. " 'Tis an unnatural mother ye be, speaking of yer babe that way."

He felt guilty at her sudden shattered expression.

"I'll never be a mother, Leith." She looked away. "I don't want a clone of myself. Maybe I'm more old-fashioned than I thought, but I'd want my child to be the product of a loving relationship with a man I . . ." She laughed self-consciously. "Before she died, Grandma Two-Z gave me the cross." She reached up to her neck as though she expected the cross to still rest there. "Anyway, she told me to always look for the *real* in life." Fortune stared down at the purring mound. "Fat chance of that."

Something stirred in him. "I swear I'll get yer cross back for ye." He pictured himself lifting the feathery curls at the base of her neck, then rubbing his knuckles against her smooth skin as he secured the chain. He'd reach around and lay his palm between the warm swell of her breasts to make sure the cross rested easily against her flesh. He'd move his palm lower. . . .

She glanced at him. "I know you will." Her voice was soft, trusting.

The moment shimmered with promise until Fortune shifted her gaze to the now snoring mound. "That's it. Nap time's over." She whipped back the sheet, lifted the sleeping cat off her stomach, then plopped him onto the floor.

Her virginal white gown had ridden up to reveal the tempting long line of her legs. Leith didn't know which image to believe.

He sucked in his breath as, in his mind, his fingers slid along the length of those legs. His imagination stripped her of the troublesome gown so his fingers could glide along her thigh and over her stomach.

"What are you staring at?"

"A man's imagination is verra powerful." He raised his lids to meet her gaze, watched her eyes widen, her expression turn cautious. She'd seen his hunger. Suddenly he realized he must know something if he were ever to fulfill his penance, one he realized he desired with growing urgency, and not only so he might return home. "Do ye fear me?"

Immediately her eyes sparked defiance at him. "Of course not. What's to be afraid of?"

More than ye could imagine, lass.

She lay quietly, watching him, and he knew his eyes must still burn with his need to touch her. In an attempt to return to normalcy, he grinned and nodded toward Ganymede, who crouched on the windowsill, glaring at them. "Ganymede isna happy."

"No."

If he hadn't looked into her eyes, he would have

133

believed the softly spoken word an answer to his comment. But he did look into her eyes, and knew she spoke of his desire.

He didn't know why it should hurt. Probably she'd only bruised his pride. After all, he'd rejected her name. What more could he expect from her? It still hurt. She'd rejected him as a man. Most likely she thought him too primitive, too savage.

Maybe she was right. But at least he knew hot blood flowed in his veins, fierce emotions made his heart pound. He *lived* life. He never wanted to be like the humans of her future world—cold, rational.

He climbed out of bed, noting with satisfaction her expression of disappointment with the briefs he wore. "Blade has spoken to Hugh Campbell's widow. She wishes to see me today. Would ye come wi' me?"

"Sounds interesting. I'd love to meet her."

He breathed out, relieved. She sounded normal once again.

"You can use the bathroom while I make breakfast." She smiled at him. "Oh, when we went shopping yesterday, I bought you a few things you'll need."

Leith frowned. He'd noticed she'd flung some objects he didn't recognize into their cart, but he hadn't questioned her. She must grow tired of his constant questions.

Besides, he hated having to ask about everything. When he asked about something others took for granted, he felt like a newborn—dependent. He needed to control his own life. Only twice before had he lost that control. He glanced bitterly around him. This was the third time.

Why did the wretched man need her to show him how to use this stuff? Couldn't he read the labels? No, maybe he couldn't.

"This is deodorant. You spray it under your arms. It makes you smell fresh and . . . I can't believe they still use this stuff. We have implants under our arms now so we never have to . . ." He watched her with gleaming eyes. "OK, this is toothpaste. Put some on this brush and scrub your teeth." He smiled at her with perfectly white teeth. Weren't primitives supposed to have nothing but blackened stumps? He probably kept them white by gnawing on the bones of now-extinct carnivores he'd killed with his bare hands. "And this is a razor. Spray this foam on your hand, put it on your face, then—"

"Ye can stop now. I understand. 'Tis no wonder yer men died. Ye drove them to exhaustion wi' all the things they must do to their bodies."

He frowned at the mirror, a towel wrapped around his waist, his torso still gleaming damply from his morning shower. He picked up the deodorant, grimacing as he lifted his arm.

Turning away, she left the room before he could notice her admiring glances. *OK, ogling.*

Fact. All the stuff she'd bought him was overkill, messing with perfection. But she was a slave to ritual. Spraying, brushing, and shaving were accepted male rituals in this time.

Speaking of rituals, her stomach told her it was time for breakfast. She'd have fruit and a cup of coffee. She tried to avoid caffeine, but she'd need it today. Resignedly, she began to cook up a dish of fat for Leith—bacon, fried eggs, and toast slathered with butter. *Yuck*. Maybe she could wean him away from some of this stuff with a few medical facts guaranteed to scare the hair off his chest. *His chest*. She busied herself with the cooking and tried not to dwell on Leith's body parts.

A piteous meow reminded her she couldn't starve Ganymede to death, even if he deserved it after this morning's debacle.

This morning. She'd avoided thinking about it. Avoided examining too closely the warm yearning she'd felt with Leith's gaze resting on her stomach, her breasts. She could find no reason for the feeling. She'd understand if she'd had a sexual response, but it hadn't been sexual. It had been a feeling of completion, of coming home. *Ridiculous*. The social scientists would call it a primal memory, something humans no longer needed. She didn't know; it had felt so . . . right.

And because it felt right, she had to make sure she didn't put herself in that situation again. She had to keep her distance from Leith. Anything that brought them closer could add up to hurt when he left her, either for his own time or when he became the property of her world state. She smiled. Leith would be a national treasure and treated as such. She stopped smiling. How would Leith feel about that? She already knew how she felt.

Fortune heard Leith's footsteps just as she set his food on the table. Hurrying back to the counter, she set a dish of salmon on the floor for Ganymede. The cat looked up at her with adoring eyes. *Right*.

The adoration would last exactly as long as the food did; then he'd be demanding something else of her.

" 'Tis a wondrous smell, lass."

Leith's deep voice directly behind her spun Fortune around, and she found herself inches from his chest. He'd put on a shirt, but it still hung open. He smelled of soap and toothpaste. "Yes, it *is* a wonderful smell," she murmured. Forever after toothpaste would trigger erotic fantasies. She knew this with every despairing inch of her soul.

He gently lifted her chin until she stared into his eyes. "Thank ye. Show me how to use these objects"—he nodded toward the appliances—"and I'll cook for ye next time."

Her amazement must have shown, because he chuckled softly. "I had no woman to cook for me, so I did it myself rather than go hungry. In the beginning, I'd as lief starve as eat what I cooked. 'Twas fit for no living thing."

Without waiting for her reply he sat down at the table. "Come, talk to me while I eat, Fortune."

Grabbing a piece of fruit, her coffee, and a cup of tea for him, she sat down at the table.

"Ye canna tell me that wee piece of fruit will satisfy ye. Why dinna ye try some of this?" He pointed to his plate.

"It's not healthy."

"*Life* isna healthy, Fortune. Doesna the smell tempt ye?"

Now that he mentioned it, his food did smell delicious. "I'll just have a little piece of your toast."

She watched with horror as he slathered more butter on the toast, then topped it off with grape jelly. "I don't think I've ever seen that many calories in one spot."

He lowered his gaze as he finished fixing the toast, and she studied his thick fringe of dark lashes. Women would kill to touch him—in any time. The thought depressed her.

"Life would be verra dull if we ate only healthful things. Here." He held out a small piece of toast. Without thinking, she opened her lips and he slid it in. For a moment his fingers touched her lips, and she forgot to breathe, let alone chew.

Something hot and elemental in his eyes told her she wasn't the only one affected. Nervously, she chewed and swallowed, then ran her tongue across her butter-smeared lips. He followed the motion with his gaze. She glanced away. Something she didn't understand, wasn't sure she wanted, flowed between them.

When she looked back, he'd placed a piece of bacon and egg on her plate. Rather than appear rude, she ate his offering. *Hmm, delicious.* "This is good. Too bad it's unhealthy."

His smile held a secret. "Forbidden fruit is the most desired. Ye must know that, lass."

OK, time for a change of subject. "If Blade is going to pick us up, we'd better get moving."

He nodded and pushed himself away from the table, but his grin said plainly that he understood her ploy.

He watched as she studied the appliances scornfully. "Primitive, but this one washes dishes." She loaded the dirty dishes, added dishwasher soap, closed the door, and pushed what she hoped was the right button. She let out her breath when she heard water pouring into the machine.

"Do they have a machine for everything?" He sounded doubtful about that possibility.

"Of course. Why, in my time—"

"I know. Ye've told me several hundred times about the wonders of yer world. But if machines do all the work for ye, what do ye do wi' yer time?"

"Without manual labor, we're free to use our minds, to create." She felt proud of her answer. He couldn't help realizing the benefits of living in a society where one could pursue one's dreams without wasting energy on things like washing dishes. Maybe if she made her time sound wonderful enough, he wouldn't hate her when she took him there.

" 'Tis sad."

"Huh?" Had she missed something?

"Ye can create many wondrous things, but ye canna create the most wondrous thing of all."

"What? Whatever it is, I'm sure our scientists are working on it."

"The love between a man and woman." With that undeniable truth, he left the room.

Leith watched the massive gate swing open and wondered why Hugh Campbell's widow seemed so anxious to meet him. She knew not what he was, would probably run screaming if she did know.

He glanced at Fortune, who sat with Ganymede in her lap, staring out the opposite window of the taxi at the gravel road leading to Mary Campbell's home.

Ganymede had won again. If Leith's clan had even a crumb of the determination that cat had, they'd have wiped out the MacDonalds years ago. Ganymede stood up for what he saw as his rights, and if the wee demon were a man, Leith would be proud to fight beside him.

Leith forgot about Ganymede when the Campbell home came into view. God's teeth, Mary Campbell lived in a castle.

"Impressive, huh?" Blade glanced over his shoulder at his passengers in the backseat. "She's rolling in dough."

"Rolling in dough? I dinna—"

"Well, isn't this beautiful?" Fortune cast him a warning glance.

She was right. He mustn't call any more attention to his lack of knowledge.

"Yeah, hard to believe, but this here is an authentic Scottish castle. Campbell had it brought over from Scotland stone by stone and set up on his land. Waste of money, if you ask me. Bet it costs a bundle to air-condition something that big."

Leith turned to Fortune. "Air-condition?" he mouthed.

"Later," she mouthed back.

Now that he was looking at her mouth, he had to admit her lips were tempting. The more he saw of Fortune, the more tempting *all* of her became. Almost tempting enough to make him forget she was, after all, a cursed MacDonald.

"I'll drop you guys off here. Call me when it's time to pick you up. Have fun." Blade glanced in the mirror, then frowned. "Oh, don't forget to take that damned cat with you."

"That damned cat" had no intention of being left

behind. When Leith climbed out of the taxi, then held the door open for Fortune, Ganymede leaped out, too.

Leith stared at the castle. This had stood on Scottish soil. It was a part of him, and the very stones spoke to him. If he could've embraced it, he would have.

"Well, now what?" Fortune sounded a little uncertain, and that somehow pleased him.

Even she felt the spirit, the essence of all those who'd walked this castle's halls. Had he stood, three hundred years ago, gazing from its battlement? He closed his mind to the possibility.

"We'll . . ." He paused as the massive front door slowly swung open.

Leith didn't know what to expect, but the small woman who hurried out to greet them surprised him. Blade had called her old, but her hair was . . . yellow. Not a gray strand showed anywhere. Dressed in a short skirt and some sort of jacket, she hardly looked the old crone of his imagination. She ignored Fortune as she stopped directly in front of Leith and stared.

He couldn't hold his tongue. " 'Tis amazing. Yer hair isna gray anywhere. Ye dinna look old, but Blade said ye were at least sixty-five." He closed his eyes. God's teeth, he must learn to guard his speech. Not everyone would be as accepting of his foolish words as was Blade.

He opened his eyes at her amused chuckle. "Old age will have to fight me for every wrinkle and gray hair. I don't believe in growing old gracefully. Now let me look at you." Her voice turned soft.

She reached up and touched the side of his face.

141

"Yes, you look exactly like him. You look exactly like my Hugh."

Leith almost squirmed at the sound of tears in her voice. He didn't know how to react to women's tears. He never had. Hugh had called him soft. He didn't think it softness to hate seeing a woman unhappy.

She seemed hard-pressed to drag her gaze from Leith as she glanced at Fortune. "I've forgotten my manners. I'm Mary Campbell, and this is Tootsie." She glanced down.

They all glanced down. Beside her sat the strangest animal Leith had ever seen. It resembled a cat, but looked like nothing more than a huge ball of white fur with a tiny pushed-in face dominated by round green eyes. Eyes that at the moment were fixed on Ganymede with a predatory gleam. Meanwhile Ganymede, he of the fearless heart, did his best to hide behind Fortune's jean-clad legs. "What manner of cat is that?"

Mary cast him a puzzled look, then explained. "She's a Persian. Hmm. Your cat seems shy. Is he fixed?"

Leith grinned. He could guess what *fixed* meant. "No, but mayhap we should think about it."

He would swear that Ganymede winced. As a fellow male, he sympathized. Leith watched with interest as Tootsie edged toward Ganymede. Suddenly Ganymede bolted. He raced for the open door and disappeared into the castle with Tootsie in hot pursuit. Leith shook his head. He didn't know if he blamed Ganymede. He might run if Tootsie chased him, too.

He glanced away from the castle to meet Mary's

concerned frown. "I'll have to send someone after Tootsie. I'm not prepared for a litter of kittens."

"I dinna think ye need worry overmuch. Ganymede doesna seem verra eager." He dragged his thoughts from the cats. "Dinna mind my poor manners. This is Fortune, and I'm Leith Campbell."

"Fortune. An unusual name. What's your last name, dear?"

The silence stretched on a little too long until Leith spoke up. "Her last name is . . . Campbell. She's my wife. We havena been married verra long, so she doesna always remember she's a *Campbell* now." He stared pointedly at Fortune.

Fortune glared back at him, but she said nothing.

"How nice. Why don't you come inside and we'll talk. I'm so excited. I can't wait to tell you about Hugh." She turned and led them into the castle.

"Why in heaven's name did you lie about my name?" Fortune's whisper spoke of future retribution.

"She seems a gentlewoman. She wouldna understand an unmarried woman traveling with a man. Besides, no Campbell would welcome a MacDonald."

"You are incredibly old-fashioned."

He saw by her eyes that she regretted her angry words, but she couldn't recall them.

"I am. 'Tis something ye must accept. But dinna condemn me for not understanding yer ways when ye dinna want to understand mine." Her criticism hurt. He knew it shouldn't. Nothing a MacDonald said should make any difference.

She sighed. "Fine. It won't do any good arguing. You go with Mary while I make sure Ganymede's okay. Tootsie looked sort of scary."

He nodded. His words had angered Fortune, but he'd spoken only the truth. For the time he remained in this castle, he'd pretend she was a Campbell and not a cursed MacDonald. "Dinna get lost."

She offered him a cool smile. "If I do, I'll just ask a passing ghost for directions."

"Have a care, lass, that the ghost isna me."

She chose not to comment as she turned in the direction Ganymede had fled.

Inside the castle, he passed painting after painting of Scotland. Leith felt the yearning for the rugged beauty of his homeland rise in waves and wash over him. He had to believe he would once again roam his beloved Highlands or he would go mad.

But when he reached a hall with row after row of portraits, Leith knew he must stop. He walked over to stare at one in particular.

Mary Campbell stood beside him. "That's Hugh Campbell, the ancestor of my Hugh. He was one of those who massacred the MacDonalds at Glencoe." She spoke in an almost reverent whisper.

Leith could tell her that she need show no reverence for Hugh. The picture was of a younger Hugh, the brother Leith remembered from his youth, the one who'd laughed with him, who'd always had time for him. Hugh had done little laughing since Glencoe. The painting didn't show the damage of too much drink, too much regret.

He followed Mary into a small, cozy room with a full-wall window that looked out over a tree-shaded garden. The air was pleasantly cool and bright with sunshine. Looking around, he admitted that modern improvements had made this a great deal more comfortable than the original castle would have been.

"Have a seat." Mary pointed to a wooden table placed near the window. "I'll get you something to drink."

He watched Mary leave the room as an exuberant Fortune entered. She held a disgruntled Tootsie in one arm. Throwing her other arm into the air, she spun in a circle. "You should see this place. I can't believe it. A *real* castle!" She set the cat on the floor. Tootsie stalked over to the window and curled up in an offended ball.

Leith pulled his attention away from his thoughts of Hugh long enough to smile at her. "Ye mean there is something yer time doesna have?"

Fortune slanted him a thoughtful stare. "Well, we have castles, but—"

"I know, I know. They're scientifically formulated to look like the real thing." He sat down at the table and stared out at a lone yellow flower blooming near the window. Flowers looked the same everywhere, in every time. But he didn't see heather in the garden, and he had to consider the idea that he might never see heather again. "Ye wouldna be verra excited about the real thing. In the winter the cold would seep through the crannies and chill ye to the bone. Ye'd have only a fire to keep ye warm. There wouldna be a fine bathroom, or kitchen wi' all yer . . . appliances."

"And yet you'd go back in a minute." Her soft words stated what they both knew.

145

He stared at the yellow flower, felt its rightness in this garden. "Aye, I'd go back in a minute." He turned to look at her. " 'Tis my home; 'tis where I belong."

She only nodded, and he sensed a sadness in her. Perhaps she thought of her own home. Though the home she described had sounded bereft of love and emotion, she had her work. He frowned. Her work. He must remember to ask her about this making of men.

Fortune sat down beside him as Mary Campbell returned to the room with several drinks in her hands and a large book tucked under her arm.

"I brought along some pictures of Hugh when he was younger. He looked so much like you he could've been your brother." She set the drinks down, then carefully placed the book on the table in front of Leith.

He studied the book for a long moment, not daring to look, not wanting to see. But as Mary's expectant silence stretched on, he knew he couldn't avoid it. Slowly, he opened the book and stared at . . . himself.

He wanted to slam the book shut and run from this place, this time. He didn't understand—Lord, he didn't understand anything that had happened to him!

"Let me see." Fortune's soft demand gave him the excuse to rid himself of the picture. He shoved it over to her.

"Amazing," she said softly.

He wanted to shout, *Dinna ye see? Dinna ye understand? 'Tis because of this man I'm here and I dinna know why.*

146

"Tell me about yourself, Leith." Mary placed her hand over his where it lay clenched on the table. "Blade only said your name was Leith Campbell, you sounded like a Scot, and you looked exactly like my Hugh." She smiled. "He rattled on about Tibet, but I couldn't make sense of it, and it doesn't matter anyway."

He looked at her warily. *Be careful,* he warned himself. *Don't say the wrong thing.* "There isna much to tell. Ye're right; I do look like yer Hugh, but mayhap we're distant relatives." *More distant than ye'll ever know.*

"Let me tell you something about Hugh, about myself, so you don't think I'm a crazy old lady." She patted his hand once, then withdrew hers.

"Hugh spent his whole life studying Scottish history, particularly anything pertaining to the Glencoe massacre. It wasn't the Campbells' finest hour, but Hugh had to know about the original Hugh Campbell—what he thought, was he the monster some said." She half closed her eyes, lost in her memories. "Up until the day he died, my Hugh was knee-deep in research. In fact, the night he was killed, he was hurrying home from Rice University with new information about a supposed brother the original Hugh Campbell had. He'd found the brother's name—"

" 'Twas Leith," he murmured.

Mary's gaze turned intent. "Yes, and I won't ask just yet how you knew." She stared down at her hand with its plain gold band on one finger. "He said he'd never rest easy until he knew if the brother took part in the killing—"

"He didna." Leith's reply was torn from an agony

that would never heal, could only scab over, to be torn open again and again. "But he didna stop the killing either. And afterward, Hugh called him traitor to his clan. They didna speak again for eight years; then Leith . . . went away."

"And never returned." Mary's face turned parchment white. Her hands trembled uncontrollably as she pushed the book out of her way. She leaned across the table, an expression of fearful urgency on her face. "How did you know that? Hugh had just made the discovery. He had the papers with him when . . . when . . ."

Never returned. No, he wouldn't believe that. Leith closed his eyes. He'd made a mistake. He'd let his emotions rule him once again, and he'd made a terrible mistake.

"Look at me, Leith Campbell." Mary's voice grew strong with a fierceness Leith couldn't deny. He opened his eyes.

"No one in the entire academic world knew that. Only my Hugh. It was his great discovery. How did you know Leith Campbell's part in the Glencoe massacre?"

He couldn't lie to this woman if his life depended on it.

"Because I was there," he whispered.

Chapter Seven

No! I'm not hearin' this. See, I'm puttin' my fingers in my ears so I don't hear it. Rats. No fingers.

Tell me Leith didn't blow his cover big-time.

I'm gettin' too old for this job. I finally escape the lovin' claws of Titillating Tootsie, and check in with Leith to find he's put his Scottish foot in his Campbell mouth. You leave humans alone for even a minute and zap, it's all over.

Of course, that's why this whole thing's such a challenge. You can't predict what they'll do.

OK, so once in a while they have a good moment. Like Leith makin' sure I got something decent to eat. Hey, he owed me. If I hadn't made my power dive off the Jockey shorts to stop the dirty thief tryin' to steal their dough, Fortune would still be standin' around wrapped in a curtain. Leith appreciates me.

That's why I chose him. He pays his debts. Just like me.

What can I say about Fortune? She's a sweetheart. Last night I had the best sleep I've had in centuries. And how do you like the way I fixed it so she'd crawl into bed with Leith? Took me hours to round up those roaches-on-steroids. Wasted effort. Leith didn't bite. Ask me if I'll ever understand humans.

Hey, no sweat, I'm makin' progress with those two. There's something funny about this Mary Campbell deal, though. Things like that don't fall into place without some outside help, and that outside help ain't me. I wonder who—

Do I hear an ice-cream truck? Hmm. Let me just look out this window. Yep, that's our friendly dumb-as-a-rock ice-cream jerk. Hey, he's got a sense of humor. I like his choice of songs. Something about me bein' a hound dog. Should I take that personal? Think I'll go out and investigate.

Fortune sat, unable to move, unable to tear her gaze from Leith. He'd been there, witnessed death at its most violent. For this moment in time, she shared his pain. Maybe this was the only way she would ever know such deep emotion—vicariously.

Vicariously. It made her feel like an outsider, always looking in but never knowing the real thing. But did she really want the kind of soul-wrenching sorrow she saw in Leith's eyes?

Fortune dragged her thoughts from the path they'd chosen. She didn't have time for inner contemplation. She had to say something quickly before Mary Campbell decided they were crazy and threw them out on their collective bottoms. "I don't think Leith meant he was actually *there*. He probably meant that he—"

"Be still, Fortune." He didn't even look at her.

Fortune stared at him openmouthed. *Be still?* Sure, he was stressed, but somebody had better say something soon to save this situation from disaster. She wondered how civilized mental institutions were in this time period.

Mary broke the silence with a heavy sigh, leaned back in her chair, and closed her eyes. Tears slipped from under her closed lids. "I believe you. Hugh always said I trusted too easily, but he never stopped me when I got a feeling here." She tapped her heart. "I don't know how, but I know why." She opened eyes brilliant with tears to stare at Leith. "My Hugh was a good man, and the only thing he ever wanted in life was to write a true account of the Glencoe massacre." She swiped at her eyes with one hand. "I prayed that . . ." She smiled through her tears. "Call me a foolish old woman, but I believe in miracles, and I believe a miracle brought you to me, Leith Campbell."

Leith only nodded, and Fortune knew he was still back with the blood and death. Suddenly, she, who'd never nurtured a maternal bone in her body, wanted fiercely to protect him from further hurt. "I realize how much you want this, Mrs. Campbell, but I'm afraid Leith can't—"

"Dinna speak for me, lass." His harsh voice shocked her into silence.

Uh-oh. She hoped he didn't do something foolish, like agree to help Mary Campbell. He wouldn't be here long enough to finish a book, and where would that leave Mary?

151

"I'll help ye write yer book." His expression spoke of how much it would hurt to relive those long-ago moments. Of course, they weren't so long ago for Leith.

"Don't you think you should consider this, Leith?" Fortune tried to sound calm, understanding.

"I must do this, Fortune. Dinna try to stop me." He looked at her out of eyes that had seen horrors she couldn't conceive, eyes that told her not to meddle in what she didn't understand.

Mary leaned across the table to touch his hand, as though by touching him she could touch the past she yearned to know about. "Thank you, Leith Campbell, for making my husband's dream a reality." She stood and walked to the window. "Maybe someday you'll tell me how this happened, but until then I'll make sure you're rewarded well for your time. Hugh's study is comfortable and has a computer you can use." She frowned. "But perhaps a computer will present a problem."

"I'll help him." Fortune blinked. Had she said that?

Mary smiled. "Leith is lucky to have a wife like you."

Wife. The tingle of excitement surprised her.

The sound of footsteps interrupted her thoughts.

The man who walked into the room convinced her that if Leith was a tiger in the male gene pool, then here was a pampered house cat—sleek, handsome, and civilized.

"Sorry I'm late, Aunt Mary, but I got involved in the Rowan account and lost track of time. You know how I love numbers. They're always logical.

Wish people could be that way." He smiled at Fortune with boyish charm she didn't need a history disk to interpret. "Oh, hi. I'm Michael." He offered her one hand, using the other to smooth short brown hair that looked as if it had never been tousled by the wind or a woman's fingers.

As she shook his hand, Fortune glanced at Leith's shaggy mane. She knew which *she'd* rather run her fingers through.

Michael followed her gaze to Leith, then froze. "My God, you look just like Uncle Hugh."

While he stared openmouthed at Leith, Fortune studied Michael. Shorter than Leith, with narrower shoulders, he still wore his suit well. No bulging muscles to get in the way. His even features were good-looking in an unremarkable way. She could bring him back to her time without causing riots.

Once again she glanced at Leith. Now *he'd* cause riots, even with his angry scowl. *Angry?*

Michael recovered, and his charming smile returned. "Sorry to stare. I'm Michael Campbell and you're . . . ?" He offered his hand.

Leith rose with a feral smile and clasped Michael's hand. "Leith Campbell."

Uh-oh. For some reason, this had a bad feel to it.

Leith remained smiling as Michael's face paled. Lord, she hoped Leith didn't crush every bone in Michael's fingers. When Leith finally released him, she breathed a sigh of relief.

Michael surreptitiously shook his hand to restore the blood flow, then cast Leith a puzzled stare. "Pleased to meet you." His expression said *pleased* didn't exactly describe his feelings.

Here was the perfect man to take back with her. Logical, neat, nonviolent, and nonthreatening, he'd fit well into her society. She frowned. So what was the problem?

For one, she hadn't found Michael in bed with her, so cosmic forces didn't want him. She watched Leith glaring at Michael. For another . . . She couldn't think of another. Michael had no faults, unlike someone else she knew. He'd be the logical choice. And absolutely no temptation at all.

Mary stepped between the two men. "This is Leith and Fortune Campbell, Michael. Leith is an expert on the Glencoe massacre. He's going to complete Hugh's book."

Fortune could see the swirling questions in Michael's gaze, but once again he was too polite to question his aunt in front of her guests. Why hadn't the cosmic forces chosen Michael? He was so civilized he'd need almost no sensitivity training.

Fortune sighed. She'd bet the cosmic forces were female.

Michael smiled, a sincere if shaky smile. "With your face, Leith, you have to be family. Campbells stick together. We're having a party in two weeks, and I'd like you guys to come."

Funny, but Leith's face didn't say *family* to Fortune. He looked like an angry Scottish warrior, and she couldn't for the life of her figure out why he was so furious. She smiled at Michael. "A party sounds like fun. We'll be there."

Michael nodded. "I'll talk to you later, Aunt Mary." As he left the room, Leith's glare followed him.

Fortune stood as Leith walked over to stand beside Mary.

"Would ye mind if I got something from yer garden?"

She didn't wait for Mary's reply. She'd had enough castle life for one day. Besides, darling Tootsie had disappeared, and Fortune wanted to make sure she hadn't devoured Ganymede whole. "Would someone call Blade?" She let herself out the door.

Lost in thought, she'd almost reached the driveway before she realized what was happening. The now-familiar ice-cream man stood beside his truck, his loudspeaker blaring a tinny rendition of, "I Want You, I Need You, I Love You." Fortune recognized the singer's voice. Didn't the driver ever try someone else?

Thoughts of the singer fled as Fortune glimpsed Ganymede padding purposefully toward the truck. She drew in her breath with a sudden sense of danger. Not pausing to question the feeling, she began running. "Ganymede! Come here. Bad cat!"

The "bad cat" ignored her as he bore down on the truck.

Puffing, Fortune managed to cut Ganymede off. She scooped the growling cat off the ground, then turned to the man. "I don't know why he's so grouchy. He's usually a friendly cat." *Liar.* Ganymede might be many things, but friendly wasn't one of them. She had the gut feeling Ganymede tolerated them, but was always working on his own agenda.

The man winked at her. "Maybe he doesn't like Elvis."

"Elvis?"

He nodded. "The King. Elvis Presley. That's all I play on my loudspeaker. Didn't you notice?"

She grinned. "I couldn't help but notice. You keep popping up everywhere. Is this your normal route?"

"Occasionally."

Fortune frowned. "You can't sell much ice cream here."

His eyes—what color *were* they?—sparkled with suppressed mirth. "You'd be surprised. I find customers in the strangest places." He glanced at the still-growling Ganymede. "And in the strangest company." He offered her an ice-cream cup. "This one's on me. It'll help you cool off. You might want to share it with your furry friend. He needs some cooling down, too."

Her furry friend growled his thoughts on the matter.

The man climbed into his truck. "Gotta go now. I have some other customers waiting. Take care, Fortune."

He drove off, leaving Fortune to wonder how he knew her name. Absently, she dropped a still-grumbling Ganymede and pulled the top from her ice cream. She dove in, for the moment oblivious to the fat content. As the creamy vanilla ice cream melted in her mouth, she closed her eyes in ecstasy. *Heavenly*. Did this really taste so much better than what she was used to, or had her senses taken a hit when she bounced into this time?

Fortune had just scooped up the last spoonful when Leith emerged from the castle. He strode toward her—dark, dangerous. In her mind's eye, she pictured him striding from the carnage of Glencoe. What had he thought with death surrounding him?

He stopped beside her, and she felt dwarfed by his size, his past. Bringing Leith back to her time would be like bringing a long-extinct tiger into a herd of sheep. But women would baa their fascination and still flock to him, to their doom. At least he would bring new life and vitality to a staleness she'd never realized existed before spending time here.

Bringing Leith back to my time. She had to tell him. Even though Leith thought they might be sent back to their respective worlds at any time or place, Fortune still felt they should return to the rest-over for their best shot.

She was tempted to lure him to the rest-over with a lie, but when they both ended up in her time, she'd have to face him. And she hated lies. No matter how much easier life would be if she didn't tell Leith her plans, she couldn't lie to him.

He'd need her help with the computer, so maybe he wouldn't walk away when she told him. Then again, she was a MacDonald, and her plan would be exactly what he'd expect from a MacDonald. It didn't matter. Tonight. She'd tell him tonight.

Leith had been strangely quiet as he stared out across Mary Campbell's meticulously cared-for grounds. Finally he gazed down at her. "Ye like Michael, do ye not?"

Michael? What did Michael have to do with anything? "Yes, I suppose—"

"He would fit well in yer time."

From his dark glance, she assumed the thought angered him. *Why*? "Yes, I guess he would. He'd give his offspring logical minds and nonviolent behavior." Warming up to her subject, she smiled at Leith. "He'd probably pass on his even features and—"

Leith looked like a man pushed to his limit. "To hell wi' what he would give to his bairns. Could he give ye this?"

Her mouth was already a round *O* of surprise, so when Leith lowered his lips to hers, he found no resistance.

She didn't even have the presence of mind to drop the ice-cream cup, now crushed between them.

This was no time for comparison shopping, but Fortune thought briefly that Michael's kiss would be sugar water next to Leith's—smooth rich vanilla, a thousand times sweeter than the ice cream she'd savored, and a whole lot hotter.

Hot. Leith deepened the kiss, his tongue tangling with hers as he pulled her against his hard body. She couldn't breathe, didn't want to breathe if it meant ending the magic.

Hot. Her heart raced, and if her mouth hadn't been fully engaged, she would've gasped for air as she had yesterday when she'd sampled Leith's hot-and-spicy salsa. Leith and the salsa had a lot in common: an addictive taste that kept her coming back while at the same time flooding her body with liquid flame. Heat that refused to die. Heat that brought tears to her eyes.

Tears? Was she crazy? The same thought must have occurred to Leith, because he suddenly broke away with a muttered curse.

"This isna right." He raked his fingers through

his hair. "I canna let ye distract me now that I know Mary Campbell is my real reason for being here."

For a moment she couldn't think past the fact that she had the power to distract him. Why should that make her so ridiculously pleased? *Never mind*. She had more serious things to ponder. Like how was she going to tell him his real reason for being here had nothing to do with Mary Campbell?

She couldn't meet his intense stare, knowing what she planned for him. He'd just given her a perfect lead-in. She should tell him now. But she couldn't; she just couldn't. She'd never thought of herself as a coward, but he'd proved that was exactly what she was. She couldn't tell him yet. But soon. She'd tell him soon. "Why *did* you think you were sent here?"

His slight flush of embarrassment surprised her. "I thought I was meant to teach ye the joys of love between a man and a woman." He glanced away from her. "Of course, 'twas before I knew ye were a MacDonald."

The joys of love. For a minisecond, the thought sent silver shards of excitement slicing through her. Then the full implication of what he'd said penetrated.

She'd kill him. "Of course." She'd kill him, then stomp on the remains, and enjoy every violent moment of it. Here she'd been agonizing over his tender feelings, while he'd coldly planned to have sex with her because he felt it was his duty.

Maybe she wouldn't tell him her plans. Maybe she'd let it be a MacDonald surprise. "I'm sure

159

you're relieved to have that responsibility lifted from your shoulders."

He grinned. "Ye're angry." He seemed disgustingly pleased by his observation. "Ye would have enjoyed my lovemaking, lass."

"I wouldn't." What an egotistical, overbearing—

"Ye still dinna lie well." He shook his head in mock dismay, and his wind-tangled hair framed his face—the face of a dark god. "I would've pulled ye, naked, to my body and I—"

Like a child, she dropped the empty ice-cream cup and clapped her hands over her ears. "I can't hear you, so don't bother telling me any more."

He reached for her hands, but Blade's taxi appeared and spared her the ignominy of wrestling for possession of her ears.

"Ye'll not escape that easily, Fortune," he promised in a whisper that tingled along her nerve endings.

It hadn't taken him long to forget she wasn't supposed to distract him.

She'd fight him. *Not too hard, not too long*. No, she hadn't thought that. This whole thing was ridiculous. He wanted to tease her, and he knew his words angered her. Of course anger was the only emotion she felt. Maybe tonight she would tell him her plan. That should guarantee he'd leave her alone permanently. She'd be happy then. Wouldn't she?

Problem. She didn't have a plan. At least not a plan for getting this wild Scottish warrior back to the rest-over room. Maybe she'd better think of one quickly.

Blade pulled his taxi to a stop beside them, and

Leith silently held the door open. Fortune picked up Ganymede and climbed into the backseat. Climbing in beside her, Leith slammed the door, then slid over the few inches it took to touch her.

She wouldn't give him the satisfaction of asking him to move. Valiantly she attempted to ignore the warmth of his side pressed against her. She tried to concentrate on how to reveal his fate in such a way that he wouldn't storm from the house.

She could still feel him. Shifting, he placed his arm across her shoulders. Pressed against the door, she had nowhere to go. Ganymede lay in her lap and watched the proceedings with slit-eyed approval. Fat lot of protection she'd get from him. What she needed was a huge, ferocious carnitak that—

"What place is that, Blade?"

She couldn't believe it. He was more interested in the scenery than his effect on her.

"The SPCA." Blade didn't elaborate.

Leith opened his mouth to ask for a more indepth explanation, but she dug her elbow sharply into his side. He grunted his surprise.

She'd enjoyed that. She could almost begin to understand the siren call of violence.

"They have dogs in cages." His tone spoke of dank dungeons and sadistic jailers.

"Keep your voice down." She glanced out the window as the cab whipped past the small building and outside cages. "I can see only a few dogs, and they look well fed. And they're in a safe environment, free from fear of predators."

He didn't look convinced. "Mayhap they'd

choose to run from predators in exchange for freedom."

"I can't imagine why."

He turned to stare at her. " 'Tis like that in yer world, isn't it? Ye live in yer wee cages with no excitement to make yer heart pound, yer breath come in mighty gasps."

She glanced nervously at Blade. "Not so loud. Cages? That's ridiculous. We go wherever we want."

He smiled at her, but there was no humor in it. "The cage is in yer heart. I could ne'er live in yer world, bound by the rules that govern ye."

Now he'd made her mad. "You know nothing of my world. I wouldn't want to live in *your* world, where massacres like Glencoe are a way of life. I wouldn't want to be near people who could kill like that."

He grew still, and his face paled. "Glencoe should ne'er have happened. But sometimes ye must kill or be killed. Which would ye choose, lass?"

"The choice would never come up." Why was she arguing about killing or being killed? Sighing, she admitted she knew the answer. This was about their completely different mind-sets, and the ability of one of them to exist in the other's world.

He shook his head. "I dinna think I would fit into yer society."

She turned from him and stared out the window. There it was. He didn't want any part of her world. And yet she had to bring him back. She had a duty to the human race. But she'd probably hate herself as much as he'd hate his new home, a cage from which there'd be no escape, where he'd feel totally alien.

"What're you guys arguing about?" Blade's curious stare in the mirror pulled her back to reality.

"Nothing." Nothing but the future of the human race as opposed to the future of one man's life.

Leith worried. Fortune had remained quiet for the whole day. Even his excitement over the magic of television hadn't drawn a sarcastic comment about primitiveness from her.

Now she lay in bed, the cover pulled up to her chin, her head turned from him. He shouldn't mind her withdrawal. It would make it easier to ignore his body's demands.

That was a lie. His body didn't care what feelings she had for him. It wanted her.

He pulled off his shirt and rescued the small object that rested against his chest. Smiling, he wondered at his silliness. Small and wilted, it hardly made a fine offering to a lady.

Without warning, she turned her head and caught him holding the foolish thing in his hands.

"A flower?"

" 'Tis a bit wilted." Lord, he was embarrassed. He could feel warmth flooding his face. He loved women, but he couldn't remember any who had managed to embarrass him.

"For me?" Sudden tears shone in her eyes.

God's teeth, the woman was going to cry. Panic filled his soul. He'd rather fight a battle one-armed than face a woman's tears. "It isna much of a gift. 'Twas beautiful when I saw it in Mary's garden, but I left it too long inside my shirt."

"It's still beautiful."

It wasn't really. He looked down at it to avoid staring into Fortune's glistening blue eyes and saw only a shriveled yellow flower. "I shouldna have picked it. Every living thing is best left in its rightful place." He looked up to find tears rolling down her cheeks. She looked stricken. What had he said?

He should throw the flower out the open window and close his mouth, but he rushed into more speech rather than examine the tension filling the room. "It was alone in the garden, with no others of its kind nearby, no one to admire it." He realized he spoke not about the flower. Lord grant that Fortune would not recognize herself in the crushed yellow bloom. She wouldn't want his admiration. Admiration? No, that didn't describe his feelings at all. He grinned and feared it was a foolish grin.

"What? No red flowers?" She smiled through her tears.

Desperate for anything that would lighten her mood, he smiled back. "I didna see any red ones, but yellow suits ye also. 'Tis a sunny color, and wi' yer red hair and blue eyes, ye remind me of a sunny day." Had those ridiculous words come from his lips? The many women he'd bedded wouldn't believe he'd said such a thing. He brought passion and expertise to his lovemaking, but never foolish compliments.

He shifted from foot to foot. " 'Tis a poor offering." He wished the wretched flower would disappear.

"It's a wonderful gift." Her voice was soft, her eyes luminous. She held out her hand for the flower.

He walked to her side of the bed with caution born of the belief that she might again break into tears, leaving him as helpless as a man with no weapon. He shoved the flower at her with all the grace of a fledgling swordsman.

She wrapped her smaller hand around his fist. Drawing his hand to her mouth, she softly kissed his whitened knuckles, then removed the flower from his suddenly lax fingers.

He closed his eyes. A flash of memory. His mother standing behind their cottage, her dark hair blowing around her face, her eyes smiling with love as he toddled toward her with a handful of heather clutched in his baby fist. His mother. Why did he remember her now? Since she'd died, he'd driven her memory from his mind, his soul, afraid he'd remember only the way she'd looked in death on that long-ago morn.

He opened his eyes and reached for his normal response to a woman. "Dinna tempt me, lass. Ye might get more than ye expected." He hoped he'd struck the light tone he wanted.

She smiled at him. Fortunately, her tears had dried. "How often does a Campbell give a Mac-Donald flowers?"

He returned her smile and relaxed. "Only when they're placed on a MacDonald grave." He switched off the light—it was amazing how quickly he'd adapted to such modern comforts—and finished stripping off his clothes.

He climbed into bed beside her, then lay still.

"Leith . . . how would you feel if you knew you'd never return home again?" Her voice sounded tentative, unsure.

He thought before answering. This present time had wondrous things, but he still felt apart from it, a bumbling stranger who might say or do something stupid at any moment. Granted, he now had friends in Blade and Lily, interesting work, and . . . Fortune. But he missed the land, his land, with all its rugged beauty. He also knew he must make his peace with his brother if he were ever to feel whole again.

He would miss Fortune, though. He could not believe he was thinking that about a MacDonald, but it was true.

Why had the powers sent her to this time with him if they didn't intend that he teach her the joys of love? They certainly couldn't expect someone like Michael to— The idea filled him with unreasoning rage.

Maybe he had two reasons for being here. The thought that he might still join with her made his blood sing as it did right before he rushed into battle.

Perhaps when he returned he could take her with him. No, she would never survive the primitiveness of his time. She'd be like the wilted yellow flower he'd ripped from its rightful place in the garden. It would be far better if she returned to her own time. His sudden feeling of loss surprised him.

"Well," she prompted. "How would you feel?"

"I'd rather die."

She sighed. "That's what I thought."

"Why did ye ask?" He knew what answer he wished from her. *Fool.* Even if she said she wanted him to remain with her, it meant nothing, nothing at all, because he still had to return to his time, to Hugh.

"No reason." She turned her back to him, but he sensed she wasn't asleep. He could feel her stiffness, her restlessness, across the width of the bed.

He gave in to temptation without even a small fight. He shoved aside his hate for the Mac-Donalds, ground into his very soul by mutual raids and murders, and slid across the centuries of distrust to mold his body to her back. Before she could react, he put his arms around her and held her still.

"Dinna fear. I mean only to warm ye."

"It isn't cold." Her voice sounded strangely choked, and she held herself stiff and unyielding.

"Use yer imagination, lass. Believe in things that aren't real, that dinna have logical explanations." He gave her a slight squeeze to punctuate his command.

"I thought that's what I was doing ever since I met you."

He would have sworn he heard laughter in her voice, felt her relax slightly. He couldn't help himself; he moved his hips more tightly against her. Immediately he felt her stiffen again.

"Maybe you should go back to your side of the bed."

He could kick himself. She was a virgin, no matter how advanced her civilization. One more move from him and she'd return to her lumpy couch. Slowly. He must move slowly.

Startled, he realized what he planned. It didn't matter that her name was MacDonald, or that he'd been sent to this time for the sake of Mary Campbell. He wanted to make love with this particular woman, and he wanted it beyond all reasoning.

But not tonight. She wasn't ready. If they made love tonight, she'd blame him tomorrow, and he knew already he'd want Fortune more than once.

Already feeling the pain of denial, he forced himself to move his hips away from her. But denying himself now would garner greater pleasure later. "Dinna fear, lass. I willna ask of ye anything ye're not willing to give freely. I can wait."

"Then you'll wait a long time."

Her statement lacked conviction, and he smiled into the darkness. But he smiled through pain. He had to distract himself from the throbbing demands of his body. "Ye've said several times that ye make men. Tell me about this."

He felt her relax again as she prepared to discuss something familiar, something nonthreatening.

"Jan Kredski's mistake opened a new area of opportunity. I have my own business, Creature Comforts. I create custom-made men to fit the desires of individual customers. Sort of like a sculptor is commissioned to do a specific likeness. I make body types, facial features, and hair colors geared to appeal to each woman's fantasy."

He frowned. Something about this sounded unnatural. "And these men you create, they work for the women?"

She shook her head. "Oh, no. Robots do the work. My men are used only for sexual fulfillment."

He swallowed hard. "You mean . . . women . . ."

There was laughter in her voice. "We don't have men, remember. We need . . . release. My men look, move, and talk like real men. They're programmed to respond sexually to the desires of their owner. You'd never guess they weren't real."

Anger seeped around the edges of his discomfort. "And when ye first saw me, ye thought I was . . ."

"Mm-hmm." There was actually a purr in her voice. "I thought you were the ultimate creation." Her tone turned thoughtful. "And in a way I was right, wasn't I?"

He could find no words to say.

Seemingly forgetful of her fear, she turned over to face him. "So what do you think?"

Rage built in him, and he knew in some rational corner of his mind he was about to say something he'd regret. "I think it is an abomination before God."

She sighed. "You really have to stop reacting so emotionally to everything. I provide a needed service."

"Do ye have . . ." God's teeth, he could hardly get the question out. "Do ye have a . . . man for yerself?"

Dimly in the dark room, he could see her bite her lip in indecision. "No. It's sort of like if you work in a bakery and have to see and smell the baked goods all day long, you lose your desire for them. Since I make them, it's hard for me to forget they're not real. I can't lose myself in the fantasy."

"Thank God," he murmured. "I wasna sure before, but I think 'tis past time ye experienced the real thing. Tonight."

Without warning, he reached out and pulled her hard against him. "The dance of love between a man and woman ne'er changes, lass, and six hundred years between us means nothing tonight." *And may I return to Scotland with no regrets.*

Somehow he sensed that he wished in vain.

Chapter Eight

Uh-oh. Now she'd done it. Flash point. Or rather, *flesh* point, because every place his body touched hers burned with a heat that convinced her she might go up in flames at any moment. *Real.* Like a greedy child, she wanted every part of him pressed to her, wanted to memorize his scent, his taste, his *realness.*

Why not, just this once? Enjoying this man's body just once would be like trying to eat just one of those potato chips she'd bought yesterday—totally bad for her, totally addictive. Besides, there was more involved here than just sexual satisfaction. She wasn't quite sure what it was, but if he'd only stop touching her for a moment, she'd think of it.

Why not go for it? There's no guarantee you'll ever get another chance to be with a real man. Do you want to die not knowing what it's like? Once back in her time, he wouldn't want anything to do with the woman who'd betrayed him. Besides, he'd have millions of women to choose from. And she'd wanted this, craved it, ever since waking to find him beside her, no matter what she said to the contrary. *Just this once.*

Her inner battle came to a screeching halt when she realized he'd managed to slip her gown off while she fought the good fight. "I haven't decided yet. I'm still thinking."

His soft chuckle was familiar, expected. "There's nothing to think about, lass. Ye had to know this would happen when ye climbed into bed wi' me. 'Tis the way of men and women."

She gulped back tears. Not fear, but anticipated loss. She'd grown used to his laughter, the cadence of his speech. When he was gone forever, would she carry his memory like an unhealed wound the rest of her life? She suspected she would.

As she stared across the chasm of time at his face—the harshness, the beauty—she knew she'd made her decision long ago. "Okay, what do I do?"

His smile flashed whitely in the darkness. "Ye dinna do anything, lass. This is yer first time. Let me—"

"Absolutely not. We share responsibility for everything in my society." Who was she trying to kid? This wasn't about responsibility, but about having a part in what happened between them. If she took an active part, she'd still feel in control.

He actually groaned. "This isna a responsibility. I canna believe we're discussing this."

"I still think—"

"Dinna think. 'Tis the curse of women."

He gave her no time to refute his claim as he lowered his lips to hers.

She'd expected his mouth to be hard, eager—if the feel of him against her hip was any indication of his readiness. But the softness of his touch took her breath away. He caressed, reassured, offered himself, and she couldn't resist pressing her mouth against his lips, memorizing his texture, the tangy lemon taste that lingered from the lemonade he'd drunk.

His kiss reached down to light a flame that had lain dormant, unrecognized. What she'd believed to be desire had been merely flickering candlelight. This . . . this was the fiery explosion of a rocket blast, hurling her into an uncharted universe. When he broke contact with her lips she wanted to cry with frustration. She wanted more, damn it, more.

He feathered kisses around her lips and she parted them. He took her offering and delved deeply. She met him, touching him as he touched her. Never had she guessed a mouth could trigger the spiraling need that wrung a shattered gasp from her.

But it wasn't enough, could never be enough. Not when this might have to last forever.

When he withdrew, she barely had time to murmur a protest before he trailed a searing path of kisses down the side of her neck.

She'd made so many men and believed them life-like, able to fulfill a woman's deepest need. She'd been wrong. *This* was real—moist heat spreading through her like the fire lakes of Tanar, her breaths coming in harsh gasps as though sucked from her by Roshun's swirling wind demons. But she couldn't let go until . . . until . . .

She rolled on top of him.

He stopped kissing her, and she sensed his puzzlement. " 'Tis not a position I'd choose to give ye the greatest pleasure for yer first time, lass." His voice, harsh with need, belied his calm words.

Now she was puzzled. "You've . . . touched me. It's time to mate, isn't it? And I have to be on top for that."

"Why?" His tone had gone beyond puzzlement to incredulousness.

"When I send out the instruction manual with my men I suggest this as the optimum position for—" Why was she babbling when hunger shrieked and beat at the walls of her heart?

"Damn it to hell." His muttered expletive didn't sound promising. "Dinna compare me to one of yer fake men. Ye canna sit on top of me like . . . like the queen of the mountain and tell me how and when to pleasure ye."

He rolled her over, and she found herself looking up into his fierce glare. " 'Tis not time until I say 'tis time."

"Why not?" She'd studied behavioral disks on the sexual relationships between men and women, and they all stated that mating could take place when the woman was ready. "I'm ready."

"Ye havena the experience to know if ye're ready. I've made love to scores . . . to a few women, and I know. Ye're not ready." His savage assertion made her burrow deeper into the bed.

"You seem kind of arbitrary to me," she murmured from her cocoon beneath him. She reached for some scathing remark about his need to control their mating, but when he touched one nipple with his tongue, she almost shot from the bed.

"Number four," she managed to gasp.

"Can ye not save yer voice for womanly cries of satisfaction?" The sandpaper edge of his voice spoke of barely leashed hunger.

Satisfaction? What a pale, washed-out word for the exploding star-shades of red his touch—

He drew the nipple into the warmth of his mouth and suckled.

"Number five!" Her voice was a cry of despair torn from the knowledge that her life's work had been a failure.

"God's teeth, will ye stop blathering, woman." His words came in biting gasps.

She wanted to explain, but right now she couldn't think, couldn't concentrate on anything except what he was doing to her.

As he softly kissed a line of blistering heat down her stomach, she silently counted—six, seven. *Useless*. Everything she'd ever done was useless.

She lifted her hips in an instinctual offering. History disks said— She couldn't remember, didn't want to remember.

"Ye're a beautiful woman, Fortune."

The soft touch of breath from his whisper told her he'd moved lower. She felt like a loose-jointed doll as he gently parted her legs and touched her with his mouth.

"Twenty!" she screamed, arching from the bed— pleading, sobbing, aching for . . .

"Stop counting." His grunted order was one part

leashed tiger and two parts angry male.

"I . . . I can't." My God, were those tears sliding down her face? "That's number twenty in my manual." What was she saying? Why was she saying it? "You skipped steps eight through nineteen. But it doesn't matter. Doesn't matter at all."

His muttered curse was crudely primitive and particularly fitting for the situation. But for all his obvious aggravation, his fingers skimming the inside of her thighs were whisper light.

She shivered, and he moved his head up to lay it on her stomach. Why had he stopped when every inch of her flesh vibrated with need, when her body clenched with unbearable anticipation? "Please . . ." She couldn't voice what she wanted, because she wanted too much. *Now*.

His soft chuckle sent a puff of warm breath across her skin, and she drew in her stomach on a startled gasp. She'd never thought her body could be so sensitized to his touch that even his breath could . . .

"Ye shouldna rush, lass. 'Tis the enjoyment of the journey that makes the end so glorious."

Hmmph. Fancy words, but his voice sounded strained, strung tight with the same need that made her long to beg. "My men don't wait. When the woman is ready—and I'm ready—they do it." Her voice quavered, further proof she'd lost control, a control that had been the cornerstone of her existence until Leith.

"Do it? 'Tis a cold way of describing the wondrous feeling when a man and woman join."

His fingers drifted over her stomach and softly circled her breasts, leaving a trail of molten heat in their wake. A totally irrelevant tear slid down her cheek, but she couldn't summon the courage to reach up and wipe it away for fear her movement might stop the wonderful things he was doing.

"Ye think ye're ready, but ye're not, lass. That is the difference between yer fakes and a real man. Ye've made them to fit yer own imagination, but I can take ye beyond what ye've ever imagined."

And he did.

An eternity beyond number twenty, she clung to his sweat-slicked body, every inch of her own skin an extension of his, her universe centered on the almost-pain ecstasy of his finger rubbing her swollen nub, then slipping into her, the in-out thrust that made her moan her inability to stand any more.

She felt the quiver in his body, his hands, as he parted her legs, then settled between her thighs. His raw power, his heat, his scent of sex and hot male, overwhelmed the last of her control, and she shook with need. If he didn't take her now, she'd splinter into a million star-fire sparks.

But even through her haze of desire, she knew that when he lifted his hips and slowly entered her, it was with a care for her newness.

She didn't close her eyes as he slid into her. Wincing at the momentary pain, she watched his expression, memorizing it for lonely winter nights in a pale, meaningless future. Wrapping her memories around his fullness deep within her, she cried out as he withdrew only to plunge deeply again and again, each strong thrust sparking a blue-lit flame that burned higher, hotter. She had no voice left as the sensation built, quivered, then exploded in a comet-streak of white light and heat. On some other plane, she was aware of Leith's cry joining hers.

And afterward she lay still beside him, listening to his harsh breathing, and cried. Silent tears slid down her cheeks—because she might never experience this wonder again, because she'd been foolish enough to think she could capture this solar flash within her poor imitations of men.

"Do ye have a number for the last?" His tone held no anger, only faint curiosity.

"No." Was that wimpy voice hers? "I never realized it could be so . . . so . . ."

"Aye. 'Twas the same for me." He gently kissed her damp forehead. "But I canna believe ye counted the steps. Ye must tell me what comes between seven and twenty. No real man would last so long." He playfully squeezed her. "I dinna think I would want to be a man in yer world."

"Without that last step, the others don't matter, and none of my men could come close to . . . to . . ."

"A machine canna touch yer heart, Fortune."

Her life's work, a failure. How could she tell women her men were lifelike when they didn't even come close?

It would be best if this never happened again, because she somehow knew the explosion of joy would come only with Leith, and Leith was forever out of reach. If he returned with her, he'd belong to the world, as he should. Besides, he'd hate her for dragging him there. And if he returned to his time . . . Either way, this could never happen again. She sensed that each time it did, her agony at Leith's loss would increase.

Wrapped in his embrace, she felt his breathing ease. He snuggled closer and touched the tip of her ear with his tongue. " 'Twas wondrous." His low murmur sent shivers of longing to nerve endings that should be suffering overload by now.

"Yes." There was nothing more to say. The thought of returning to her sterile workroom to create more fakes—fakes that seemed tawdry and inadequate measured against Leith—depressed her. Would she go through the rest of her life knowing her greatest joy had happened three hundred years in the past—never to be experienced again, never to be forgotten?

"It didna matter that ye were not on top?"

She heard the laughter in his voice and for once didn't react angrily. "Oh, but I was." She reached out and traced the line of his strong jaw. Her hand shook. "Not only was I on top, but I floated free, beyond the stars, beyond eternity."

"Aye." His soft chuckle reached all the way to her toes. "Ye're like no other, lass. Ye remind me of a loch near my home. 'Tis small and verra blue. A foolish man would think it shallow and cold. As a lad, I fell into it one bitter winter day. 'Twas amazing. The water was warm. A man could close his eyes and sink into its heat." Leith kissed the sensitive skin beneath her ear, and she shivered.

"But when I tried to stand, I couldna touch bottom. I still dinna know how deep the loch is, but some things are best left to imagine." His lips touched the base of her throat where her pulse

179

pounded a mad rhythm. "The loch's mystery still draws me."

She believed him, and felt a warm spurt of happiness, knowing how many women he'd probably sampled, how many he had to compare her with. Women who'd felt his touch the same way she'd felt it, touched him in ways she hadn't.

She hadn't touched him. "I'm sorry, Leith. I didn't do anything to give you pleasure. My men are programmed to do everything, and I forgot. I lay there like a big lump of emotional dough." The thought of running her hands over the hard planes of his body brought an excited shiver. She would remember that when she went back to work. Maybe if she made her models more interactive, she'd increase her clients' enjoyment. Then again, maybe not. Running her hands over a lifeless fake couldn't begin to compare with sliding her fingers across the body of a vibrant, living man. A real man. This man.

"Dinna fash yerself, lass."

His laughter vibrated in her heart, and she stored the memory to pull out later, years later.

"Ye didna need to touch me. Yer response pleasured me." He pulled her closer against him, and she fought the rising tide of hysterical tears.

No! She couldn't take it. Instinctively, she knew each time they became one, the memories would double in intensity, torturing her, reminding her of a future she could never have.

She also knew she wouldn't be able to resist if he wanted her again, and from the feel of his body, that would be very soon. *No.* She couldn't resist him, so she had to make sure he stopped wanting her.

She had the perfect weapon. The only one that would allow her to walk away from this with her emotions reasonably intact.

Say it. Just say it. "You're very good. The women back home are in for a real treat."

She felt his sudden stillness, his emotional withdrawal. "I dinna understand."

"Isn't it obvious? Ever since we woke up together, I've wondered what the point of our meeting was. Well, it doesn't take a rocket scientist to get the picture. From everything I've observed, you're a potent male, just what we need to bring healthy genes back to our society. Think of yourself as the second coming of Adam." She hated the words, hated herself for saying them.

" 'Twas an experiment?" The warm huskiness of his voice turned glacial. "Ye meant only to prove I was *potent*?"

"Actually, this didn't prove your sperm count was adequate, but you performed well, and I don't see any problem. You'll do nicely. Now that you understand, I suppose we can just go back to the rest-over room and get ourselves beamed to my time." She cringed at her chirpy tone. *I'm sorry, Leith. So sorry.* She'd never hurt a living thing in her life, but she was hurting Leith, and the knowledge sickened her.

She felt the bed give as he rolled away from her, shivered as cool air replaced the warmth of his body.

"Ye would take me back to be a prisoner in yer society, a bull to service yer women?" He'd wiped all emotion from his voice, and that frightened her more than his rage could.

"That's a little dramatic. You'd be an honored guest. Of course you wouldn't have to physically impregnate all the women. We could collect your sperm and artificially—"

"I dinna want to hear any more. 'Tis unnatural."

She was glad he'd interrupted her. Every word she uttered shattered into a razor-sharp shard of agony that tore at her heart. Only a few days ago the thought of bringing this man back to the world's women had thrilled her. What had happened? Leith had happened. His smile, the tilt of his head, the musical roll of his words. He was *real* now, not just a male body to be manipulated for the good of humanity.

"And if I didna want to *share* my body with the women of your world, would they force me?" He'd swung his feet to the floor, and was sitting on the edge of the bed, his strong back a muscled wall of rejection.

"I . . ." *Yes, they would.* Everyone practiced nonviolence, but for the survival of the human race, they'd sacrifice Leith.

"Answer me!" She'd never heard this note in his voice before—cold rage, danger. "Would they strip me, bind me to a table, and take what I wouldna give them?"

She flinched away from the whip-sting of his accusation. "It wouldn't be like that. They'd put you to sleep for a while, and—"

"And they'd rape me."

The ugliness of the word hung between them. She couldn't make herself speak past that word.

"Ye'd let them do that to me, lass?" The softness of his question stretched between them with the intensity of a laser beam in the hands of an unpredictable madman.

Where had this conversation gone wrong? She'd never meant it to get so out of hand. She'd just wanted to distance herself physically, emotionally from him. She'd thought he'd get angry, then calm down and tell her she was crazy to think he'd go with her, and dismiss the whole idea. She should've remembered how intense he'd become when discussing Glencoe.

But he'd asked a question, and her innate honesty wouldn't let her lie. "I'd . . . I'd have to do what was best for the continuation of the human race. It would be my duty."

"Aye, and duty, of course, would come first." He sounded deeply sad, disappointed. "Ye havena lived long enough to understand there are things ye must put before duty."

"What could possibly come before the survival of the human race?" She wanted to cry, even though she knew she was right.

"What indeed?" His murmured question seemed almost a musing, not connected to her.

She couldn't take this anymore. Why had she started it? Her reasons didn't seem quite so urgent now. "Look, let's drop it. If you don't want to go, I'll . . . I'll find someone else." *Right.* Sure she would. Even now, facing his wrath, she knew he was the only one she'd want to bring back with her.

"Ye willna. Ye believe powers have chosen *me* as yer sacrifice. But I willna go, Fortune. I willna make myself a captive in yer world. But dinna worry about the survival of the human race. Yer race is no longer human."

Stung, she lashed back. "At least we're dedicated to continuing life, not ending it."

The silence between them vibrated with sorrow, regret—for what she'd said, for what he'd done, or failed to do.

"Ye're right, lass." He reached for his clothes. A few seconds later, dressed in shirt and jeans, he faced her.

She couldn't see his expression in the darkened room, but that didn't stop her sudden spurt of fear. "You're not leaving, are you? Where would you go? You won't have anyone to help you understand things." *Stupid*. He'd survived in the savagery of his world, and he'd survive in this time, also.

"I dinna need anyone to help me understand things. I understand things fine. 'Tis ye who dinna understand, lass."

Speechless, she watched him leave the room, listened to his footsteps fade away, heard the slam of the front door.

A low, angry growl drew her attention to the foot of the bed, where Ganymede crouched. OK, what was *his* problem? She distinctly remembered feeding him. Oh, who understood cats? For that matter, who understood men?

Turning her head on the pillow, Fortune for a moment failed to recognize the velvety-soft touch against her cheek. Lifting her head, she stared at the crushed yellow petals of Leith's flower. She closed her eyes and accepted the pain of its symbolism—her crushed hopes and the color of cowardice.

*   *   *

Leith slouched over his table at the Cajun Café and considered his situation. After walking and fuming in the darkness, he'd stuck out his thumb as he'd seen someone doing on the day they'd arrived in this cursed time. A car finally stopped, and Leith asked to be left here. He knew no other place. When the driver commented on his surly attitude, Leith felt obliged to admit he'd fought with a woman, and that he was in a mood to crack some heads. The man laughed.

He felt at ease with men. They were honest and said what they thought. He understood men.

Ye understand women, too. 'Tis only a certain red-haired vixen ye dinna understand. He exhaled sharply. His problem was that for all the times Fortune befuddled him, this once her motive was clear. Duty. He might hate what she intended for him, but he had to respect her motivation. The same duty drew him back to Hugh, to his clan.

Then why was he so angry? He closed his eyes in recognition of the truth. If she'd chosen any other man, he would've understood, accepted. But that she would do this to *him* . . . that she would make passionate love with him, then calmly announce she intended to hand him into slavery . . .

"I dinna understand women, Blade." When he'd entered the cafe, he'd found Blade and Lily. He lifted the drink Blade had bought him, emptied it, then slammed it down on the table for emphasis.

"What's to understand?" Blade shrugged, then glanced over at Lily, who was returning after soundly thrashing a host of men at a game of darts.

Leith stared at Blade with newfound admiration. "Mayhap ye can help me. What would make a woman turn on ye after the two of ye had just finished being verra . . . friendly?"

"Hmm," Blade offered in thoughtful comment.

"You probably scared her." Lily sat down next to Blade.

"Scared her? How can ye be scared when ye're still joined to a man ye've made love wi', and after screaming yer pleasure . . . ?"

He noticed their avid interest, and realized perhaps he'd said too much. "She'd no reason to be frightened," he grumbled.

Lily sat back and studied him with eyes that saw too much. "When you make great love, you lose control. Fortune looks like a lady who wants to be in control. Maybe she felt threatened." She winked at Leith. "You look like the kind of man who'd be dangerous to any woman's peace of mind." She threw her arms around Blade and squeezed. Blade winced. "Just like my man."

Doubtful, Leith shook his head. "I dinna think she felt me a threat."

Lily's expression softened. "I've never known a man who really knew what a woman was thinking. Go with the flow, handsome."

Go with the flow? He refused to ask what that meant. Besides, he thought Lily was wrong. She hadn't been there, heard the coldness in Fortune's voice. He'd misjudged Fortune. If she had her way, he'd spend the rest of his life playing stud to a world of sex-starved women. Once he might've welcomed that thought. Not now. Not since Fortune. *Curse the woman!*

She would not make a fool of him. Even though

he still wanted her, he'd be damned if he'd give in to his body's demands. He would stay with her because he needed her help with his work, and also because, as much as he wanted to deny it, he felt the need to keep her safe. At least until she returned to her world. *Alone*.

"Hey, big guy, if you need extra protection, look in the top drawer next to the bed." Blade's quiet offer interrupted Leith's dark thoughts. "I know how it is. Just married and all, you sorta forget things like that. But you folks don't need the patter of little feet right now, except for that damned cat."

Leith closed his eyes. *A child*. He'd wanted Fortune so badly he hadn't considered the consequences. He forced away soft thoughts of Fortune and him together with their bairn. It wouldn't happen. Even if Fortune was with child, there was no future for them as a family.

His resolve hardened. He couldn't control much, but if Fortune bore his child while they still remained together, he would make sure of one thing.

"We got trouble outside, Blade."

Leith opened his eyes at the urgent whisper. A stranger leaned over Blade, and Blade looked worried. Without a word, Blade stood and walked toward the door. Leith rose and followed him. *Trouble*. He needed some trouble now to clear his mind.

Outside, Tank stood facing a massive man who wore a leather jacket with what looked like a skull and crossbones. Behind the man stood more men who looked as dangerous as their leader.

Leith took in the situation at a glance. The huge man must belong to a rival clan . . . no, motorcycle club. He was looking for trouble, hoping to find it in Tank. Leith knew the type.

Leith moved up to stand beside Tank, who cast him a grateful glance. "Ye should pick on those closer to yer size." Up close, Leith realized how really big the man was. He would have a hard time finding anyone his own size. *Fine.* Leith needed a physical challenge, something he could pound with his fists, kick with his feet, something he could understand no matter what the time.

The man cast Leith a contemptuous glare. "He a new member of yours, Tank?"

Tank started to answer, but Leith broke in. "I take care of special . . . problems."

The man nodded and reached toward his boot, but Leith was quicker. He knew what the man reached for, and as the man brought the knife up toward Leith, Leith kicked it from his hand. The man's shocked expression whetted Leith's appetite for battle.

The fight was not overlong. The big man was strong, but he didn't have a lifetime of experience behind him. He didn't carry with him the need to beat his opponent to a pulp in order to rid himself of the image of a red-haired vixen whose lips were still swollen with his kisses, and who calmly spoke of taking him back to her time, not for herself, but for humanity. He didn't feel the rage of knowing she'd not wanted him at all, but had simply been testing him to see if he'd be an adequate stud.

When it was over, they stood with feet apart, breathing hard, and swaying. But the big man breathed harder and swayed like an old oak in a killing wind.

Leith grinned through a cut and bleeding lip. He turned his head so he could see his opponent out of his one good eye.

The big man glared at Leith from a bruised and swollen face. "Another time." He didn't spare Tank a glance as he nodded to his followers, who muttered threats but climbed on their bikes and roared away from the café.

Tank grinned and slapped Leith across the back. Leith almost fell over. The fight had felt good, but he was exhausted. The big man had been a worthy opponent. He'd known the same dirty tricks as Leith, and tried every one. Yes, men were predictable. Only women changed with every breeze.

"Let me buy you a drink. You deserve it."

Leith shook his head. " 'Tis time I went home."

Tank nodded and studied Leith. "Look, if you ever need any help, you can call on me. I owe you."

Blade shoved aside the milling crowd of well-wishers to reach Leith. "I'll drive you home, big guy. You want to get cleaned up before we leave?"

Leith shook his head again. Let Fortune see him a bloody mess. With the way she felt about violence, she'd probably never come near him again. *Good.*

Leith followed Blade and Lily out to the taxi, then climbed into the back. He stretched out his legs and leaned his head against the seat. Now that the thrill of battle had drained away, he felt like hell. Everything hurt, including his head. Luckily, no one tried to make conversation with him.

A short distance away from the house, he made a decision. "Blade, wi' ye let me out here?"

Blade pulled the taxi over and turned to stare at him. "Here? Beside the lake?"

Leith nodded. "I need time to think. 'Tis quiet here. None will bother me. 'Twill be a short walk when I'm ready to go home." *Go home.* Going home would take more than a short walk, but Blade would never know that.

He knew Blade and Lily watched as he stumbled from the taxi. He must be getting old, or just out of practice. It had not been much of a brawl, but he felt like he'd been kicked by a horse. Considering the size of the man he'd fought, he was lucky to have no broken bones. And if the man had reached his knife a bit faster, Leith would have a few new scars.

He listened to the taxi drive away as he sat down with his back against a tree. A cool breeze moved over his skin—soothing, calming. He closed his eyes and listened to the quiet slap of water against the bank. Maybe he'd sleep here tonight.

The knock galvanized Fortune. *Leith.* He'd been gone so long she'd been afraid . . . afraid he wouldn't come home, because no matter what had passed between them, she couldn't conceive of life in this new world without him. Afraid he *would* come home, because even though she got a sick feeling every time she thought of the angry words he'd flung at her, she still had to bring him back to her time. She had a duty to her world, one she couldn't cast aside because of personal feelings.

She flung open the door to find Blade and Lily standing there. She took in the somber expressions on both faces. "Leith! Something's happened to

Leith." Her heart pounded out a terrified rhythm, and her mouth felt suddenly dry.

"Your man's OK, honey. Calm down." Lily's words didn't reassure Fortune. "He mixed it up with another guy down at the bar. He's got a few cuts and bruises, but nothing the loving care of his woman won't cure." She cast Fortune a meaningful glance.

"I . . . I don't understand. Where is he?" Only slightly reassured, she still couldn't control her feeling of panic.

Blade patted her on the shoulder. "He's sitting down by the lake. He'll come home when he's ready."

Lily made a rude noise. "Let's not beat around the bush, sugar. You got yourself a good man there. Go take care of him." She turned, grabbed Blade by the arm, and started pulling him back toward the taxi. "Let's get out of here, dumpling, and let Fortune do her thing."

Fortune didn't even wait to see them drive away before she locked the door and ran toward the lake.

Breathing hard from the unaccustomed exercise, she stopped to peer into the darkness. Then she saw him, a dark silhouette leaning against a tree by the shoreline. He'd flung his head back against the trunk, and she hesitated, studying him. Once again she marveled at the pure masculine lines of him, and the way the mere sight of him could cause her breath to catch, her heart to pound, even when she hadn't been running like crazy.

He must've sensed her approach, because he turned his face toward her and watched silently.

Hurrying to his side, she dropped to her knees beside him. Only then did she notice his torn shirt and bloodied face. "Oh, my God."

He shook his head solemnly. "God didna do this, although the man who did was uncommonly strong."

She didn't smile. With shaking fingers, she reached out to touch his bruised face. "Your poor face."

He tried to make a wry expression, but it didn't quite work with his cut lip. "My face doesna feel good, but I dinna think any bones are broken, so it isna so bad. I've had worse."

"Why?" She could manage only one word though lips that were beginning to tremble in spite of her attempt to control them.

"For the joy of it." Once again he tried to smile at her, this time with more success. "And dinna preach to me of violence. 'Twas my way of ridding myself of anger, and I willna apologize for it."

She sat back on her heels and stared at him. "I don't understand."

He nodded as though they'd actually agreed on something important. "Then ye know why I would ne'er fit in yer world. I would die of boredom."

"It's not like that. There are wonderful things in my time. You could—"

He reached out and touched her lips with one rough finger, effectively silencing her. "Hear me, Fortune. While breath remains in me, I willna live in yer world." His stare pierced her. "Nor will any child of mine."

Child? Could there be a child? She hadn't thought, hadn't . . . No, she wouldn't consider the possibility, couldn't conceive of what it would mean. And she absolutely did *not* feel a warm glow at the thought of having Leith's baby.

His total rejection of her world, and her duty to humanity, hung between them like a yawning chasm. She mourned for what had almost been, for what would never be again.

Chapter Nine

*I swear to . . . Oops. Almost said the G word. Gettin'
careless. But hey, I'm allowed. The Chicago fire was
a breeze compared to these two humans. A little cow
manipulatin' and poof, Chicago flambé. That fire
was one of my masterpieces.*

*Okay, so cows are easy—limited brain cells. But
gimme a break. Fortune and Leith are makin' me
sweat. Nothing makes me sweat. I mean, I really
thought old Leith was gonna take a hike. I wouldn't
blame the guy.*

*Here we have some great lovin'. Don't get me
wrong, I didn't peek. OK, so I peeked a little. Anyway,
I really thought this would be my big moment. Fortune had him in the palm of her hand, figuratively
speaking, of course, and she blows it.*

*Why the hell'd she spout all that garbage about
bringing him back to her time? After all, a man has*

his pride. Now I've gotta start over again, and time's tickin' away.

Maybe I shouldn't have set that time limit, but who woulda thought two ordinary humans would be a problem? You gotta give them credit, though. Two tough cookies, just like me.

I gotta do somethin' about that ice-cream peddler. I don't get a real good feelin' about him. He looks familiar, but I can't place him. When you've been around as long as I have, a lotta faces look familiar. Give me time, and I'll remember.

So now what? At least Leith didn't fly the coop. They're still together, even if he's sleepin' on the floor. Don't blame him. That couch makes an iron maiden feel like sleepin' on air.

Maybe I can do my thing when they go back to Mary Campbell's. That's if I can escape the lovin' claws of Tootsie. If that cat was human, she'd be wearin' men out by the thousands. I guess no one said my life would be easy, but there are trials that try my tiny store of patience. If Tootsie isn't careful, she'll be lookin' outa the wrong side of a mouse hole.

I gotta tell you, I sorta like Fortune and Leith. I never spent much time up close and personal with humans before, and I've kinda . . . bonded with them. Don't get me wrong, I won't blink when I zap them back to their own times. I have my professional integrity.

But you know, they're . . . OK. Leith admires my guts, and I like a man who's not afraid to be a man. Just like me. And Fortune's . . . She's a kind lady, even if she has this stupid idea about lugging Leith back to her time. She thinks about my comfort. I like that in a woman.

Not that I'm goin' soft. Hey, I've been around for a long time, and nothin's gonna keep me from doin' what I've gotta do.

Fortune woke slowly, stretching her arms out in a languorous search for . . . Empty. The other side of the bed was empty. Memory flooded her. *Of course*. She'd burned her transport beams last night. Leith wouldn't share her bed again. He considered her nothing short of a slave trader.

She sighed and sat up. That was what she'd wanted him to think, so why the stab of disappointment?

She'd think logically. She didn't actually miss Leith, but the comfort of his physical presence, the physical aspect of their relationship. After all, she'd mated for the first time in her life, and it had been spectacular. So why shouldn't she feel a sense of loss knowing it wouldn't happen again? Leith represented only her physical need. *There*. She'd explained everything logically. She felt better. Didn't she?

The sound of music wafting in from the living room interrupted her thoughts of logic and reasonableness. Leith had risen early. She couldn't contain an uncharitable hope that he'd found the floor a hard mistress. But on the other hand, she knew if he returned to their bed he'd create a whole new set of problems, at least for her peace of mind.

Reluctantly, she climbed from bed and headed for the bathroom. Closing the door, she stared bleakly into the mirror above the sink. Was that the face of a woman who'd found ecstasy in the arms of a man who loved her? Hardly. Leith would never love someone who'd sacrifice him on the altar of duty.

A familiar cramp assured her that motherhood didn't hover on her horizon. Her monthly flow. She breathed out a sigh of disappointment, and the mirror momentarily fogged. It cleared, and she wished her own mixed feelings would clear as easily.

She should be overjoyed that she wouldn't have a child to complicate her return home. A daughter would most likely live a life very like her own, one in which she'd never know the love of a real man.

And a boy? If she had a boy, he'd be coddled, pampered, and . . . stifled. He'd never know the freedom his father reveled in. He'd know only his duty to humanity and to an endless stream of faceless women.

So she should feel thrilled she didn't have to worry about a child. As she climbed into the shower, she knew it would take more than the stream of hot water to wash away her soul-deep disappointment . . . and her memories. Memories of a hard, passion-slicked body awakening her to— *Stop! Just stop.* She wouldn't think about what she couldn't have.

A short time later, clean but not refreshed, she pulled on her jeans and a top, then padded into the living room. She found Leith lying on the floor, propped up on one elbow, his attention riveted to the television.

She glanced at the screen, then frowned. A man and woman, locked in each other's arms, moved to the slow rhythm of a song. There wasn't enough space between them to fit a microchip.

Leith glanced up at her. " 'Tis a strange way of dancing." She thought she detected a gleam of laughter in his eyes. "Do people still dance so in yer time?"

Fortune chose to ignore the humor. "Of course not. Without men it wouldn't make much sense. We still dance, but with a little more space between us."

He glanced solemnly at her. "Aye, I understand." The flash of humor returned. "Still, mayhap we can try it one day."

Her start of pleasure was all out of proportion to his suggestion. She shouldn't get close to him again. She didn't think logically when he was near—a disruption of her brain wave patterns. No, she would never dance like that with him. "I don't think that would be wise."

His glance touched her with a secret promise. "We will dance, lass. When 'tis time."

He frowned. How could he want to touch her when he knew what she planned for him? His body didn't understand the situation. She would try to use his body to capture his soul.

"You think because of what we did together you can dictate what happens between us?" Her eyes narrowed in defiance; her lips thinned in anger. "Not in this lifetime."

What they'd *done* together? *Damn the woman*. They'd made love. But he'd forgotten: for her it had simply been a mating.

"Ye're right, lass. 'Tis best we not touch again. I'd forgotten ye have but one purpose for my body, and 'tis not pleasure for yerself." He tried to feel satisfaction with his rejection of her, but could only drag up a dull acceptance.

Fortune walked over and clicked off the television, effectively ending the discussion on dancing and at the same time asserting her control. Leith almost smiled at her transparency, except he'd never felt less like smiling.

"What time will you leave for Mary Campbell's?" She threw the question over her shoulder as she headed toward the kitchen.

He rose and followed her, stretching his complaining muscles as he went. He was growing soft. The fight had been short, and he'd slept on the cold ground many times and still risen eager for battle.

"I'll bathe, then dress. Can ye be ready by then?"

She nodded as she poured herself a glass of orange juice.

" 'Tis amazing. Most women would spend more time making themselves presentable." Why had he goaded her? Did he want her to refuse to go with him? More likely he hoped to shatter her cold manner, expose the warm, soft woman beneath. But perhaps there was no warm woman beneath. Had her concern last night for his injuries been real, or merely worry that her chosen stud might be marred before she could get him home?

"Presentable?" She smiled sweetly at him, but no sweetness reached her eyes. "Now who would I want to be presentable for?"

"Aye. Ye can look like a hag for all I care." He strode toward the bathroom, angrily aware his outburst had been akin to a lad sticking his tongue out at an adversary he could defeat in no other way.

After a hot shower and even hotter thoughts, he hurried to the bedroom to dress.

Glancing at the shorts he'd dragged from his drawer, he allowed himself a satisfied smile. To put the shorts on before his jeans was the civilized thing to do. *To hell with civilized things*. Dropping the shorts into the trash basket, he defiantly slid the jeans over his bare skin. He pulled up the zipper with extra care, for a careless jerk of those metal teeth could make him useless to Fortune or any woman that came after her.

As he headed back to the living room, his act of childish defiance almost embarrassed him. Almost. Even though Fortune would never know what he did or didn't wear beneath his jeans, *he* knew, and felt he'd struck a blow for all males.

When he reached the living room, Fortune awaited him. Her tousled hair framed her face and looked as though she'd only dragged her fingers through it. She wore her shirt hanging loose to hide her body, but she couldn't hide the angry pink of her cheeks or the defiant sparkle of her eyes. He almost laughed. She'd purposely attempted to make herself unattractive, and instead she'd made herself beautiful.

"Ye look bonny. 'Tis a compliment that ye made yerself beautiful for me, but I didna think ye could do it so quickly."

"Drop dead." Her bosom heaved, probably with the effort to keep from attacking him.

He followed the motion with his gaze. He remembered the soft fullness of her breasts as he'd cupped them in his palms, the hot taste of woman and desire as he'd suckled each nipple. *Damn!* If he didn't stop such thoughts he'd be forced to release his zipper and horrify Fortune with his lack of shorts.

He shook his head in mock sorrow. " 'Tis sad that ye'd wish violence on me, and ye coming from such a peaceful society."

Her beauty shone as brightly as her anger. This was almost as much fun as . . . No, it wasn't even close. The thought of their lovemaking sobered him immediately. "Are ye ready?"

"Yes. I've already called a taxi. I hope this job pays well, because our money won't last long if we have to take taxis everywhere."

The sound of the taxi stopping in front of the house pulled him from his dangerous memories of her body, their lovemaking. As he followed Fortune into the vehicle, he didn't even attempt to stop Ganymede when the cat leaped in behind him. Ganymede was a male, and he needed all the male support he could get.

When they stopped in front of Mary's castle, Ganymede leaped out before they could stop him and disappeared into the shrubbery. Leith smiled. Ganymede didn't fear thieves, but an amorous Tootsie was a different matter altogether. He cast a sideways glance at Fortune, who sat primly against the far door, refusing even to look at him. Leith understood Ganymede. A wise male retreated to fight another day.

But he'd never claimed to be a wise male. He slid across the seat until he almost touched her. She didn't wait for explanations. Jerking the door next to her open, she practically fell out in her anxiety to be away from him. *Hmm. Interesting.*

Climbing out behind her, he watched as she hurried toward the castle's entrance. The sway of her hips drew his attention like tender spring grass tempted a hungry ram. She'd almost reached the door when Mary opened it.

Smiling at Fortune, Mary turned her gaze on Leith. "I'm glad you could make it today. Come with me, and I'll show you where you'll work. We need to talk about money, too."

A movement at Mary's feet drew his attention. Tootsie slipped out the door. He hoped Ganymede was fleet of foot today.

After showing them to the study, Mary left them alone. Leith glanced down at the piece of paper she'd given him. "I dinna understand this."

Fortune walked over to one of the strange machines. "It's a computer, primitive but adequate for what we need."

He looked up, puzzled. "No, I mean this piece of paper Mary gave me. It doesna look like dough."

Preoccupied, Fortune turned on the machine, then sat down in front of it. "That's a check. You go to a bank and turn it in for money." She stopped playing with the machine and glanced over her shoulder at him. "I got a look at the amount. If I remember correctly, that's a lot of money for this time period." She turned her attention back to the machine. "Of course, we won't be here long enough to take advantage of all that money."

Folding the paper carefully, he put it in his pocket. "What if ye ne'er return home, Fortune?"

Fortune swiveled her chair to stare at him. The thought felt like a splash of cold water on a hot day—unexpected enough to make her catch her breath, but after the initial shock, not as unpleasant as she'd thought.

She watched him walk toward her with the easy grace of a man who'd pushed his body to the limits of physical endurance and understood its power. He'd still find physical challenges in the year 2000, but in 2300 he'd be an anomaly, a freak who didn't understand the only muscle that counted was in your index finger, the one for pushing buttons. Sure, there were still primitive worlds, but he wouldn't be allowed to leave Earth. He'd be much too valuable to trust to the vagaries of space travel. *A dark predator in a golden cage.*

She hated the thought, but the human race had to continue. "We have to return. It's my—"

"Aye. It's yer duty. But if ye had no duty, would it trouble ye greatly to stay?" He peered curiously over her shoulder at the monitor.

Never return to her work? Strange that her first thought wasn't for her mother, her friends. To be honest, her mother had no place in her life, had never wanted a place in her life. Friends? None she couldn't face a future without.

She raised her gaze to meet Leith's. If she were really honest, she'd admit this man seemed closer, more real than anyone in her other life. *Other life.* There was a discovery waiting in those words, but she couldn't think with him so close.

"Staying isn't an option." Her words were cold and clipped, but the sooner he accepted her position, the sooner he could accept how important it was he return with her. That return would happen in the rest-over room; she was convinced of it.

"Hmm." He watched as she accessed the Internet, then typed in *Glencoe Massacre*.

With calm deliberation, she clicked on search, then waited for a list of websites to appear. *Return.* That said it all. Lost in her need to bring him back with her was his desire to return to Scotland. The thought of sitting in her studio, creating men who would never come close to imitating the life force of her Scottish warrior, and realizing Leith had been dead for over five hundred years, lost to her forever, made her feel suddenly empty, futile.

"We . . . we have to return to the rest-over. Can't you see how important you are to humanity? How can you be so selfish?" She blindly pulled up information about the Glencoe massacre on the screen, but she couldn't read the words.

He straightened and she heard him move away. "Ye dinna understand at all, lass. Is it selfish to want to see yer own land again? There is someone I . . ." She almost leaped from her seat as he punched the wall, then glanced disinterestedly at his bleeding knuckles. "Mayhap 'tis selfishness, but ye can find someone else to take wi' ye."

There is someone. Had he left a woman he loved back in his time? She'd been so intent on her own agenda, she hadn't stopped to think about him. Why? *Because you didn't want anything interfering with your plans to take him, and only him, back.*

She rose shakily and walked over to him. *Don't let him see your uncertainty.* "Let's take care of those knuckles."

A smile touched his lips, those lips she wanted to—

"Dinna ye want to lecture me on the evils of violence?"

She led him to the bathroom, and he stood behind her as she rooted through the medicine cabinet. "If I willna go willingly wi' ye to the hotel, how will ye force me wi'out violence?"

Intent on dabbing peroxide on his cut knuckles, and wincing for him at the pain he must feel, she didn't consider her answer. "There's always medication, I suppose, but if cosmic forces get tired of waiting they'll probably send us back from wherever we happen to be at the moment." Then why her determination to return to the rest-over? If she returned to the rest-over of her own volition, she'd have some control over her destiny. Unlike everything else that had happened so far.

"Medication? Do ye mean a potion?" He sounded horrified. "Ye would resort to such evil in the name of yer duty?"

She'd had enough. She'd simply had enough. Curse Jan Kredski and her cloning experiments. Not only had the scientist bartered away humanity's future, but she was doing a pretty good job of messing up the past as well.

Angrily, she heaved the peroxide bottle into the sink. "Damn it! Leave me alone. Leave me the hell alone." Storming out of the bathroom, she returned to the computer, breathing deeply to calm herself. Had she said those things, lost control? What was this world doing to her? What was *he* doing to her?

She stiffened at the first stroke of his hand along the length of her hair, but when he said nothing she gradually relaxed into the rhythm of his caress.

"Dinna fash yerself, lass." His low murmur soothed her, made her feel everything would be all right, even though she knew that whatever happened, nothing would ever be all right again. "Ye'll do what ye have to do. I willna blame ye."

Somehow his words of acceptance made her feel all the worse. A Sornian earth burrower couldn't have felt lower. "Let's start your report." *When in doubt, throw yourself into your work.*

With her mind reasonably clear, she read the words on the screen . . . then froze. *No!* What she saw there shouldn't shock her, not after what she'd gone through already, but it did.

"Why?" She refused to look up at him. "Why didn't you tell me you'd slaughtered MacDonalds at Glencoe? After everything else you told me, why keep that from me?"

She felt rather than heard his harsh exhalation. "Ye wouldna understand. When horror piles atop horror, ye must keep a small piece of it to yerself for fear that final bit will drive ye to madness, or make those ye care for turn from ye."

She looked up in time to see his shrug.

"I didna know if ye could forgive the killing of yer ancestors."

Where was her outrage at his withholding of such important information, her fury at what he'd been a part of? *Those ye care for.* Did he care for her? The thought was new, tender, and needed to be protected until she could examine it.

She should've considered how she could use this to bring him to her time, but as soon as the thought surfaced, she dismissed it. Logic had nothing to do with what she felt, and that was a danger she'd have to face at a calmer moment.

She willed her pounding heart to slow, her voice to give away no emotion. "We've wasted enough time."

Methodically, she showed him everything she could find about the massacre. Finally he walked away from the computer. "I dinna need to see any more. 'Tis half-truths and lies. Neither Campbell nor MacDonald were free of guilt." She heard him ease himself onto the leather couch that sat against the far wall. "I'll tell ye what really happened."

She abandoned the Internet to take down his story.

He lived it again—the unexpected awakening, his groggy response to Hugh's whispered orders, his disbelief when he realized what Hugh planned. He couldn't forget. Closing his eyes, he recalled the horror of watching those he'd thought he knew turn to animals in a killing frenzy. What he should have done, what he didn't do, and then his final betrayal of his brother, his clan—all the memories he called up to scourge himself, and rightly so.

When he'd ended, he sat there, wrapped in the dark dungeon of his yesterdays until she touched him. Slowly, he returned—to the room, the time, the woman.

She leaned over him until her soft breath touched his face. He longed to bury himself in her warmth . . . and forget. She placed her hand over his. As from a distance, he noted her hand's delicateness beside his, the paleness of her skin next to the sun-darkened roughness of his. He shivered

as his sweat-dampened shirt clung to him, but the
shiver had nothing to do with coldness, unless it
was the coldness of his heart.

"You're a very brave man, Leith Campbell." She
absently stroked his cut knuckles.

"No." His denial was bitter.

"Yes. In the end, you did what was right."

"I did too little, too late; then I betrayed my clan,
my brother. What would ye know of that?" He refused to allow her to make him into a false hero.

She sighed. "Nothing. I have no clan to be loyal
to. I've never had a difficult decision to make in my
life." She smiled. "No, I lied. I've tried for ages to
decide if I should make a man with red hair." She
wrinkled her nose. "I hate red hair."

He recognized her attempt to lighten his mood
and rose to his feet. Reaching out, he fingered one
strand of her hair. "Ne'er doubt it, lass. Red hair is
beautiful . . . on a woman." He grinned. "I wouldna
wish it on a son."

She returned to the computer and shut it off.
"Let's get out of here. We've done enough for today." Pausing for a moment, she turned toward the
door. "Do you hear Elvis?"

"Elvis? I dinna know an Elvis." Striding out of
the room, he headed for the stairs with her beside
him. He was anxious to leave behind the events
he'd had to tell today. Could this also be part of his
penance, being forced to relive what he'd tried so
unsuccessfully to forget? Would the telling of his
part in the massacre purge him of his guilt? He
doubted it.

Deep in his own gloomy thoughts, he started
down the stairs. Suddenly a howl worthy of a ber-

serk piper jerked him from his reverie. Glancing behind him, he saw Ganymede leap down the stairs and launch himself past them. Had the cat gone mad?

But the cat was forgotten as Leith heard Fortune's startled yelp. He glanced at her in time to see her lose her balance and start to fall. Instinctively, Leith flung himself in front of her, and they tumbled down the stairs together.

As Leith lay at the bottom of the staircase, he considered the irony that in his short time here he'd received more cuts and bruises than he had in years lived in his "savage" past.

"What . . . what happened?"

Fortune's breathless question brought his attention to the fact that she was sprawled atop him, not an entirely unpleasant position for him. "We tumbled down the stairs."

Surprisingly, she didn't scramble to remove herself from contact with his body. His body noted that fact with growing interest.

"You're a master at stating the obvious. What I meant was, *why* did we tumble down the stairs?"

He breathed deeply. She still made no attempt to roll off him, but merely wiggled into a more comfortable position. A particular part of his body rose to study the situation. "Ganymede was in an uncommon hurry and tripped ye on his way down the steps." He glanced around. "Tootsie seems verra determined to have his manhood. 'Twould make any man run for his life."

He felt her indrawn breath, her sudden alertness. "Elvis. The ice-cream man."

He didn't know what she was babbling about,

209

but it didn't matter because all he could think of was the torture of her breasts brushing against his chest, the agony of her hips pressed between his thighs, and the pain of too-tight jeans that allowed no room for a man's . . . He longed to rip open his shirt, rip open her shirt, and allow her breasts to touch his flesh, her nipples to harden against him. He gritted his teeth, fighting the need to pull down the cursed zipper on his jeans and take her like the barbarian she thought him.

Fortune sighed deeply, and Leith closed his eyes to keep from groaning at the renewed pressure on sensitive areas.

"I suppose I should get off you."

He opened his eyes. "Dinna feel the need to hurry." He didn't smile when he said that.

Hurry was exactly what she had to do, before she gave in to temptation, before she touched him in ways she'd sworn never to touch him again. She took a deep breath, then rolled off him. She had to remember that even though there was an obvious physical attraction between them, that couldn't deter her from what she had to do. And if she allowed herself to become addicted to the wonders of his body, it would be all the harder when he rejected her in the end.

Fortune smiled weakly. "Hey, this time I got to be on top."

He returned her smile. "Aye, but next time—"

"There'll be no next time." Her voice was harsh with regret. "Nothing has changed, Leith. I still intend to take you back with me."

"Ye can try." He didn't stop smiling as he rose in one lithe motion.

"Are you OK?" She frowned. She'd been so intent on the feel of his body beneath her, she'd forgotten how he'd gotten there. It said a lot about Leith that he'd instinctively tried to protect her. And this wasn't the first time he'd put himself in danger for her. Protecting women must be second nature to him, because if he'd stopped to think who he was saving, he probably wouldn't have bothered. "I appreciate that you tried to cushion my fall. Thanks."

He didn't acknowledge her belated thanks. "Only a few more bruises. I dinna have any broken bones."

The sound of footsteps swung Fortune's attention to the doorway. She groaned inwardly as Michael walked into view, then stopped to stare at them. *Great. Just great.*

"My God, what happened?" Michael's horror was sincere. In her time, women valued sincerity.

"We fell down the bloody stairs." Leith glared at Michael. Sincerity mustn't rank very high on the primitive scale.

"Did you hurt yourself? Here, let me help you up." Michael rushed over to Fortune and carefully lifted her to her feet, then gently smoothed down her hair. "Why don't you sit down and rest for a few moments?"

Michael was so empathic. Her society put great store in empathy for others.

"She doesna need rest. She had a verra soft landing." Leith's glower was a thunderhead rising above a mountain.

How could she compare the two men? Michael was cheerful and sincere. Leith was cranky and . . .

211

sexy. Michael was soft and sympathetic. Leith was hard and . . . sexy. Michael was perfect for her world. Leith was perfect for her bed. *Good*. She was glad she'd settled that.

"I suppose now isn't the best time for introductions, but I'd like you to meet my fiancée, Stephanie." Michael stepped aside, and the woman standing behind him moved forward.

Fortune's eyes widened. Stephanie was . . . extraordinary. Tall, regal, with long black hair and green eyes that moved over Leith's body with . . . *Hmm*.

It was Fortune's turn to glare. Leith's tongue was practically hanging out over Stephanie. OK, so Stephanie was magnificent in an obvious sort of way. OK, so Stephanie didn't even look dumb. Fortune would've felt a little more charitable if Stephanie looked dumb as a dwerb. Yes, she admitted she wanted Stephanie to do or say something stupid to offset her other assets.

Fortune glared harder at Leith. It was all his fault. If she hadn't seen the way he ogled Stephanie, she wouldn't care what the woman looked like. Fortune was . . . jealous? *No*. She couldn't possibly be jealous. Jealousy was an undesirable trait. She absolutely, positively wasn't jealous.

She looked at Stephanie again. Stephanie was busy undressing Leith with her hot gaze. Fine, she was jealous.

"It's so nice to meet both of you." Stephanie didn't even glance at Fortune. "I hope I'll see more of you." Her gaze locked on the parts of Leith she hoped to see more of.

"Well, now that you're safe, we'll be on our way."

Michael smiled a sincere smile. "I'll have someone check those stairs."

" 'Twas a warrior's gallant dash for freedom." Leith glanced away from Stephanie.

"Huh?" Michael blinked owlishly at him.

Leith grinned with the first sign of good humor he'd shown since Michael showed up. "Have ye seen Tootsie lately?"

"No, I haven't, but I'm sure she'll show up." Shaking his head in puzzlement, Michael guided Stephanie down the hallway.

Fortune ignored Leith as he held the door open. She stepped outside with him close behind. They stopped at the same moment.

Closing her eyes, she counted to ten, then opened them again. Nothing had changed.

Melting ice cream littered the driveway and lawn. Ice-cream wrappers hung from tree branches and festooned nearby bushes. And crouched in the middle of the havoc was Ganymede, happily lapping up a cone. Ominously, their favorite ice-cream man was nowhere to be seen.

"Oh, my God!" Fortune murmured.

"God's teeth!" Leith muttered.

"Meow," Ganymede explained.

Chapter Ten

" 'Tis passing strange." Leith walked over and peered behind a tall hedge. "I dinna see a body."

"What could've happened?" Ganymede, the only witness, wound around Fortune's legs, purring his description of the battle.

"Mayhap someone mugged him." Leith stared at the branches of a towering live oak, its leaves dripping a colorful pattern of vanilla, chocolate, and strawberry ice cream.

"Mugged?" Fortune turned in a dazed circle, wondering who could've done something like this to a harmless ice-cream man. Glancing down, she shook her head at Ganymede, who looked distinguished with his vanilla-coated whiskers.

"Aye. I heard the word on television. 'Tis when criminals attack a person while he walks along the street." He turned to give her a tight smile. "Dinna worry, ye're safe wi' me."

Forgetting the ice-cream man for a moment, she realized she believed him. She felt safe with Leith, a warm, glowing feeling of security in a world that offered precious little of that commodity. What had he done to earn her trust? Nothing that would give him superhero status. But her heart knew and trusted him to protect her more than anyone she'd ever known.

The admission made her uncomfortable, as though she'd given him a piece of herself. She'd already given him a piece of herself when she'd mated with him. How many pieces did she have left?

"I'll tell Mary." He started back toward the door.

"Wait. I'll go with you." She felt vulnerable for some reason, more vulnerable than she'd felt since first waking in this past time, as though if she took her gaze from Leith for a moment he'd be whisked back to his time, and she'd never see him again. And today, in this place, the thought sent shivers of fear trailing down her spine. Fear? Fear of being alone in the year 2000, fear of never touching him again. "I . . . I just remembered that I left something up in the study."

He nodded, and she followed him back into the castle.

Climbing the winding stairs, she thought of her growing hunger for him. She, who'd never hungered for much of anything in her life other than models with tighter tushes and bigger biceps, found she couldn't satisfy this new yearning. She

215

could never be close enough, touch him enough.

Her life's mantra had been control, and now she couldn't control her need. It was like a black hole in space—dark, impenetrable, drawing her against her will into its depths.

Think of something else. Why had the ice-cream man been here, and what had happened to him? Nothing made any sense. Of course, the very fact that she stood here in this time and place made no sense. Cosmic forces had picked a dud for a delivery person.

Fortune descended the stairs to join Leith and Mary, who stood in the doorway looking out at the destruction.

Mary shook her head. "Where did this come from?"

" 'Twas from the ice-cream truck." Leith walked out to look behind a large statue of an angel, still searching for a body.

"Ice-cream truck?" Mary looked bewildered. "Ice-cream trucks never come here. They couldn't get past the gate."

Leith frowned. " 'Twas here today."

Mary turned brisk. "You must be mistaken, but who could have done this?"

"I don't know, but if I were you I'd get a scan-glow protection system with corvan-repel beams as soon as it's invented." Fortune mentally clapped her hand across her lips.

"Corvan-repel beams?" Mary stared at her as though she'd just announced that a Moccan giant had landed on Earth.

Thoughtfully, Leith's gaze settled on Ganymede.

" 'Twas the fall. Fortune tumbled down yer stairs, and her wits are addled."

Mary seemed to forget about the repel beams in her concern for Fortune. "I'm so sorry, dear. Are you all right?"

"Fine. I'm just fine." She glanced helplessly at Leith. "Here comes our taxi. It's been . . . interesting." She smiled inanely at Mary. "See you tomorrow."

"Of course." Mary smiled. "I'll get someone to clean up this mess, then look into a security system for that gate. I don't like the idea of strangers wandering in."

Leith and Fortune waited silently for the taxi to stop. Preoccupied, Leith held the door while Fortune and Ganymede climbed in. Leith told the driver where to take them, and quiet reigned again.

Fortune almost sighed. She'd expected Leith to be gleefully triumphant at her blunder, would've preferred it. Brooding silences irritated her.

All she'd done was make one little slip. He had a lot of nerve getting mad at her after all the times she'd had to cover for him.

She waited until they were finally in the privacy of their house before she let him have it. "I don't know why you're all bent out of shape. So I made one mistake. So what? I mean, is this some sort of primitive code where the man gets to make all the mistakes, and the woman has to be perfect?"

He seemed weary as he collapsed onto the lumpy couch. "Ye canna leave my primitive nature alone, can ye, lass? I wasna angry wi' ye, and I dinna know why ye thought such."

"Oh." Talk about feeling stupid. "But you didn't say anything."

"I was thinking." His gaze challenged her. "Even primitives think, but 'tis a chore that drains a man's strength and leaves none for speaking."

Fortune dropped her gaze. "I'm sorry." She deserved his sarcasm.

He rested his head against the back of the couch and stared at a corner where a hopeful spider spun its silky web. "Dinna fash yerself. I know I've asked many foolish questions, and I dinna blame ye for saying what ye said." He continued to stare at the spider, which had decided to add a deck to its home. "That is not what bothers me." He turned his gaze on her.

"Why were we sent here together, Fortune?"

"I thought we'd worked all that out. I believe cosmic forces want me to bring you back to my time to save humanity. You believe the powers that be want you to help Mary Campbell and teach me the . . . well, you know." The only thing they'd managed so far was the "well, you know."

He returned his attention to the spider, which had now expanded its living space to include a two-hovercraft garage. "Ye dinna understand me. When ye spoke to Mary about repel beams and such, I realized how truly far apart we were. We dinna have anything in common."

We have one thing in common.

"If ye're right about my purpose here, then I dinna understand why yer cosmic forces chose me. I'm a savage, by yer standards. Why didna these forces choose someone closer to yer time, someone who would understand yer way of life?" He abandoned the spider's ongoing construction to shift his gaze back to Fortune.

"Hmm. Let me think." *Your eyes, green like the evening light on Chima, beautiful, mesmerizing. Your lips, masculine, but with a full lower lip that would tempt a holy woman of Sirent. Your body, warm skin and hard muscle, sheathed in power.* "Your mind. They definitely chose you for your mind."

"Hmmph." She didn't need to see the amused slant of those great lips to know what he thought of *that*. "If 'twas my mind ye were thinking of, ye were staring 'at the wrong part of me, lass."

She was blushing. She could feel the heat rising to her cheeks. She never blushed, even when explaining to customers how to get the greatest pleasure out of her models' most intimate parts. "OK, so they probably checked out your genes too."

"Jeans?" He frowned. "Why would they care what I wore?"

She sighed. He was right. Cosmic forces had gone back a long way to find the right man. But he *was* the right man; she was convinced of that. *For the world or for you?*

"And what about ye? Why did they send ye?"

"That's obvious." She felt on firmer ground here. "I know all there is to know about men. I make their bodies. I've studied their habits on history disks. I've listened to women's fantasies about their ideas of what the perfect man should be."

He smiled and shook his head. The dark silk of his hair settled across one broad shoulder, and she yearned to slide her fingers through the shining strands.

"Ye dinna know men at all. Not here." He tapped his chest. "Do ye want me to tell ye why I think ye were sent here wi' me?"

No. She shrugged.

"Ye need loving more than any woman I've ever known."

Love? The word exploded in her heart; then her logic kicked in. He didn't mean love; he meant sex. "That's ridiculous. I could've mated with any man." *Wrong*.

Patiently, he shook his head. "Nay, lass. Ye needed the right man for *ye*."

Arrogance, thy name is Leith. "Okay, smart guy, tell me why you're the right man for me."

"Nay, *ye* tell me." His whisper sliced through her acid thoughts of a particular Highlander's astounding pride.

Her mind zipped right past her previous catalog of his physical attributes to something deeper, more profound, and completely unexpected. She stared at him in surprised realization. "You gave me a yellow flower. No one ever gave me a flower before, not in my whole life."

He smiled at her, a smile filled with mystery and hidden knowledge. "Mayhap ye needed that flower."

"Ridiculous. I mean, it doesn't make any sense. I'm a grown woman. I don't need a flower to fulfill me." Uncertainly, she reached down to pet Ganymede, who wound around her feet, purring his support.

"Ye're right. 'Tis not a flower that makes a man and woman right for each other, but the many small things they share each day, things they dinna notice until 'tis too late."

Nevermore. For some reason, the closing word of an ancient poem she could hardly remember popped into her head. Would she sit years from now watching the rain beat against her workroom window and think of all the small things she'd done with Leith, regretting all the small things she'd never done?

She blinked. No, she wouldn't let her thoughts meander fruitlessly down that path. She'd forgotten the original point of this conversation. Something about security systems and a missing ice-cream man.

There was a knock at the door, and she turned to open it.

"Stop. Ye're too trusting. Ne'er open a door till ye're certain a friend stands on the other side." He offered her a self-deprecating smile. "I forgot. Ye come from a time where people have nothing to fear." His smile turned grim. "Unless ye're male," he amended.

Fortune tried to ignore his last dig. She swung the door wide and smiled a welcome as Blade and Lily entered the room. "I'm glad you stopped by."

Turning to lead them into the room, she caught Leith's dour expression and heard his muttered comment. "I dinna blame ye for being glad. No doubt ye couldna wait to get relief from our talk."

Blade grinned and walked over to sit on the couch beside Leith. Lily paused to pet Ganymede.

"Why do ye think women canna let that cursed cat alone?" Leith mumbled to Blade.

Ganymede stared at the men. For a moment,

Fortune saw amused intelligence in the cat's amber gaze. Then Ganymede returned his attention to a cooing Lily. Fortune drew a deep breath. She'd obviously worked too hard today.

Blade reached over and clapped Leith on the shoulder. "Lily and I were talking about you guys. We know you're trying to get on your feet, so we thought we could help you get your act together. How about talking it over? We can go to dinner, then take in a movie at the mall."

"I'd love that." Fortune knew she sounded over-eager. "How about you, Leith?" She needed some time to relax, forget.

Leith rose and walked to her side. He put an arm across her shoulder and leaned close. She controlled her urge to move away. His knowing smile mocked her; his husky whisper taunted her. "When ye look at me that way, ye could almost convince me to return to yer time. Almost."

Straightening, he nodded at Blade. "Aye. 'Tis a good idea." He frowned. "What is a . . . mall?"

Both Blade and Lily looked at him as though he'd just sprouted another head. "They dinna have malls in Tibet," he hurriedly explained, and Fortune could tell he was trying to avoid making eye contact with her.

Fortune's reaction surprised her. Before this, she would have bemoaned his carelessness, and thought nothing more of it. Now? She sympathized with his puzzlement, yearned to ease his embarrassment. "You'll find out soon enough." She forced a laugh. "Let it be a surprise." She hooked her arm through his—offering her support, her promise that she was on his side.

Blade glanced at his watch. "Great. Let's go." He paused to let Fortune join Lily, then fell into step beside Leith. "By the way, noticed any strangers around here?" His quiet words didn't reach the women walking in front.

Leith shook his head. "Why?"

"Bones, that big guy you took a chunk out of, won't let it rest. You whipped him in front of everyone. That's never happened before. He won't forget it. Better watch your back."

"Bones?" Leith wasn't worried for himself. He'd dealt with men bent on vengeance before. But he must make sure Fortune saw none of it. His deep need to protect her didn't surprise him. Nothing about his feelings for Fortune shocked him anymore.

"Yeah, Bones. That's usually all that's left after he gets through with someone."

Leith nodded his understanding. "Thank ye for yer warning."

As they all climbed into Blade's taxi, Ganymede made an attempt to leap in behind them. Leith took great pleasure in slamming the door shut in the cat's face. It was small of him, he knew, but it made up a little for the attention Fortune had lavished on Ganymede instead of him. He refused to contemplate what this said about his vaunted skill with women, that he felt threatened by a cat.

It was only a short drive to the mall, and he barely had time to examine the wonders of the many stores before Blade steered them into the restaurant.

As Leith studied the varied food choices, he realized if it were not for his desire to make peace with Hugh and his love of Scotland, he'd almost be content to remain here. If Fortune remained also.

He glanced at Fortune. Why would he want to remain with someone who planned to—

"Ready to order, big guy?"

Blade's question startled him. Order? He didn't understand half of what was on this . . . menu.

Fortune leaned over to look at his menu. "Beef seems to be their specialty. I bet they have good prime rib, if you like red meat. You probably like it rare—barely cooked." She wrinkled her nose at him. "A baked potato would go well with prime rib. And I always enjoy the salad bar." She smiled up at him, then returned to her own menu.

Thank you. Leith wanted to kiss her soundly. She'd saved him the embarrassment of asking for help, and for this he owed her.

When she peeked over the top of her menu, he offered her a smile—one that suggested he always paid his debts. She immediately took refuge behind the menu again.

Leith glanced up at the woman waiting to take his order. "I'll have prime rib—rare, a baked potato with everything on it, and the salad bar." He smiled up at her and she smiled back, a smile he'd recognize across any time barrier. Amazingly, it had no effect on him, and he waited impatiently as she fluttered around him like a drunken butterfly.

He glanced over at Fortune in time to see her eyes emerge from over the top of her menu—angry eyes. Suddenly he felt wonderful and rewarded the waitress with another smile that had her fluttering all the more.

When the food arrived, he lost himself in the flavor and texture of it—the meat was juicy and tender, the potato moist and oozing butter. His whole body sang with the glory of it. He glanced across at Fortune, who picked at a large salad. He was wrong. One body part didn't join in the chorus, but yearned to sing alone. He attacked his meal with renewed gusto.

"That food will kill you." She pushed a piece of lettuce into her mouth and chewed as though it were her duty.

He cut off a piece of rare meat and put it into his mouth. He chewed slowly before answering. "At least I won't die a rabbit." He sent her a sideways glance. "Mayhap 'tis my imagination, but are yer ears a wee bit longer and yer nose a wee bit pink?"

Lily's laugh cut across whatever sharp retort Fortune had been planning. "Leave the man alone, honey. He needs his strength." She winked at Leith, and he grinned back.

Lily reminded him of Moira—earthy, with common sense and an unquenchable sexual appetite. Exactly the kind of woman he'd pictured himself settling down with on some Scottish hillside.

Then why couldn't he keep his gaze from Fortune—she of the lettuce leaves and carrot sticks, of the disapproving glances and evil plans? He shrugged and put another piece of meat into his mouth. Who could understand the vagaries of sexual attraction?

He refused to allow dark thoughts to ruin possibly the best meal he'd ever had.

When his dessert arrived, he thought he might simply die from the joy of it. Scooping up a large spoonful of vanilla ice cream covered with hot fudge sauce, he slitted his eyes as he savored every creamy drop, then slowly licked his lips clean.

Looking up, he caught Fortune's gaze riveted on his lips, her eyes wide saucers of interest.

"Would ye like to taste this, lass? 'Tis delicious."

She shook her head, her stare still locked on his lips, almost as though she hadn't the power to look away.

"One spoonful wouldna harm ye," he wheedled.

"No." She blinked and finally glanced away. "It's bad for me, and . . . I couldn't stop at one spoonful. I'd want more and more. So . . . I think I'll pass."

Carefully he placed the spoon on his plate. "Why do I get the feeling ye're not talking about the ice cream?"

Startled, she dared a look at him. "What else would I be talking about?"

His appetite suddenly gone, he pushed the remainder of the dessert away. "What indeed?"

"Hey, guys, let's not get so intense over a dish of ice cream." Blade glanced at his watch. "Besides, it's almost time for the movie."

God's teeth, would he never learn what all these words meant? Rising, Leith followed Blade and Lily from the restaurant. Fortune walked beside him.

Glancing up with a mischievous glint in her eyes, she stood for a moment on tiptoe to reach his ear. "Movies are moving pictures projected onto a large screen. They tell a story." She grinned. "And thank you for not asking Blade."

"Besides primitive, ye also think me a fool. 'Twas a mistake asking about the mall. I willna do it again." He knew he sounded stiff and defensive, but he couldn't help it. No matter how he tried to deny it, her opinion of him mattered.

She moved a small distance away from him, but it symbolized much more. Six centuries, to be exact. "I'm sorry if you thought I was making fun of you. I know I have an advantage because I studied history disks and understand a lot of what's happening. That doesn't mean I think you're a fool."

"Only primitive?" He was regaining his sense of humor.

She considered this as she waited for Blade to pay for their meal. "Well, you *are* primitive. That's not a put-down, just a fact. I'd think of anyone from your time period as primitive."

He put his arm across her shoulders and pulled her close to him. He could feel her stiffen and then slowly relax against his side. She felt good, and he almost lost his train of thought. "Dinna mistake me, lass. I may not understand yer modern inventions, but I understand human nature verra well. I've lived thirty-two years, *survived* thirty-two years. I've known fear, hate, pain, but I've always survived. Ye have yet to be tested, Fortune. Ye trust too much." *Especially me.* "For example, ye were unwise to tell me yer plans to take me home wi' ye. Now I will guard myself from ye."

Her eyes were wide, confused. "I don't like to lie."

He pounced. "Aye. And because ye dinna like to lie, ye've warned the enemy." Something wasn't quite right about those words. He frowned.

Her gaze turned stricken. "Is that how you see me, Leith? The enemy?"

227

He stopped, rooted to the spot. Gazing into her eyes, he gazed into his own soul—fearful, confused. "I dinna know, lass." Those words, perhaps the most truthful he'd spoken since landing in this time, were painful to speak.

Even worse was the resigned sadness in her gaze. "I see." Her tone expressionless, she turned from him and headed for the door even as Blade flung it open.

"Quit jawin' and come on, big guy. We're gonna be late for the show."

Leith followed them into the theater, glancing at the movie's title as he did so. "*Highlander*?"

"Yeah. The latest one. I thought of you as soon as I saw it was playing. Lily and I decided since you were Scottish, maybe you'd like to see the old homeland."

No! Leith could feel his heartbeat quickening.

"It's about this guy who's immortal, and they have flashbacks to things that happened in Scotland hundreds of years ago. We thought you'd enjoy it." Blade paused, waiting, no doubt, for Leith's exclamations of pleasure.

No! He didn't want to deal with the emotions— loss, sorrow. But gazing at Blade's and Lily's expectant smiles, he couldn't disappoint them. "Aye, I can hardly wait."

Only Fortune wasn't smiling. She looked worried. "I don't feel too well. Maybe we should skip the movie."

Leith narrowed his gaze on her. She looked healthy. Could she be trying to protect him? Even after his comment about her being his enemy?

Unlikely. "If Fortune feels unwell, mayhap we could—"

Lily reached into her purse and pulled out a small package. "Here, have a Tums. You probably just ate a little too much. Happens to me all the time." Handing her the package, Lily proceeded into the movie.

Fortune cast Leith an *I tried* look, shrugged, then followed Lily into the theater.

Leith was perplexed. Fortune *had* tried to shield him. Strange that she could sense his feelings. Even stranger that she'd want to help him after what he'd said.

Finding his seat in the darkness, Leith stared at the huge screen suddenly filled with larger-than-life figures; then the story catapulted him back to Scotland.

For an instant he closed his eyes, then opened them to scenes of . . . Glencoe. Clutching the arms of the seat, he held on tightly to keep from shaking. This then was also part of his penance, to experience again and again the horror. How many times could he relive it before he went mad?

The faces were different, but everything else was the same—the blood, the despair, the regret. He blinked away sudden moisture. He had not wept since his parents' deaths, and would not weep for this. But he would grieve forever.

Only his vow never to hide again kept him from exploding out of his seat and racing from the theater.

Just when he thought he could stand no more, he felt her hand. As she had done in the taxi that first day, she pried his fingers open and gripped his hand tightly in the warmth of her own.

"Hold tight; it'll be over soon." Her whisper fanned his neck, a blessed breath of heat to battle the coldness spreading from his heart.

Without warning, a weight landed in his lap. Only the training of a lifetime kept him from shouting his surprise. The weight curled into a ball and proceeded to purr loudly.

"What the . . . ?" He stared down into Ganymede's gleaming eyes. And even though he should be shocked, he wasn't.

Fortune leaned closer. "Is that . . . ?"

"Yes."

She asked nothing more, and Leith reached down to pet the cat. The repetitive motion of his hand down Ganymede's smooth body calmed him, slowed his heartbeat, allowed him to get through the last of the movie.

More than how Ganymede had found them, Leith wondered why he had chosen his lap this time when he usually favored Fortune. But whatever the reason, between Fortune's warm hand and Ganymede's comforting purr, he managed to stumble from the dark theater and his even darker memories with his soul still intact. Barely. He would have to make sure Blade didn't choose any more movies he thought would remind Leith of home.

As he left the theater with Ganymede in his arms, he met Blade's astonished gaze. "Where the hell'd he come from?"

Leith shrugged. "I dinna know. I left him at home wi' the window open only a wee bit."

Blade nodded sagely. "Yeah. Even a roach

couldn't crawl through. Know the feeling."

Fortune was quiet on the way back to the house, and Leith felt unable to say anything. But Blade made up for the silence in the backseat. "Great movie. Lots of action. Real men. That fight at Glencoe was something else. I know those Campbells were probably your ancestors, but ya gotta admit they didn't play fair." He glanced at Leith in his rearview mirror. "You look a lot like that Highlander, big guy. Different eye color, but real intense, just like him. Hair's the same, too."

Leith shifted his gaze from Blade's. "He was only playing a part." *But I've lived the part—smelled the blood, felt the cut of the blade, known the rage, the helplessness. At the end, the dead did not rise, brush themselves off, and go home. The keening didn't stop, will never stop. It echoes down through the centuries, pulling me back to Scotland, to Hugh.* "And ye're right, the Campbells didna play fair."

Lily turned to glance at him. "Not to change the subject, but we've gotta get one of you guys a driver's license. Even if you're not staying in Texas very long, you'll need a vehicle. Get your ID together, and we'll take you down to the Department of Motor Vehicles tomorrow."

Fortune gave him no time to reply. "Leith can't get a license. He has . . . seizures. Not often, but they won't give him a license, since he can't predict when they'll happen. And I . . . I lost my license."

"Lost your license?" Blade sounded scandalized. "What could a sweet little thing like you have done to lose—"

Lily gave him a not-too-gentle shove. "Leave her alone dumpling. That's none of our business."

231

"Hmmph." Blade's comment was less than gracious, but he asked nothing more.

Fortune relaxed against the seat, limp with relief. They'd dodged another potentially disastrous situation. No matter how friendly Blade and Lily were, they'd get suspicious if they learned that not only didn't Leith and she have identification, but they didn't even exist so far as the world knew.

Thank heavens Leith didn't challenge her assertions. But he hadn't said much of anything since the movie ended. How would she feel if something horrific had happened in her life, and then she went to the movies and had to watch the whole thing reenacted on a giant screen for all the world to see?

She breathed a sigh of relief when they finally pulled to a stop in front of their house. Climbing out, she walked toward the door with Leith right behind her. Ganymede wound between their legs so he could be first inside.

Leith reached around her to unlock the door. "Let me go inside first, lass."

Puzzled, she stepped back. "Why?"

"'Tis wise to be careful. We dinna know how safe this area is. Remember the ice-cream man. 'Tis possible he was the victim of foul play." Leith eased the door open, then motioned her to stay still until he'd gone through the house.

She stood fuming until he came back. "Aren't you being a little paranoid, Leith? I don't think we have anything that would get us to the top of someone's hit list."

"Hit list?" He glanced at the couch with distaste. "What is a hit list?" He began dragging his shirt off, and she realized he intended to sleep on the couch.

Not tonight. "A hit list is a list of people scheduled for assassination." She walked over and put her hand over his as he unfastened the last button. "Wait. Sleep in the bed tonight. We're adults. You need a good night's sleep after that movie."

He slanted her a tired smile. "Aye. 'Tis a good idea. It willna bother ye?"

She threw a glance over her shoulder as she entered the bedroom. "It willna bother me."

She was a liar. An hour later she lay in the dark staring at the ceiling. He hadn't moved, but she knew he wasn't asleep. *OK. Get it over with.* "Come here, Leith." Would he move over or would he simply laugh at her order?

Wordlessly he rolled toward her. Wiggling her arm beneath his head, she cradled him to her. He molded his body to hers and she felt his heat seep into every crevice of her heart. "Sleep, dark warrior. I'll keep you safe tonight."

She felt his shudder. "Not even ye could keep me safe from my demons tonight, lass."

Laying her hand against his bare chest, she rubbed in soothing circular strokes until she felt him begin to relax. Eventually, she thought he slept.

Just as her lids drooped shut, he laughed. His face pressed to the side of her breast, she felt his laughter rather than heard it. "What're you laughing at?"

"Ganymede. Dinna ye wonder how the cursed cat appears wherever we go? How did he follow us to the mall? How did he get into the theater and find us?" Propping himself up on one elbow, he stared down at her. "And why did he climb into my lap at the movie? He ne'er chooses me over ye."

"Maybe you needed him more."

"Ye're daft, woman." She heard the amusement in his voice.

She could barely keep her eyes open. "I don't know, but can't we discuss this tomorrow?"

Leith lowered himself until his mouth almost touched hers. "Do ye know what I think?"

Something in his tone had her suddenly alert. "What?"

"I think Ganymede has something to do wi' our trip through time."

At the foot of the bed, a dark shape rose from the covers to watch them with gleaming amber eyes.

Chapter Eleven

Uh-oh. The cat's outa the bag, no pun intended. I didn't expect them to catch on so quick. I shoulda known. Leith's smart, just like me. Maybe I overplayed my hand a little.

I shoulda stayed away from the mall, but I gotta admit I like bein' with them. Don't get me wrong; I'm not goin' all mushy, but I'm a normal kinda guy. After all those centuries of bein' alone, I could get used to havin' some company.

So what can I say; I felt sorry for Leith. Look, I've got some things in my own closet I wish coulda gone in a different direction. Don't tell the Big Guy this, but sometimes I sorta yearn for a different job description.

Guess we all do what we gotta do, though. Right now I'd better take care of business. But I'll work on bein' more careful.

Good thing humans never look too much past externals. They look at me and see a cat. A cat couldn't have caused all their misery, could it? Nah.

They don't even suspect that ice-cream man, and he's pretty obvious. At least I took care of him for a while. Did you see the look on his face? No, of course you didn't. Hey, he was lucky. A few more seconds and his skinny butt would've decorated the potted ferns along with his drivetrain.

But his kind never gives up easy. He'll be back as soon as he restocks. Bet he doesn't do too much messin' around with me anymore. He wants to get to Leith and Fortune. He can try, but I'm tellin' you he'll have to go through me first, and that won't be easy. They're my humans, and he'd better keep his mitts off them or else I'll stuff his Fudgsicles . . .

Relax. Forget the ice-cream jerk. Think happy thoughts like that last great earthquake.

So I guess I'd better cool it with Leith and Fortune from now on. Besides, looks like they're doin' OK without me. Who woulda believed? I mean, I busted my butt to find a touch-me-and-you're-dead virgin and a man who lives to love. Complete opposites, right? Should hate each other's guts, right? Looked great on paper. Never can figure with humans, though.

"Ganymede? You think Ganymede's responsible for this?" He had her full attention now. "He's only a cat, Leith."

As though he realized they were talking about him, Ganymede crept up from his resting place at the foot of the bed and lay purring on top of Fortune. She reached up to scratch behind his ears. "Is Leith picking on my kitty?"

"God's teeth, woman, think about it." Leith winced as Ganymede transferred his ample body to Leith's bare torso and began to knead contentedly with his sharp claws. "Where did Ganymede come from?"

"There has to be a logical explanation."

"Look around ye, Fortune, and tell me about yer logical explanations."

Leith could sense her worrying at the problem. "He must be a stray that wandered into the room somehow. That's it."

"Dinna ye think it strange that he goes where'er we go? How did he find us in the mall?"

"I . . . I don't know, but I refuse to believe he's some evil demon responsible for all this."

Ganymede seemed to suddenly lose his zest for digging holes in Leith's flesh and crept back to the foot of the bed.

Leith couldn't keep himself from asking, "Is this so verra unpleasant, Fortune?" He'd wanted the question to come out firm, direct. Instead it sounded soft, tentative. He grimaced.

From the silence, he assumed she was thinking.

"This has been the most exciting time of my life, but I don't feel right here. I miss the familiarity of home, people I know, places I go, my work. I really miss my work."

"Making men?" Would he be just a fading memory once she returned to her time?

"Yes. It's fulfilling."

"Aye." Did she get more pleasure from a fantasy than from the real thing? A fantasy was perfect. It didn't argue, didn't grow old, and would never embarrass her with "primitive" behavior.

Could he compete with a fantasy? *Bloody hell, yes*. No fantasy could've wrung the cries of ecstasy from her that he had as she'd wrapped her long legs tightly around him. . . . He took a deep breath. Just thinking about it made him hard.

"OK, let's back up. It's not particularly the making of men that's fulfilling. It's the creative process. I miss it."

He didn't want to examine his feeling of relief. "Ye could do the same thing here. Mayhap not men, but something that would satisfy ye."

"I won't be here long enough to need a career." She moved closer to him. An indication she didn't feel as certain as she sounded? "If I didn't need to take you with me, I could probably go back to the rest-over room and be home by morning."

"According to yer belief, if it werena for me ye wouldna be here at all." He wrapped his arms around her and pulled her close. She didn't fight him. "I will ne'er go back to that room wi' ye. So what will ye do? Will ye take some other poor man, one wi' a family, children? Do ye think ye have the right?"

"I don't know, Leith. God, I don't know." She snuggled closer to his side, drawing strength from his warmth, his solidness. From the memory of his powerful, sweat-sheened body poised above her, filling her. *No*. She had to erase that memory, because remembering would increase the wanting, the need. And she knew with a certainty born of a woman's instinct that desire for Leith, and only Leith, would destroy her.

Before being catapulted into this time, everything had been black-and-white. Either something was right or wrong, and differences were always clear-cut. Now? Did the end justify the means? Did she have the right to force Leith into the future for the survival of the human race, for the good of humanity? Probably. Did she want him to return with her? Definitely. Then why did she feel like the worst kind of traitor?

She'd have to make up her mind soon, though. Before she got too used to having him with her. Before she couldn't do what had to be done.

And what had to be done? He wouldn't go on his own, so she'd have to force him somehow. *Force him*. Even the thought made her feel dirty, and not just because it went against everything she'd ever been taught. He was . . . a friend. And you didn't force friends. *And is he more than a friend? Would you have mated with someone who was just a friend?*

Mated. Such a cold word for what had been explosive white light and searing blue flame. Even the iron will she'd used to survive a loveless childhood, to forge a successful business out of women's needs, couldn't hold back her memories of Leith. The warm, salty taste of his skin, the slick glide of smooth muscles and hard flesh across her body, the scent of hot male, sex, and . . . the sweet perfume of a small yellow flower.

She had to distract her thoughts right now or risk everything by begging him to mate with her again. Either that or return to the hard floor and its beady-eyed inhabitants.

Fine. She'd start making plans. Relaxing into

239

him, she listened to his even breathing, knew he'd fallen asleep. OK, not tonight. She wouldn't make plans tonight. Maybe tomorrow.

A dark shadow leaped from the foot of the bed and disappeared through the open window. Ganymede. Had her small furry friend merely wandered into their rest-over room; was he a hitchhiker on time's endless highway? Or could there be a more sinister reason for the black cat's presence?

The brooding, starless night, combined with the cool breeze smelling of rain, was putting her in a fanciful mood. She needed the bright sunlight of morning to get her back on track.

Leith would be just a man, one her world desperately needed. Everything would seem reasonable then. Ganymede would be just a stray cat, one she'd hate to leave behind, but just a cat.

She edged closer to Leith and stared at the curtains blowing softly in the night breeze. *Just a man? Never.*

Leith climbed out of the taxi and stared at the castle while Fortune paid the taxi driver. At least by tomorrow they'd have more money. He'd given Mary's check to Blade, and Blade had promised he'd have money for Leith by tonight.

He heard the taxi pull away and walked toward the door without waiting for Fortune to join him. He didn't want her to see his face, his pain. The powers asked much of him if they expected him to tear open the healing wounds of Glencoe day after day. But if he must do so to return to Scotland, so be it.

An Original Sin

He heard Fortune's running steps, and then she was beside him, tucking her arm through his. "We have all day, remember?"

Her laughter washed away his dour thoughts. She brought with her the present—a sunny day with a clear blue sky, a green stretch of lawn dotted with live oak trees.

If he never returned to Scotland, could he find peace here? He was stuck in this time, if Fortune's theory was right, because he'd never go back to the hotel room with her.

He cast her a sideways glance and caught her watching him. She smiled up at him. Yes, he'd always miss Scotland, and yes, there'd always be a feeling of things left unfinished. But if Fortune stayed . . .

What if Fortune was wrong? What if, in the middle of the night with her body warm beside him, she suddenly disappeared? He shivered, a cool breeze trailing over his skin. Clenching his fists, he rejected the idea. It wouldn't happen. But what if it did?

Ignoring the doorbell, he raised his fists to pound on the massive wooden door. He needed to beat on something, and the door was convenient. But he was cheated of the satisfaction as the door swung open before he could touch it.

Stephanie. Her gaze swept slowly over his body. He felt the urge to place his hands protectively over his manhood. He'd met women like her, and even enjoyed a few, but it had been like mating with a she-wolf—exciting if you liked being eaten alive. His manhood indicated no interest in repeating the experience.

Fortune leaned into his side and smiled at Stephanie. "Could you tell Mary we're here?"

"Umm." She licked her lips and dragged her gaze from Leith. "That's okay. You can come in. Mary's expecting you." She stopped and blinked. "You brought your cat?"

Leith frowned. By unspoken agreement, they'd ignored Ganymede as he'd leaped into the taxi with them. Manipulated by a cat. *A cat*? Suspicion again poked at him. Ganymede's appearance had been so convenient, his tenaciousness in staying with them so determined. Ganymede stared at him with large, guileless eyes, or as guileless as any cat's eyes could be.

"We canna leave him home." *Truer than ye know.* "He's part of our family, and would feel insulted." *Family*?

"Whatever floats your boat, I suppose."

He could hear the shrug in her voice . . . and the amusement. The sudden fierce flare of protectiveness toward his "family" surprised him. The sound of footsteps kept him from an examination of his feelings.

"There you are." Mary Campbell pulled off the gloves she wore and stuffed them in the pocket of her jeans. She grasped Leith's hand warmly and smiled at Fortune. "I was just working with my plants. The gardener does most of the tough stuff, but I like to putter around." Still holding Leith's hand, she led him toward the stairs. "I have to confess to being nosy. I couldn't wait to see what you'd written, so I took a peek." She squeezed his hand. "Marvelous. Absolutely marvelous."

Releasing his hand, she paused at the bottom of

the stairs and turned to face him. "I've decided to take full advantage of your time here, Leith. I don't want just a bare-bones list of events. I want everything." She flung her hands in a wide arc. "People's emotions. How did they feel during the massacre, afterward? And the consequences. How did the massacre affect the lives of ordinary people? Can you do it?"

"Aye." *By ripping out my heart and soul.*

"Good, good." She bent down to brush soil from the knees of her jeans. "You'll be happy to know the mystery of the ice-cream man is solved. I talked to a few neighbors after you left. Carol Davis said he stopped by her house right after her husband had open-heart surgery. She was feeling pretty worried, and before she knew what was happening she'd told the ice-cream man everything. He gave her a free cone along with some advice that calmed her right down. Same thing happened when Joan Carlson's little boy fell out of a tree and broke his leg. The ice-cream man was right there to help. Strange that I've never seen him. But no matter how many good deeds he's done, he'll still have to answer to me for the mess he made of my lawn."

Satisfied no dirt remained on her jeans, she smiled at Fortune and Leith. "Well, have a good day with your work, and lunch will be at noon." She turned just before leaving the room. "Oh, I almost forgot. I borrowed several books from the library that you might need for research. I thought you'd want to find out what happened years later, get a wider historical perspective on the whole thing. I think I left them on the couch." For the first time, she seemed to realize Stephanie stood

Nina Bangs

watching them. "Come along, Stephanie. You can help me with my plants."

The expression on Stephanie's face as she followed Mary from the room didn't bode well for the plants.

Deep in his own thoughts of wounds he must probe to satisfy Mary's desire for "emotion," Leith trailed Fortune up the winding stairs. But even those thoughts couldn't stop his gaze from following the tantalizing sway of her hips. And so when she suddenly stumbled, fell forward, and braced her hands on the step above her, he found himself at eye level with that most intriguing part of her body, her nicely rounded bottom. Instinctively, he reached out with both hands to steady that bottom. Then, of course, he had to smooth his fingers over each wondrous curve to make sure it had suffered no damage.

With a startled gasp, Fortune straightened, then promptly fell backward.

Leith caught her and pulled her tightly against him. A part of his body that was always alert to possibilities swelled in anticipation. " 'Tis lucky I was here to catch ye."

"I was fine until you grabbed me."

He didn't imagine the slight breathlessness of her voice, and for all her outraged words, she didn't move away from him.

"I dinna need thanks. 'Tis part of a warrior's calling to save clumsy women who canna go up or down steps wi'out tripping." Leaning down, he gently kissed the side of her neck where her pulse pounded a rapid beat. He breathed in her scent of warm woman and—

"Clumsy women!"

She turned in his embrace to glare up at him with blue eyes sparking danger, and full lips pursed in anger. So close. So tempting. "Mayhap *clumsy* isna the right word." If he leaned a little closer, he could touch those lips with his—

"It's these stupid stairs." She scowled at him as though he were personally responsible for crafting each step. "They're narrow. They're winding. They're dumb. Who in their right mind would build stairs like these?"

Her words momentarily diverted his thoughts from her lips. "Men who had to defend this castle from enemies. Narrow, winding stairs allowed a man to protect himself from any who tried to climb them."

"Right. I should've known. Everything in your time comes back to violence."

Backing down a step, he stared up at her. "Ye dinna find much to admire about my time, lass." *Ye dinna find much to admire about me.*

An emotion he couldn't identify flickered in her gaze, then disappeared. "Leith, I come from six hundred years in your future. Everything in our lives is different. How can I admire what I don't understand?"

"There is one thing that hasna changed." Reaching up, he pulled her down to him and covered her mouth with his. He kissed her deeply, hungrily. There was no gentleness in his kiss, only the savage need welling in him, the need to prove his time had something hers would never have, that *he* had something her time would never have.

Surprised, he realized she met him with the

same urgency. Her tongue tangled with his, searching, drawing the very breath from him. And as her fingers clasped the back of his head, pulling him closer, he thought she'd made a fitting mate for a warrior, a woman who'd stand beside her man and not behind him.

The shock of the thought made him pull back to stare at her. He knew he must wear the same glazed expression as Fortune. Her lips swollen from his kiss and the soft glow in her eyes made him groan with his need to take more, but he must stop now. It would not do to tumble down these stairs a second time.

He smoothed back several curls that had fallen across her forehead. "Mayhap these stairs are haunted, lass."

"Haunted?" Her breathy reply sounded bemused.

"Aye. Haunted by all the lusty warriors who followed fair maidens up these steps, watching the wondrous sway of their—"

"You mean all the dirty old men who groped fair maidens on these steps and got knocked on their behinds for their trouble. Now I understand who's tripping me. It's the spirits of all those lechers who cracked their skulls when they hit the bottom step. Served them right."

Her smile lit up his heart and scared the bloody hell out of him. " 'Tis certain ye'd ne'er choose to live in my time."

She still smiled, but her gaze had turned serious, assessing. "Only if my life depended on it, Leith."

"Aye." He didn't understand his stab of disappointment. After all, he'd expected no other answer. And he'd never ask her to suffer the primitiveness of his life. So why . . .

She sighed. "We'd better get some work done." Turning, she continued up the stairs and into the study. Glancing at the couch, she made an impatient sound. "Mary must've put the library books somewhere else. We'll need them to get the big picture. Why don't you do a little exploring on the computer while I go downstairs and hunt up those books?"

"I dinna know how." He kept his tone even, unemotional, and tried to quell the strange hurt. She wouldn't expect him to understand modern machines, but he couldn't help his feeling of inadequacy. He didn't belong here. Lord, let him return to Scotland soon. *Even if it means never seeing Fortune again?* He realized he wasn't sure.

Hunching her shoulders, she rubbed the back of her hand across her eyes, then smiled up at him. "Sorry, of course you don't. How could you? But you can learn. Why don't I show you how to get on the Internet, and you can do some surfing while I go down and get Mary to find those books for me."

"Aye." He'd seen the many things one could learn about on the " 'Net," although it resembled no net he'd ever seen. " 'Twould keep me amused." Like a child. Was that how she thought of him? A primitive child to be kept amused while the adult did the really important work? He ran his fingers through his hair. He must stop being so sensitive. She'd meant only to be thoughtful. "Thank you, Fortune."

Her brilliant smile rewarded him. "Here." She

247

beckoned him to sit beside her as she showed him what he needed to know.

Several minutes later he had the basics, and she rose to leave the room. "When I get back we can go over what we covered yesterday. Since we've already done an outline of the massacre, layering in the emotion and other details should be easier."

He could tell her the story would never get easier for him.

She'd barely left the room before he'd turned eagerly back to the computer. Where should he start—history, science? Perhaps he should start with something simple.

Downstairs, Fortune hunted fruitlessly for the books. She didn't see Mary, but she did find Stephanie grimacing as she washed soil from her hands.

Fortune grinned. "Escaped garden duty, I see."

Stephanie sighed and offered her a glimmer of a smile. "Plants hate me. I touch them, and they shrivel up and die."

Fortune stared at her. That faint smile . . . Stephanie seemed familiar, but she didn't know why. Must be her imagination.

They were alone. With no one around, Fortune could ask the question eating at her. There was no need for politeness. "Stephanie, if you love Michael, why do you look at Leith like he's your favorite dessert?"

Stephanie's gaze turned cautious. "Who said I loved Michael? We have an . . . arrangement. We'll have a kind of modern marriage of convenience."

Surprised, Fortune stared at her. "Why?"

248

"My name. It goes back generations, and every generation has passed it on with pride."

"So?"

"It's my turn now. I'm the last of our line, and it's up to me to make sure the name continues."

First Leith and now Stephanie. How could anyone be obsessed with a name?

"Michael understands. He's agreed I can keep my own last name after marriage. And every child I have will understand the importance of carrying on my name. In return, I'll give Michael an intelligent, glamorous wife who'll further his career."

Fortune thought of the millions of women in her time who'd kill for the love of a man. Her horror must've shown because Stephanie looked defensive.

"I have an obligation to the family name."

"Is there a man you really love, Stephanie?"

Surprised, Fortune watched Stephanie's eyes fill with tears.

"Yes, but . . . I can't marry him."

"Does he love you?"

Stephanie nodded as a tear slid down her cheek. "But he's sterile. The family name would die with me."

Fortune absorbed her bitter stab of envy—that here was a woman free to marry the man she loved—and her anger that Stephanie chose to reject her love.

In her need to influence Stephanie, she put her hand on the other woman's arm. Stephanie didn't move away.

"Don't do this. Your family name won't keep you warm on a cold winter night. Your family name won't comfort or hold you during the hard times."

"But my name is—"

"A name is *nothing*." Fortune tightened her grip on Stephanie's arm. "When you're old with nothing but memories, would you rather remember your name or a lifetime spent with the man you loved? Choose love, Stephanie. It's too precious to throw away."

"You . . . you sound like you've had a lot of experience."

Fortune knew her smile was bitter. "A lifetime."

"But you have Leith now."

"Yes, I have Leith now." *But I still don't have love, will never have love*.

Stephanie gazed at her with uncertainty. "I'll . . . I'll think about it."

"Follow your heart, Stephanie." Strangely embarrassed by her outburst, Fortune resumed her search for Mary and the books.

A short while later, carefully watching each step she took, Fortune hurried up the stairs. Finding the books had taken longer than she'd expected.

Had Leith missed her? Would she find him pacing the floor, anxious for her return?

She didn't know whether to feel relieved or insulted when she found his attention still riveted to the monitor. What could hold his concentration so completely that he didn't know she'd entered the room? Maybe he'd discovered information about Glencoe. Moving up behind him, she peered over his shoulder.

"Oh!" She clamped her hand over her mouth and resisted the urge to fling her other hand across her eyes.

"What?" He glanced at her over one broad shoulder.

"That . . . that . . ." Her vocabulary didn't include words to describe what he had on the screen.

"Aye, 'tis interesting." He returned his attention to the screen. "Although I dinna know if I could enjoy making love in that position. Mayhap when I was younger I could have—"

"I can't believe . . ." Her gaze trailed down the graphic description beneath the picture. "How . . . ? Where . . . ?"

"I typed in *sex*." He turned to face her, his eyes dancing with amusement. "Ye must remember that primitive humans dinna spell words of more than four letters, and I couldna think of a more interesting short word. Ye look bonny when ye blush, lass."

She reached around him to remove the objectionable picture, and he gently but firmly grasped her wrist. The easy strength in his grip reminded her of what he was, what he could do if he chose. Something in her expression must have mirrored her thoughts because his smile died. He dropped her wrist.

"Ye dinna need to remind me, lass. Ye think me a barbarian, and mayhap ye're right, but I find nothing to embarrass me in a picture of a man and woman making love."

While he spoke, Fortune read the rest of the page. "Have you read this?"

A glimmer of his smile returned. "Barbarians dinna read. They just look at pictures."

Hmm. She had to finish that last sentence. Scrolling down to the next page, she continued

reading. *Interesting. Outrageous, but interesting.*
"You know, I can use this stuff."

"How?"

She couldn't mistake his hopeful tone. Making
note of the website, she clicked off the Internet.
Waving him out of her chair, she set up the page
for today's writing.

The intense stab of desire when she thought of
field-testing with Leith some of the things she'd
read about had caught her by surprise. She'd tried
so hard to be rational, to reason away the roiling
need he stirred just by being near, but no amount
of logic meant a thing where her body was concerned.

"I've never even thought of some of that stuff. I
bet I could program my men to—"

His swift exhalation spoke of disgust. "And this
is the world ye would take me to, where a man is
nothing but a thing to be programmed? What
would they do to me, lass, when I didna perform
the way they wished?"

Surprised, she glanced up at him. "We're not
talking real men here. There's no emotion involved."

"If ye think that, then ye dinna know yer own sex
verra well. For a woman to find satisfaction with
a man that isna real, she must have a fantasy. She
must picture a man growing hard beneath only *her*
touch, moaning only *her* name as he spills his seed,
needing only *her*. The physical act wouldna be
enough."

He was starting to make her mad. Turning to
face him, she placed her hands on her hips. "Oh,

and I suppose you know all there is to know about women?"

"I know a great deal more about women than ye know about men." His frown had disappeared, and the glitter in his eyes suggested he was enjoying their argument.

She tilted her head and glared up at him. "I wouldn't count on it. For example, I can tell you from personal experience the physical act is quite enough." When had she become such a liar? *He* was her only personal experience.

He stared at her intently. "Ye think mounting one of yer fakes could make ye scream yer pleasure the way ye did when ye lay beneath me? I dinna believe it."

She didn't believe it either, but now that she'd taken her stand, nothing would make her recant. *Stubbornness*. Her many flaws continued to amaze her.

"Don't get me wrong, Leith. You're a very attractive man, and I'm sure that had a lot to do with my pleasure. But I certainly didn't feel an emotional involvement." *Right*. If she was going to lie, she might as well tell a big, juicy one.

Dark color gathered along his cheekbones. He looked angry. She immediately felt more cheerful.

"I suppose ye could have mated wi' Michael and enjoyed it as well?"

Don't say it. Don't even think about saying it. She said it. "Possibly." Had that word come from her mouth? How could an out-and-out lie feel so exciting?

His eyes narrowed to stormy green slits. "Aye.

He could whisper sweet numbers in yer ear. Excite ye wi' tales of logic."

She smiled sweetly. "Perhaps." Her enjoyment escalated in direct proportion to his anger. That said something about her character she didn't want to examine right now.

His voice was low, hoarse with emotion. "Take Michael back wi' ye. He would fit in yer world. He would ne'er grow emotional, ne'er become violent. Ye'd be perfect for each other."

But he'd never make me feel like this. She felt she might explode with the joy of battle, the undercurrent of fear. He looked as though he wanted to wrap his hands around her neck and—

The sound of footsteps swung her gaze to the door.

"Sorry to interrupt your . . . academic discussion, but lunch is ready." Stephanie gave Leith a long glance before leaving the room.

"Well, that was a productive morning." Surprisingly, Fortune meant it. She rose and stretched. She felt amazingly energized, and hadn't the slightest idea why. Yes, she did. As strange as it might seem, she'd had a wonderful time arguing with Leith. And best of all, she'd won! She almost floated down the stairs on a fluffy cloud of triumph.

While she soared high on a cumulus cloud, Leith rumbled along on a black thunderhead of displeasure. She gloried in that displeasure because . . . because . . . Pausing before entering the kitchen, she considered why she was so happy. His anger had focused on her attitude toward their mating and Michael. All of which pointed to a bit of jealousy. Why should his jealousy make her happy? They didn't have a future together, so what was the point? The point was that she no longer understood herself, and that was a dangerous situation.

"Do ye intend to stand here all day?"

His snarled question propelled her into the room. Maybe he wasn't jealous at all. Maybe she'd just pricked his overblown male ego. "Forgive me, Your Nastiness," she muttered as she purposely took a seat next to Michael.

Stephanie sat on Michael's other side while Leith strode around the table and sat directly across from Fortune. From this strategic spot, he glared into her eyes. *Oh, great, nothing like a nice, relaxing meal among friends.*

"I'm sorry I wasted so much of your research time this morning." Mary's cheerful apology went unnoticed among the darts zinging across the table.

Fortune studied her salad, then carefully stabbed a piece of lettuce and brought it to her mouth. She glanced at Leith. *This is you.* She smiled.

Leith picked up his knife and cut a piece of tomato with controlled ferocity. Holding up the mangled remains, he glared at it before popping it into his mouth. Then he smiled at her.

Message received.

"So?" Mary encouraged. "What did you learn this morning?"

Leith pushed aside his salad and stared morosely at his sandwich. "I learned the MacDonalds are heartless users who dinna care who they hurt• to get what they want."

Fortune almost choked on her lettuce. Coughing discreetly, she abandoned her attempt to eat the salad. "I discovered the Campbells have overactive hormones and overdeveloped egos."

Leith didn't deign to comment. He methodically ate his sandwich with the same enthusiasm he'd reserve for chewing on a cardboard box.

"All fascinating information, I'm sure, but what did you learn of academic interest?" Michael, impeccably dressed in perfectly creased slacks and an understated neutral shirt and tie, smiled at her encouragingly.

She wondered why he didn't cause so much as a ripple in her yum-yum index of attractive males. "You're right. It was just an interesting sidebar. We didn't get as much done as we'd like because of a slight disagreement over Internet research sources. Some of the graphics we found weren't very pertinent to our topic." Gleefully, she noticed Leith's slight flush as he concentrated on eating his pie. Humble pie, she hoped.

Michael leaned closer as he offered her an understanding glance out of brilliant blue eyes. Brilliant blue eyes with the depth of a rain puddle.

"Feel free to call on me if you need any technical assistance. I can fix any problem." His expression suggested he could fix problems in a variety of areas.

Fortune tried to ignore what sounded like a low growl from across the table. "I'll remember that." She leaned back as Michael swayed closer. The growl grew louder.

"Michael's taught me a lot about computers, so

yell if you need help." Stephanie's offer was a welcome tension breaker.

"Do ye hear music, Fortune?" Leith had stopped growling.

"I think . . ." She smiled. "Yes! It sounds like . . . Elvis."

"Elvis?" Michael sounded puzzled. "No one plays Elvis in this house. We have a few Beatles CDs, but that's—"

"The ice-cream man! It's the ice-cream man." Her happy relief surprised Fortune. She hadn't realized how worried she'd been over that stupid truck.

Michael's smile was charming and sincere. "Such childlike enthusiasm for ice cream is delightful."

Fortune knew that if she decided to take Michael back with her, she could hand him over to the rest of her world without even a thought of possessing him herself. But even though his attitude would fit perfectly in her time, she didn't want to take him back. There was something—

"Have ye seen Ganymede?"

Fortune didn't understand the urgency in Leith's voice.

"No. I suppose he's still outside—"

Leith pushed his chair back so quickly it fell over as he rose to his feet and strode toward the front door.

Fortune rose and ran to catch him while the rest of the family followed at a more leisurely pace.

"Leith." She grabbed his arm in an attempt to slow him down. "What's the hurry?"

He threw her a worried glance. "Dinna try to stop me, Fortune. I must save the ice-cream man."

Chapter Twelve

Leith took in the scene at a glance.

The ice-cream truck, dented and scraped, was parked in front of the castle. Ganymede crouched on the roof, his head hanging over the edge as he glared at the man inside. Leith recognized the man's expression of fatalistic acceptance. He'd seen it worn by comrades he'd fought beside in battle, men who knew their end was near.

Leith's instincts had kept him alive longer than many a friend, so he didn't hesitate to listen to them now. He didn't bother to shout as he raced across the lawn, praying he'd reach the truck in time.

An arm's span from the vehicle, a blast of heat almost knocked him backward. He could see the truck taking on a faint red glow. If he hesitated, all would be lost. Leaping high in the air, he scooped

Ganymede off the roof and, mindless of claws that ripped at his exposed arms, stumbled away from the truck.

Wasting no time in thank-yous, the driver pulled from the curb with a screech of tires. As the truck chugged into the distance, he heard Elvis bemoaning "Suspicious Minds."

Breathing hard, Leith transferred his attention to a suddenly quiet Ganymede, and looked into the eyes of . . . His breath stopped; his hands began to shake so badly he almost dropped the cat. But he'd honed his courage in a multitude of battles, and so he held tightly, daring Ganymede to vent the fury, the unspeakable power he'd glimpsed in those eyes.

Leith met the cat's gaze, then felt the animal relax. *Safe.* He didn't know how, but he recognized that the danger was over—for the ice-cream man, for himself. He dropped the cat to the ground from hands that seemed to have lost all feeling. Ganymede immediately sat down next to him and proceeded to groom himself. Leith allowed himself a shaky laugh.

Leith heard running footsteps and turned to face Fortune. The other members of the family hadn't bothered to come outside once they saw that Leith was only getting his cat.

"What . . . what happened?" Uncertain, she picked Ganymede off the ground and cuddled him under her chin. His loud purr announced the return of his good humor.

"I saved a man's life." He stared intently at Ganymede.

She smiled. "Aren't you exaggerating a little?"

He watched her gaze reach his arms, and her horrified expression satisfied him completely. "Oh, Leith! Your arms." She held Ganymede away from her and scowled at him. "Did you do that, you bad kitty?"

Leith could almost imagine regret in those amber eyes. Then again, the whole thing had been so unbelievable he didn't know what to think about the bloody cat.

"I think he's sorry, Leith." Ganymede purred his agreement. "Let's get something on those scratches."

He couldn't help it; he laughed. And if the laugh held a bit of hysteria, who could blame him? He'd looked into the eyes of death, and Fortune was worrying about a few scratches.

"What're you laughing about?"

He shook his head. "I didna know driving an ice-cream truck could be so dangerous."

"What really happened, Leith?" She stared at him, her glance searching.

He looked away. Would she even believe him? Did he even know himself? "We can talk about it tonight. 'Tis past time we went back to work."

Following Fortune up the castle steps, he realized he looked forward to the work. No matter how painful, he understood Glencoe. There was no mystery, no danger, only undying regret.

But Ganymede presented a different problem. If he told Fortune, would she dismiss his tale as the imaginings of a man who came from a time when superstition ran rampant? And if she did accept his story, what then?

With Ganymede still in her arms, Fortune led

Leith into the bathroom next to where they worked. Setting the cat down, she opened the cabinet door and pulled what she needed from inside. Leith sat on the edge of the tub and waited for her.

Finally ready, she turned to him. "Hold out your arms so I can clean those scratches."

While she worked, Leith kept a wary eye on Ganymede, who seemed interested in the proceedings. He felt her turn his arm over and heard her small gasp. He looked up to see her suddenly pale face, then down to note the deep cut on the inside of his arm. As he held the arm up, blood flowed from the open wound down to his elbow. From there it dripped onto the floor, where it made a jagged pattern on the gray tile. He noted the depth of the cut dispassionately. He'd had much worse.

A sudden movement caught his attention. Amazed, he watched Ganymede scramble behind the toilet, where he enthusiastically and noisily threw up.

He glanced up at Fortune with a wry smile. "Our wee friend doesna seem to appreciate his own handiwork."

Fortune gave Ganymede barely a glance before returning her attention to Leith's arm. "More likely one of the poor birds he caught in the garden didn't agree with him. Serves the little savage right. Look what he did to your arm."

Leith basked in the glow of her concern. From the way she frowned as she dabbed at his cut, he thought that it pained her more than it did him. Many women had shown interest in a particular part of his body, but none had worried overmuch about his health. He could grow used to Fortune's cosseting.

Fortune took pride in always having a reason for what she did, but she could think of none to explain why she slid the tips of her fingers down the length of the inside of his arm. She remembered the strength of his arms as he'd held her safe against the night. Her fingers paused, then traced the ridge of a scar that ran across his arm near his elbow. She winced, imagining his agony, wishing she'd been there to ease his pain.

When she reached his wrist, she followed the pale blue line of a vein. He clenched his fist and the vein stood out, a thing too fragile to sustain life. Her fingers lingered on the vein, feeling somehow connected to the hot flow of blood that gave Leith life, that made him vulnerable. Real.

On a level she'd never explored, she recognized his vulnerability—to painful memories, to his feelings of powerlessness. She recognized his vulnerability because it was her own. For a moment she closed her eyes against the shock of that realization. Across six hundred years of differences, they shared one thing—a common pain.

She opened her eyes to meet Leith's fiery gaze. His green eyes glowed with the searing heat of rock flung from the heart of a volcano—primal, dangerous, inevitable.

Fortune jerked her fingers from his skin. She could almost hear the sizzle, feel the blistering heat.

"If ye touch me like that, lass, I canna answer for

my actions." He held her captive with his unblinking stare.

"I . . . I was only touching your arm." How did he manage to make her feel so defensive, unsure?

"Ye touched much more than that, and ye know it well." His husky voice spoke of dark nights, tangled sheets, and bodies entwined in passion's eternal dance.

She took a deep breath, gathering her wits. "I can't imagine why anything I'd do would affect you. You already think of me as a slave trader." With unsteady fingers, she busied herself with putting away the peroxide. Pulling an adhesive bandage from a box, she almost flung it at him. "Here. Put this on." She'd be damned if she'd touch him again.

But by the power of the universe, how she wanted to, with a need that gnawed at her resolve with ever-increasing ferocity. When he was near she couldn't think, couldn't plan, could only feel . . . and want.

He smiled grimly. "Ye're a caring, beautiful woman, and sometimes I think it wouldna be so verra bad to be yer slave." He reached up and cupped the side of her face in the warmth of his rough hand. "But only for ye, no others." His whisper feathered along the length of her neck, and she swallowed against the strangely intimate touch. "In the deepest night, slave and mistress become one, bound by a need that has only one end."

"Stop it!" She backed away from him. "Just stop it. Words don't change anything. What I want doesn't matter. Only the continuation of the human race matters." This was starting to sound like a memorized speech, but she must keep saying it in order to combat his quiet seduction. She knew what he was trying to do. He understood the power of physical desire. If she gave in now, she'd keep giving in, and he wouldn't have to worry about her scheming to take him back to her time. But she couldn't turn her back on her duty. *Duty*. A word she'd grown to hate.

"Let's get back to work." Who cared if he knew she was in full retreat? His threat was too potent, her defenses too weak.

He threw her a knowing smile and nodded. "Ye can get ready while I clean up Ganymede's wee accident."

Relieved that she'd have a moment alone to pull herself together, she rushed from the bathroom and settled down at the computer. She didn't quite know what had happened back there, but it had scared her. That didn't make sense, though. She'd already lost her virginity when she'd mated with Leith. What more was there to lose? *Your heart, your soul*.

She made a face at the monitor and saw it reflected back at her. Now she was being melodramatic. She'd formed a tenuous relationship with Leith, but that was only natural because they needed each other. Yes, he made her heart pound and her mouth go dry, but that was physical desire. She could handle that. OK, she got a little emotional thinking about never seeing him again, but she'd get over it. The face staring back from the monitor looked doubtful.

"I'm ready, lass." His voice startled her, and she swung to stare into eyes that promised a readiness for whatever she wished. She wished for a cold shower and a few hours away from his sensual assault, but she wouldn't get it, so she'd better pull herself together fast.

"Fine." She didn't trust herself to say more. Turning the computer on, she tried to block out everything except the words on the screen. *Problem*. Every word took her back to Leith—his life, his world, his pain.

Gradually she immersed herself in the events of Glencoe and relaxed. In between her questions, Leith thumbed through one of Mary's research books.

Feeling good about the day's work, she was almost ready to call it quits when she sensed a sudden change in Leith. She'd just asked her last question and sat with fingers poised over the keys to type in his answer. No answer came. Puzzled, she glanced over to where he sat on the leather couch.

He stared down at the open book, his fingers gripping the edges like a space traveler who feared he would float off into the dark reaches of the universe if he let go. She couldn't see his eyes, but his jaw was clenched and the lines of his face were a study in savage despair.

"My God, Leith, what's the matter?" She stood and quickly moved to his side.

" 'Tis nothing ye need to fash yerself about." He didn't look up at her, didn't move.

"Don't shut me out. We're in this together. Whatever it is, we'll work it out." Tentatively, she put her arm across his shoulder, expecting him to flinch away from her touch.

Instead, he leaned into her, and she tightened her grip as though she could hold him afloat in whatever dark sea he struggled.

"There are some things that canna be worked out." He closed the book with a finality that said louder than words that the subject was closed. " 'Tis time to go home." As though ashamed of his momentary weakness, he pulled away from her and rose, then picked up a sleeping Ganymede and strode from the room.

Fortune glanced at the book he'd flung to the couch, then picked it up. She remembered the page he'd been reading, and this was one time she didn't intend to let him play a silent game with her. He needed to talk, even if he didn't realize it. Maybe in 1700 it was considered strong to bottle up emotion, but in 2300 it was considered unhealthy. Besides, she had to admit, she couldn't stand the agony she'd glimpsed in his eyes before he walked away.

Like a nervous filly, she'd danced and pawed around his silence all night. What could he tell her that she'd understand? What did he *want* her to understand? Perhaps it would be best for everyone if she simply thought that, unlike her perfect men, he had moods, and this was one of his moods.

He crawled into bed and, with a mumbled goodnight, turned his back to her. He felt the bed give as she climbed in beside him. Lying completely still, he hoped she'd think him asleep.

"Do you mind if I read for a while?"

"No." Perhaps one-word answers would discourage her.

Minutes later he began to relax. Evidently engrossed in her reading, she'd forgotten him.

"What did you say your brother's name was, Leith?"

The question cut him like the slash of a sword, and he realized what book she must be reading. He could pretend he was asleep, but he doubted she'd accept his playacting.

"Hugh." Even saying his brother's name aloud hurt.

"It says here that a Hugh Campbell who took part in the Glencoe massacre died in 1716. Is that your brother?"

"Yes." He spoke through gritted teeth. Would the woman never leave him alone?

"Is that what upset you today?"

"Yes." She was like one of those damnable mosquitoes this Texas had in overabundance, buzzing in his ear, defying every effort to get rid of it until the only recourse was to bury his head under the covers. He suspected even that wouldn't work with Fortune. She'd simply follow him with her endless questions.

"You saw the date of his death. Did that bother you so much?"

"Yes."

"OK, I can understand that—"

"Can ye? Can ye really understand the feeling when ye see the date someone ye loved died?" Unable to control his churning emotions, he turned over and found himself face-to-face with her wide-eyed concern. "I dinna think ye can. All yer loved ones havena even been born yet."

"I have no loved ones." Her statement was calm,

emotionless. "But we're not talking about me. I'd started to say there has to be more to it than you're telling me. I saw the look on your face this afternoon. Talk to me, Leith."

There was nothing for it; he must tell her something, even if in the telling he tore a secret part from himself. "Hugh and I havena spoken since Glencoe. He thinks me a traitor to the clan, and he has every right to think so."

"I don't understand."

"Loyalty to clan is everything. 'Tis yer family, and ye're expected to give yer life for it if need be."

"So?"

She looked at him from puzzled eyes, and he clenched his hands into fists as his frustration mounted. How could he make someone who'd never known family loyalty understand the scope of his betrayal? "I betrayed my clan when I helped Ian MacDonald escape into the hills during the massacre. Hugh said afterward that I wasna a brother to him, nor would I ever be again."

Her eyes were deep pools of sympathy as she reached out to touch his face. Damn it, he didn't want her pity. Roughly he pushed her hand away. "I gave aid to my clan's sworn enemy, and nothing can change that—not time, not regret."

"You showed mercy. There's nothing wrong—"

He was breathing as though he'd run a race. "I must return so I can make peace with Hugh before . . . He is all I have."

"You have me." She looked as though she couldn't believe what she'd said.

Her words hung between them. He watched her swallow and followed the smooth line of her neck down to the soft swell of her breast. His groin tightened, and he knew he could easily spend his emotion on her body. But he couldn't do that to her, to himself. She must remain separate from his memories of Scotland. He didn't know why that was important, but it was. Besides, he doubted she'd been offering her body.

"Thank ye, lass." He forced a smile, and she relaxed. "I dinna feel like sleeping. Would ye like to go somewhere wi' me?"

"Now?" She glanced at the clock.

"It isna so late." He slid from the bed, then playfully pulled the covers from her. "Come wi' me."

She smiled up at him. "Sure. Why not?"

She glanced up at the Cajun Café sign with its erratic pattern of burned-out bulbs, then down at the people crowding into the small building, and felt the first twinge of unease. "I don't know about this, Leith. These people look kind of . . ."

He held the door open for her. "They wouldna fit in wi' people like Michael and Stephanie. Is that what ye mean?"

She gulped as the largest human she'd ever seen stalked over to Leith. He reminded her of a Quintian mountain-gross, an angry mountain-gross, an ugly, angry mountain-gross.

"You and me, we still got somethin' to settle, man." He spit on the floor. "But I'll decide the time and place. Just so you know it's comin'." He grinned at Leith.

Fortune couldn't stop herself. "Aggressive feelings are bad for your cardiovascular system. I'd sign up for sensitivity training, if I were you. And you really need to do something about your oral hygiene. Bad teeth can affect your whole—"

The human mountain-gross shifted his attention to her and spit on the floor again to punctuate the transition. "This your old lady?"

"Old lady!" She should thank her lucky stars that cosmic forces hadn't just picked a name out of a hat for their chosen male. She could picture a world populated by . . . Of course, it would never happen, because no woman would mate with . . . *Wrong.* She knew some women who would mate with a Nodern fizzle-gopper if one would stand still long enough. "*Old* is an insensitive term. *Mature* is the accepted description, and I won't be mature for another hundred years."

The human mountain-gross returned his attention to Leith. "I feel sorry for you, man." He walked away.

Now why would he feel sorry for Leith? "Who was that person, and why did he sound so negative?"

She could see a smile tugging at Leith's lips, and for a moment she lost her train of thought in the contemplation of those lips, how they'd felt pressed against hers.

"His name is Bones, and he's the one I fought wi' on the night ye came to me at the lake."

"Oh." Then what were they doing here? She tried to push back her panic. "Let's get out of here before—"

"Lass, lass." His voice soothed as he smoothed his fingers over her clenched jaw. "Ye canna run from some things. Ye must stand and fight or feel less than a man."

270

"That's what I'm afraid of, getting back less than a man once that mountain-gross is finished with you." She hated the pleading sound of her voice.

His chuckle made light of her fear. "Ye dinna have much faith in me, lass, if ye think yon warrior can best me. What is a mountain-gross?"

"Never mind." He was hardheaded, obstinate, and she wanted to keep him safe so badly it hurt. So much for her staying emotionally uninvolved in this little cosmic quest.

"Yo! Over here." The sound of Blade's voice lowered her anxiety level somewhat. Gratefully, she followed Leith.

"Have a seat, little lady." Blade grinned up at her.

She frowned. If Blade's lopsided grin was any indication, he'd sipped a bit too much happy juice. They drank alcohol at home, but only in moderation. Everything at home was in moderation. *Moderately happy, moderately satisfied.*

Not like here, where everything had been breathtaking highs and lows. A kaleidoscope of brilliant colors as opposed to faded sepia shades. She knew which made her feel more alive.

Fortune cast a sideways glance at Leith, who'd seated himself next to her and was ordering something from a gum-chewing woman. He'd add brilliant color to her world, with its many shades of pale, but would he fade in the process? His babies would revitalize humanity, but would he survive to see it?

She stared for a long time at the large glass of amber liquid the woman put in front of her. One sniff assured her of its alcohol content. The glass was too large for her. She didn't have much tolerance for alcohol. In her other life, she would have demanded a smaller glass. *Moderation*.

But she wasn't in her other life. If she wanted to drink this whole glass, she could do it. Picking up the glass, she savored her sudden heady feeling of freedom. She took a greedy gulp of the liquid and sighed her satisfaction.

A short while later, she stared at the empty glass and tried not to giggle. She didn't know why she wanted to giggle, but who cared? She grinned at Blade. The grin felt sort of crooked, but she couldn't be bothered straightening it. "You know, the men here give me some great ideas for *my* men."

"Your men?" Lily leaned closer.

She almost grunted as Leith elbowed her sharply. Throwing him a resentful glance, she transferred her attention back to Lily and Blade. "I make men, but they're all pretty tame compared to the men here."

"You make *men*?" Both Lily and Blade watched her with rapt attention.

Leith wore a pained expression. What was his problem?

"Yep." She took a careful sip of the full glass of . . . beer the woman had plunked in front of her. "Perfect men. OK, I do make them with really big—Oomph!" She turned and glared at Leith. "How about keeping your elbow to yourself, mister."

Taking another gulp, she focused on Blade and Lily. Focusing was becoming a little hard. "Where was I?"

"The men with the really big oomphs," Lily offered.

"Oh, yeah. Other than that, my men are perfect." She frowned as she tried to prod her lethargic thought processes. "They're sorta boring, though." She brightened. "Except for Humongous Hoss. He doesn't say anything, but I guess when you have a two-foot penis you don't have to worry about small talk. I mean, you have your own built-in conversation piece." She leaned toward Lily. "Some women will buy anything. I made him as a joke, and would you believe, he's my biggest seller."

"Bloody hell!" Leith propped his elbows on the table and covered his eyes with one hand.

Fortune blinked. What was he muttering about? "I'll never understand. I mean, there's just so much you can use. But I guess some women have to have the biggest everything."

She sighed. "Anyway, the rest of my models are pretty ordinary. They always say the right things, do the right things. That can get kinda old after a while. Not much imagination in bed—" The rest of her comment was cut off when a large hand was placed over her mouth.

"Dinna listen to her. She's had a wee too much to drink."

Fortune pulled his hand from her mouth. What was he talking about? She felt great. She leaned away from him, and the world tilted. Leith pulled her to an upright position again.

Lily wore a puzzled expression. "Where're you from, honey?"

Suddenly Fortune felt maudlin. Tears sprang to her eyes and slid down her cheeks. "Far, far away.

I don't know if I can ever go home. Home is perfect. No one gets mad, no one fights, everyone follows the rules—"

Blade's snort interrupted her litany of praise. "Doesn't sound like much fun to me."

Fun? She blinked at him. Come to think of it, she didn't remember much fun in her life. Not like . . . She slid her gaze to Leith, then quickly away.

Her tears dried as fast as they'd started, and she smiled shakily. "Hey, if I can't go home then I don't have to worry about Leith being a slave—" Leith's hand was back. Glancing sideways, she noticed that all four of his eyes looked desperate.

" 'Tis time we went home, Fortune." He removed his hand and started to push back his chair.

"But we just got here. Why do—"

"Sit down, Leith." Blade's order cut her off in midwhine.

Suprisingly, Leith complied.

"OK, let's level with each other. There's something strange goin' on. Where are you guys really from? And don't give me that Tibet garbage."

Fortune felt too woozy to answer. Leith looked grim. Why did everyone look so serious?

Finally Leith relaxed, as though he'd made a decision. "I'm from Scotland. The Highlands. I canna return there, and I canna tell ye why." He paused and waited.

Blade nodded. "Go on."

"We dinna have . . . identification. Can ye help us?"

Lily's laugh was shaky. "Who'd you murder?"

"We did nothing wrong, ye ken."

Fortune found that the room stopped whirling when she focused on one object, so she concentrated on Leith's hand. Maybe she could figure out why he had the arm of his chair in a white-knuckled grip when she'd never felt so relaxed in her life.

Blade stared across the table at Leith. "Running?"

Leith nodded.

Fortune frowned. She guessed they were sort of running—from the past, the future. It was a shame they couldn't run away from their memories. There was something profound in that thought, if she could hold it long enough. She blinked. *Nope, gone.*

Maybe she should tell Blade about herself. "I'm from—"

No hand this time. Leith leaned over and kissed her. For a moment his body shielded her from Blade's view. "God's teeth, woman, hold yer tongue."

Deepening the kiss, she decided that would be hard. She'd never realized how essential the tongue was to a great kiss.

Leith broke the kiss with a groan. Fortune sat back, puzzled. Why had he stopped a perfectly good kiss?

He turned back to Blade. "Fortune is in this wi' me."

Blade and Lily exchanged glances; then Blade grinned. "OK, big guy, we'll see what we can do. You've been straight with us. Driving a taxi I meet lots of people. Learn to judge character pretty

275

good. I've liked you and the little lady since the first time I saw you."

Leith nodded, and Fortune decided that since there was a break in the conversation, she'd try to tell Blade and Lily about herself again. "I'm—"

"Fortune's a sculptor. 'Tis amazing what she can make."

Damned right. Fortune scowled. She'd never realized Leith had this annoying habit of interrupting people.

Lily turned an interested gaze on her. "That right? Hey, Caryn does a little of that. Why don't I see if I can get some stuff for you?"

The euphoria from her drink was wearing off, and Fortune didn't feel too well, but she could think more clearly. "I don't have enough money to pay—"

Lily waved a dismissive hand at her. "Don't sweat it. Just do me a sculpture of handsome here"—she nodded at a grinning Blade—"and that'll be payment enough."

"OK." Fortune *really* didn't feel well. She turned to Leith, but she didn't need to say anything.

" 'Tis time ye went home, Fortune."

She could only nod.

"We're heading out of here, too. We'll drop you at your place." Blade and Lily stood.

Fortune remembered Leith leading her to the taxi and helping her into the backseat. She remembered curling into a ball of misery with Leith's arms wrapped around her. She remembered him helping her into the house and into the bathroom, where she humiliated herself. That was all she remembered, but she decided it was quite enough for one night.

It was impossible to feel this bad and still be alive.

Fortune rolled over and moaned into her pillow. What had she done last night? What had she said? She remembered just enough to know she couldn't face Leith.

She sat up and looked at the time. They'd be late for work. She clasped both sides of her head with her hands, as though by doing so she might keep it from flying off.

"Ye look a wee bit pale, lass."

Turning her head carefully, she stared at Leith. How could he look so alive when she was at death's door? He'd drunk the same thing as she. Primitive stomachs must be lined with steel.

Then she saw what he held in his hand, and whatever blood still remained in her face dribbled down to her toes.

"I cooked ye breakfast."

His crooked smile of hopeful pride was endearing, but she couldn't, she just couldn't. "It looks . . . delicious, but I don't think I can put anything into my stomach right now."

He sat down on the bed beside her and placed the tray on the bedside table. "Ye'll feel much better if ye eat something. Trust me, lass. I know how ye feel." He reached out and gently pushed a strand of hair away from her face.

Something fluttered in her stomach, and it had nothing to do with her unwise drinking. Suddenly shy, she turned her face away. "I . . . I must look terrible."

277

"Aye, I did ask the powers to send me a shriveled crone so I wouldna be tempted, but I thought they'd forgotten."

She turned back to glare at him, and met the sparkle of humor in his gaze.

"I'm certain they've forgotten, because ye're still here." He fluffed her pillow up behind her, and she relaxed against it.

"What did I say last night, Leith?"

"Before or after ye danced on the table? 'Twas wondrously entertaining."

Groaning, she slapped at him. He caught her hand in his and slowly brought it to his lips. Her breath caught as she held his hot gaze. Gently his lips brushed the inside of her wrist. The flutter in her stomach grew, and she placed her other hand protectively over it.

Immediate concern filled his eyes. "Do ye feel sick, lass?"

She grasped the easy out. Nodding, she broke eye contact.

He put the tray on her lap. "Ye'll feel better once ye've eaten. 'Tis the empty stomach making ye feel poorly."

Picking up the juice, she took a careful sip. "I'll try. After all, who'd know better than you how to combat excesses?"

He grinned and helped himself to a piece of bacon. "Ye must toughen up, lass, if ye expect to live in this time."

She put the glass down and studied him. "You think we'll be here for a long time, don't you?"

His expression turned serious. "I dinna know. Ye think forces will send ye back as soon as ye convince a man to go wi' ye. I think I'll be sent back when I've done suitable penance." He shrugged. "Mayhap we're both wrong. Who can guess what the Fates have planned for us?"

Could he be right? No, she was sure why she'd been sent here. There could be no other reason. One thing still niggled at her consciousness, though. If she was supposed to bring Leith back with her, why hadn't she been sent directly to his time? Why had *he* been sent to this time? At first she'd believed this was a sort of halfway house, but now she wasn't sure. It would've saved a lot of wear and tear on everyone if cosmic forces had just sent Leith directly to the year 2300.

Her head hurt too much to think. Besides, if she were honest, she didn't want to consider anything right now that confused her. She was already confused enough by her feelings for Leith. "I'll eat quickly so we're not too late for work."

"Dinna hurry. I called Mary and told her we'd be late."

"OK, but it won't take me long—"

He placed his finger gently against her lips. "Shush. We must talk."

She stared up at his somber expression. "About what?"

"Ganymede."

"Ganymede?" Now would be a nice time to throw a tantrum. *I want to talk about us. Us!*

Instead, she stared at Leith with stoic resignation. *There can't be an us. Ever.*

Chapter Thirteen

*Did I blow it, or what? This is what I get for messin'
with humans. They're emotional time bombs. Least
little thing and they go off like fireworks on the
Fourth of July.*

*So what happens? I'm around them for a week—a
week, for cryin' out loud—and I start actin' like
them. You'd think a couple of thousand years
woulda made me a little smarter.*

*I take that back. Sure, I'm smart, but I have feel-
ings just like every other guy. OK, maybe not exactly
like every other guy.*

*Yeah, yeah, so I lost my temper with that ice-
cream jerk. And when Leith took me out of the action, well, it made me mad. That's when I made my
biggest mistake. I let him look into my eyes, and he
saw the real me. Major blip in my brain wave.*

I never have these problems with my other oper-

ations. Hey, it's hard to get emotional over a sand-storm.

Wonder what they'll do? Who gives a damn? I'm still the man in command. I'm hangin' in till the end. Every time they look around, I'll be there. Every time they open a door, I'll be there. Hmm, sounds sorta like a song title.

I still have a deadline. Only two more weeks to make it happen, but I'm gettin' close.

Then there's our I'm-so-dumb-I-don't-know-when-to-cut-and-run ice-cream man. He'll be back, and I want a piece of him.

I'm not gonna make it easy for Fortune and Leith. I'll sit right here on their bed while they decide what to do. Then I'll decide what I'm gonna do.

Leith read Fortune's reluctance to discuss Ganymede in her eyes. Maybe he should wait to talk about the cat.

But if he didn't think about Ganymede, then he'd be forced to think about Fortune—how she'd looked last night, her cheeks flushed and eyes sparkling, how even when she was sick as a dog he'd found her lovable. *Lovable.* He didn't want to think of love and Fortune in the same breath.

It would take no more than two weeks to finish his work for Mary; then he'd return to Scotland and fall in love with some Highland lass, just as he'd always planned. For the first time in his life, the thought of a Highland lass in his bed brought no feeling of joy, anticipation.

But he had no future with Fortune. Love with Fortune would simply mean going back to her world, and that he would never do.

What if they stayed here? If they found no way to return to their times, then what? He shook his head. There could be no what-ifs. He *must* return to make his peace with Hugh, to help his brother make peace with himself. Beyond Hugh, there was his clan. The Campbells needed him, and he owed them his loyalty. Besides, with the knowledge he'd found on the Internet, he might be able to improve their lives, even if only in a small way.

"OK, let's talk about Ganymede." The set of her mouth indicated her unwillingness to believe what he was about to say.

He drew in a deep breath, strengthening himself for what he must tell her. "Fortune, I think yer cosmic force is sitting at the foot of yer bed cleaning his whiskers."

"You're joking." She didn't smile.

"I wouldna joke about this. When I took Ganymede from the roof of the truck, I looked into his eyes. I saw there a power that . . . frightened me." Putting his fears into words sounded foolish in the bright light of morning. Fortune would laugh.

She didn't laugh. "How do you see power in someone's eyes? You've been under a lot of stress, maybe—"

"I know what I saw, lass." He stopped and raked his fingers through his hair. Losing his patience wouldn't accomplish anything. "There was more. When I reached the truck, a wave of heat pushed me back. The cursed truck had begun to glow red. I didna imagine that."

Fortune still looked doubtful. "I don't know. . . ."

"Think, Fortune. Has he ever acted like an ordinary cat? Do ye truly believe him a stray?"

For the first time, he saw fear touch her eyes. "Come to think of it, when I woke up in that rest-over room, Ganymede wasn't there, because I remember looking at the bureau. And the door was shut, so he couldn't have wandered in. But when I looked back a minute later, he was there."

Leith nodded. He glanced at the last piece of bacon, but for some reason his appetite had fled.

"What is he, Leith?" Her question was hushed. She glanced nervously at the foot of the bed, where Ganymede watched them with unblinking amber eyes. "Should we be discussing this in front of him?"

Leith smiled and shook his head. "I dinna think it matters where we discuss him. He'll know."

Fortune closed her eyes for a moment. When she opened them, they glistened with tears. "Should we . . . get rid of him?"

Leith had no idea why he saw humor in this situation. "We havena had much luck in getting rid of the wee beastie so far. What makes ye think we can do so now?"

Fortune didn't share his humor. "I want a serious answer. What do you think we should do with him?"

Leith took a long moment before answering. What *did* he think? How did he really feel about Ganymede? His decision surprised him. "I think we should keep him. I dinna know who or what he is, and I dinna know what part he has played in all this, but he has proved a brave friend when we needed one. One doesna get rid of a friend." He smiled. "Besides, if the wee devil brought us here,

283

'twould be wise to keep him near. Mayhap we can ply him wi' food to win his favor."

She smiled weakly. "That shouldn't be hard. I think we should keep him, too. He kind of feels like family." She shrugged. "But what would I know about family?"

"Ye have a mother." He held a finger to her lips when she would've interrupted. "I ken that ye and yer mother havena been close, but she's still yer mum, and ye must love her or she wouldna have the power to hurt ye."

"I . . . I don't even think of her anymore." She glanced away from him.

He smiled gently. "I think I've told ye before that ye dinna lie well." Placing his hand beneath her chin, he tipped her face up to meet his gaze. "We canna choose our families, and our families are not always what we'd wish, but they are still our families. They will always hold a part of our hearts."

She shook her head. "You don't understand."

"Time doesna change the human heart. I understand yer feelings for yer mother because of Hugh." Would speaking of his brother never grow easier? "I canna forget what he did at Glencoe, but I also canna forget that he raised me, kept me safe. He is still my brother, and I love him."

He nodded toward Ganymede, who gazed back at them with unblinking intensity. " 'Tis the same wi' the wee beastie. It doesna matter what he's done. Ganymede is part of our family, and he will stay wi' us."

Emotion flooded him. Perhaps he was being given another chance, a chance to defend his second family when he'd failed so dismally with his first.

Her smile was one he'd remember, no matter how old he grew. On a chill Highland night when the mist drifted in from the sea, he'd see her smile in the flames of the fire that warmed his old bones, and she'd be there in his memory.

"You're right. You and Ganymede are family to me and . . . and dammit, we'll stick together."

He couldn't help it; he leaned forward and kissed her forehead. She lifted her face, and he transferred his lips to her mouth. She tasted of orange juice and warm woman, a combination he found irresistible.

He'd just begun to deepen his kiss when a knock came at the front door. With a groan of frustration, he pulled away. Her lips, swollen from his kiss, tempted him back, but he couldn't ignore the renewed pounding. "Ye can get ready whilst I see who is at the door." He couldn't look at her again or else he might leave their visitor banging at the door forever.

Fortune watched him leave and softly close the bedroom door behind him.

Now that she was alone, the silence gathered around her as she forced herself to look at Ganymede, who still crouched at the foot of the bed. For a moment fear intruded, but she pushed it away. "I feel sort of silly calling you kitty, but old habits die hard."

At the sound of her voice, Ganymede rose and crept over the covers toward her. Taking a deep breath, she reached out and scratched behind his ears. "Who are you, kitty? Where did you come from? What have you done?"

Ganymede met her gaze, and she looked into amber eyes that reflected . . . nothing. So what had she expected, a demon's evil glare? Ganymede curled into a ball against her side and began to purr. Releasing her fear, she listened to the sound of the front door closing and Leith's returning footsteps.

He flung open the bedroom door and hurried to her side. Embracing her in a bear hug, he nuzzled the side of her neck. "Blade brought the money from my check, and he also brought a great many things he said ye could use for creating sculptures."

She laughed at his exuberance, and he tickled her. Squealing her dismay, she rolled away from him, but he followed. Pulling her on top of him, he tangled his hands in her hair and kissed her hard. "Blade said he talked to some people who can get us new identities, but 'twill cost money. Mayhap we should talk to Mary. She's the only one who understands our need."

Catching her breath after his kiss, she lay still atop him, content to remain there all day, if that were feasible. "What Blade intends to do is illegal; I know it is." *What you do to me should be illegal.*

Rolling to the side, he took her with him, still clasped in his arms. "Lass, we must survive in this time. And we canna survive wi'out identification. We canna get a license to drive a vehicle, nor can we cash a check."

She watched his gaze drift away from her. "I spoke wi' Blade, and he said we canna leave this

286

country wi'out a passport. And for this we need identification."

She grew still beside him. "Leave the country? Why would we leave the country?"

He looked at her, and she couldn't meet his gaze. "If we dinna return to our own time, then I would choose to live out my life in Scotland." His smile slid across her heart, leaving a trail of sadness. "All those I know will be gone."

He looked at her, but she knew he didn't see her. *All those I know*. She knew he thought of his brother, and her heart ached for him. What must it feel like to love that deeply?

"But the land will remain. I must see the Highlands again—the hills, the lochs, the heather."

"I understand." Where would this leave her? Would she have to go home by herself while he stood atop some hill in Scotland, his dark hair whipping tangles around the savage beauty of his face? Would he think of her?

"Aye, and ye'll come wi' me, lass." His gaze was intense, searching. "If ye still remain in this time."

Heartlessly, she trampled her sudden burst of joy that he'd want her to stay with him. It didn't matter, didn't matter at all. "Do you really believe we'll stay in this time?" Her question was a harsh whisper.

He stared at her for endless moments, then shook his head. "Nay. The powers wouldna be so forgetful. 'Twill take me no more than two weeks to finish my work wi' Mary. Then . . ." He shrugged.

Panic stirred. For the first time she forced herself to face squarely the realization that she'd lose him, and not in some nebulous future, but soon, too soon. "No. Two weeks isn't nearly enough. You were supposed to teach me the joys of love. OK, I've had a few giggles, but it's not in the *joy* category yet. We need a lot more time to work on the joy part."

His smile was tinged with sadness. "Ye're trying to pretend, as I was, that this willna end. But 'twill."

She could only nod.

"When will ye make plans to take a man back wi' ye?" His gaze searched her soul. "Or mayhap ye've aleady made yer plans and need only capture yer . . . victim."

"You do have a talent for melodrama, Leith." Her cool words covered the heat of denial, a denial that was false. He was right. She had to take a man back with her, and cosmic forces had chosen Leith. But why, *why* out of all the women in the world had they chosen her for this job? She'd thought she knew the answer to that question at the beginning. But now? Mentally she might be diamond hard, but emotionally . . . ? Emotionally she was powdered talc, blowing away in a firestorm of feelings she didn't understand.

So what would she do? Whether she returned home with Leith or a dozen substitutes, she'd still return alone. Alone with her guilt, her memories. Alone to live out her life making fake men who would all probably end up looking like Leith, but would never even come close to *being* Leith.

"Let's talk about this later, when I've recovered from last night." She knew her smile was wan. "Besides, Mary will wonder where we are." *Mary*

doesn't give a dingdong what time we come to work.
When had she become such a coward?

After such a strange beginning, the week had
improved considerably. Fortune felt like singing
and . . . dancing. Yes, like dancing. She'd never
tried to dance before. Humming a little tune, she
took a few skipping steps in time to the rhythm.

Leith glanced at her. "And what are ye so happy
about, lass?"

She punched him playfully in the side. "Lighten
up, Campbell. The last few days have been wonderful. Ganymede decided to stay home, the writing went great, and now we get to shop." She flung
her arms in the air to encompass the mall they'd
been strolling through for the last five minutes.

"Buying things. 'Tis what a woman does best."
Smiling, he reached down to clasp her hand in his.
Pausing for a moment, he gazed into a store window. " 'Twould take me a lifetime to understand
all that I see."

"Umm." She leaned forward to study the objects
in the display. CDs. Music. Blade had loaned them
a combination radio and CD player. "Maybe I'll
look around."

"Dinna hurry." His attention had already shifted
to a display of knives in the next window.

With the help of a salesman, it didn't take her
long to make her purchase; then she left the store
to rejoin Leith.

"What did ye buy?"

He pulled her hand into the warmth of his again,
and she suddenly realized she was happy. *Happy*.

Go figure. "It's a surprise. You'll find out when we get home."

They lingered in front of a jewelry store, and Fortune sighed as she looked at the sparkling gems. "This reminds me of my cross. As soon as you get another paycheck under your belt, I can get it out of hock."

He scowled. "Ye should ne'er have had to leave it at that cursed place."

Uh-oh. He was starting to sound intense again. "Look, I have to go into this store and shop for something to wear to Michael's party."

"I dinna want to go to his party." He eyed an ice-cream stand hungrily, then fished in his pocket for some change. "Do ye want some ice cream?"

She shook her head. "Stay here and eat your ice cream while I go into this store. You know that's pure fat, don't you?"

He grinned. " 'Tis why I want it."

She watched as he bought a chocolate cone.

"Would ye like a lick?" He slowly swept his tongue across one side of the ice cream, and his eyes slitted in bliss. She watched, mesmerized, as he then licked his lips.

The serpent in the Garden of Eden. She knew exactly how Eve had felt. Chocolate. She could have resisted any other flavor. Leith. She could've resisted any other mouth, any other tongue.

"OK, just one lick." Taking a quick lick, she let the guilty pleasure slide down her throat. Then her gaze caught Leith's, and the sudden pounding of her heart convinced her that her arteries were in no danger of clogging anytime soon.

When she'd finished, he watched her with

hooded eyes, then purposely licked the same spot. Slowly. Her lips tingled and her hands grew clammy as she watched that incredible mouth in action, imagined herself plunked in a sugar cone with Leith sliding his tongue sensuously across her. . . . "I'll . . . I'll be right back." Before he could offer to go with her, she rushed toward the store. His warm chuckle stayed with her all the way to the women's-wear department.

When she finally came out, she was feeling really stupid. How could anyone get worked up watching a man eat an ice-cream cone? OK, not just any man. A man with a sexy mouth that—

She spotted him sitting on a bench with a bulky package clutched in his large hands. There was something warm and comfortable about knowing a man waited for you.

If only he would go back with her. No, that was a fool's dream. If he went back with her it would be against his will, and he would never again be able to sit unnoticed in a crowded place.

Frowning, she watched the sideways glances women cast him as they swayed past. He wasn't doing such a great job of going unnoticed now.

He stood as he saw her approach, and she couldn't control the rush of pleasure just being with him gave her. What would she do when she knew for certain she'd never walk toward him again, never see him smile in greeting again, never look into his eyes again? Something like real pain tore at her.

"Did ye not find what ye sought, Fortune? Ye dinna look verra happy."

Forcing a smile, she held up her package. "I

found exactly what I wanted. Looks like you did some shopping, too. Let's see."

He held his package out of reach as she grabbed for it. "Two can have secrets, lass. Ye'll find out soon enough."

She took a deep breath and let herself relax into the moment. *Enjoy the present. But keep your memories safe*. "Ready to go home?" *Home? Where is home?*

"Aye. Ganymede willna be happy wi' us gone so long."

He walked to a nearby phone to call a cab. He'd adapted easily, much more easily than she, in some ways. Of course, he didn't have the future of humanity resting on his shoulders. That was unfair. He had the pain of his bitter past to deal with.

He returned and automatically grasped her hand as they walked toward the exit. "I hope Blade can get this identification soon. We canna afford so many taxis. How do ye feel about riding a Harley?" He turned a hopeful glance her way.

I don't want to return to 2300. I'd rather stay here with Leith, even if I have to learn to ride a Harley. Amazing how momentous revelations came in the darnedest places. She'd always remember that her revelation came in front of the Godiva chocolate shop.

She couldn't answer his question, couldn't go along with his what-if game. Cosmic forces wouldn't leave them here long enough for her to have to worry about riding Harleys, no matter what she wanted. "Wait a minute, Leith. I'd like to get a small box of these chocolates."

He paced impatiently as she made her purchase.

Wow, talk about expensive. They'd better be worth it. She'd wait until tonight to savor them while she lolled in bed.

She almost chuckled to herself. A week ago all she would've thought about was the Godiva's fat content, but gradually a product's pleasure index was becoming more important.

Pleasure index. Where would Leith rate? She glanced at other men hurrying past, then looked at Leith, who now leaned against the wall outside the store. He looked like a dark predator among a sea of rabbits. She smiled at her comparison. A few weeks ago, she'd never have believed she was a woman who'd choose dark and dangerous over warm and fuzzy. Yes, Leith's pleasure index would rate very high.

Leaving the mall, they hurried to the taxi. In the backseat, Leith automatically pulled her to him, and she sighed as she settled comfortably against him. She'd miss his warm companionship, the feel of his body next to hers. She, who'd done so little touching in her life, couldn't seem to get enough.

When she went home, everyone's hands-off attitude would seem cold, unfeeling. *When she went home.* Which brought her back to her personal revelation. She took it out and examined it. She didn't want to go home. Clear Lake had become her home. Yes, she'd miss certain things about her own time, but that was all they were—things. There were no people. Her mother? No, she'd realized the truth long ago about her mother. Fortune's disappearance would only be a minor blip on her mother's life-screen. After her discussion with Leith about family, Fortune could face that knowledge without bitterness. Her friends? None who'd remember her with anything more than faint fondness.

She closed her eyes and sighed. What was she thinking about? Her trip into this time had nothing to do with her personal choices; it had to do with the continuation of the human race. She felt the burn of tears behind her closed eyelids. God, she'd miss Leith.

"Ye havena answered my question."

"Huh?" She opened her eyes to look at him.

"How would ye feel about riding on a Harley?" He reached over to push a stray strand of hair from her face.

"Well, it's so . . . open. I mean, you'd get wet when it rained, and cold in the winter, and—"

" 'Tis not about comfort, lass. 'Tis about adventure, the thrill of the wind whipping yer hair, the oneness wi' everything around ye." She felt his smile in the darkness.

"I suppose so." She didn't think so. She couldn't imagine straddling the strange machine and roaring away. Her hovercraft had all the comforts of her own home. She simply set her destination and forgot about it.

"Life isna about comfort, lass. When ye're old and gray, ye willna remember the comfortable things ye did. Ye'll remember the things that made yer heart sing."

I'll remember you. "You could be right. But I suspect your question had a purpose."

"Hmm." He laid his chin on top of her head. "Blade said he could get me a Harley. I think I would like one."

294

Oh, Leith. The emptiness inside frightened her. "It sounds right for you."

Leith felt her disbelief, her refusal to consider that they might have a chance for a life together. She was ever the logical one, and he knew in his mind she was right. But it wasn't his mind that drove him into more foolish speech.

"Stay wi' me, Fortune. Stay wi' me in this time, or return wi' me to my time. I promise I'll keep ye safe," he whispered in her ear. Now why had he said that? It wasn't as though he loved her. Yes, he admired her, felt comfortable with her, desired her, but she wouldn't fit in his world. He'd have to listen to her constant complaints about its primitiveness. His offer must have stemmed from his wish to protect her. That was it. He felt better now that he understood his reason.

"I appreciate your offer, Leith, but I can't. I have to return to my time. I have a—"

"Duty. Aye, I know." As a warrior, he understood and even admired her determination to return to her time with a man, with him. Then why his anger? Because his heart knew she'd rejected him, would never want to stay with him. Why should she? He had nothing to offer her other than his body, and she wanted that for her world, not herself.

He was still in a roaring bad mood when the taxi stopped.

He paid the taxi driver, picked up all their packages, then climbed out behind Fortune. It was amazing how watching her wondrous bottom in motion eased his anger, or at least distracted it. As the taxi sped away, he started walking toward the house.

Then a remembered feeling hit him, a sense of something being wrong. Perhaps it was an instinct honed in a time when failure to notice something out of place, something not as it should be, could mean death. But whatever it was, he felt it now.

He quickly set the packages down, then put his arm out to stop Fortune. "Dinna go any farther."

"What?" Clearly puzzled, she stopped.

"Mayhap there is hope for ye yet. 'Tis the first time ye've listened to me since we met."

"Oh, I don't know about—"

"Shush, woman. Someone has been here who doesna belong."

He finally had her full attention. "How do you know?"

He moved slowly forward, his body tense, ready. Now he had a full view of the house. "The window by the door has been broken, and the door is open."

"Ohmigod, Ganymede's inside! We have to save him."

Leith paused as the incongruity of her statement hit him. "I dinna think Ganymede will be the one needing to be saved. Besides, whoever was inside is gone."

"Are you sure?" She moved up beside him, her body pressed to his side.

Even with the vibrations of danger still strong, his body acknowledged her closeness. This would not be a woman to take into battle, where a moment's distraction could be a man's last. "I dinna feel a presence."

"A presence? We're not talking spirits here."

"When ye've lived wi' danger yer whole life, ye know when 'tis near. Whoever was here has gone." Still cautious, he held up his hand when they reached the door. "I'll go inside. Ye stay here until I've searched."

He could see her nod in the darkness.

Keeping to the shadows, he crept into the house. Long practice made his entrance silent. Moving through the darkened house, he watched for movement, listened for an unfamiliar sound. By the time he reached the kitchen, he felt confident he'd been right. The house was empty.

Turning to search for the lights, he met gleaming amber eyes. At least Ganymede had survived. Not that he'd ever had a doubt. Switching on the light, he found the cat crouched atop the microwave oven. Leave it to Ganymede to protect that which affected his stomach.

Before he could do more, he heard Fortune coming. So much for her promise to stay outside. He winced as he heard her stumble over furniture.

"Where's Ganymede? Is he OK?" She rushed into the room, blinking at the sudden light. Locating the cat, she scooped him into her arms. "He's my kitty," she crooned as she hugged him to her. "Did those big, bad burglars frighten him?"

Leith didn't know who was more embarrassed, Ganymede or him. But considering the attention Fortune was showering on the cat, Ganymede probably thought the embarrassment worth it.

"I thought I told ye to stay outside."

She blinked at him. "You expected me to listen to you?"

"What would ye have done if ye found a burglar still here?"

"You said no one was here. I believed you. Shouldn't I believe you?"

He spoke through gritted teeth. "Pretend ye charged into the kitchen and found a strange man here. What would ye do?"

"I wouldn't have charged in if I didn't know you were here, but hypothetically, I'd talk to him and explain the lack of logic in what he was doing." She bent her head and made soft cooing sounds to Ganymede. The cat's expression had turned blissful.

"Talk! Ye'd talk to the bastard? I canna believe ye."

Her expression turned grim. "What would you do, Leith?"

"I'd bash him wi' anything I could lay my hands on."

"Exactly the response I'd expect from you." She looked as though she'd confirmed her worst fears.

He wouldn't be able to leave her alone for a minute for fear she was trying to reason with some madman. "Isn't there anything that would drive ye to violence?"

"Almost every problem can be solved without violence." Her expression had turned stubborn. "We've wasted enough time. Let's call the police."

"I dinna think that's such a good idea. We shouldna call attention to ourselves until Blade can get us identification." As he spoke, he strode back into the living room, then peered at the floor near the front door. Bending down, he noticed several tufts of black cat hair and a few drops of blood.

298

Hmm. He hadn't seen any wounds on Ganymede, so he could only assume . . .

"Do you think this was a regular burglary, or is it connected to that mountain-gross who threatened you?" She bent down to see what had caught his attention.

His respect for her reasoning powers, if not her common sense, rose. "I didna notice anything missing. There's blood on the floor, so Ganymede marked him."

She nodded. "We have to get the packages."

He followed her out the door, and as he stooped to retrieve their packages, he saw what he'd missed in his previous concentration on the house itself.

"What happened here, Leith?" Fortune's hushed question mirrored his own thoughts exactly.

Someone or something had fought a war on their lawn. Plants were uprooted and chunks of sod were flung everywhere. Bits of cloth and tufts of black fur trailed a path to where the deep grooves dug by the wheels of a motorcycle told the tale of a frantic escape.

"The mountain-gross lost."

Fortune's comment was a statement of fact— one that Leith agreed with. He would say nothing of his plans to Fortune. He would deal with the man in his own way. But he somehow felt that Bones would not be coming back to this house.

Silently, they returned to the living room. Fortune didn't ask what he intended. Perhaps she feared he might tell her.

She headed for the bedroom, clutching her packages, but turned before leaving the room. "Thank you for being there, Leith. No matter what I say, you make me feel safe." With that surprising announcement, she closed the door behind her.

Leith's pleasure in her admission made him feel ridiculously lighthearted, considering the circumstances. Her compliments had been few and far between. Of course, he hadn't overwhelmed her with admiration either. Perhaps he should, while he still had the chance. *While he still had the chance*. His lighthearted mood evaporated.

Before following Fortune into the bedroom, he glanced at Ganymede. Ganymede stared back with eyes that gave nothing away. " 'Twas a brave thing ye did tonight. Fortune doesna understand the need for violence. Men understand such things. I thank ye."

Ganymede seemed to swell with pride right before his eyes. Whatever else Leith believed, he believed that he spoke with a fellow warrior.

Turning out the light, he paused at the bedroom door to glance back. Amber eyes glowed in the darkness, watching him with . . . approval. He laughed and shook his head at his whimsy.

Chapter Fourteen

Last night, Fortune hadn't given Leith the gift she'd bought for him at the mall. Instead they'd lain on their own sides of the bed, only feet apart, but in actuality, centuries apart.

What had he thought of in the hot Texas night? Had he drifted back to his beloved Scotland, his land of cool mists and dark memories? Or had he wrestled with the problem of what to do about the mountain-gross who'd broken into their house? Had he thought of her?

She'd thought of him. Thought of his confidence even when dealing with an alien world. Thought of his vulnerability when he spoke of the Highlands, his brother. Thought of his soft voice soothing her, his hard body driving her to sobbing ecstasy. Thought only of him.

She should've given him his present last night.

Nina Bangs

She should've held him, stroked him. Because she never knew when she'd wake to find him gone, a distant memory of a time long past. And she knew with a certainty born in her heart she'd regret the things she hadn't done, could never do again.

Two weeks. He'd said he'd be finished in two weeks. Was that how long they had? Maybe she could delete what she'd done, tell him she didn't have a copy, make him start over again. No, in her heart she knew all her wishes, her plans, would mean nothing when their time was up.

Her plans. The truth? She had no plans.

Now she sat in front of Mary's computer once again, ready to record more of his memories. Memories that tugged at her heart, made him more precious to her.

"What worries ye, lass?"

The soft huskiness of his voice startled her, and she turned to find him standing behind her, staring at the blank screen. "Oh, nothing. I was just thinking about what I wrote yesterday." When had she, who prided herself on her truthfulness, become such an accomplished liar?

Pulling a chair up beside her, he sat down. "Ye dinna like what I've told ye of Scotland, do ye?" He reached up to tuck a stray strand of her hair behind her ear. The automatic gesture brought tears to her eyes.

She concentrated on the screen, as blank as her future hopes. "The country sounds beautiful, but the people seem so . . . savage." No, *savage* was the wrong word. He was part of that time, and she no longer thought of him as savage.

"Each age has its own kind of savagery, Fortune. Think of yer own time."

She didn't want to think of her own time, didn't want to think of a time before Leith or after Leith. And somehow she knew that no matter what finally happened, home would never be a comfortable place again.

"I don't understand." Without permission, her fingers typed in the word *home* on the screen.

"Savagery has many faces. Ye dinna speak of yer mother wi' love. Why?"

She didn't see the connection, and she didn't want to talk about her mother, but because he'd shared so much of his pain with her, she told him. "Each woman in our society has a duty to produce one child. I was an obligation to my mother, nothing more. Once she gave me life she abandoned me to the care of robot nannies." At least now she could speak of her mother without bitterness. Leith had done that for her. "I'll give her credit, though. She never pretended. I've sort of thought that the cloning process doesn't lend itself to the growth of maternal feelings. Who knows?" Once she would've shrugged a pretended nonchalance while she tried to suppress her roiling anger. Now? She could never forget her mother's lack of love, but perhaps she could begin to understand it.

"I dinna know what 'robot nannies' are, but they dinna have a warm sound. Did no one hold ye, hug ye?"

The outrage in his voice was for her. *Her*. The realization triggered a warm glow that expanded with each beat of her heart.

"Our society as a whole doesn't do much hugging or kissing."

"Why?" Wrapping his arms around her, he pulled her tightly against him. " 'Tis a wonderful custom." He kissed her ear.

Shivers rippled from her ear to pool in dark, hidden lakes of desire. She tried to ignore the heat threatening to overflow its banks and drown her. "I'm not sure, but I think after men disappeared, physical signs of affection didn't have the meaning they once did. Even birth had a different significance. Babies were no longer a manifestation of the love between a man and woman. They were just an extension of one's self."

He released her, and she fought the urge to turn and pull him back, sink into his warmth.

"Would ye consider getting yerself wi' a male child here, then taking him back to yer time?"

She glanced at him. He watched her with a deep intensity that gave away none of his thoughts.

Fortune had briefly thought of this solution to the human race's problem. It made sense. Bring back a child and raise him with the intention of repopulating the world with males. It made perfect sense. Then why did the idea make her cringe with horror? "I . . . I couldn't do that, Leith. I couldn't bring a child back to that kind of attention, isolation. He'd never get to play with other little boys, never be free of constant scrutiny, examinations." She shook her head. "No, I wouldn't do that to my child." *Our child.* The thought alone made her weak.

She thought she glimpsed approval in his eyes,

but his expression remained hooded. "But ye'd do it to me, lass?"

No! Her heart screamed the word, but she couldn't say it aloud, because no matter what her heart suffered, she still had to sacrifice him for the future of mankind. "I . . ."

Maybe she could still find a suitable male to re-place— *Stop it!* The logic she'd rarely used lately told her Leith was the chosen one, no other. Trying to slip through a crack to escape her duty would only catapult her into a black hole of indecision. She couldn't allow that now. But she needed a plan. She hadn't even tried to think of one. *You don't want to think of one.*

Leith rubbed his hand across his eyes and turned away. "Dinna try to think of a lie, lass. 'Twould do no good." He sounded unutterably weary.

"I see Aunt Mary has made you comfortable here."

Michael's voice spun Leith and Fortune around. He stood in the doorway, impeccably dressed in suit and tie, every hair in place, shoes shined to a mirror finish. In contrast, Leith wore old jeans, a shirt open halfway down his chest, and scuffed boots that Blade had given him, but she realized Michael didn't have a chance in the same room with Leith.

"I just wanted to remind you guys about the party next Saturday. You're still coming, aren't you?" He wandered over to the computer and stared over Fortune's shoulder as she pulled up yesterday's work on the screen. "Wow, pretty in-tense stuff. People really lived this way?"

Fortune knew when Leith moved closer, felt his heat, his passion.

"Aye. Lived, loved, died this way. 'Twas not a time for the weak of spirit."

His harsh reply was aimed at Michael, so why did she feel he spoke only to her? Challenged only her?

Michael leaned closer, then shook his head. "I bet it wasn't." He straightened. "Got to go. Don't forget the party."

She listened to his footsteps leave the room, listened to the silence wrap around her until she felt suffocated by it, until she had to say something. "We've wasted too much time already. Yesterday we left off—" She paused as a distant sound caught her attention.

"What is it?" His voice was expressionless, as though they'd never discussed her decision for his future.

She listened for a few more seconds, then shrugged. "Nothing. I thought I heard the ice-cream man, but it was something else." She started to type, then paused again. "Why do you think Ganymede hates the ice-cream man so much?"

She turned to see Leith gazing out the window at the garden below. "I think the ice-cream man has a part in this, but I dinna know what." He glanced at her. "It does no good to worry about things I canna understand."

"Why not?" She'd done nothing but worry since she'd set foot here. Who wouldn't worry? *A man who'd watched his parents killed in a raid and then had taken part in a bloody massacre. What could there possibly be to worry about after that*? "Forget I said that. I'll do the worrying for both of us."

Leith leaned back against the wooden bench and watched the people stream by. Fortune sat beside him, still breathing hard from their walk to the mall.

"Why are we here, and why did we have to walk? My legs feel like they're about to fall off, and I'm starved. Ganymede will wonder where we are. Why—"

Leith raised his eyes to the heavens. "Lord save me from a complaining woman."

Fortune's expression turned offended. "Who's complaining? I'm asking reasonable questions. We spent a long day at Mary's and I'm tired. So here we sit watching people go by."

"I needed the exercise. I canna sit around all day staring at a computer." He watched a woman walk by leading a small boy by the hand while clasping an oversize stuffed bear with her other. He automatically pictured Fortune in place of the woman.

He must stop his fantasies. Even if they could remain in this time, she would never consent to have his child. Not with so many other men more suited to her. "Since I willna go back to yer time, mayhap we can choose one of these men to return wi' ye." He smiled at her, inviting her to join him in his game.

"Hmm. Good idea." She relaxed against his shoulder and studied the passing men. "How about that one? He's well built, has a good face. . . ."

Leith shook his head. "He looks wi' affection on

307

the man beside him. I dinna think a lass would interest him."

"Oh." She looked confused. "How can you tell?"

"I understand such things. Keep looking."

"OK." She pointed to another passing man. "He looks good—healthy, nice bone structure."

Leith shook his head sadly. "Married."

Fortune's expression turned mutinous. "Give me a break. There's no way you can tell he's married."

" 'Tis obvious. He wears a look of servitude. Any man would see it." Leith noted her angry glance and controlled his grin. There was nothing more glorious than a red-haired woman when she was furious.

"Fine. How about him?" She jabbed her finger at another man.

"Stubborn. Ye can tell by his bushy eyebrows."

She turned and impaled Leith with her stare. "Don't look now, Mr. Smart Guy, but your eyebrows aren't exactly neat and narrow."

"Aye. I admit to a certain amount of stubbornness. 'Tis how I recognize it in others. Like recognizes like." He ignored her derisive snort. "Keep searching."

"There. Look at that man. He's perfect." Her narrowed gaze dared him to find fault.

" 'Tis too bad." He hoped his expression was suitably dejected.

"What? What's wrong with him?"

"Do ye see the shape of his ear? 'Tis a sign of impotence. He'll do yer world no good at all."

She exhaled in disgust. "That's the most ridiculous thing I've ever heard."

"Aye, well, ye're a city lass, and ye wouldna understand such things." If he didn't laugh soon, he'd explode.

Fortune straightened, then turned her face from him so he couldn't see her expression. "Maybe I'm wrong, but I'm beginning to see a certain pattern here. You won't go back with me, but you find fault with everyone else I suggest. I wonder why?"

He didn't feel like laughing anymore. "I was only trying to help ye."

"Right." She turned her face to him, and he read the truth they both knew in her eyes. "You don't want me, but you won't let me take back someone I might find attractive. Don't you find that attitude a little selfish?"

Don't want you? He'd want her till he died. The realization rocked him. " 'Tis yer imagination. Ye can take whatever man ye want, if he agrees."

"What would it take for *you* to agree to go back with me?" Her soft question held wistful hope.

"Nothing. If I loved ye beyond all reason, it would take nothing." His gaze locked with hers. "But even if I loved ye, I'd have to return to my time."

"Why?" Her expression was carefully blank.

"It doesna matter. 'Tis time for us to go." He rose and walked away from her—hating himself for his brusqueness, hating her for creating doubts in his mind.

She caught up with him quickly. "This is about Hugh, isn't it? I know how you feel about him, but you can't sacrifice—"

"I dinna want to talk about it." He continued walking.

"OK. Forget I asked. Your life is your business."

Leith winced at the hurt he heard in her voice. He stopped to call a taxi, then walked to an exit, all the time trying not to meet Fortune's gaze. She deserved an answer, but how could he expect her to understand the mixture of anger and guilt he felt toward Hugh when he didn't completely understand it himself?

Relieved, he watched Blade's taxi pull to a stop. They could not discuss personal matters with Blade in the taxi. He held the door as she climbed in.

"I was hoping to have a chance to talk to you guys." Blade grinned at them over his shoulder. "Talked to some people about fake IDs. It's all set up as soon as they get some dough."

Leith nodded. "Once we get identification, I would like to see about purchasing a Harley." He ignored Fortune's pointed stare.

Blade transferred his attention to the road as they pulled into traffic. "No problem. I know a guy who wants to sell his. He'll take payments." He glanced at Fortune in his mirror. "How do you feel about the big guy gettin' a bike, little lady?"

"I'd hate it." Fortune stared out the window at a passing motorcycle. "It's so open and . . ."

" 'Tisna safe, is it, Fortune?"

Her expression told him how right he was.

"Exactly. I like being enclosed, safe. I've always been safe. I . . . I could never climb on one of those." She looked almost embarrassed by her declaration.

He leaned over and whispered for her ears only.

"I am not safe, Fortune. Ye seemed to like climbing on me verra well."

Her face flamed red, and he almost felt ashamed at the words he'd said. Almost.

She stared straight ahead, refusing to answer him, to even look at him.

Blade glanced again in the mirror. "Heard you had some excitement last night."

"What did ye hear?" Fortune grew still beside him.

"Well, the way I heard it, Bones and a big old panther had a go-around on your front lawn last night."

"Panther?" Leith and Fortune spoke in unison.

"Saber-toothed panther. Know Bones got the worst of it 'cause I saw him today. Looks like someone took the working end of a rake to his face and arms. He's stomping and swearing he'll take care of you when your pet's not around to protect you." Blade chuckled. "He was real entertaining."

Leith glanced at Fortune. He wasn't surprised to see the look of panic growing in her eyes at the mention of violence. "Did Bones tell ye about the . . . panther?" He returned his attention to Blade.

"Don't forget the saber-toothed part." He gave Leith a grin. "No, it was Mrs. Hyperstein down the street. She was walking her poodle and saw the whole thing. Swears you're lettin' a panther run loose in the neighborhood. Called me to let me know she doesn't think folks are allowed to keep exotic pets around Clear Lake." He winked at Leith. "Truth is, she's afraid your panther might have a taste for poodles."

311

Nina Bangs

"A panther?" Fortune had recovered her voice. "All we have is Ganymede."

Blade's good humor disappeared. "Close enough. Course, Mrs. Hyperstein's eyesight ain't so good anymore. Won't wear glasses."

Leith nudged Fortune. He thought it might be best to say nothing more about this. Fortune nodded her agreement.

Thankfully, Leith realized they'd reached home. As he helped Fortune from the taxi, he made a quick visual survey of the house to make sure they'd had no more uninvited guests. Relieved, he found nothing disturbed.

He unlocked the door, stepped inside, and was immediately met by Ganymede, who seemed intent on imparting all the news of the day.

Fortune laughed as she picked the cat from the floor. "Did our panther stay out of trouble today?" She scratched behind Ganymede's ears, and he broke into a rumbling purr. Fortune looked up at Leith with eyes that sparkled with pleasure. "He's glad to see us."

Leith shook his head, but he couldn't help smiling. "The wee beastie is happy to see *ye*. I'd guess he wants to eat. 'Tis late."

"Poor baby." She rubbed her head against the cat's glossy coat.

Leith rolled his eyes at the cat. With calm deliberation, Ganymede yawned in Leith's face.

"If ye were a man, ye'd nurse a broken head for a week," he muttered.

"What did you say, Leith?" Fortune stopped rubbing her head against the appreciative cat long enough to stare at him.

312

"I said ye should put the cat down so I can feed him."

"Oh, thank you." She plunked a grumbling Ganymede onto the floor, then headed for the bedroom. "I'll get us something to eat as soon as I take a quick shower."

Leith followed Ganymede's waving tail into the kitchen. "Tread carefully, ye wee demon." He opened the refrigerator and took out a piece of salmon. "No matter what form ye take, I dinna believe ye're a cat."

He'd gotten Ganymede's complete attention. The cat's amber eyes seemed suddenly intense, searching.

There'd been a time when Leith would have laughed at holding a conversation with a cat, at believing what he now believed. But after being sent forward three hundred years, nothing seemed impossible.

" 'Tis strange that Fortune still treats ye as a cat, even suspecting what ye truly are." Leith smiled at Ganymede. "Whate'er that may be."

Leith couldn't name the moment Ganymede's amber gaze became something more than a cat's, but suddenly Leith sensed he'd finally seen the real Ganymede. Wicked humor and a knowledge as old as man's earliest memories were visible in the hypnotic eyes. And a warning.

Leith had never reacted well to warnings. "When ye've finished amusing yerself wi' us, find yerself a place wi' enough foolish humans to satisfy ye." He clenched his hands into fists and met Ganymede's fixed stare. "But dinna hurt Fortune or ye willna be able to hide from me." His threat seemed foolish

313

Nina Bangs

in the face of the power he believed Ganymede possessed.

It wasn't fear of Ganymede's retribution that made him close his eyes, but rather the possibility that Fortune would no longer be his to protect, that she would be forever lost to him.

When Leith opened his eyes, Ganymede's gaze held no fury, but rather a strangely satisfied expression. And Leith had a feeling he'd walked into a well-laid trap. Not a comfortable thought.

By the time Leith ate dinner and finished his shower, Fortune had turned on the CD player and was curled snugly on the pink couch. Excitement made it hard for her to sit still.

When he finally entered the room, she patted the seat beside her. Without comment, he lowered himself to the couch. She tried not to let his presence distract her, a difficult task. He'd put on jeans, but nothing else. His torso still gleamed damply, and he smelled of Irish Spring and temptation.

"I have a surprise for you." She unwound from the couch, carefully lit a lone candle she'd placed on the coffee table, then turned off the lights. Returning to the couch, she clicked "play" on the remote. The room glowed with soft candlelight and her expectation of his response to her gift.

As she folded her legs beneath her, Leith moved over and pulled her against him. Wrapping his arms around her, he nuzzled her ear. "What is this wondrous surprise?"

She reached up and placed a finger against his lips. "Shush. Listen."

When he softly kissed her finger, then drew it

into his mouth to suckle, she felt the warm liquid flow begin and gather in delicious pools of want. "Stop." *Don't stop.* "You have to listen."

"Umm." He transferred his attention to the sensitive skin on the inside of her wrist.

She closed her eyes and fought the need to clench her thighs against the anticipation his touch loosed.

Suddenly the darkened room filled with the haunting sound of a lone bagpipe, and Leith grew still beside her. She opened her eyes to the flicker of the candle flame, a flame that almost seemed to move to the lonely melody the piper played. What memories lived in its orange and yellow depths, crouched in its hot blue center?

Leith's tension thrummed through her, and for the first time she considered that her gift might not be the success she'd expected. "Should I turn it off?"

"No. I would like to hear all of it." His soft murmur spoke of an infinite sadness that tore at her heart.

She felt him relax against her, and she sighed her relief even as she moved closer to him, a closeness she hoped would in some way protect him from the memories that tortured him.

"I wasna sure I would ever hear the pipes again." He kept one arm wrapped around her while he clasped her hand tightly with the other.

She held his hand with the desperate wish that she could take his pain as her own, reach into his soul and soothe it. "You miss it a lot, don't you?" *What a stupid question. Of course he missed it.* The knowledge hurt in the same way an old wound

315

would hurt—a constant ache that would forever be a reminder of searing pain. He would always miss Scotland, his home. And she would never be a part of those memories.

"I miss the purple mountains, the burns that run wi' water so cold it would make yer teeth ache, the mist moving in from the sea. I miss . . ."

He paused so long that Fortune thought he'd say no more. She felt him draw in a deep breath.

" 'Tis time I explained about Hugh."

"Don't do this to yourself." She raised her finger to his lips, and he kissed it. "You've told me enough about Hugh for me to understand—"

He touched the tip of his tongue to her finger, then gently grasped her finger and held it against her own lips. "Ye dinna know all, and ye must know all to understand."

She watched him with eyes that shone blue fire in the candlelight's glow.

"Ye have to understand that Hugh was the most important person in my life, Fortune. I was only a bairn when our parents died in the raid. Hugh raised me. He was a fine brother." He felt the need to affirm this—to himself, to Hugh—before he went on. "But he hated the MacDonalds beyond all reason. They became an obsession wi' him. I didna realize how deep his hate ran until Glencoe."

"You don't have to tell me the rest, Leith." Her voice soft with sympathy, she rested her head against his chest. He smoothed the silky strands of her hair with fingers that trembled slightly.

"I do, lass. Ye need know why I must leave ye." *Even though 'twill tear me apart*. The realization didn't materialize in a jagged streak of blue-white lightning. It had been there all along, teasing him with shadowy glimpses. Finally it emerged in the soft orange glow of a single candle.

"You have to leave . . . because of Hugh." Her voice sounded fatalistic.

He would rather she had ranted and raved against heartless forces, but that wasn't Fortune's way. Her society taught calm acceptance. He didn't want to consider the idea that she just didn't care enough about his leaving.

"At Glencoe he became an avenging force, killing any MacDonalds he found." As she lifted her face to him, Leith watched horror fill her eyes and felt his own gorge rise at the remembered screams, the remembered smell of blood, the remembered feel of death.

Staring into her eyes, he saw the exact moment the horror died, to be replaced by stubborn conviction. "But that wasn't *you*. We each have to take responsibility for our own actions."

He resisted the urge to cover her mouth with his, to gain surcease from his agony in the sweetness of her body. "I didna stop him, lass. I stood frozen wi' horror and watched the slaughter turn the earth red around me." He made a conscious effort to loosen his grip on her hand. He'd probably hurt her, but she hadn't said a word.

"When I finally did try to stop Hugh, he turned on me, called me a craven—"

"A *craven!* And was it brave to kill unarmed men?"

"A craven who wouldna fight for my clan."

"Stop, Leith. You're just hurting yourself." He felt the dampness of her tears against his chest.

He needed to hurt himself. He needed to remember always. "I stumbled away from the carnage and met wi' Ian MacDonald, who was trying to escape into the hills wi' some of his clan. The Campbells were pursuing them and would've cut them down. I pulled my sword free. I knew what Hugh expected of me, but . . ." He drew in a deep breath along with the courage to continue. "I couldna stand the thought of any more senseless bloodshed, so I helped them."

"Any person with a conscience would've done the same. How dare Hugh condemn you."

Her outrage on his behalf touched him. "If that had been the only thing, mayhap Hugh might have forgiven me. But shortly after the massacre, Hugh met Ian MacDonald in the hills. Ian wounded Hugh sorely. When Hugh finally healed, he was left wi' a scarred face and a permanent limp. He didna blame Ian; he blamed me. He said 'twas the price he paid for my traitorous acts. Hugh ne'er spoke to me again."

"That's why you hate the MacDonalds so much, isn't it? Not because they're the enemies of your clan, but because of how they destroyed your relationship with your only relative. Oh, Leith." She wrapped her arms around him and hugged him with all of her strength, as if she could squeeze all the bitterness from his soul.

" 'Tis rumored that after his wounds healed, Hugh took to drink. I canna change what I did at Glencoe, and if truth be told I would do the same again, but I must make my peace wi' the brother of my childhood, even though I fear he's gone forever."

"I understand." Her quiet acceptance defeated him, defeated his foolish resolve never to join with her again, never to give her power over him. The truth? She'd held power over him from the moment she'd thrown back the cover in that hotel bed and gazed at him with those wide blue eyes.

Chapter Fifteen

Rats! I missed something important. I make one quick popcorn run, burn the damn popcorn, rush back, and find out I've missed something juicy. Look at their faces. It must've been great. Tell me. I gotta know.

Right. I shouldn't listen. Yeah, yeah, a better person would butt out. But what the hell, I'm not a better person. Though you know what they say about curiosity and the cat.

Besides, I have a stake in this. I'm part of the family. I've never been part of anyone's family. Feels sorta good. Makes me kinda wish I'd picked two turkeys to jerk around instead of Leith and Fortune. OK, I'll admit it's gonna hurt when I have to rip them apart. They're good people. I know, I know. That shouldn't matter. But for some reason it does matter this time. When you're up close and personal with two people day after day, you start to care.

I don't think I'll try something like this again. It's dangerous to my moral fiber. OK, so I don't have any moral fiber. But if I did, I'd say this whole thing stinks. I need to wrap things up and move on. Forget about Leith and Fortune.

Speakin' of wrapping things up . . . I wonder where the ice-cream jerk went? Haven't seen him around lately. I felt sure he'd stick to Leith and Fortune like a tick to a hound dog. If he's supposed to save their hides, he's doin' a piss-poor job of it. There've been a couple of times he could've caught them when I wasn't around. Oh, well, I'll worry about him when he shows up again. And he will show up.

Final detail. This Bones character. Gives Neanderthals a bad name. Leith needs to watch out for him. You don't back a rat into a corner, and Bones is gettin' desperate. His reputation is dog poop after Leith worked him over and I did my thing. I'd take care of him myself, but I don't think Leith would appreciate it. Male pride and all that stuff. Hey, I understand. Us males gotta do what we gotta do.

Hmm. Doesn't look like much is goin' down here, and I'm still hungry. Burned popcorn isn't gonna do the job. I'll just mosey on down to the nearest steak house. Get me a great prime rib—rare—and a bottle of fine wine. Hey, it works for me.

"Leith, if I could go back with you to your time for one hour, just one hour, what would you show me?"

She smiled up at him, and he appreciated her attempt to lighten his mood. "I thought you wouldna go back to my time unless yer life depended on it?"

"Well, I guess I could take one hour. After an hour, though, I'd have to find some buttons to push or go crazy. So what would you show me?"

"I wouldna waste our precious hour showing ye anything. I would draw ye down to the heather and love ye."

She still kept her arms wrapped around him as he slid to the worn carpet. But in his mind he lay upon a purple carpet of heather, a soft breeze blowing that carried the scent of Scotland. He rolled over so she lay beneath him.

"Umm, wouldn't the heather be sort of scratchy?"

He stored her playful grin with his other memories of her—too few to last the rest of his life.

He shook his head in mock sadness. "Ye have much to learn, lass." He ran his fingers down the side of her face, and she shivered. "Passion runs strong, like the crash of storm waves against the cliffs. It doesna feel, doesna know anything but its need." His voice dropped to a husky murmur. "And its need is relentless, hungry."

She looked into his jade eyes and saw there her past, her future—at least for this moment. No matter what happened, she would have this, a memory none could share, none could take from her. She wouldn't worry how this would affect the future of the human race, didn't care. This night she'd live as though there'd be no other. And who knew, there might not be.

"Will ye remember me, lass, if we part?"

For a moment the closeness of his thoughts to

hers startled her. But she forgot everything when she saw the sadness in his gaze. "Will we be allowed to remember, Leith? Or will our memories be wiped clean?" The very thought drove a lance of cold dread through her. *Not remember Leith?*

"I willna let it happen. I will remember ye, always."

His savage declaration hung between them, igniting her own determination. She'd no more forget Leith than she'd forget how to breathe. She would imprint his touch, his soul, so deeply in her heart that nothing could erase it.

Reaching up, she smoothed a strand of dark hair from his face. He grasped her hand and stilled it, then softly kissed her palm. The touch of his mouth fanned a spark that waited with blue-flamed heat within her, fanned it to glowing life, anticipation.

Suddenly he pushed away from her and rose in one lithe motion. "Dinna move. There are two things I must get."

Before she could protest, he was gone. Trying to control her racing heart, her rapid breathing, she fought for logical thought. The bed. Reasonable people mated in bed. She frowned. Something was wrong with that sentence.

Then she smiled, a slow smile. Not mating. Making love. She was ready to admit she'd make love with Leith tonight. But not on the floor. In the nice, soft bed.

She'd started to rise when Leith's shadow loomed over her.

"Where do ye think ye're going, lass?"

"In to the bed. It's soft, comfortable. This floor is—"

With a disgusted grunt, he leaned down and scooped her up. Ignoring her startled cry, he headed for the back door.

"What're you doing? Put me down." She winced as he kicked the back door open and carried her into the yard.

"Ye must learn to use yer imagination for other things besides making men." Setting her on her feet, he spread the blanket he'd brought on the ground beneath the large live oak tree. "Ye must have a sense of adventure, live dangerously." He put down a bag he'd slung over his shoulder.

"Someone will see us."

"No one will see us."

"There're bugs out here."

"Ye have a fearless warrior wi' ye who will protect ye against such things."

"Inside is better." She turned toward the house, but she'd barely taken two steps before he'd picked her back up with the same ease he would Ganymede, then deposited her on the blanket.

"Stay there, woman."

She huffed and puffed, then stared up at him as he towered over her. "Don't you dare use that tone of voice with me, Leith Campbell. Maybe that caveman technique goes over well in 1700, but it doesn't cut any ice with a woman from 2300."

Silently, he reached for the snap on his jeans.

She swallowed hard, barely daring to breathe as he paused with his fingers on the metal snap, teasing, drawing out the tension until she was ready to do her own kind of snapping. *Finally!* The tiny pop of the released snap allowed her to exhale, and the sound of the zipper brought with it a promise—a promise that was reinforced by the arrow of male skin the open zipper revealed.

That mouthwatering vee of flesh was telling her something, but she couldn't think above the raucous prelaunch party her hormones were holding. Never subtle, never subdued.

Glancing up, she slid her gaze across his bare torso, which gleamed in the pale glow of the full moon. "I bet all those rippling muscles really impressed the milkmaid set, but they don't do much for . . . I mean they don't actually excite . . ." It would start growing any minute. She almost reached up to check the length of her nose.

He still said nothing as he slid his jeans down over his lean hips and strong legs. He kicked them away from his already bare feet. Would he just as easily kick her heart away if it became a nuisance? Her heart? What did her heart have to do with this?

She shifted her gaze and her thoughts. "No shorts." She knew that open zipper had been trying to tell her something. "Why don't you wear shorts? You bought plenty. A different color for each day of the week. I notice these things." Of course she noticed those things, small, unimportant things, like all the small, unimportant details that had made up the fabric of her whole life. *Until Leith*. "All civilized people wear . . ." She blinked at the pure inaneness of her comment.

His white smile flashed in the darkness. "I ne'er claimed to be civilized. When ye return to yer time, ye can amuse yer friends wi' tales of how ye made love wi' a savage." His lips still smiled, but there was no smile in his voice.

The moonlight painted him in shades of gray, a dark warrior come to live in her memories forever. "Forget what I said." She smiled up at him. "Come here." *My fierce Scottish lover*.

She sensed his body relaxing as he dropped to his knees beside her. "Ye try my patience, lass." He shook his head in mock sadness. "But I think ye worth the aggravation ye give me."

"I'll try not to comment on that." She couldn't help herself. She reached out and laid her hand against his chest. Closing her eyes, she felt the strong beat of his heart, the warm flesh and solid muscle. "But you don't play fair. You took away half my fun." She opened her eyes to gaze into his—amused, inviting. "I didn't get a chance to undress you."

"Ach, another one of life's wee disappointments." He reached into his bag and pulled something from it. "To make up for it, I have a gift for ye." Uncertainty suddenly clouded his gaze. " 'Tis a silly thing, but when I saw it I thought of ye."

He held it out and watched for her reaction as though he expected her to break into gales of laughter.

She finally focused on what he clasped in his large hands, and her breath escaped her in a cry of recognition. "Skirky! You found Skirky for me." No matter that the tag said Cuddle-Me Caterpillar, it was *Skirky*.

Trembling, she took the tubular yellow toy from him, gazed into its huge purple eyes, then clasped it to her and rocked back and forth as tears coursed down her face.

"God's teeth, I didna mean to upset ye, lass." She heard the panic in his voice and smiled through her tears.

"You are a wonderful man, Leith Campbell." *And I love you*. When had she known, really known? Was it when he'd sat beside her at the computer and told her of his life, a life only a man with his inner strength could've survived? Was it when he'd offered her a wilted yellow flower he'd rescued from loneliness in Mary's garden? Or maybe it was when he'd shielded her body with his that first day. Most likely it was when she rolled over in the rest-over bed and saw him for the first time, his dark hair spread across the pillow, his face one of savage beauty even in sleep.

Through the emotion that tore at her, she recognized the irony. She sat clasping her first love to her chest while she gazed at her last love. And he *would* be her last, for she would never feel this love for another. Never.

His smile held none of its usual wickedness. "Ye like him? I know he's not the same as the one ye had as a bairn, but—"

"He's exactly the same." *In my heart*.

Leith's smile warmed every dark, frozen corner of her soul—the ones untouched by a parent's love, a friend's understanding, a lover's tenderness. She could almost hear the cracking of ice as the loneliness of her childhood melted into a sea of heated desire—for only one man.

Carefully setting her new Skirky on the blanket, she looked at Leith. "I want you, Leith Campbell, with every atom of my MacDonald body."

"Atom?" He frowned, then realizing what she'd said, froze. "Are ye sure, lass?"

She tried to think of her oh-so-logical reason for never making love with him again, but like a greedy child, she could think of nothing except the man kneeling in front of her—and her need, her hunger, her love. "I've never been so sure of anything in my life."

He touched her then, sliding his finger down the side of her neck until he reached the top button of her blouse. Carefully, as though he were opening an infinitely fragile package, he released the buttons.

She didn't move, didn't breathe as he peeled the blouse away from her, then released the clasp on her bra. Bared to his view, she sat without moving—waiting.

With a muffled groan, he moved away from her and lay down on the blanket. Stretching his arms above his head, he met her puzzled gaze. "Ye wanted to be on top last time, Fortune. Do what ye will wi' me."

His power to tangle her thoughts amazed Fortune. She couldn't concentrate on his words, only on him: The muscular line of his arms leading down to his thick, dark hair spread across the blanket like temptation in silk. His jade eyes glittering with expectation, with hidden promises. His lips, parted, begging for her touch.

As her gaze slid past his throat, he swallowed hard, a sign of vulnerability that she longed to smooth away with her fingertips, her lips.

His wide shoulders, flat stomach . . . She knew

his body, and yet she didn't. The long, ridged scar that ran from beneath his right arm in a straight line to his waist. Tonight she'd trace with kisses the healed agony of that sword cut, yet never know what battle caused it, what he'd felt when the blade pierced his flesh, never know his emotions as his lifeblood soaked into the Scottish earth. She wouldn't ask him about it tonight, with magic all around them, and she suspected they wouldn't be together long enough for her to learn the stories of so many scars, the stories that made up the flow of his life.

Following the line of his body, she noted the relaxed strength of his slightly spread legs—waiting.

He was completely relaxed. He trusted her, knew he was safe in her presence. Somehow that knowledge made her want to . . . *Do what ye will wi' me.* The full import of his words hit her.

He lay before her, offering her the one thing he'd always refused to relinquish—control. She felt like some ancient goddess being honored with the supreme sacrifice. But instead of a sacrificial knife, she'd wield something far more potent.

Standing, she slowly stripped off her jeans with hands that shook. Running her gaze down his body, she let her glance linger between his thighs, glorying in the hard length that proclaimed his readiness for her.

Reacting to her gaze, he lifted his hips from the ground in an instinctual offering that needed no explanation. "Ye *do* wear underthings." His voice was harsh, urgent. "Get rid of them."

Her glorious savage hadn't quite learned humility yet. She smiled sweetly as she slowly, carefully,

329

slid her red panties over her hips, down her legs, then paused for effect before stepping out of them.

As he groaned like a man on the rack, she lifted her arms above her head in a leisurely stretch. She didn't know who she was torturing more. She barely resisted the urge to leap upon his mouth-wateringly naked body and devour him alive.

"Lass, dinna do this to me."

"What?" She smiled innocently down at him. "I haven't done a thing." Her smile turned wicked. "Yet."

Slipping to her knees beside him, she placed her palm against his heart—felt the quickened beat, heard his harsh breathing. For her.

She didn't think she could ever go back to making her pale imitations of men with their programmed responses, because she'd never be able to duplicate this—the emotion, the truth.

Leith started to reach for her, but she shook her head. "Don't. Let me bring you pleasure this time."

"Touching ye brings me pleasure, Fortune." He dropped his hand while his gaze turned smoky. "Ye will ask me to touch ye soon enough."

She looked at him from under lowered lids. "You talk too much, Campbell." Leaning down, she touched her mouth to his, then immediately deepened the kiss. She had no control where he was concerned. With his hands above his head, and his body bared to her, he pushed the buttons that left her panting like an overeager puppy at the sight of a new toy.

When she finally broke the kiss, she breathed as though she'd run miles. The hot taste of male and desire lingered on her lips. The searing response of his lips, his tongue, tempted her. She barely stopped herself from begging him to touch her.

"Ye have the look of a woman who needs to feel her man's hands on her, lass."

Looking into his eyes, she saw the triumph there. Never let it be said she couldn't accept a challenge. "Not until I drive you crazy, Campbell."

Easing down beside his prone body, she kissed a delicious trail along the side of his neck, glorying in the salty tang of warm, living male. She let her lips linger where his pulse beat fast and strong. She savored this proof of his life force, would close her eyes in future years and pull out the memory of his blood coursing through his body—his pulsing realness. She suspected she'd have a sad lack of realness in a life that didn't include Leith Campbell.

Fortune felt rather than saw impatient need writhing in him. "Hang on to your force field; I'm going as fast as I can."

"For a woman who lives in such a fast time, ye set a verra slow pace." His words were a hungry gasp.

Hunger. Her own body turned liquid with it. She carefully explored his nipples, licking, then rolling each one between her fingers until she could hear his harsh panting.

Suffer, Leith. But she knew in his suffering lay the seeds of her own destruction. Her hands shook as she slid them across his lower abdomen, down the inside of his hard, sweat-dampened thighs. Her lips followed the same path; then, when she reached the pulsing heart of her need, she paused. She wanted to, wanted to with every deprived cry echoing from her past, a past that had bound her

331

with silken rules—soft, comfortable, until you tried to break them. She'd never hungered to break them, until Leith. But rules meant nothing now. She was free—free to follow the path of her desire.

She put her mouth on him. His pleasure-pain groan encouraged her. Lingeringly, she ran her tongue the length of him. His hips bucked, rising to offer more of himself, begging for more of her. She couldn't resist. She took him deeply into her mouth, heat within heat. And when finally she moved from him, she knew.

She hadn't experienced teleportation, but she'd heard that in the moment before you became nothing, you had to face the fear that upon reappearance somewhere else, you'd never be the same person. This time she knew. She loved Leith Campbell, and their lovemaking tonight, in this time and place, would forever change her heart and soul. "Touch me, Leith. Please . . . touch me." *Touch the person I was, the person I'll be forever after*.

Without a sound he turned to her. He needed no words. She read his soul in his touch—his mouth on her nipples, teasing them with his lips, his tongue, until she moaned. His fingers—stroking her body until she thrummed with sobbing desire—her stomach, the insides of her thighs, then finally the spot that opened the door to a paradise she'd never thought to walk through again. She wouldn't walk through it alone.

"Now, please, now!" He was on top again and she was begging, but who gave a damn.

She closed her eyes and waited until she thought she'd explode. When she opened her eyes to make sure he hadn't dissolved into an unfulfilled dream, she found him watching her. His taut smile challenged her. "Know me, Fortune. Know who makes love to ye tonight. 'Tis not one of yer creations. I'm real. Remember the realness always."

Then he rose above her, blotting out her yesterdays, her tomorrows. Power rode his thrust, plunging deep to touch the center of her universe. And like an exploding star, she arched to meet the heat and light that flung her to the farthest corner of sensation, where for one searing moment in time she touched eternity.

Drifting through a soft black euphoria, she listened to the rasping of his breath beside her, felt his body still a part of hers, and felt a surprising tear slide down her cheek.

How much longer? And how could she live in a world without him? She didn't know; she just didn't know.

She opened her eyes to meet his warm gaze. For a moment she glimpsed something there that made her catch her breath; then it was gone, replaced by his smile.

"I must cross out the marks I've made." He ran his finger lightly down the middle of her nose, then leaned over to kiss the end of it.

"Marks?"

He nodded solemnly. "A mark for every time ye've climbed into bed beside me and havena made love wi' me." His gaze turned smoky. "A mark for every night of torture ye've put me through, lass."

Beyond all belief, she could feel him growing within her.

"But tonight ye made all the marks mean nothing, the waiting worthwhile. Tonight, lass, ye were wondrous." His voice was a contented growl.

"Really?" She felt like Ganymede, arching in the hope of receiving further strokes.

"Aye." His gaze turned suddenly serious. "There has ne'er been another who touched me as ye touched me, Fortune."

What she longed to say reached too deeply into her heart, exposed a small, quivering hope that blinked in the light, then retreated to its own familiar spot, still afraid, still unsure.

"Strange, you ended up on top again, in control, but it didn't matter." She smiled weakly and stroked the side of his face. "It didn't matter at all." What mattered was the feel of him beginning to move within her.

"This was ne'er about control, lass, but the sharing of pleasure between a man and a woman."

His quickened breathing told her of his desire to share more pleasure with her. "Doesn't it bother you that you found all this pleasure with a Mac-Donald?"

He stopped the slow, rhythmic movements that were beginning to make her breathe a little more quickly, too, and grinned at her. "It hasna bothered me for some time." His grin faded and he buried his face in the curve of her neck. " 'Twas ne'er the MacDonalds I hated, but myself. Even though I would do the same again, I felt I'd betrayed my clan, my brother. Ye must understand, lass, that I felt I did nothing to help my parents when they were killed during the raid. Glencoe only added to my guilt."

"You were only a child when your parents died. You couldn't do anything." This was one feeling she could share with him. She understood the helplessness of childhood, the feeling that if she could only do the right things, say the right things, her mother would love her. She realized now that her mother had never loved anyone, was probably incapable of loving anyone but herself.

She softly stroked Leith's hair. Now she knew the power of love, and she pitied her mother. Relief flooded her as she finally released the last of her lifetime's resentment.

" 'Twas safer to blame the MacDonalds than to question my brother's love, but mayhap I understand now. After the massacre, many who took no part condemned Hugh. My brother ever found it hard to admit wrong, but guilt couldna help but visit him in his dark moments. Mayhap Hugh saw in me the face of his own guilt. Hugh couldna fight the many, but he could fight the one—me."

His muffled words tore at her heart, a heart already lacerated by fear of their separation. His warm breath fanned her neck, and she ran her hand down his back in a comforting gesture.

"Love me, Fortune." His movements turned fierce, demanding.

Always. Tonight she'd give him enough love to wipe Hugh from his mind, his heart. At least until dawn ended this magic night.

She met his fierceness with her own, driving all memories of guilt and sadness away. "I love you, Leith."

Her murmur was lost in the rhythmic surge of fulfillment.

Afterward, he carried her to their bed, where she lay beside him, watching as he drifted toward sleep. At least for tonight, he'd found peace.

When his steady breathing told her he slept, she rose and threw on her robe. She felt restless and wide-awake with her need to think about tonight, about all her tomorrows. Wandering into the living room, she looked at the materials Blade had brought. Maybe she could start Blade's sculpture tonight.

Hours later, she realized how much she'd missed her work. But she could be happy in this time creating dynamic sculptures. Stopping to study what she'd done, she suddenly realized there was another sculpture waiting to be born—born of her love, her dreams. She'd work on it at the same time she did Blade's.

As the sun peeked above the horizon, Fortune glanced at Blade's head. She'd finish this quickly. Then she turned to stare at the second sculpture, the one she'd barely started. Walking over, she carefully covered it.

Chapter Sixteen

Leith dreamed sweet dreams that night, dreams that for once didn't include slaughter. Instead, he walked down a Highland path that led to a small cottage. In his dream he smiled, knowing his sweet, compliant wife awaited him with shy innocence and a homemade meal.

The cottage door swung open, and he saw silhouetted in the sunset's last rays . . . a red-haired vixen clothed in a clinging red dress. She smiled at him, a smile full of wicked promise.

"I sent out for pizza, lover. Why don't you get comfortable while we wait? I have a feeling the driver might be a little late. It's a long drive from Houston."

Leith woke with a silly grin on his face and a body part hard with anticipation. Rolling over, he reached for the red-haired vixen in question, only to find her side of the bed empty.

He groaned, flopped disgustedly onto his back, and tried to calm the agitated body part that insisted on standing up for its rights. "Relax, lad. Ye'll have to live on hope for a wee bit."

After climbing from bed, he showered quickly, dressed, then headed for the living room. He found Fortune humming happily and working on Blade's head.

Forgetting his disappointment for the moment, he circled the sculpture and peered closely at the detail. " 'Tis amazing, lass. It looks remarkably like Blade."

"How fortunate for me."

He glanced at her, and she grinned playfully at him.

"Of course it looks like Blade, dummy. After all the years I've made men, I should hope I could sculpt a faint resemblance."

He didn't quite know how to handle Fortune in this mood. After last night he'd expected . . . what? Regret? Anger? He'd known women who would blame the man when the lovemaking didn't meet their expectations, and sometimes when it did.

Fortune seemed vibrant this morning. Leith studied her. There was something in her eyes—a soft glow, a new vulnerability. He wasn't sure what it meant, but he decided it boded well for him.

A plaintive meow from outside drew his attention. "His lordship demands entrance. Shall we let him in?"

Fortune pursed her lips as though in deep thought. Then she smiled brightly. "Oh, why not?

May as well live dangerously. Let's hope he hasn't brought any ice-cream men home with him."

Leith swung the door open, and Ganymede paced regally in.

Fortune blinked, then stared at Leith. "Where'd he get that collar?"

Kneeling down, Leith touched the shiny red collar and the silver tag attached to it. Lifting the tag, he peered at the engraving. "It has his name, address, and our phone number on it."

Fortune abandoned her sculpture to kneel beside him, and he controlled his need to clasp her in his arms. Things were in a sorry state when even in an impersonal situation he couldn't stop thoughts of lust from intruding.

She ran her fingers along the collar's smooth surface. "Who put this on him?"

Leith remembered the feel of those fingers on his body, and his breathing quickened. Forcing the memory aside, he shrugged. "I dinna know. Mayhap the wee beastie put it on himself."

Ganymede cast him a sudden wary glance.

Leith decided he'd imagined the look. Perhaps he read too much into all of Ganymede's actions. Meeting Fortune's incredulous stare, he grinned. " 'Twas only a joke. Most likely Mrs. Hyperstein put the collar on him so all would know where to complain if he caused havoc among the neighborhood poodles."

Fortune smiled and shook her head. "You're probably right. Should we leave it on?"

"Aye. It wouldna do to have him lost." He grinned at Ganymede. "Though I dinna think we could lose him if we tried."

Nina Bangs

Ganymede swiped at him with unsheathed claws, and Leith jerked his hand away. "Ye understand me well, cat. 'Tis lucky I admire yer spirit. Most men wouldna put up wi' yer antics."

Ganymede stared at him out of large amber eyes that glittered with evil laughter, and Leith forced himself to hold the cat's gaze.

Finally he stood and mentally shook himself. What were the words for what he must do? Now he remembered. He must . . . get a grip.

Since Fortune showed no desire to speak of what had happened last night, he would allow her to think and come to terms with their new relationship. For after the wonder of last night, he couldn't leave her untouched on her side of the bed. He would go crazy if he tried.

"Ye can work on yer sculpture today. I must speak wi' Mary about money for our IDs." If the powers had any compassion, they'd leave him here with Fortune long enough to need identification. If not . . . "Then I must do some shopping. Ye wouldna be interested."

He noted the flicker of disappointment in her eyes and yearned to tell her how much he wanted her with him. It was becoming an obsession, this need to have her near. When he looked at her, touched her, he forgot everything else. Even his memories of Hugh paled in comparison to the pleasure Fortune brought him. But today he must be alone.

Leith stood on the sidewalk and looked at the money in his hand. Enough to purchase identification and something equally as important.

340

He'd purposely left Fortune at home because he knew she wouldn't approve of what he intended to do. She'd argue that they had more important things to do with their money right now.

But she was wrong. He wasn't blinded by what he wanted, and he wanted Fortune to remain forever with him. He no longer tried to fool himself about that. But the Fates were nothing if not fickle, and he must face the fact that Fortune might very well be sent back to her time without warning.

The thought made his stomach cramp with sick dread. He didn't want to think of it, but he must, for Fortune's sake. If she returned to her own time, he wanted her to take with her this memory.

Pushing the money into his pocket, he entered the pawnshop.

When he again stood outside the shop, he clasped Fortune's chain and cross in his hand. He longed to crush the cross so tightly in his hand that its imprint would forever remain in his flesh—the only physical memory he'd have of Fortune. But that was impossible. He opened his hand and studied the intricate silver design, then idly turned it over.

He narrowed his gaze as he brought the cross closer to his eyes. There seemed to be some faint words chiseled on the back. Squinting, he finally made out the message.

When at last he lowered the cross, disbelief and wonder fought for dominance. *Impossible*. What he'd read was impossible.

But why not? Everything that had happened to him in the last few weeks had been impossible.

Throwing his head back, he laughed—laughed at a fate that arranged things so neatly, manipulated them so completely. The whole thing was brilliant, and he offered a silent salute to its planner.

Fortune heard him whistling as he approached the door. The carefree sound fueled her sense of outrage. Here she'd been worried sick about him, and he could *whistle*. Well, she'd see how Mr. Happy-go-lucky felt in a few minutes.

The door swung open, and she attacked. "How nice of you to show up occasionally." She hoped he recognized the phoniness of her smile. "I suppose I can cancel the missing-person's report?"

He stared uncomprehendingly. "Missing-person's report?"

She felt like gnashing her teeth. How could she crush him with her witty sarcasm when he didn't understand her meaning? "Let me rephrase that in more primitive terms."

Gleefully, she noticed she had his full attention now. He glared at her, and she smiled back. "It's almost six o'clock. It's the day of Michael's party. It's been eight hours since you left. It's . . . it's . . ."

" 'Twas a grand day, lass, until now. I have money for our identification." He pulled the bills from his pocket and waved them at her. "I dinna know anything that can destroy a man's happiness faster than a nagging wife." He slapped the money down on the coffee table, then strode toward the kitchen.

Surprised, Fortune stood staring after him. *Nagging wife*? The nagging part made her feel guilty, but the wife part . . . The wife part sounded right. She closed her eyes. Who was she kidding? She had as much chance of marrying Leith as she had of understanding him. He'd want a wife who didn't defy him, insult him, argue with him. Sighing, she trailed him into the kitchen.

She watched him cut up a tomato for the sandwich he was making with the same precision he'd probably use to cut out an enemy's heart. Her heart, to be exact. "I'm sorry I called you primitive. I only said it because I was angry."

He didn't take his attention from the hapless tomato. "Dinna fash yerself, lass. I didna even notice yer insult."

Tell that to the tomato. "OK, if you *had* noticed that I called you primitive, I'd like to apologize. I lashed out at you because I was . . . worried." *There*. She'd said it. Now he'd laugh at her.

He paused from his tomato dissecting to gaze at her. "Ye were worried?" His warm gaze caressed her, assured her she'd said something wonderful. "Why?"

She fidgeted with the place mat on the worn wooden table. "Anything could happen to you out there. Someone could mug you." She abandoned the place mat and clung to the back of a chair. "I know. It sounds dumb. I mean, you've survived a lot more than a mugging, but I still worry." This was getting worse and worse. Any minute now she'd resort to babbling.

"Ye'd care?" The husky softness of his voice held a note of tension.

They seemed to be talking in circles. "Of course I'd care."

"Why?"

Didn't the blasted man know any other words?

"Because . . ." She should lie, tell him she didn't

343

want to manage alone, that she needed the money he made. She told the truth. "Because it would hurt me." Unconsciously, she placed a hand over her heart.

"Aye." He smiled as though she'd imparted some great secret.

"Well, I'd better get ready for the party." She fled the kitchen as though pursued by alien invaders, but glanced back to see that he'd stopped savaging the tomato and was standing staring into space with a bemused expression on his face.

She lifted her arms to the star-filled sky and twirled happily. The short skirt of her new red dress flared in the light breeze. Even Ganymede's sober presence couldn't dent her joy in the party. Everything had been wonderful, from the smoldering appreciation in Leith's gaze when he first saw her dress to the hungry glances he'd thrown her all night. Who cared if red wasn't her color? Leith liked it, and that was all that mattered.

She stopped twirling to stare at the dark shapes of live oak trees and the gaily lighted castle in the pale silver glow of the full moon. The fiercely independent Four-Two-N would never have worn something just to please a man. But Fortune? Fortune would make the most of the time she had with her man. *Her man*. Possessiveness. She'd have a lot of negative traits to purge when she returned home.

Home? Home was here, in the year 2000, with Leith Campbell. And nothing would ever change that.

Her mood shattered, she stood and stared at the

castle's door. Leith had said he'd be out in a moment. What would it feel like to know that Leith would never again open a door and come toward her? With his work for Mary almost complete, maybe she should start getting used to the idea.

The sound of the door opening distracted her from that distressing thought. She watched as Leith strode toward her.

In his jeans and white shirt, he was the sexiest man there. Not that she'd even looked at the other men except when politeness demanded it.

" 'Tis a beautiful night." He lifted his gaze to the sky, and she stored the memory of the man, the night, the emotion.

His hair lifted gently in the soft breeze as he lowered his gaze to stare at her. "Ye look bonny tonight, lass." His husky murmur gave sensuality to the silence.

In another time, she would have felt unsure, nervous. But tonight was magic, and she felt able to topple empires or mesmerize princes in her red dress. Of course, the only man she wanted to mesmerize stood in front of her.

A distant melody broke the night's quiet. Puzzled, she stared into the darkness. "What's that?"

" 'Tis the ice-cream truck. I canna imagine he'll sell much ice cream at this time of night." He glanced around him. "I dinna see Ganymede. We would be wise to see that the wee devil doesna get near the truck."

They listened silently as the music grew louder.

Fortune smiled at Leith. "The song Elvis is singing . . . It's beautiful."

"I canna help falling in love with ye." Leith murmured the song's words.

Fortune closed her eyes against the sudden pain. She would trade all her yesterdays, barter all her tomorrows, to hear Leith speak those words—from his heart, from his soul.

"We didna dance tonight, Fortune. Will ye dance wi' me now?"

Fortune opened her eyes and blinked away her sudden emotion. Knowing she couldn't speak without her voice quavering, she only nodded.

He moved close to her and she absorbed the heat, the special feel of him that would allow her to recognize him forever.

"I havena done this before, but I know I must put my arms around ye, and *that* I can do verra well."

The music swelled, and the words flowed over her as he embraced her—blotting out the moon, the stars, the universe. "I've never done this either, but I think you have the right idea."

She tilted her head to look up at him. His hair framed his face—a dark halo in a moonlit paradise. He stared down at her, his eyes warm, compelling. Then he smiled, a rueful slant of his lips, and she wanted to stand on tiptoe and touch those lips with hers.

"Ye have my permission to curse me if I step on yer toes." His smile broadened. "But then, yer curses are no curses at all, lass."

He pulled her tightly against him, and she wrapped both arms around him. She didn't think this position was technically correct, but it sure did feel good.

Feel. She ran her fingers across the muscles of his back, gloried in the tactile sensations of firm flesh and controlled power, longed to sink into him until no line of separation remained.

He began to sway to the music, and his hands smoothed their way to the small of her back, then gently rubbed an up-and-down rhythm of their own.

She was sure that wasn't where his fingers should be, but when his hands moved lower to cup her buttocks and urge her closer, she forgot all about traditional dancing positions.

This was the right way. And as his steps guided her across the moon-silvered lawn, she gloried in the lithe movement of his body against hers.

Lifting her head, she met his heavy-lidded stare. No laughter glittered in his eyes, only searing intensity, and a need that seemed more than physical. Wishful thinking? She didn't know. "This moment is perfect, Leith." She reached up to stroke a strand of his dark hair that lay on his shoulder.

" 'Tis what I'll remember, lass." Leaning over, he gently kissed her forehead. "The moon, yer eyes, and . . . the music." He glanced away as he swung her in a circle that lifted her hair in the breeze, but not before she saw his sudden flush.

Her heart turned to mush. He was embarrassed, and she loved him so much she could cry. "Just my eyes? What about my dress? It's red. I mean, I don't wear red for just anyone, you know."

His gaze returned to her, and he smiled. But his smile didn't touch the sadness she saw in his eyes.

"I dinna know where the Fates will fling us, lass, but I want to stay wi' ye."

She started to speak, but he lightly kissed her lips, effectively silencing her.

"Every year on this night, I will dance wi' ye in the moonlight." As he swept her into another circle, the skirt of her dress billowed in a scarlet cloud around them. "And ye'll wear this dress for me."

Suddenly the night sparkled with diamond shards of hope and happiness. She laughed and buried her face in the warm hollow of his neck, felt his pulse beating strong beneath her lips. "It's a deal, Campbell."

He hadn't said he loved her, but surely the fact that he wanted to stay with her meant something. She felt like a child again, with the world alive to wonderful possibilities, all of which centered around her Highland warrior.

The magic faded as the castle door swung open, allowing light to stream onto the lawn. A couple they'd met at the party walked toward them. The man grinned at Leith. "Hey, you guys left a while ago. Aren't you ever going home?"

Fortune searched her brain for a reasonable excuse, but she might as well not have bothered.

" 'Tis a beautiful night. Fortune and I were enjoying it together." Leith's easy smile made everything perfectly reasonable.

"Gotcha. How about a ride home? Michael said you don't have wheels yet."

"Aye. If ye dinna mind taking our cat home also." Leith nodded his head toward where Ganymede sat beside a lion statue.

The woman spoke for the first time. "Of course

he can come." She walked over and scooped Ganymede into her arms. "Is him my widdle kitty?"

Her "widdle kitty" wore a pained expression as the woman squeezed him to her chest.

Fortune climbed into the car's backseat beside Leith. She remained quiet while Leith carried on a companionable conversation with their new friends. Right now she didn't want to talk. All she wanted to do was absorb the solid feel of Leith's arm around her and his side pressed against her. And think. She had a lot to think about.

She was still thinking when they reached the house. Automatically, she scooped up Ganymede and headed for the door. She'd already swung the door open when she realized Leith wasn't behind her. Turning, she saw he'd stopped to speak with an older woman who held a bored-looking poodle on a leash. Mrs. Hyperstein must be taking her nightly walk.

Fortune grinned, then continued into the house. Poor Leith. Mrs. Hyperstein probably wanted to warn him about the dangers of keeping saber-toothed panthers on his front lawn. Fortune counted herself lucky to have escaped the inquisition. Setting Ganymede down, she walked into the bedroom to wait for Leith.

Tonight was a magical night, and it would end magically with Leith in her arms. Tonight was made for love. She grimaced. And love was making her think in clichés. Or maybe clichés were simply universal truths.

Hmm. Leith had been gone quite a while. Maybe she should take pity on the man and rescue him.

When she stepped out of the house, it took only

a quick glance up and down the road to realize Leith was nowhere in sight. Mrs. Hyperstein was wending her way down the street, stopping at every tree or bush to let her poodle do his thing.

Where . . . ? She ran quickly to the backyard. No Leith. He wouldn't just leave without telling her where he was going. Unless . . . The thought rocked her, and for a moment she forgot to breathe. Cosmic forces wouldn't do this, not with her mission unfulfilled. She couldn't believe he'd been sent back to his own time. Not like this.

With panic born of despair, she raced down the street in pursuit of Mrs. Hyperstein.

Completely out of breath, Fortune could only tap Mrs. Hyperstein on the shoulder when she reached her. The woman dropped the leash, then spun with a cry that sounded sort of like those martial-arts movies Leith liked to watch.

Fortune stared blankly at the objects Mrs. Hyperstein clutched in each hand.

"I'm armed and dangerous, scumball. If the hat pin doesn't get you, the pepper spray will." Mrs. Hyperstein blinked at her, then smiled. "Oh, it's only you, dearie. A helpless old woman can't be too careful nowadays."

If Fortune hadn't been so terrified, she would've laughed. She pitied any muggers who tried to work this street. "Mrs. Hyperstein, you were just talking to my husband. Do you know where he went?"

Mrs. Hyperstein reached down and picked up her poodle's leash. "Of course, dearie." She carefully put her lethal weapons away.

Fortune counted years off her life while she waited for the woman to continue.

"I gave him a message from that man, Bones. Then your husband rushed right off to meet him." She frowned. "I suppose this Bones didn't want to wait on your lawn because of your panther. Can't say that I blame him." She brightened. "Anyway, I happened to be nearby, so this Bones asked if I'd give your husband a neighborly message."

Get to the point! "What message?"

"Hmm. Let me get this exactly right." She dragged her dog over to a promising-looking bush. "This Bones—who is a seedy-looking character if I ever saw one, but who am I to comment on your friends—wanted your husband to meet him down by the lake." She frowned at the poodle, who showed no interest in the bush. "Oh, and he wanted him to come alone."

Damn you, Leith Campbell. Damn you for thinking you could keep me safe by going off to meet him alone. Didn't Leith know she'd never feel safe again without him?

Not even stopping to thank Mrs. Hyperstein, she spun and raced back to the house. Picking up the phone with a trembling hand, she quickly punched in a number.

A few minutes later, still clutching the phone, she ran out to the lawn to wait. If a phone made a good enough weapon for Leith Campbell, then it was good enough for Fortune MacDonald. Vaguely, she wondered where Four-Two-N had gone. She glanced down as she felt the weight of a body against her leg, then smiled weakly. "You should've gone with him, Ganymede. He needs you."

Ganymede's amber eyes locked with hers, and

351

she could've sworn worry moved in their depths. More likely she merely saw a reflection of her own distress.

Thoughts of Ganymede disappeared at the approaching rumble of powerful motors. When they finally broke into view, she started to tremble. She couldn't do this. But she had to, for Leith. Taking a deep breath, she stepped to the curb and waited.

Ganymede waited beside her.

Leith had miscalculated. He'd underestimated how much Bones wanted to get rid of him—permanently. He'd thought they'd simply beat each other to a bloody pulp and that would be that. Honor would've been served.

Staring at the gun Bones held, Leith tried to gauge the deadliness of the threat. He knew how fast a gun could kill, and he doubted Bones would hesitate to pull the trigger.

"I dinna understand why ye feel the need to threaten me wi' death." Leith shifted his weight, preparatory to diving for the gun. "Why canna we fight like men?"

"Shut up." Hate shone from Bones's eyes. "They kicked me outa my own club, and it's all your fault."

Leith frowned, trying to follow Bones's logic. "They wouldna do that just because I won the fight, nor because ye had a wee tussle wi' my cat."

"Enemies. The club was full of dirty sneakin' enemies. They wanted to get rid of me, but they were afraid. They knew I'd kick their asses if they made a move." His voice was a vicious snarl. "But when you beat me, you made me lose face. And when I tried to tell them your panther messed me up, they laughed. Laughed at me!" He was almost shouting, and his gun hand shook. "Blade spread it around that all you had was an ordinary black cat. It was a panther! I know a friggin' panther when I see one."

Leith could hear Bones's control slipping, and he considered how fast he could reach the knife strapped to his ankle. Not fast enough to avoid a bullet. He eyed the distance to the water. Too far. "If ye shoot me, all will know who did it. Ye'll have to run, ne'er knowing when the police will find ye."

"The cops won't find me. I'm good at goin' to ground." His grin was an evil twist of his lips. "Maybe I'll kill your old lady for good measure before I go. Yeah, I like that idea."

Bones had just made a mortal mistake. Leith felt the icy stillness flow through him, the current of death he'd felt so many times in the heat of battle. No one threatened his woman.

His woman. The words echoed in his mind, in his heart, and they sounded right. Fortune wouldn't appreciate their possessiveness, but he came from a world where a man protected his woman with his life, if need be.

Leith's smile promised death; his narrowed gaze suggested it would be soon.

Bones reacted to the silent threat by waving his gun wildly. "Don't move, Campbell."

Leith's plans for how best to tear Bones limb from limb were shattered by the sudden roar of distant motors.

"What the hell . . . ?" Bones glanced nervously to each side.

Leith peered into the darkness. Those were motorcycles. Lots of them. What were they doing on this road at midnight?

Then he saw the lights. Shading his eyes against the glare, he squinted to make out who was driving the front bike.

He made out a silhouette that looked like Tank. There was something braced against the front of the bike, and someone riding behind Tank.

God's teeth! He didn't believe it. Briefly closing his eyes, he prayed to whatever gods protected foolish women and demon cats. He would need all the help he could get tonight.

Chapter Seventeen

I am really not happy. How unhappy am I? Thank you for asking. I'm butt-kickin', where's-a-plague-of-locusts-when-you-need-it unhappy.

Right. They don't have locust plagues in Houston. What would I do without you to point out these minor, unimportant details?

Why don't humans ever do what you expect? Who woulda guessed Leith would go off to tackle Bones without his compadre, his fellow warrior, me?

Okay, no excuses. I messed up. Now I'm payin' for my mistake. I've had comfier rides on camels during sandstorms. Humans have weird ideas of fun. Give me a big Mercedes with a leather interior, and I'll die happy.

But this isn't about my comfort. I gotta get to Leith before anything bad happens. I promise you, if Bones hurts Leith, I'll tear Bones apart, use his head

*for a bowling ball, stomp on his liver. . . . Then I'll
really get nasty.*

*So I'm gettin' a little carried away. But no one
messes with my human. And Leith is my human. I
mean, we understand each other. He takes care of
my needs, even though he knows I'm not your regular garden-variety puss. Hey, he can look past our
differences and see the real me—loving, loyal. Yeah,
I guess you don't buy that crap, but I do have feelings
for him. I'm not quite sure what they are, but until
I figure them out, everyone had better keep their
hands off my man.*

*Once I make sure Leith is okay, I gotta start plan-
nin' the final act in this play. October 31 is . . . hmm.
Only one more week. How time flies when you're
havin' fun. Look, I'll level with you. Somehow I
don't have the enthusiasm for this like I had at the
beginning. But I can't back out now. The Big Guy
frowns on changes of heart.*

*Right. I don't have a heart. I forgot. Anyway, I've
got a reputation to uphold, and Halloween is the big
payoff.*

*You know, I don't feel too hot. Must be motion
sickness.*

Leith blinked to clear his vision. No, he wasn't seeing things.

An army of leather-vested warriors rode to his
rescue. Two by two, a long line of Harleys roared
toward him out of the darkness.

But he had eyes only for the front bikes, the ones
Tank and Blade were riding. Behind Blade sat
Lily—majestic, larger than life—with a knife that
glinted in the moonlight raised above her head and

another knife gripped between her teeth.

And behind Tank . . . Behind Tank sat Fortune, every inch of her body language screaming her fear. He remembered her vow never to climb on a motorcycle and felt humbled by her courage.

She'd conquered her fear for *him*. Somewhere in the darkest corner of his heart, the last stones of the wall he'd built to protect himself from her crumbled forever.

His woman was coming for him. Then he noticed something else. The front of Tank's bike had gained a new figurehead.

Ganymede stood on his hind legs, his front paws braced against the bike's handlebars. His ears were pinned back, and fury gleamed in his amber eyes.

And even though Bones still held his gun, Leith felt wrapped in triumph. His friends, his *family*, were ready to do battle for him.

Then reality intruded. Leith could see panic growing in Bones's eyes. A frightened bully was far more dangerous than a calm, seasoned warrior. He must get the gun from Bones.

Bones swung the gun in an arc, trying to cover both Leith and the new danger. "Tell them to go away, Campbell, or your old lady gets it first."

"I dinna think so," Leith murmured as he dived for the gun.

Bones brought the gun over to aim at Leith, and as Leith's fingers closed over the weapon, Bones pulled the trigger.

A sudden burning pain in his upper left arm sent Leith to his knees, but he didn't release the gun. Forcing the muzzle aside, Leith gathered his strength to launch himself at Bones again. He knew his own power, and if he could land one solid punch with all his fury behind it, Bones would drop the gun.

Leith didn't need to bother. Suddenly he heard a shrill, savage scream and saw a flash of red. Before he could even blink in surprise, Fortune had leaped onto Bones's back and was pummeling him with . . . a phone?

Unable to cope with this new attack, Bones dropped his gun. Fortune didn't seem to notice.

"You hurt him, you bastard!" She emphasized her observation with a whack from her phone. "You son of a bitch!"

Leith winced at the sound of the phone connecting with bone.

Abandoning all pretense of aggression, Bones tried to protect his head from Fortune's lethal attack. Suddenly he screamed and started shaking his leg in a bizarre jig of pain.

Glancing down, Leith grinned. Ganymede had his claws firmly attached to Bones's leg and was climbing methodically toward his goal. Leith followed Ganymede's obvious route up Bones's leg and realized what would happen in a matter of seconds.

As enjoyable as this was to watch, he'd better stop it now before Fortune and Ganymede reduced Bones to a battered eunuch. There was no need for further violence. Fortune would be proud of his decision.

Struggling to his feet, Leith pulled Ganymede from Bones's leg. Damn, the wee beast had dug in like a starving tick on a fat dog.

Ganymede growled his displeasure at having his

attack aborted. But Leith couldn't worry about him.

Moving around behind Bones, Leith grabbed Fortune's arm just as she was about to deliver another phone message. "Ye can stop now, lass. 'Tis over."

She stared at him out of eyes glazed with fury and fear. "He hurt you. I'll kill him."

He watched as her gaze grew calmer, and when he felt it was safe, he released her.

Now free from attack, Bones turned to flee, only to find himself ringed by angry bikers. Tank climbed off his bike and walked over to Bones. "You're alone, Bones. You don't have anyone to stand behind you. Everyone in your club is glad to see you gone. If I were you, I'd get out of Texas fast. Oh, and if you ever come back, we'll know." Tank smiled—not a nice smile. "And we'll find you wherever you try to hide."

Like a whipped puppy, Bones nodded, then ran to his bike. They listened as the sound of his motorcycle faded into the distance.

Bones's public humiliation could almost make Leith feel sorry for him. Almost. Until he remembered that Bones had threatened Fortune. His lips tightened as he thought of the punishment he would have liked to mete out.

Tank moved over to Leith. "Are you okay? We can take you to the hospital."

Leith shook his head. " 'Tis not serious. I've seen on television that a doctor must report bullet wounds, and I dinna want to answer questions from the police."

Tank nodded his understanding.

With mounting panic, Fortune watched Leith's lips tighten. He was in pain. Even if his wound was serious, he wouldn't admit it to Tank because he didn't want to involve the police. She had to see his arm for herself.

"Let me help you get that shirt off, Leith. I want to see your arm." Without waiting for permission, she unbuttoned his shirt and slid it off his shoulders.

Wincing, he let the shirt slip completely off.

She drew in her breath at all the blood. One of the bikers handed her a clean cloth, which she used to dab at the wound. Out of the corner of her eye, she saw Ganymede race into the bushes, but she couldn't worry about the cat now.

When she'd finally wiped enough blood away to see the injury, she sighed with relief. The bullet had gouged a shallow groove in his upper arm, but the cut didn't look serious.

For the first time since she'd realized what Leith planned, she allowed herself to relax, to release the terrible fear that she might lose him, not to the past, but to death. She refused to admit they were one and the same, that if they both returned to their own times, Leith would've been dead for almost six hundred years.

"Let's go home so I can take care of this, Leith," she murmured softly. Without conscious thought, she wrapped her arms tightly around his waist and laid her head against his chest, glorying in the steady beat of his heart. *Alive*. She blinked rapidly to keep the tears at bay.

"Aye. Home." She felt his hand glide over her hair in a gentle caress.

"We'll give you guys a ride home." Tank's voice shattered the moment. "Someone will drop your cat off as soon as he gets through throwing up behind the bushes."

Leith shook his head. "Dinna bother. I'll get him. He deserves to go home wi' us. He fought bravely today."

Tank looked puzzled, but then shrugged. "Whatever you say."

Soon they were home, and with Leith settled in bed, Fortune could breathe easily again. Sitting on the bed beside him, she still shook with the horror of how close they'd come to—

She couldn't even form the possibility in her mind, couldn't conceive of losing him. But the probability was that it would happen. She'd been sent for a purpose, and even if she failed in that purpose she'd be called back.

No! She clenched the sheet tightly in her fist, the way she wanted to squeeze every last moment of joy with Leith, make it last forever. But there were no forevers, not in this lifetime.

Leaning over, she smoothed his hair away from his face, touched his cheek with her lips.

He opened his eyes and stared at her.

If she could sink into him, become part of him, then there'd be no good-byes, no tearing pain of separation. She didn't attempt to hide her need, her fear, her love. In her eyes he could read all the emotions she didn't dare speak.

Pushing the sheet down to his waist, he continued to hold her gaze. She'd seen so many emotions in his eyes since they'd met, but now, when it mattered most, she saw . . . nothing. It was as though he'd pulled a mask over his soul. Why? What did he fear she'd see?

"For a woman who swore she'd ne'er resort to violence, ye played the warrior queen well." He pulled the mask slightly aside for a moment, exposing something hotter, more elemental than his teasing words indicated. "And yer curses were fine, lass. I couldna have done better myself."

"You'll never let me forget this, will you?" She tried unsuccessfully to match his light tone.

"I'll remember it always, Fortune." He reached up to trace the line of her jaw with his callused finger. "I'll remember *you* always."

She knew at any moment she could explode with the emotions struggling to escape her. "It's amazing. When I knew you were in danger, nothing mattered. Not values instilled in me since birth, not anyone's opinion of me. Nothing mattered except you."

He moved his hand behind her neck and gently massaged the tense muscles there. "Ye are the first person to come to my rescue armed only wi' . . ."

Love? Say it! Damn you, say it.

". . . a phone."

Even as he said the words, the mask fell away and she looked into the tortured depths of his soul. She spun like a leaf in a maelstrom—with no beginning, no end, just the endless battering by emotions he'd never admit, wouldn't want her to see if he could control them.

But he couldn't control them, and she gloried in his weakness. His inability to hide all his feelings from her was a small victory, but a victory nonetheless.

He gave her no time to think further as his grip tightened on her neck and he pulled her down to him. His lips touched hers with need, hunger— searching for something.

Remembering his injured arm, she held his face in her hands and kissed him deeply, letting her lips speak of her love.

The phone rang. Pulling away from him, she allowed the shimmering colors of love to fade into reality. She heard Leith's harsh curse as she picked up the receiver. "Hello?"

"Hi. It's Blade. I forgot to tell you guys we're having a Halloween party next week at the Cajun Café. Y'all get costumes and come on down." He chuckled. "You were great tonight, kid. Fastest phone in the West. And what about that damned cat? Tank said he'd trade his Rottweiler straight up for that cat. Oh, and Lily says for you to take good care of your man. See ya."

Fortune hung up the phone and savored the warm glow from Blade's praise. How could she return to her time, where emotions ran cool and contained, after experiencing the hot and explosive feelings she'd gotten used to in just two weeks?

She met Leith's questioning gaze. "That was Blade. We're invited to a Halloween party next week. We have to come in costume. Any ideas?" She gently touched the bandage on his arm. Never would she get her fill of touching him.

"Aye." His gaze sizzled with ideas. "But not about costumes."

Something pulled at the corner of her conscious-

ness, and she fought its insistent demand, but to
no avail. "You'll . . . you'll be finished with Mary's
work by next week, won't you?"

He simply nodded, and the silence said all that
needed saying. Could one week be all that remained of the universe he'd forged in her heart?
Would she try to take him back with her? How
could she do that to the man she loved? How could
she *not* bring him back, knowing that humanity's
very existence hung in the balance? And even if
duty won, how would she convince him to return
to the rest-over room with her? The multitude of
questions swirled in her mind, her heart, making
her feel slightly nauseous.

"Come back to me, Fortune."

For a moment, his demand eerily mirrored the
battle she fought in her soul; then she saw the concern in his eyes and tried to relax. "I'm . . . I'm fine.
So what costume do you think you'll wear?"

She saw his sigh and knew he'd humor her need
to avoid the subject that writhed between them like
a poisonous Tiran cloud.

"Mary's husband collected copies of Campbell
clothing. Mayhap she'll let me borrow something.
What will ye wear?"

Who cares? Just don't leave me, Leith Campbell.
"OK, if you're going to dress like a Scottish warrior, I'll dress as your common ordinary woman in
2300."

He captured her hand where it lay on the sheet
and brought it to his lips. "Ne'er common, lass.
Ne'er ordinary." He softly kissed the inside of her
wrist, and shivers of desire worked their magic until her entire body thrummed with want.

Forcing herself to stand, she moved a safe distance from the bed. Fine, so no distance would ever be safe enough from him. *How about six hundred years?* She shoved the thought aside.

Trying to ignore the disappointed glint in his eyes, she walked toward the bedroom door. "If I stay here, I'm going to eat you alive."

His expression brightened.

"Forget it, tough guy. You've lost some blood, and I won't take a chance of doing more damage to your arm."

" 'Tis not my arm that needs attention. Come to me, lass."

And she did. Turning off the light, she returned to the bed, now spotlighted in the moon's cool silver glow. But there was nothing cool about the man awaiting her. Flinging off her clothes, she slid into the bed beside him and wrapped herself in his heat, his passion.

She rode him fiercely, glorying in the feel of hard male beneath her, lifting her to the stars like the fabled winged horse, Pegasus. Clasping him tightly between her thighs, she urged him on with a sense that she must squeeze every last drop of emotion, sensation, from him, enough to last forever, knowing that forever could begin soon, too soon. And when he bucked beneath her, she cried out for more of him. He answered by driving so deeply into her, she felt the shudder all the way to her heart. His final thrust was power and light, filling her as she'd never been filled before, would never be again. When she heard his hoarse cry and felt the warm spill of his seed, she shattered her silent fears with a primal scream that echoed down the

Nina Bangs

corridors of time as completion shook her.

How long she lay wrapped in his arms while her pounding heart slowed and her breathing grew normal, she couldn't guess. They needed no speech, because words couldn't describe what they'd shared. She waited until his even breathing assured her he slept before slipping from the bed and padding silently into the living room. If she stayed in bed, she wouldn't sleep. All the decisions she'd avoided making would howl at her like rabid carnitaks, demanding her attention, refusing to go away.

She might as well work on Blade's sculpture for a while. It should be done by next week. Would everything be done by next week? She couldn't handle that thought now.

She might even have time to work on the other sculpture, the one that wouldn't be done by next week, might never be done.

Fortune turned the living room light on and studied the almost completed head. She could always lose herself in her work, and she needed that badly tonight. She didn't want to think, only feel and remember.

A week. How could a week pass so quickly? Agitated, Fortune paced the floor while darkness gathered outside the living room window. The silky white pantaloons bothered her as she moved, reminded her of things she'd tried to push aside, reminded her of a home that no longer seemed like home.

The distant laughter of children trick-or-treating mocked her somber mood. "Curse you, Leith

366

Campbell. Where are you when I need you?" *I'll always need you*.

As though in answer to her entreaty, she heard Leith's key in the door. She turned to greet him.

But the man who walked into the living room wasn't the Leith she knew. Hard eyed, with his plaid flung across one broad shoulder, he was a warrior from a time she'd never known, would never know.

Leith Campbell was dressed to go home.

She swallowed hard against the creeping sense of dread that made her shiver even in the still-warm Texas night.

Then he smiled and reached her in one stride. Gathering her into his arms, he kissed her hard, not bothering to hide his desire. "Dinna look at me like that, lass." Gently grasping her wrist, he moved her hand down the length of his body until she felt his readiness for her. "Clothes dinna change the man." He held her away from him for a moment while he studied what she wore. "Or the woman." He frowned. "Ye need to wear strong colors, lass, to go wi' yer passionate nature." He placed a finger over her lips before she could retort. "I've held ye in my arms, so dinna deny yer passion."

"I'm afraid this is what I'd wear if I were home." She smiled up at him, but her smile was bitter-sweet. "Leith, I have to go somewhere before the party."

" 'Tis no problem. I will go wi' ye."

Fortune shook her head. "I'd . . . I'd rather go alone." She longed to ease the suddenly worried gleam in his eyes.

"What has happened, Fortune, and where are ye going?"

She took a deep breath and tried to dispel her cold fear. "Ganymede disappeared right after you left, and I just got a call that someone found him."

"Fine. We will bring him home."

She clasped and unclasped her hands, then purposely held them still. She had to make him understand.

"He's at the rest-over."

She watched a shuttered expression once again change him into a stranger, a stranger she'd known only three weeks but who'd managed to fill her universe.

He nodded. "We will go together to get him." His tone was implacable, uncompromising.

No! He couldn't go. If this was it, the time for her to return, she didn't want to face the decision she must make. If he stayed here, there was no decision. When had she become such a coward? *When you fell in love.* "I don't want you to go with me."

His lips lifted in a wry grin. "I dinna think ye have a choice, lass." He moved away from her, already distancing himself, it seemed. "Let us speak plainly. We could have someone bring him home, but 'twould only be postponing what must be. I would rather stand and fight than run away like a craven."

She'd never felt so proud of him as she did at that moment. She forced aside the weak arguments that fought to tumble from her in a frantic attempt to hold back the inevitable. If he could face with such courage whatever waited for them at the rest-over, could she do less?

Besides, if they only went into the lobby, grabbed Ganymede, then left, probably nothing would happen. Maybe she could convince Leith to wait for her outside. He hated the thought of returning to her time. Hadn't he sworn he'd never set foot in the rest-over again? *But without him, what will happen to humanity?*

She tried to calm herself, tried to think logically. If she failed, cosmic forces would simply find someone else to do their dirty work, wouldn't they? *Are you willing to sacrifice humanity if you're wrong?*

What happened to her didn't matter so long as Leith was happy. Whether he stayed in this time or returned to his own time, he'd survive and make a place for himself. Maybe he'd find a woman who'd love him. *Never as much as I will. Never as long as I will.*

She tried to force aside thoughts of humanity's fate.

The phone's shrill ring vibrated along nerve endings already stretched taut with tension.

"Ye need not answer. I'll speak wi' the person, then call for a taxi."

She watched numbly as he picked up the phone and left the room. She understood. Each of them needed a few minutes alone—to think, to come to terms with what this night might bring.

She wandered over to the bust she'd done of Blade. He would find it when he went through the house and know it was for him, a thank-you for his kindness to two people who'd traveled farther than he could possibly imagine. Two people who for three short weeks had put aside the differences of six hundred years to live and lo— No, that was wrong. She loved Leith, but she didn't know what Leith felt, wouldn't try to force him to say something he didn't feel.

Slowly she walked to the second sculpture and pulled off the cover. The unfinished work mocked her. Their family—Leith, Ganymede, and herself. Perhaps it was fitting that it remain unfinished, just as their life together remained unfinished. A time that in a few years would fade to a sepia memory. *Liar.*

She fought the temptation to take it with her. Even if she went back to her time tonight, it was unlikely any object could go with her. Last time she'd managed to keep only her cross. Her cross. She knew a sharp stab of regret. She'd have to return without it. The pawnshop was closed for the night.

But *things* didn't matter in the scheme of life. She realized that now. Only people mattered. She looked at the unfinished sculpture. It belonged here, where they'd been together. It was part of this time, this life.

She took a deep breath and rushed outside to wait for Leith. If she stayed inside for one more minute she'd break down. And tonight she had to be strong—for Leith, for herself.

As she stood in the comforting darkness, she could see the taxi's lights coming down the street. She turned for one last look at the house.

Leith opened the door and stepped out.

This would be one of her most precious memories—her fierce warrior poised in front of the shabby little house where she'd found happiness. She quickly turned from the sight and held her breath until the tears that clogged her throat grew bearable.

As the taxi pulled to a stop in front of her, she felt Leith behind her—his quiet breathing, the scent of cool night and warm male, the rough caress of his hair as he bent to kiss the side of her neck.

"Mayhap this isna what we think, Fortune. But if 'tis, we will face it together." He wrapped her in his quiet strength, shielding her with his promise.

No, love, we can't face this together. I have to do this alone. For you.

As he held the taxi door open, she climbed in and slid to the far window. He got in behind her and moved to her side. Then he pulled her into his arms.

" 'Twas Stephanie on the phone."

"Stephanie?" Stephanie, who could turn from Michael and walk into the arms of the man she really loved, but wouldn't because he couldn't give her a child. Stephanie, who would sacrifice all her tomorrows because of a name. Campbell. Mac-Donald. In three short weeks, Fortune had learned how little a name meant in the face of love. She envied Stephanie's freedom of choice.

"Aye. Stephanie Kredski, Michael's lass. She wanted ye to know she'd thought about what ye said. I told her ye couldna speak to her right now, but that ye would call her later."

Kredski. Fortune remembered her feeling that Stephanie looked familiar. Of course she did. How

371

often had Fortune seen the face of Jan Kredski on history disks? If she wasn't so close to tears, she'd laugh. By marrying Michael, Stephanie had succeeded in immortalizing her name. But immortality was a double-edged sword. Because of Jan Kredski, there might soon be no humans left to remember the Kredski name.

Fortune felt too numb even to question the coincidence of Stephanie crossing her path. Nothing surprised her anymore.

The ride to the rest-over seemed only a second, and she'd longed to have it last forever. She couldn't string two coherent thoughts together before the taxi stopped, and Leith helped her out. She touched his cheek, feeling the roughness of beard stubble and the hardness of his clenched jaw. "You stay here while I go in and get our little monster."

He didn't even honor her with a reply, but simply walked into the rest-over and left her to tag behind. She allowed herself a small smile of remembrance. This was how it had all started, with him charging through the rest-over while she frantically hurried to keep up with his long strides. Some things never changed.

They reached the desk where a woman cast them an inquiring look. "Great costumes." She dragged her admiring glance from Leith long enough to ask Fortune. "What're you supposed to be?"

This once, Fortune refused to lie. "I'm from the year 2300."

"If you say so." The woman laughed and turned her attention back to Leith. "What can I do to help you?" Her tone suggested her help could encompass a wide spectrum of services.

Fortune glanced away from the woman's eagerness. Leith would have no trouble finding a woman to replace her once she'd left. *Don't cry. Not here. Not now*.

"We've come to claim a black cat ye're holding."

The woman grinned. "Hey, you're really Scottish. Great accent." Her smile faded as she realized what he'd said. "Oh, the cat belongs to you. Well, we have a small problem. He got loose on us. Someone was cleaning room three thirty-three, and he ran in there. Hid under the bureau and wouldn't come out. Since we knew you were coming, we decided to let you deal with the little horror." She held up her right hand to show them a set of livid scratches. "Good luck."

Fortune watched Leith's face pale and knew her own looked the same. But she'd expected this, and she didn't need to point out to Leith that she'd been right all along. She'd return from the same room where she'd entered. There was a certain cosmic balance to the thought.

For just a moment she considered grabbing Leith's hand and dragging him from the rest-over, leaving Ganymede to his fate. But she abandoned the idea with a deep sigh. It didn't matter. Cosmic forces wouldn't be cheated.

The woman pulled some paperwork from under the desk and pushed it at Leith. "Please fill this out. Just some papers we need to show who picked the cat up."

Leith leaned over the counter and studied the questions.

Fortune saw her chance and took it. While his attention was engaged by the form, she turned and raced for the open elevator. By the time he realized she was gone, she'd be in the room. He wouldn't follow her. He'd made it clear he'd never go back to her time, would never allow himself to be used, kept a virtual prisoner.

She stepped into the elevator, then punched in the third floor. As the door slid closed, she took one last look at the man she'd always love. Her final glimpse was of his strong back bent over the form, his night-dark hair fanned across his broad shoulders. The elevator rose silently toward the third floor while Fortune allowed tears to slide unchecked down her face.

When the elevator doors slid open, she wiped at the tears streaming down her face, then hurried toward the room. Opening the door, she slipped inside, then shut it quietly behind her. She didn't even bother looking for Ganymede. He wouldn't be here. He'd simply served as an instrument, and his job was finished.

She moved as though in a trance to the side of the bed she'd occupied when she'd opened her eyes to find herself in another time. Slowly she sat down on the edge of the bed facing the window. If she didn't sit down she knew she'd fall down.

She closed her eyes. *Do it, damn you, just do it*.

Suddenly she heard the soft click of the door and knew someone had come in.

She knew him, as she would over an infinity of years, untold lifetimes. His presence reached out to her across the width of this room, this eternity that trembled on the brink of discovery.

"Why are you here, Leith?" She didn't open her eyes.

"Ye know, lass. Ye must always have known."

She listened to his quiet footsteps draw near, pause on the other side of the bed.

What would it take, Leith, to make you go back with me?

I would have to love ye beyond all reason, lass.

She opened her eyes to stare at the blurred image of the window through her tears. Then slowly she turned her head to look at him. "Yes, I know."

Chapter Eighteen

Houston, we've got a problem.

I can't believe I didn't see this coming. Look, I'm always prepared. That's how I reached the top rung—the baddest of the bad, the meanest of the mean.

Sure, I wanted them to fall in love, but not this in love. Not I'll-die-for-you in love. Know what I mean?

Why'd I ever think breakin' their hearts would be fun? I musta been nuts. I shoulda stuck to exploding galaxies, creating black holes. Lots of bang for your buck without much effort.

This emotional stuff is killin' me.

Fine. Go ahead. Laugh. I'll be straight with you. I like Leith and Fortune. Really like them. I've never liked anyone or anything. Tolerate is about the closest I ever got.

Talk about tolerating, the ice-cream jerk's back. Parked across the street. Guess he figures he'll rush in and save their butts at the last minute. Fat chance.

I finally remembered where I've seen him before. He's one of those cosmic do-gooders always runnin' around trying to save people from the evil clutches of troublemakers like me. We've never locked horns before because I always deal in mass destruction, not individuals.

He'll need a new pair of Rollerblades if he expects to keep up with me.

Damn, he distracted me from my problem. How do I keep Leith and Fortune apart long enough to send them back to their own times? How do I make sure Leith doesn't go back with Fortune?

Hey, I'm doin' this for Leith. He'd hate Fortune's world. All those sex-starved women. Hmm.

Anyway, I waited too long. I shoulda zapped Fortune back before Leith got to the room. But I didn't think he'd come. I didn't think he loved her that much.

OK, I can handle this. When I'm ready, I'll just make sure they can't get to each other. I'd better do it before they touch. I don't know if I can do it when they're touching.

Kick me in the butt if I ever suggest doin' anything like this again. I think I'm gettin' a migraine, and the ice-cream jerk is playin' . . . "Blue Christmas"? Give me a break. It's Halloween, for cryin' out loud.

"I love ye, Fortune, and I willna let ye go back to yer time alone." When had he decided? Had he known as they danced in the moonlight, her red dress flaring around her long legs, or when she fearlessly attacked Bones to protect him? Perhaps it had been a gradual realization, growing and spreading like the ageless branches of the live oak they'd danced beneath. But he'd known for sure when he'd turned from filling out the form to find her gone. A part of him had died in that moment, a part he could ill afford to lose: his heart.

"Please don't force this decision on me, Leith. How can I take you back with me? How can I do that to you? I'd hate myself for every moment you spent in a life you hated. And you *would* hate it." She stared across the width of the bed at him, and it was as though the breadth of the universe stretched between them. "But I have a duty to humanity. How can I sacrifice the entire human race for you, for me?" Her anguished whisper was an echo of her inner torment.

His soft chuckle chided her. "Ye havena listened to me, lass. Ye dinna need to make a decision. I've made it for ye. I will come wi' ye whether ye want me or not."

"Not want you? Not want you?" She attempted a weak smile. "You haven't been paying attention, Campbell. Don't you *know* how I feel about you?"

"I dinna give a bloody damn about duty or the wishes of the Fates." He couldn't control the harsh desperation in his voice. "I will defy them to be wi' ye."

She looked at him then, really looked, her eyes glowing with wonder and something so beautiful it made him gasp. "You'd do that for me?"

He felt like tearing the room apart, howling his frustration to whatever gods were responsible for this. "Aye, Fortune. Ye willna leave me behind. I dinna care if they chain my body and use it for their own needs. They canna touch my heart. 'Twill always belong to ye, lass."

He knew she was mustering her final argument. It would do no good.

"What about . . . Hugh? If you don't return to your time, you can never make peace with him."

He could see in her eyes the hope that he'd accept her reasoning. The fear that he would.

He knew his hand shook as he raked it through his hair. His heart felt torn asunder by the decision he must make, one that was no decision at all. "I love Hugh wi' all my heart, but ye have my soul, Fortune. I will go wi' ye." He took one step, then another toward her side of the bed, toward her time.

Then he stopped. What real proof did he have that she loved him? She'd never said the words. He strengthened his resolve. That mattered not. He'd make her love him.

And what if going to her side meant nothing? What if the Fates were simply amusing themselves, and now that the game was ended they decided to send them each back to their own time in a puff of smoke?

No matter how determined he was, he had no weapons to fight such power. He must give her something just in case. Carefully, he pulled out her chain and Celtic cross, then held it out to her. "I dinna fool myself, Fortune. No matter what I wish, mayhap we will be swept apart. I would have ye take this wi' ye. To remember."

With shaking fingers, she reached for the cross. Her fingers touched his and seared every doubt from his heart. She was his woman, and he'd fight for her.

"Look on the back, lass."

Puzzled, she turned the cross over. "I never paid much attention to the back. I know there's a date and some faint words, but I never bothered . . ." She brought the cross close to her eyes and squinted at the faint inscription.

He knew the exact moment she realized the import of the words. She turned pale, then raised shocked eyes to meet his gaze. "It . . . it says Ian MacDonald, Glencoe, 1692. But it can't be. That means . . ."

His voice was soft. "Aye. It means ye wouldna be if I hadna saved Ian MacDonald's life. Our destinies were forged in the blood of Glencoe, lass."

She stared at him with eyes that pleaded, that made him eager to slay dragons for her. But a man couldn't slay what he couldn't see, didn't understand.

"Who planned this, Leith?" She held up the cross, and the silver gleamed softly in the dim glow of the overhead light. "What did they want to prove?"

"I dinna know." He clenched his fists. "But it doesna matter." He took a step toward her, a step that would allow him to gather her into his arms, hold her safe forever.

Suddenly two doors appeared on opposite sides of the room. In a part of his mind that seemed disconnected to the unfolding drama, Leith noted that the Fates had made the doors look very ordinary, like all the others in the hotel. Somehow he

thought they should look like the gates to heaven—
or hell.

Even as Leith prepared to fling himself across
the short space separating him from Fortune,
there was a whoosh, and a wall of flame erupted
between them. The sudden blast of heat flung him
back to his side of the room, and the strident ring-
ing of an alarm sounded a death knell to his
dreams.

Slowly the doors swung open.

For a moment Leith couldn't think, couldn't
feel. He turned to stare at his open door, a door he
had only to step through to return to his beloved
land . . . and Hugh.

He saw his home, and beyond he saw Hugh
walking slowly down the path that would lead to
his door. Even though he was distant, he could still
see Hugh's expression—pensive, sad.

Leith's heart contracted. If he stepped through
the door now, he could meet Hugh. They could
talk. And with the look on Hugh's face, Leith might
at long last have a chance to convince Hugh that
brothers shouldn't hate.

Leith took a step toward the door. He'd yearned
for this chance for eight bitter years. Now he need
take only a few more steps. He'd be home, and the
door would close behind him.

He'd never see Fortune again.

Leith swung from the open door. Through the
flames he saw her. She watched him with blue eyes
widened in shock. She still held the cross clutched
in both hands. Shaking her head as though waking
from a dream, she turned to look at her door.

No! Leith's cry echoed in his mind, his heart. No

man should have to make such a choice, but his heart had made the choice for him. He took two staggering steps away from his door, away from Hugh. His breath came in deep gulps. "Forgive me, Hugh." His voice dropped to a whisper. "Forgive me."

Turning, he faced the wall of flame. "Fortune, I love ye! Dinna leave me," he shouted above the fire's deadly crackle and the alarm's shrill warning.

Fortune stared in unblinking wonder at her open door. She could see her workroom, but where were her unfinished creations? All she saw were sculptures of animals and abstract objects.

It didn't matter, though, because there'd never again be a sense of coming home in the room.

She stepped toward the door, away from everything she'd ever love, away from Leith. Frantically, she dredged up all the reasons she had for leaving him. It was for the best. He couldn't make good on his promise to go with her now, so if she walked through her door he'd give up and return to his time, to his brother. He'd be safe. As for her, there was nothing she could do to change her fate, and if her fate didn't include Leith, she didn't care what happened to her.

She took another step toward the door. Funny, even though her life was disintegrating around her, her mind still registered other things, ordinary things. Outside the rest-over's window, she could see fire trucks with men rushing to do battle with the blaze, a blaze that seemed to exist only in this room.

There was something else. Something important. A black cat raced frenziedly back and forth among the fire-fighting equipment.

A smile touched Fortune's lips. At least Ganymede was safe. Even though she suspected he'd had his sneaky paw in this whole thing, she couldn't hate him.

She hesitated at the door's threshold. All she had to do was step through, and the door would close behind her. Forever.

Then she heard his shout.

She spun to face him, unable even now to walk away without one last glimpse.

Through the wall of flame, his gaze challenged her, flung his love across the deadly barrier like a gauntlet. "I willna leave ye!"

As though sleepwalking, she slowly returned to the bed. She looked at the man who would die for her. For die he would if he stayed in this room or tried to cross to her.

She turned her head for one last look at the door. All her reasons for walking away from Leith rang hollow in the face of his love, *her* love.

If Leith refused to return to his time, and she couldn't take him to her time, then what reason did she have for leaving? None. Fortune smiled, suddenly feeling as though an unbearable weight had been lifted from her shoulders. She felt as if she could fly.

With the Celtic cross still clutched in her hand, and somehow protecting her from the flames, she reached through the fire to Leith. "I love you, Leith Campbell, and I'll never leave you."

He grasped her hand, and they clung together with the cross between them. Fortune could only think that at last, after six hundred years, Campbell and MacDonald had closed the circle of hate, joined by the cross passed down from Ian MacDonald.

Flames crackled and hissed their threats while searing heat beat against her in waves of agony. She gasped for breath in the haze of deadly smoke. Still, the cross felt strangely cool in her grasp. But she knew it was only a matter of minutes before fire engulfed the room. She wondered why it hadn't happened already.

Gazing across the inches between them that might as well have been a million light-years, she watched a single tear slide down Leith's cheek, then another. She felt she'd explode with love for this man—strong yet tender, willing literally to brave the fires of hell for her. Humbled, she wondered what she'd ever done to deserve such love, but she fiercely vowed to return it—if they survived. She had to believe their love could conquer time. Belief and their love were now their only weapons.

Chapter Nineteen

No! I don't believe this. After all my planning. All they had to do was walk through the damn doors. Where'd I go wrong?

This never happened to me before. I mean, when I whip up a tornado, the wind blows. Period. So what the hell happened here?

Humans. You can control all the externals, but it doesn't mean diddly-squat once their emotions are involved.

I can't hold back the flames much longer. Once I set a disaster in motion, I can't turn it off. It's taking all my power to keep that fire from turning them into a pile of cinders.

They'll die. Once the fire escapes my control they'll die.

I don't want them to die.

"Why don't you want them to die, Ganymede?"

How did the ice-cream jerk know what I was thinking? Come to think of it, why doesn't he save them? That's his job. I don't have any pride left. Someone has to save them, and I don't care who.

"No, it's your job, Ganymede. You started it; you end it."

Fat lotta help he'll be. Think! There hasta be a way. Damn, the fire's startin' to get away from me.

"You still haven't answered my question, Ganymede. Why do you care if they die?"

Just what I need right now, a philosophical discussion about life and death. I have to save them because . . . because I love them.

Love. Why didn't I recognize it? Because I never felt it before, that's why. An eternity of existence and I never felt love before.

I'm doomed. It's the big Crockpot Down Under for me. The Big Guy doesn't tolerate weak emotions in his ranks. But this isn't weak. It hurts.

Fortune and Leith love me. No one in the universe ever loved me before. OK, so I'm not a lovable guy. Sue me.

I could let them fry, and the Big Guy would probably forgive me. I mean, I've given him a lot of good times.

But you know something, he can go to hell. Oops, forgot. He's already there.

Nothing matters now. I'm toast. But I'm gonna go out in a blaze of glory. No pun intended.

I've never tried to manage two natural forces at once. Don't have much strength left, but I didn't get to be the best without guts. Time to pull out all the stops. Nothin' left to lose now.

Hey, if Leith and Fortune live, it'll be worth gettin' zapped.

"I'd help if I could, Ganymede, but Fortune and Leith aren't my assignment."

Right. Doesn't this guy ever give up? He's like a pain-in-the-butt mosquito buzzin' in your ear.

"Don't you want to know what my assignment is?"

No. Now get lost and let me concentrate.

"*You*, Ganymede. My assignment is you. This good deed will, uh, terminate your present employment, but I've been authorized to offer you a Gold Card with unlimited credit to do good."

Too much stress. I'm hallucinatin'. How does a cosmic troublemaker do good?

"Well, you've done a great job of helping Fortune and Leith fall in love."

Yeah. A cosmic Cupid. I can get a little shop, hang out a sign, charge a nominal fee. . . . One question, though. This whole operation fell together like a giant jigsaw puzzle, and I was just one of the pieces. Who . . . ?

"Top-level decision."

OK, I get the picture.

"Do we have a deal?"

You're on. If I survive the next few minutes.

Hold on, guys. Your old pal won't let you down. Remember me.

Fortune didn't know at what point external noise interrupted the sounds of her soul. She'd heard that your life flashed before you at the point of death. *Wrong.* She was so focused on Leith that nothing, not her past or her doubtful future, could interfere with her last few moments with him.

But gradually outside noises battered at her. Thunder shattered the thick silence now broken only by the crackling flames, and lightening flashed, competing with the eerie glow of the fire. The sound of the wind rose to a wail of torment.

Suddenly the gale's force shattered the room's large window, and the storm entered in a shower of broken glass. A wall of wind-driven rain hit her, and she staggered beneath its strength.

Leith tightened his grip on her hand. "Dinna worry, lass. I willna let ye go."

And while the wind, rain, and fire battled for supremacy, Fortune clung to Leith—her warrior. Had it been only a few weeks ago that she'd arrogantly thought she didn't need him? How could she have been so wrong? He'd always be her anchor in whatever life chose to fling at them.

Suddenly it was over. The fire died with an angry hiss of defeat, and the wind became a soft whisper of encouragement.

Now that she was safe, reaction set in. Shaking, Fortune turned to look at her time portal. The door started to swing shut, too quickly for them to reach it.

Gazing one last time at the world she'd never see again, Fortune felt only a sad regret for the women who'd never experience the kind of love she shared with Leith.

Fortune had started to turn away when Leith's startled oath swung her attention back to her workroom.

A man carrying a small sculpture moved into view. A woman followed closely by another man carried material to a counter, where they began to discuss something.

Men. There were men in her time. *What . . . ?*

Then she remembered.

Is there a man you really love, Stephanie?

Yes, but I can't marry him. He's sterile. The family name would die with me.

Fortune *had* saved humanity, but not in the way she'd expected. Jan Kredski and her catastrophic cloning method never existed because Stephanie had followed her heart.

The door shut with a quiet click.

" 'Tis ended, Fortune."

Without speaking, she pulled Leith over to his time portal, which had started to slowly close. "I want to take a peek at your Scotland, Leith."

She felt his reluctance, his sadness right up to the moment she shoved him with all her strength, and he stumbled through the door. "You're wrong, Campbell. It's just the beginning." She held on to him, tumbling, pitching forward until they landed in a tangled heap on the heather-covered hillside.

Turning her head, she watched the time portal close. Forever. For a millisecond, panic intruded. No buttons to push. She'd go into button-pushing withdrawal, maybe have to make some artificial buttons to ease the craving.

Looking back at Leith, she watched the wonder, the joy transform his face. *To hell with buttons*. She smiled at him through tears of happiness, then wrapped her arms tightly around him and felt his fingers stroking her hair.

"Why, Fortune?"

His warm breath teased the side of her neck, and

she shivered in growing excitement. A new world, a new time, but she could handle anything so long as she could reach out and touch him. Forever.

"You had to come back because you'd always feel a sense of incompleteness without Hugh, without the Highlands. You belong here."

" 'Tis not what I'm asking, and ye know it well." His lips touched the sensitive skin behind her ear.

She turned her head to stare into his jade eyes, and it felt like the first time, when she'd emerged from beneath the rest-over cover to meet his startled gaze. Only now there was a sense of coming home. "I love you, Leith Campbell, and I want to be where you are. Always."

His face blurred, and she took a shaky breath, filling her heart with the scents of her new home. Earth, rain, and . . . "Hey, we're in Scotland. We're sitting on heather! At least I guess that's what this purple stuff is. You promised me we'd make love here, right in the middle of it. Pay up, Campbell."

His slow smile washed over her—warm, sexy, *real*. "Do ye love me beyond all reason, lass?"

Reaching up, she pulled his head down to her. "Beyond all reason. Beyond all time."

"Ye willna miss yer other life?"

Even though his soft murmur was teasing, Fortune sensed the importance of his question.

"I have no other life. Only you."

And just before his mouth covered hers, she grinned at him. "Besides, man-maker conventions were hell."

Epilogue

Leith allowed Fortune's love to flow through him as she clasped his hand tightly in hers.

What had he ever done to deserve her—his wife, his lover, his strength? And how he'd needed her strength during the past year.

They'd both mourned the loss of Ganymede, although Leith thought the wee demon had probably found other innocent humans to torment.

He'd made peace with Hugh, even though Leith knew Glencoe would always stand as a silent ghost between them. Mayhap someday they would discuss it, but not now.

And Fortune? She seemed happy with her carvings and her plans for their castle. *God's teeth, a castle*? But if she wanted a castle, he'd get her one. Even if it meant collecting favors from all who owed him. She already had some ideas for making it more comfortable. He hoped none of her ideas involved pushing buttons.

Lately he'd often look up to find her gaze on him. She would offer him a small, secret smile, and he'd wonder what mischief his beautiful vixen planned.

He raised his gaze to the midnight dark Highland sky, then closed his eyes as he savored the smells of home—the scent of woodsmoke, the land, the rising mist. Peace settled over him, peace he hadn't felt for many long years.

She moved closer, snuggling against his side. He glanced down at her, a blue-eyed sprite wearing a red dress, the same dress she'd worn in another time, another world.

"I willna ask how ye made yer dress look so like the other. It canna be the same one. 'Tis certain ye didna wear it the day we arrived, for I stripped every piece of clothing from ye before we made love in the heather." He grinned at the memory, and she blushed.

"I . . . I thought *you* had someone make it as a surprise. I found it among my other clothes a few days ago." She frowned as she puzzled over the dress.

"We'll speak of the dress later. Ye should've worn something more to keep ye warm, love." He wrapped his arms around her, sharing his heat, his protection.

She looked up at him with a love that humbled him. "I think it's probably a sin to feel this wonderful. You've given me so much, Leith, and now I can give you—"

" 'Tisn't needed, lass." He glanced at the surrounding hills silhouetted in darkness, drank in the silent Highland night. "Ye've given me what no other could: peace to accept what I couldna change, more happiness than I ever hoped for."

He smiled. "Last year on this night, I swore ye'd wear yer red dress and dance again wi' me. 'Tis time, Fortune."

She slipped from his embrace, then flung her arms into the air. Her red dress floating above her knees as she whirled in a circle, Fortune hummed the Elvis tune the ice-cream truck had played that night. "I'm ready, Campbell," she murmured as she returned to him.

They danced, as he'd promised her they would, beneath the dark Highland sky.

"You interrupted me a minute ago, and I had something important to tell you."

"Hmm." He lowered his head to kiss the side of her neck.

Reaching up, she pulled his hand down the length of her body, then stopped when his palm rested against her stomach. "By this time next year, we'll be an odd number."

Odd number? For a moment he stared at her, perplexed; then his heart began to pound as understanding dawned. "Ye're wi' child?" He didn't wait for her to confirm his statement, but lifted her into the air and swung her around.

She laughed joyously as he finally returned her to her feet. "I've been thinking of names already. If it's a boy we can name him Hugh, and a girl . . . a girl we could call Four-Two-O."

"We'd better pray for a boy, then, because I couldna see a wee lass wi' such a name."

She made a mock moue of disappointment. "We

393

could always name a boy Ganymede."

"Ganymede Campbell. It doesna flow, lass."

And as Leith laughingly swung her back into the dance, he caught a glimpse of the shadowy figure of a black cat, amber eyes glaring at him. The cat twitched its tail at him twice, then faded into the night.

Into the future.

Leith grinned. "There are some, of course, who would think Ganymede Campbell a fine Scottish name."

Night Bites

Nina Bangs

Cindy Harper has an ice-cream flavor for every emotion. But no sweet treat from her freezer is smooth, creamy, or tempting enough to cool down her dark fantasies about über alpha male Thrain Davis.

This is a man to be enjoyed on a strictly primitive level. Every woman who ever sees him smile wonders about the pleasure his mouth can give her. Too late she realizes the danger of inviting an ancient vampire into her inn. He forces her to examine her past when she is just fine with her present. He does have an upside, though. Who needs ice cream when you have a hot and yummy dark immortal in your bed?

THE BEWITCHED VIKING

Wink & Kiss

SANDRA HILL

'Tis enough to drive a sane Viking mad, the things Tykir Thorksson is forced to do—capturing a red-headed virago, putting up with the flock of sheep that follow her everywhere, chasing off her bumbling brothers. But what can a man expect from the sorceress who put a kink in the King of Norway's most precious body part? If that isn't bad enough, he is beginning to realize he isn't at all immune to the enchantment of brash red hair and freckles. But he is not called Tykir the Great for nothing. Perhaps he can reverse the spell and hold her captive, not with his mighty sword, but with a Viking man's greatest magic: a wink and a smile.

___52311-6 $5.99 US/$6.99 CAN

NINA BANGS
Master of Ecstasy

Her trip back in time to 1785 Scotland is supposed to be a vacation, so why does Blythe feel that her stay at the MacKenzie castle will be anything but? The gloomy old pile of stones has her imagination working overtime.

The first hunk she meets turns out to be Mr. Dark-Evil-and-Deadly himself, an honest-to-goodness vampire. His voice is a tempting slide of sin, and his body raises her temperature, but when Darach whispers, "To waste a neck such as yours would be a terrible thing," she decides his pillow talk leaves a lot to be desired.

Dangerous? You bet. To die for? Definitely. Soul mate? Just wait and see.

SANDRA HILL

HOT & HEAVY

As Lieutenant Ian MacLean prepares for his special ops mission in Northern Iraq, he sees no reason the insertion should not go down as planned. He leads a team of highly trained Navy SEALs, the toughest, buffest fighting men in the world. As a 34-year-old bachelor he has nothing to lose. He has the brains, guts, and brawn to out-maneuver, out-gun and just plain run circles around any enemy.

Madrene Olgadottir comes from a time a thousand years before Ian was born, and she has no idea she's landed in the future. After giving him a tongue lashing that makes a drill sergeant sound like a kindergarten teacher, she lets him know she has her own special way of dealing with over-confident males…

The Reluctant Miss Van Helsing

Minda Webber

Having lived long amongst London's *ton*, Ethel Jane Van Helsing is an astute female who well knows her faults. She has a face unremarkable in its plainness. And yet…at a masquerade ball, anything can happen. There, even an ugly duckling can become a swan.

But tonight is not for fowl play. You see, plain or not, Jane comes from distinguished stock: Van Helsings. And Van Helsings are slayers. Her father, the Major, showed her very early on how to use the sharp end of a stick. Tonight, everything is at stake. Something is going to get driven very deep into a heart, or she isn't…

The Reluctant Miss Van Helsing
